BITTER HOMECOMING

Wade swallowed the rest of the whiskey and slammed the glass down on the rock hearth. "Don't you think I want my memory back?"

Sandrine shrugged. "I don't know. Sometimes it seems like you're glad you don't remember."

Wade walked to the cupboard and grabbed the bottle. She watched as he took a long swig. "You're not the man I fell in love with. You're nothing like him."

Wade took a quick step toward her, startling her, but he only reached out and lifted her hair off her neck. His fingertips brushed her skin. Why was he doing this to her? "Do you hate me?" she asked aloud.

Abruptly Wade took her into his arms. "Hate you?" he whispered against her cheek. "I could never hate you." Suddenly his lips were on hers, hard and demanding. Desperately she struggled to get away from him, twisting and turning her body. But even as she struggled, she felt Wade's hands as they touched and stroked her, and slowly she felt her body betray her.

TODAY'S HOTTEST READS
ARE TOMORROW'S SUPERSTARS

VICTORY'S WOMAN (4484, $4.50)
by Gretchen Genet
Andrew—the carefree soldier who sought glory on the battlefield, and returned a shattered man... Niall—the legandary frontiersman and a former Shawnee captive, tormented by his past... Roger—the troubled youth, who would rise up to claim a shocking legacy... and Clarice—the passionate beauty bound by one man, and hopelessly in love with another. Set against the backdrop of the American revolution, three men fight for their heritage—and one woman is destined to change all their lives forever!

FORBIDDEN (4488, $4.99)
by Jo Beverley
While fleeing from her brothers, who are attempting to sell her into a loveless marriage, Serena Riverton accepts a carriage ride from a stranger—who is the handsomest man she has ever seen. Lord Middlethorpe, himself, is actually contemplating marriage to a dull daughter of the aristocracy, when he encounters the breathtaking Serena. She arouses him as no woman ever has. And after a night of thrilling intimacy—a forbidden liaison—Serena must choose between a lady's place and a woman's passion!

WINDS OF DESTINY (4489, $4.99)
by Victoria Thompson
Becky Tate is a half-breed outcast—branded by her Comanche heritage. Then she meets a rugged stranger who awakens her heart to the magic and mystery of passion. Hiding a desperate past, Texas Ranger Clint Masterson has ridden into cattle country to bring peace to a divided land. But a greater battle rages inside him when he dares to desire the beautiful Becky!

WILDEST HEART (4456, $4.99)
by Virginia Brown
Maggie Malone had come to cattle country to forge her future as a healer. Now she was faced by Devon Conrad, an outlaw wounded body and soul by his shadowy past... whose eyes blazed with fury even as his burning caress sent her spiraling with desire. They came together in a Texas town about to explode in sin and scandal. Danger was their destiny—and there was nothing they wouldn't dare for love!

Available wherever paperbacks are sold, or order direct from the Publisher. Send cover price plus 50¢ per copy for mailing and handling to Penguin USA, P.O. Box 999, c/o Dept. 17109, Bergenfield, NJ 07621. Residents of New York and Tennessee must include sales tax. DO NOT SEND CASH.

KAREN A. BALE
BRIGHT STAR'S PROMISE

ZEBRA BOOKS
KENSINGTON PUBLISHING CORP.

*For my mother, whose love, strength, and
courage constantly inspire me.*

ZEBRA BOOKS are published by

Kensington Publishing Corp.
850 Third Avenue
New York, NY 10022

Copyright © 1994 by Karen A. Bale

All rights reserved. No part of this book may be reproduced in any form or by any means without the prior written consent of the Publisher, excepting brief quotes used in reviews.

If you purchased this book without a cover you should be aware that this book is stolen property. It was reported as "unsold and destroyed" to the Publisher and neither the Author nor the Publisher has received any payment for this "stripped book."

Zebra and the Z logo Reg. U.S. Pat. & TM Off. The Lovegram logo is a trademark of Kensington Publishing Corp.

First Printing: July, 1994

Printed in the United States of America

One

Night Sun dragged in a heavy breath, his old eyes weary. He reached out with his gnarled fingers to hold onto Little Bear. "The light grows dim, grandson," Night Sun said, his voice rough and labored. He drew in another breath. "And the day grows short."

"You are strong, grandfather," Little Bear replied, forcing his voice to remain steady. He glanced across the fire. His aunt, Running Tears, sat so still that it was easy for him to forget she was there. He looked back to his grandfather's face, silently praying that the old man could not see that he was crying.

"My strength is quickly leaving me, Little Bear. It is almost time. I have had a good life here on this earth. Now I am ready to greet Napi, the Creator, and see what life is like on the other side."

Little Bear moved closer to his grandfather. "There will be many buffalo to hunt, grandfather, and the meadows will be overgrown with long grass. The streams will be filled with cool, clear water, and corn and fruit will grow everywhere." Little Bear leaned close to his grandfather's ear. "I hear that the women on the other side have such beauty that it brings tears to your eyes."

"How do you know of this?"

"I have spoken to Napi many times, grandfather. When I went to the mountain to find my medicine, Napi showed me what it was like on the other side."

"And you saw women?"

"Many women, grandfather. Smiling, beautiful women."

"I am ready for this then," Night Sun said, nodding. "But there is one more thing that I wish before I go—I wish to see my granddaughter again. My heart yearns to see Bright Star."

Little Bear caught his aunt's eye. They had been expecting this. Even though it would be difficult, Little Bear had already decided to accept the mission. He took his grandfather's hand and squeezed it. "On my life, I will bring Bright Star back here to you, grandfather."

Night Sun nodded and closed his eyes, seemingly satisfied with Little Bear's promise. When his grandfather had fallen asleep, Little Bear went outside. He stood in front of the lodge, shaking his head. He had given his word, but he wasn't sure he could keep it. How could he get Bright Star back here in time? He heard the lodge flap open behind him, and he turned to see Running Tears. She reached out and gently touched his cheek.

"He knows you will do your best, Little Bear."

"But what if I cannot bring Bright Star back here in time? It is his truest wish to see her."

"If you do not make it in time, he will die happy knowing that she is on her way to him."

Little Bear paced back and forth, finally stopping next to Running Tears. "I will miss him and his stories." He looked up at the stars. "I will miss his guidance. My heart is heavy, aunt."

"I know," Running Tears replied softly. "He has been a good father to me. There will be an empty place in my heart when he is gone from us." She touched his arm tenderly. "We have been blessed by Napi to have had such a person in our lives."

Little Bear did not try to hide his tears from his aunt. He knew that she felt the same sadness. "I will leave before the sun rises to find Bright Star. Pray for me. Pray that we both return in time to bid our grandfather goodbye."

***

Sunshine filtered into the room, bathing it in warm yellow light. Sandrine rubbed her eyes and propped herself on her elbow, looking at Wade as he slept. She reached over and pushed his blond hair back from his face. She had loved him since she was a young girl—from the moment she had seen him ride into her parents' trading post. But her love for him had grown even stronger since they had built this home together and spent their days and nights with each other.

Sandrine looked around the small bedroom. It was sparsely furnished, with only a bed, dresser, and wardrobe. Wade's gunbelt hung on a bedpost on his side of the bed. The kerosene lamp sat on the dresser next to the blue enamel wash basin.

It was quite small; they had built only two rooms. The living room contained everything that their bedroom did not—a cookstove, a large cupboard and sideboard, a small table and two chairs where they ate their dinner. The only other pieces of furniture were two rocking chairs where they sat in the evenings near the warmth of the fire.

On the wall behind the stove hung the big tin tub that they bathed in. On the opposite wall next to the north-facing window, Sandrine had hung the beautiful red and blue blanket her mother had given them as a wedding gift. The striking Blackfoot design reminded her of her Indian family. She missed them fiercely at times—her mother's laughter, her cousin's teasing, and her grandfather's stories. As much as she loved Wade and her friends here, she still got homesick. White women were bound by a rigid code of propriety that she sometimes found suffocating. She knew this was not what her father had wanted for her—if it had been up to him she would now be living in his native France. Sandrine smiled and shook her head. But that would've meant marrying Alain, and even her father had come to see that that would have been a mistake.

As much as she had come to love this little cabin, it would be wonderful when the big house was finished. Already, Wade and their friend, Jim Everett, had begun building it. The rooms would be big and airy. There would be plenty of room for children. Sandrine closed her eyes and smiled as she thought of having Wade's children.

Sandrine leaned forward and brushed her lips across Wade's cheek, and he stirred in his sleep. She kissed him again and smiled when he opened his eyes.

"You look beautiful in the morning," he said.

She felt her cheeks flush, but she wasn't embarrassed. When he reached out to touch her, she leaned forward into his embrace. Still blushing, she ran her hand over his bare chest. She felt his breath quicken against her neck, and she closed her eyes as his mouth found hers. He pulled her closer, and she could feel the urgency of her own passion rising as he parted her lips with his tongue.

"I love you," Wade whispered.

"And I love you," Sandrine whispered. She opened her eyes and found him looking at her with such love and intensity that she leaned forward and covered his mouth with hers. He moved his hands to her breasts, his fingers lightly brushing across her nipples. She felt her whole body respond to his touch, and she pulled him closer, fitting her body tightly against his. He kissed her closed eyelids, then her throat. His hands left her breasts to slide down to her hips, and she arched her back involuntarily, pressing herself against him. When he entered her, she moaned softly, lifting her hips to meet his thrusts. Together they found a rhythm that quickened, then slowed. The depth of their love and trust made their lovemaking slow and unhurried. When they finally reached their passionate fulfillment, Sandrine cried out and felt Wade's arms tighten around her.

"Sandrine," he whispered, brushing her ear with his lips.

Sandrine touched his cheek, and Wade turned his head to kiss her fingertips. "I don't think I could live without you," she said softly, pressing her cheek against his shoulder.

Wade kissed her lightly. "You won't ever have to," he said. He shifted his weight, pulling her with him. Sandrine felt herself being lifted, and a moment later, she was looking down into his gray eyes. He grinned. "You didn't think I'd let you get up and start breakfast yet, did you?" He slid his hands up her thighs, then reached out to pull her close enough to kiss. "I may never let you go."

When Sandrine awakened, Wade was gone. She reached out and touched his pillow, then on a sudden impulse, pulled it toward her. The scent of his skin was still on the cloth. She loved Wade so much, sometimes it frightened her. He had proved his love many times, and had risked his life for her. Sandrine shivered and hugged the pillow more tightly, remembering Bear Killer. He had hurt her so badly, had made her feel so filthy, but through it all, Wade's love had sustained her.

Sighing, Sandrine sat up and stretched. She could hear the sound of Wade's hammer ringing in the distance. She smiled. He worked on the house at least a little every day making time between the endless chores. Sandrine scooted to the edge of the bed, grinning. She pulled her work clothes from the wardrobe. Quickly dressing, she glanced out the window. The sun was well above the horizon. He had let her sleep in again.

When Sandrine heard the sound of hoofbeats, she shook her head. Jim was here and she hadn't even made coffee yet. She ran her fingers through her hair, trying to straighten the tangles. She hurried to the cookstove, then hesitated, listening more closely. The horse wasn't shod. She ran to the door, flung it open, and watched the rider come closer. Recognition lit her face. "Little Bear," she whispered. She had missed her cousin so much. He had always been her best friend. She ran into the yard and stood shading her eyes until he reined in his horse. He looked down at her, his handsome face a bronze impassive mask.

"It is good to see you, cousin. I have traveled a long way to find you."

Sandrine waited until Little Bear dismounted, and without hesitating, she hugged him. As always, he remained stiff and uncomfortable in her embrace, but he tolerated this white man's custom from her. She stepped back, searching his eyes, but the twinkle of humor she had been expecting was not there. "What is it? What's wrong?"

"It is grandfather. He is dying."

Sandrine held herself very still, trying to absorb Little Bear's words. Her grandfather had been an old man for as long as she could remember, but she had never allowed herself to think he could die.

"You must come with me, Bright Star. His only wish is to see you."

Without speaking, Sandrine nodded, knowing she had to go. She would do anything for her grandfather. But still, as she thought of the long, hard journey and the time it would take, an uneasiness spread through her. She glanced up the hill to where Wade was working on the house. They had been through so much to be together, and now she would have to leave him again.

"Why do you hesitate, cousin? Get your things."

"I have to talk to Wade," she said, still looking at the half-finished house on the ridge.

Little Bear followed her gaze. "I will talk to him. You get what you need for the journey."

Sandrine bristled at her cousin's words. "There is no need to order me about, Little Bear. I know what I must do." Lifting her chin, Sandrine turned on her heel and walked up the trail toward the new house. As she got closer, Sandrine wondered why Wade had not heard Little Bear's horse. But soon she realized why. Wade was singing while he hammered. Sandrine couldn't help but smile. What he lacked in musical ability, he made up for in enthusiasm. When Wade saw her, he smiled broadly and let the hammer fall silent.

"I thought you'd sleep all day," he said, his eyes twinkling.

Sandrine walked to Wade and put her arms tightly around him, pressing her cheek against his chest.

"What's wrong?"

She looked up at him. "Little Bear is here. He came to tell me that my grandfather is dying."

Wade pulled Sandrine closer, stroking her shining dark hair. "I'm sorry. I know how much you love Night Sun."

She waited, sure that he would insist on coming with her, but instead, he looked past her. The expression in his eyes was distant, remote, and it surprised her. His silence went on so long that she began to feel herself getting angry. "Come with me."

"The cows will be calving soon. Who'd take care of things around here? Besides, you wanted to move into this house before winter. I'll have to stay."

"But I don't know how long I'll be gone. It could be months."

Wade took her face in his hands. "I don't want you away from me, Sandrine," he said, kissing her softly, "but I don't see any other way. You have to be with your grandfather and I have to take care of the ranch."

Sandrine tried to hide the hurt she was feeling. She knew he was right, but still, she didn't want to be separated from him again—and he didn't seem to care. Hadn't this morning meant anything to him? She felt his arms tighten around her, pulling her closer, then just as suddenly, he released her and stepped back. Sandrine fought back tears as he smiled and patted her on the cheek.

"Try not to be too sad. He has lived a long life."

Sandrine could only stand, staring into his eyes. Why didn't he realize that it wasn't just her grandfather that she was upset about?

"If I know Little Bear, he's not going to wait for much longer. Let's go on down."

Wade took her hand and she did not resist as he led her back down the path. She felt an ache deep inside. She had been so happy here with Wade—it was too good to be true.

Emily Dodd loosened the ribbons to her bonnet and sighed heavily. Reading about bone-jarring stagecoach rides was very different from actually experiencing them. She couldn't wait to get to Santa Fe and her uncle's ranch. She was quickly tiring of what had started out as an adventure and had now turned into an ordeal.

She glanced at her fellow passengers with distaste. The good Reverend Tyley was surreptitiously taking yet another swig from the silver flask that he thought no one had noticed. Beside him, her face florid and beaded with sweat, Betsy Mulligan sat with her baby clutched to her ample breast. The child had finally stopped crying, but Emily had no doubt that it would soon start again. As much as she hated the baby's screams, Emily preferred them to Betsy's attempts at conversation. Betsy's husband, a timid man who rarely spoke, had long ago given up trying to get a word in edgewise. And even now, with no one answering her, Betsy continued to comment on everything they passed.

Emily stubbornly kept her eyes fixed on the bench across from her. As much as she disliked looking at Betsy and the reverend, it was preferable to taking a chance on making eye contact with Andrew Tobias. Smelling of cheap cologne and high ambition, he had boarded the stage the morning before and had not stopped staring at her since. When she ignored his attempts to talk to her, he had fallen silent, contenting himself with clandestine glances at her breasts.

Emily was used to men staring at her, but to be trapped in such close quarters with someone who was so utterly disgusting was almost more than she could bear. She reached up and smoothed her auburn hair, tucking the loose strands back into her chignon. Just because she was away from Boston, traveling with a group of people she would normally avoid, that was no reason for her to let herself become disheveled.

"I don't know why you do that," Betsy said, staring at Emily.

"Do what?" Emily responded, taking the hanky from her bag and wiping the trail dust from her face.

"Why are you always making yourself over so? You look perfectly put together."

"Habit, I guess," Emily replied, glancing with disdain at the milk stains on the front of Betsy's dress.

"Well, it's a habit I never had time to acquire. What with the baby and my four others, I barely have time to even brush my hair."

"Oh, really?" Emily arched her brows.

"I agree with Mrs. Mulligan. I've never seen such a vision of beauty as you," Andrew Tobias said, leaning toward Emily.

Emily sat up straighter and pressed closer to the open window. She stared out at the arid landscape, not wanting to continue the conversation with either person. She just wanted to be left alone.

She poked her head outside the window as the stagecoach jostled along. The trail seemed never ending, and the dust continued to swirl about in thick clouds. She put the hanky to her nose and kept it there, inhaling the sweet fragrance of her rose water. If she hadn't been forced to leave Boston, she would have never taken this damned trip.

"Did you hear that?" Betsy asked.

"Hear what?" Reverend Tyley asked, looking about him in confusion.

"I thought I heard shouts," Betsy said, twisting to see out the window.

Emily heard it, too. Distant shouts and then the sound of gunfire. She started to lean out of the window, but a hand on her shoulder stopped her. "Best stay away from the window, Miss Dodd. Could be Indians."

This was one time that Emily looked Andrew Tobias straight in the eye. "Indians? I was told this was supposed to be a safe journey."

"Nothing's ever safe out here in the West," said Mulligan.

Emily glanced sharply at Betsy's husband. He had finally spoken and was sitting upright, checking his revolver to make sure it was loaded.

"What will we do if we're attacked?" said Emily as calmly as she could.

"Not much we can do," Andrew said. "Just hope the stage can outrun them."

Emily heard more gunshots and involuntarily moved closer to Andrew. The shouts were getting louder. Andrew suddenly put his arms around her, and before she could protest, he had pushed her off the seat and down onto the floor next to Betsy and her crying baby. The heaving motion of the stagecoach and the sour milk smell from Betsy's dress nauseated her, but her fear kept her down. Andrew and Betsy's husband were firing out the window. Emily's whole body jerked involuntarily at the sound of each shot.

A rasping scream from the driver made Emily shrink down in terror. Outside, the world seemed to shatter in a barrage of thunderous gunfire.

Andrew dropped onto the floor beside her. "They've got us." His breath was warm on her cheek, but Emily was too scared to try to move away from him.

"They told me the Indians weren't a problem," Emily hissed, trying to control her fear and anger.

Andrew shook his head. "They're not Indians."

At that moment, the gunfire ceased, and Emily could feel the stagecoach slowing. Someone was shouting close to the window, ordering the men to throw their weapons out. As the stagecoach slowed, Mulligan and Tobias tossed their revolvers out. A few seconds later, the stagecoach rumbled to a halt and the door was jerked open. Emily struggled to get to the seat, tangled in her skirts, but found herself staring into cold, black eyes.

Sandrine stared up at the sky, her hands folded underneath her head. It had been a long time since she'd been on the trail, and she'd forgotten how tiring it was. She stretched out on the thin bedroll and pulled the blanket up to her chest. She and Little Bear had only been riding for two days, but already she longed for Wade.

"Are you still angry with me?"

Sandrine smiled in the darkness when she heard Little Bear's voice. As tough as he tried to seem, he was one of the kindest people she'd ever known. "I'm not angry with you."

"Then why have you not spoken to me? It is not like you to remain so silent, Bright Star."

Sandrine sighed. "I have much to think about."

"You miss Colter? Are you sorry you came with me?"

"You know I'm not. I want to see grandfather. It's just that . . . it's hard for me to be separated from Wade again. I can't help but think about the time I was with Bear Killer."

"Bear Killer is dead, cousin. Do not worry about him."

"I'm not worried about him, Little Bear, I'm worried that I won't see Wade for a long time. He's my husband now. I don't want to be away from him."

"So, it has happened to you, too." Little Bear's voice sounded strange.

"What're you talking about?"

"This madness has taken control of you. The madness that overtakes all women when they get married. They can think of nothing but their husbands. I did not think you would become like them."

"It is not madness, cousin. It is love."

"Please, do not talk to me of love."

"But you had it with your wife, I know you did. It's a good thing, and I know no matter how much you protest, you're happy for me. I know how much you like Wade."

"I must admit, he is not bad for a white man. I am surprised you are not already with child."

Sandrine shook her head in the dark. Little Bear had never had a problem speaking his mind. "First we're going to build a big house."

"Hmph," Little Bear grunted. "I do not understand the need for the white man's lodge. Why do you live on land where there is tall grass, trees, and a clear stream, and then you spend all of your time in the wooden lodge? It makes no sense to me."

"We will raise our family in our house, just as you'll raise your family in your lodge. There is no difference."

"There is a big difference. You are no longer one with the land as I am."

"I am tired, Little Bear, and I'm not in the mood to argue."

"Then you have changed, cousin."

Sandrine smiled again. It had always been like this between them. They had always argued, but Sandrine knew she could depend on Little Bear for the truth and more. She could depend on him for her life.

She rolled onto her side and pulled the blanket up to her neck. A sudden ache went through her body, and she wished that she had had a chance to talk to Wade before she'd left. She loved him so much. She could feel the trail weariness in her legs and arms and she closed her eyes. They had another long day ahead of them; thinking about Wade would not help her to rest.

* * *

Wade watched Jim as he paced back and forth in the street, kicking at the loose brown dirt. "Jesus, you'd think a man had nothing better to do than wait for a stagecoach all damned day."

"Just relax, Jim. It'll be here soon enough." Wade sat down on the edge of the wooden plank that served as a sidewalk and continued to watch Jim as he paced nervously back and forth. Jim Everett had been one of the best wagon masters of his time. He'd led dozens of wagon trains west and he had lost very few people. It was on one such wagon train that Wade had met him. When his parents had died, Wade was left alone in the world. He grimaced, remembering. He'd been barely thirteen years old, and he remembered how scared he had been. But Captain Everett took him west with him, saying they'd worry about what to do later. Later never came. Wade wound up staying with Jim on the various wagon trains, learning how to scout, learning how to survive among the different tribes of Indians they'd seen while traveling across the immense frontier. He had seen the vast Oregon territory, had even spent time exploring the teeming streets of San Francisco. While he was still a boy, Wade had seen more cities than most men would see in their lifetimes. With Jim he had traveled to St. Louis, New York, Boston, and finally, Santa Fe. Jim had always liked Santa Fe, and that's where he had settled down.

Wade looked up when he heard his old friend cuss again. Jim was understandably nervous. His niece Emily was coming west from Boston. People from the East were never quite ready for the hardships of the West, and Jim didn't want Emily's first trip to be unpleasant in any way.

"Well, I've had it," Jim said, looking at his pocket watch. "The stage is over an hour late. Something's wrong."

Wade followed Jim into the stagecoach office and listened

as Jim loudly inquired of Lane Davis where the hell the stage was.

"Haven't heard anything, Captain Everett," Lane said. "I sent Randy out to take a look. He should be back before too long."

"The hell with Randy. I'll go myself," Jim said, angrily stomping out of the office.

Wade shrugged his shoulders at Lane and followed Jim outside to their horses. "You're sure you're not getting all worked up over nothing?"

"If this was Sandrine, would you be so calm?" Jim asked, swinging up onto his horse.

Wade nodded silently. No, he wouldn't wait if it was Sandrine. And the truth was, the stage was seldom late. Jim had good cause to be worried.

They rode out of town at a gallop, but within a couple of miles, Wade reined his horse in, glancing over at Jim. The road was rutted and covered with tracks, but as Wade leaned down for a closer look, it was obvious that the newest wheel tracks were several days old. The stage had not made it this far. Wade caught Jim's eye and received a curt nod in return. Without exchanging a single word, the two men spurred their horses back into a gallop.

Wade saw the stage first and glanced at Jim. Together, he and Jim took in the scene and spurred their horses even faster. As they got closer, Wade's fears became real. The driver and the man who had been riding shotgun were both dead, slumped forward over the wooden seat. The horses had been cut out of their harnesses and were grazing, scattered, their reins trailing through the brush. A feeble shout led them to the other passengers. A few hundred yards from the road, three men and a buxom woman were tied, hand and foot. On the ground next to the woman, a baby lay crying. Grim-faced and tense, Wade dismounted and untied the woman. She picked up her child and held it tightly, sobbing.

"I thought they were going to kill us all," she said, cradling the baby in her arms.

"It's all right, ma'am," Wade said reassuringly.

After Wade and Jim had untied the men, they began to piece the story together. They soon found out that Emily had been on the stage and had fared worse than the other passengers. She had been kidnapped.

Jim's face clouded with worry. "Were they Indians?"

"It wasn't Indians," the older man said, lifting a silver flask to his mouth.

Wade glanced at the woman and her baby. Now that her husband could put his arms around her, she was calming down. She looked up at Wade.

"There were four of them," the woman said, patting her baby on the back. "All white. Two of them were pretty young. I could tell even with their faces covered. It was one of the young ones that talked them into taking Emily."

Wade swung back up onto his horse. "I'll circle and see if I can pick up any tracks, Jim." Bleak-faced, Jim nodded, and Wade knew what he was thinking: they had to find Emily soon.

Wade rode in a wide circle. It didn't take him long to pick up the tracks of four horses that led away from the stagecoach. They seemed to be riding in a straight line, which surprised him. They hadn't even tried to cover their tracks. He turned his horse and rode back to the stage. Jim had organized the people, and they'd already caught the team.

"They've gone east," Wade said without dismounting.

Jim nodded. "You people be all right?"

"We'll be fine," the woman answered. "You go on after your niece."

Wade and Jim rode away from the stage, following the tracks of the riders eastward. Wade was glad that the trail was so easy to follow, but it made him uneasy, too. A mile farther on he found what he'd been expecting all along: the trail split. Wade pulled up sharply, shaking his head. It was a smart move on their part.

Jim's voice brought Wade out of his thoughts. "Can you tell which horse Emily is on?"

Wade dismounted and examined the tracks carefully, running his fingers along the edges of the hoofprints. Two sets of prints were deeper than the others, indicating that the horses were carrying heavier loads. The only problem was one horse went east, the other went south. "Two of the horses have deeper prints. Could be one of them is just carrying supplies. Only problem is, we don't know which one."

"We'll have to split up then," Jim said, squatting next to Wade. "The bastards. Wasn't it enough to rob the stage?"

Wade straightened up. "We'll find her."

"You keep going east. I'll follow the tracks south."

"I don't even know what Emily looks like, Jim."

"For Chrissakes, Wade. She'll be the one wearing the skirt!"

Wade tensed, then relaxed and grinned. "If I find her, I'll take her straight to your ranch."

"Be careful, Wade."

"I'll be careful. You do the same." Wade watched as Jim rode south, then he wheeled his own mount around and kicked it into a gallop.

He rode hard but carefully. An injured horse would be the end of his search for Emily. As he rode, the land got rougher, and it was obvious that the outlaws were doing everything they could to conceal their tracks. Twice, Wade had to double back through the thick sagebrush to pick up their tracks again. But he did not slow down. By nightfall Wade had found the small camp.

The two outlaws had hidden away under an outcropping of rocks, but their small fire had given them away. He could see Emily, her hands tied behind her back, leaning against a rock, her face ashen. The two men sat close to the campfire. They were drinking from a bottle of whiskey and laughing as if they were having a night out on the town.

As he watched from behind the rocks, Wade checked his revolver to make sure it was loaded. He could easily pick off one of the men from here, but before he got off the next shot, the other man might get to Emily. He couldn't take the chance that she'd get hurt. He'd wait and watch for awhile, knowing that eventually one of these two would make a mistake.

Wade settled himself against the rough-barked trunk of a mesquite tree. For a long time, the two men passed the bottle back and forth. Their laughter became forced, then quieted. They both looked young; that worried Wade. These weren't hardened outlaws—their behavior would be quirky, unpredictable. They acted as if they wouldn't get caught.

Finally one of the men stood up and wandered unsteadily out of the camp and into the jumble of house-sized boulders. Crouching, Wade made his way forward, moving silently from rock to rock. He stopped when he got close. Just below him, the man was buttoning his pants and humming drunkenly. He stumbled slightly. He reached out to steady himself but couldn't and fell backward. As the man struggled to get up, Wade jumped him. Before the man could cry out, Wade swung hard with his left hand, landing a blow that snapped the man's head back. A second later, Wade raised the butt of his pistol and brought it down sharply on the man's temple. He slumped against the rock and began to slide to the ground. Wade broke his fall and eased him silently to the ground.

Checking to make sure the man was unconscious, Wade moved silently down the slope, keeping himself hidden. He made his way around the camp until he was behind Emily. He was so close to her, he could see the firelight glinting off her auburn hair. He could also see the face of the man who was sitting by the fire. He was too drunk to have missed his companion, but he was not too drunk to leer at Emily. His look of desire faded when Wade threw a stone that clattered among the boulders behind the camp.

"Hurry up, Dever. I'm not going to wait forever." The man stood up, walking toward Emily and roughly yanking her to her feet. "You are a pretty little thing," he said, pulling her to him and holding her against his chest.

Emily struggled, but she was unable to break free. "Leave me alone," she snarled.

"Is that an order, ma'am?" the man asked, laughing harshly.

Wade threw another stone, directing the man's attention away from Emily.

The man glanced briefly over his shoulder. "I told you to hurry up, Dever. If you ain't here in one minute, I'm taking my turn with this little lady first."

"No," Emily shrieked, twisting frantically.

Wade watched as the man dropped to his knees, forcing Emily with him. "It's time you and I got to know each other better, little lady." He pushed Emily onto the ground, and without hesitating, he climbed on top of her. Emily pounded at him, biting and scratching at his face, but he only laughed. Wade moved swiftly, coming up behind them. Holding the barrel of his pistol, he swung downward, hitting the man on the back of the head. The blow landed solidly, knocking the man sideways onto the ground.

Wade held his hand out to Emily, helping her to her feet. She wasn't crying. She stood stiffly, her arms crossed in front of her.

"It's all right," he said gently. "I'm a friend of your uncle's. We've been looking for you."

Emily looked past him to the man on the ground. "Is he dead? Are you going to shoot him?"

Wade shook his head, startled.

"He deserves it," Emily spat.

He nodded cautiously. Emily's eyes were wild, her breathing

quick and shallow. When he spoke, he used the kind of voice he would have used to calm a frightened colt. "We better get going. I don't know where the rest of those outlaws are, and we don't want to take a chance," he said, taking her arm and guiding her away from the camp toward his horse. She came reluctantly at first, then seemed to gather her wits and her dignity. He looked to the rocks where he had knocked out the first man. No movement. Then he glanced at the man in camp. He was still unconscious. Emily stumbled, and when he tried to steady her, she jerked free.

"What's your name?" she asked as she smoothed her fine auburn hair.

"The name is Wade Colter, ma'am, and I don't mean to be rude, but I think we should be going."

Emily smoothed her hair again, an angry, distracted gesture. "They robbed me. They took my mother's brooch."

"You're lucky to be alive," Wade said as he pulled her forward. "Can you ride?"

Emily stepped away. "Ride? Of course not. Didn't you hear what I said?"

Wade turned to lead the way and didn't look back until Emily called his name loudly. "Mr. Colter."

Wade paused mid-stride and said over his shoulder, "If you want to wake these two up, you just keep yelling." Wade continued walking, smiling when he heard her hurried footsteps behind him. He knew she was struggling not to stumble on the rough terrain with her cumbersome skirts and her tightly laced boots, but he fought the impulse to turn and help her. His horse stood nervously, eyeing Emily's billowing skirts with suspicion. Wade laced his fingers into a stirrup. "Step up."

"Up there?"

Wade reminded himself this was Jim's niece. "I'll help you. You won't fall." Emily looked around apprehensively, then stared at his cupped hand, frowning. "Step into my hands just like they're a stirrup." When Emily hesitated, Wade could barely contain his anger. "I'm not going to argue with you. We have to leave now."

Emily tried to step back, but Wade leaned forward quickly and grabbed her waist. Lifting her in one fluid motion, he set her roughly in the saddle, ignoring her outrage. Seconds later, he had swung up behind her and was urging his horse into a gallop. To keep her from falling, he kept one hand around Emily's waist. Through the smooth silk of her bodice, he could feel how tense she was, how frightened.

For the first few miles, Wade rode cross country, avoiding the stage road. As unlikely as it was that the outlaws would still be around, Wade didn't want to take the chance. At first he tried to reassure Emily, but her curt answers finally drove him into silence. As they got closer to town, he made his way back onto the road. He kept an eye out for Jim, hoping that he was all right.

"I'm going to take you straight to your uncle's ranch."

"How long before we get there?"

Wade shook his head. "Not long."

When they topped the rise above the ranch, Wade tried again to talk to Emily. He explained how Jim had found this land, pointing out the prize bull Jim was so proud of and the new barn he had built just the spring before. Emily barely reacted, still stiff and obviously uncomfortable. When they finally rode into the yard, he dismounted first, then lifted her off the horse. As he set her down, she lost her balance and fell against him. He tried to steady her, but she started toward the house. Again, she stumbled and he caught her. Once more she shook him free, fighting with her voluminous skirts. He could see that her hands were shaking and her face had gone pale. On an impulse, Wade bent and slipped one arm underneath her knees and the other around her waist. To his amazement, she didn't protest as he carried her into the ranch house.

"What happened? Is she all right?" Rose came out of the kitchen, wiping her hands on her apron. "Where's Jim?"

"I'll tell you about it later. She needs to rest."

Rose guided Wade to the spare room, and he laid Emily on the bed. She instantly covered her eyes with her arm, and Wade shook his head, unable to conceal his impatience with her theatrics.

"You just rest, Emily dear," Rose said gently, patting her hand. "I'll be back in a few minutes with a nice cup of tea." Rose took Wade's arm and led him out of the room to the kitchen. "What happened?"

Wade walked over to the table and cut himself a piece of cake. "The stage was robbed and Emily was kidnapped."

"My heavens, that poor thing!"

"Poor thing, my ass," Wade muttered as he took a bite of the cake.

"What did you say?"

Wade shook his head. "I can't believe she's related to Jim. I've seen trapped mountain lions that're friendlier than she is."

"I'm ashamed of you, Wade Colter. She's been through a terrible ordeal. How can you be so hard on her?" Rose went to the stove and poured Wade a cup of coffee, setting it on the table.

Wade pulled out a chair and took off his hat, hanging it on a corner of the chair. He sipped at the coffee and watched Rose as she busied herself making tea for Emily. Rose was one of the best women he'd ever known, and he respected and admired her a great deal. They'd met on one of the wagon trains Jim had been leading to Oregon when Wade was just fifteen years old. She and her husband had lagged behind, and when they hadn't been among the trains that night, Jim had sent Wade back to look for them. Wade had found the wagon a few miles away. Rose was alone in the back, ready to give birth to her child, and her husband was nowhere in sight. Wade had helped Rose deliver her baby, and Rose had been so grateful, the baby bore his middle name, Daniel. When Jim and Rose had gotten married, it was like Wade had acquired the family he had missed for so long.

"What're you thinking about?" Rose asked, sitting down at the table next to Wade.

"I was just thinking how you and Jim have become like my family. I'm real grateful."

"You must be missing Sandrine. You sound a bit melancholy, Wade."

"Maybe I am. I don't like it when she's away."

"She'll be back soon." Rose stood up and went to the stove, pouring some hot water into a cup. "I better see to Emily. She's had a rough day."

Wade watched Rose as she walked out of the room carrying the cup. Being around Rose made him miss Sandrine even more. He wondered if his wife and Little Bear were safe and if they'd reached the Blackfoot camp yet.

Two

Sandrine looked back at Little Bear for reassurance before she ducked into her grandfather's lodge. The familiar odors of sage and mint stung her nostrils as she entered, and she heard her mother chanting softly. She stopped, watching as her mother passed a bough of sage along the length of her grandfather's body and back up again. Her mother sat on her heels and began to sing, a song that Sandrine recognized as one of healing. It told of the strength that a person can draw by being close to the earth.

Sandrine moved forward slowly, feeling Little Bear's hand on her shoulder. When her mother looked up and saw her, she did not stop her song, but a slight smile lit her mouth. Sandrine knelt next to her mother, folding her hands in her lap, and biting at the inside of her lip to hold back her tears. Little Bear knelt on the other side of their grandfather. Sandrine waited patiently as her mother sang her song. She looked down at her grandfather, who was lying on a thick buffalo robe, dressed in fine elkskin pants and shirt. Feathers had been worked into the long braids that lay on his chest. He had a spot of black paint on his forehead and on his chin, and streaks of red and white were painted along both cheeks. Sandrine watched as her mother finished singing the song.

"I knew you would come in time, Bright Star," Running Tears said, reaching out to gently touch her daughter's face. "You look well. Did Wade come with you?"

"No, he did not," she said too quickly. "I did not know how long I would be needed here." She glanced at her grandfather.

"He is weak," Running Tears said. "This morning he asked to be dressed in his finest clothes, and he had me lay out his favorite weapons. He is ready to pass over to the other side. He has just been waiting to see you."

Sandrine nodded slightly, moving closer to her grandfather. She reached out and stroked his thick, gray hair, not knowing what to do or say.

"Talk to him, daughter. He will hear you."

Sandrine looked at her mother and Little Bear, and she drew strength from their faces. She put her mouth close to her grandfather's ear. "I am here, grandfather. It is Bright Star." When her grandfather did not open his eyes, Sandrine continued to speak. "You look fine today, dressed in your best clothes. I am proud to be your granddaughter." Sandrine felt the tears well up in her eyes. "I remember when you first sat me on a pony. I was so small I could barely walk. But you were determined that I should ride better than any girl and as well as all of the boys. So you put me on the pony. I wanted to cry but I did not. I remember the look of pride on your face when I sat tall, with my back straight. I tangled my fingers in the pony's mane and you led me around the camp, boasting to everyone. I never told you that I was afraid."

"I knew you were afraid, Bright Star," Night Sun said, his voice trembling slightly. He opened his eyes, blinked a few times, and focused on Sandrine. "But I knew you would overcome your fear, and you did. Was there any girl who could ride as well as you? Indeed, were there any boys?"

Sandrine smiled and shrugged her shoulders. "Not many, except for Little Bear. He was always a better rider."

"Little Bear only thinks he is a better rider." Night Sun smiled weakly.

Sandrine smiled and glanced back at her cousin. "I have missed you, grandfather."

"As I have missed you, Bright Star. So, tell me of your life in the white man's world. Does it go well?"

"Yes, grandfather, it goes very well. Wade is a good husband, and we are very happy together."

"This pleases me." Night Sun closed his eyes for a moment, then opened them again. "Do you live in one of the white man's wooden lodges and do you sleep up from the ground?"

"Yes, we live in a wooden lodge, and we sleep on a wooden frame that is up from the ground. We put our robes on top of the frame. It is comfortable."

"But it is not like this," Night Sun said, lifting his hand and pointing to the lodge.

"No, grandfather, nothing is like this." Sandrine picked up her grandfather's hand and held it in hers. "I love my life with Wade, grandfather. We live on land that has tall grass and trees, and we are close to a stream. It is beautiful there. Still, there are times when I am outside riding, or just walking, when I miss this place and my Blackfoot people. There is a freedom here that I do not feel in the white man's world."

"Do not ever lose touch with your people, Bright Star."

"I will not, grandfather." Sandrine tenderly kissed her grandfather's hand. "Will you still look after us when you have passed to the other side, grandfather?"

"Perhaps," Night Sun replied weakly. "I may be too busy. My grandson tells me he has spoken to Napi, the Creator, and he says there are many comely women on the other side."

"And what about grandmother? Will she not be there also?" Sandrine asked playfully.

"Of course, I will find your grandmother first, then I will have many other wives. As many as I please." Night Sun closed his eyes again.

Sandrine watched her grandfather, and she felt her heart

pound in her chest. He was so still. She glanced over at her mother, but she shook her head. Sandrine leaned down and kissed the old man on the cheek. "I love you, grandfather. I know you do not like the white man's words, but they are good words, true words."

"Yes, they are good words," Night Sun breathed, pulling Sandrine close to him. "When you were born," he barely whispered, "you were a beautiful baby. You did not cry. It was clear to me that you were content to be on this earth. When I saw that you and my daughter were well, I went outside the birthing lodge. I looked up at the sky. There were many, many stars, but there was one that outshone the rest. It sparkled so that it almost hurt my eyes. I knew then that Bright Star must be your name. And you have been a bright star in all of our lives."

"Thank you, grandfather," Sandrine said, unable to stop the tears. She laid her head on her grandfather's chest, listening to his slow, uneven heartbeat. She was surprised and pleased when she felt his hand come up and stroke her hair. It was not a gesture he would normally make.

"Thank you for coming, Bright Star. Now that I know you are safe, I can begin my journey."

"Must you go now, grandfather?" Sandrine asked, trying to keep from crying aloud.

"Yes, Bright Star, it is time. I am old and weary. I have had a good life. Now it is time to leave room on this earth for others who are just beginning their lives."

"Will I see you again, grandfather?" Sandrine met her grandfather's eyes.

"Yes, we will meet someday on the other side. And I will save the swiftest horse for you."

Sandrine smiled through her tears, and again she kissed her grandfather on the cheek. "Thank you for all that you have given me, grandfather. I will carry your words with me always."

BRIGHT STAR'S PROMISE

"Where are my daughter and grandson?" Night Sun asked without opening his eyes.

"They are right here, grandfather," Sandrine said, watching as her mother and Little Bear moved closer.

"My weapons are beside me, Little Bear?"

"Yes, grandfather, they are here."

"Good. I would not want to go without my favorite bow."

"Your horse will be waiting for you there, grandfather," Little Bear said.

"I do not wish to take my horse with me. There will be many of them there. I will give my horse to you, Little Bear."

"Thank you, grandfather."

"Running Tears," Night Sun whispered.

"I am here, father." Running Tears took her father's hand in hers.

Sandrine watched tearfully as Night Sun opened his eyes to look at his daughter.

"You have been a good daughter, and you have always shown great courage. Even when you married the white man, you were not afraid of me." He smiled slightly. "You have the heart of a warrior, my daughter."

Sandrine looked at her mother and saw tears streaming down her cheeks.

"I am the daughter of a great warrior. It is natural that I possess such courage," Running Tears said softly. "Rest now, father. Please."

"Soon I will be resting for eternity. Let me look on your faces once more before I take my leave."

Sandrine and Little Bear moved to either side of their grandfather, and slowly they raised him up to a sitting position, so that he was leaning against his backrest. He emitted a deep sigh and his hands were trembling, but his eyes glistened brightly.

"Yes, that is much better." Night Sun touched Little Bear's arm. "Take care of these people, Little Bear. They will need a strong leader some day. Remember to think clearly; be guided by your head and not your heart. Remember that hatred and bitterness are your worst enemies. They will always seek to destroy you."

"I will remember, grandfather."

"And you, Bright Star. Remember everything that I and your mother have taught you, and never forget your Blackfoot people. They are part of you."

"Yes, grandfather," Sandrine said, stroking her grandfather's hand.

"Come closer." Slowly, with shaking fingers, Night Sun touched each of their faces. "You both have given me much joy. I hope the same joy fills your hearts the rest of your days." Night Sun looked toward Running Tears, and he reached out for her. Running Tears took her father's hand. "Do not look so sad, daughter. Soon I will be with your mother. I long to see her." Night Sun closed his eyes and his arm went limp.

Sandrine watched as her mother bent closer to grandfather. She thought that her mother might break down and cry, but when Running Tears sat back on her heels, her face was composed. "Night Sun is gone from us."

Sandrine met Little Bear's eyes. They were moist, but he didn't look sad. Sandrine smiled slightly, thinking about her grandfather as he walked the path to the other side and finally saw her grandmother. It pleased her to think that her grandparents would finally be together after all this time. Sandrine leaned down and kissed her grandfather once more, then stood up and walked from his lodge. She knew that there would now be an emptiness in her that could never be filled.

Sandrine sat by the wide stone hearth in her parents' cabin. She watched as her father lifted the kettle off the stove, and she shook her head when he burned his finger and cursed in French.

She smiled wearily and drew her fingers through her thick hair. They had buried her grandfather that morning. People in the village had exchanged stories of Night Sun for most of the day, honoring his memory and celebrating his courage. But as the day wore on, Sandrine realized she wanted to be alone with her memories, and she had ridden to her parents' cabin. Her father crossed the room and handed her the tea he had made.

"I could've done that," Sandrine said, gratefully accepting the cup.

"It gives me pleasure to wait on you, Sandrine. It has been so long since I've seen you." He sat down in the chair next to her, reaching over and squeezing her hand. "I am just sorry that it is such a sad occasion that brings you home."

"Grandfather is content now," Sandrine said, sipping at her tea.

"That is one thing I have always liked and admired about your mother's people. They see no sadness in death. They see only a beginning to a new life."

"It is good to be here, father. I have missed you and mother very much."

"But you are happy. I can see it on your face."

Sandrine smiled broadly, hoping to cover her own uneasiness. "Yes, I am very happy. Wade is a good man. I have everything I need."

"I have always meant to ask you, Sandrine. Do you resent me for forcing you to go to Paris?"

"It doesn't matter now, father. All that matters is my life with Wade."

"You always were a forgiving child." Luc looked past her for a moment, then brought his eyes back to hers. "So, tell me about the house you are building. Will there be a room for children?"

Sandrine felt herself blush. "I don't know when we'll have

children." Sandrine fidgeted, setting down her teacup, then picking it back up again.

Luc nodded. "Perhaps your mother and I will visit you and Wade. I could help him with the house."

He gestured, and Sandrine knew what he was thinking. He had built this cabin with his own hands, and it had withstood twenty-five years of harsh winters.

"I would love it if you and mother could come to visit. You'll like it there. We could always build on an extra room if you decide to stay."

"Stay? Have you lost your mind? Your mother and I could never leave this country. Her people are here and I feel like it is my home." Luc looked at Sandrine, and he smiled. "Besides, you would tire of us quickly."

Sandrine curled her fingers around the warm china cup. "I heard talk in the village that there has been trouble with the Crows again. Have there been raids?"

"A few. A Blackfoot hunting party was attacked, and all of the men were killed. So, some of the young ones who were bent on revenge went after the Crows. They found them and mutilated them. News got back quickly to their people. I'm sure they'll retaliate somehow. It goes back and forth, just like it always has."

"Has Little Bear been involved?" Sandrine knew how much Little Bear hated the Crows. They had killed his wife and his infant son.

"You should be proud of your cousin. He used to be so hotheaded and wild. Lately he has been the voice of reason. He was the one who tried to talk the young ones out of their revenge raid, although it didn't do any good. I don't think it will be long before your cousin is a powerful chief in this tribe."

"I remember when Little Bear and I were children and he always used to tease me. He would get me so angry that I would cry. But I loved him so much, and I always looked up to him.

BRIGHT STAR'S PROMISE

When Bear Killer kidnapped me, there was never any doubt in my mind that Little Bear would find me. He will make a great chief."

"Well, perhaps I should have you speak for me, cousin." Little Bear's deep voice came from the partially opened door of the cabin. "How is it I was able to come in here unnoticed? If I was a Crow, you would both be dead by now." He came into the cabin and closed the heavy wooden door, walking across the room. He sat on the hearth next to Sandrine.

She slid toward him until their shoulders touched. "If you were a Crow, you would have never gotten this close. My brave cousin would have stopped you."

Little Bear shook his head. "See how she charms us all, uncle. I feel sorry for Colter. He has no chance against this woman." Little Bear reached out and took Sandrine's cup, taking a long drink and handing it back to her. "I have news that should interest you, cousin. Two of our men captured a Crow warrior. When he was questioned, he said he was looking for you."

"For me?" Sandrine said, looking from Little Bear to her father. "I don't know any Crows except . . ." She stopped, thinking of Gray Wolf, the old Crow warrior who had saved her life when Bear Killer was determined to kill her. "Did you see him? Was it Gray Wolf?"

"He is not Gray Wolf, and he would not speak except to say that he wanted to talk to you."

"What do you think he wants?"

"I do not know, cousin. I am a clever man, but I am not very good at hearing words before they are spoken."

Sandrine suppressed a smile. "I'd like to speak to him. You haven't hurt him, have you?"

"He is under guard, but he is well."

"Why don't you stay here tonight? Tomorrow I'll ride back to the village with you. I want to speak to this Crow warrior."

***

Sandrine followed Little Bear to his lodge, stopping when he held out his arm to prevent her from going any farther. A man stood guard outside the lodge, and Sandrine waited impatiently while Little Bear spoke to him. When he was finished, Little Bear motioned for Sandrine to wait while he went inside. Then he poked his head outside the lodge and motioned for her to come in.

It was a warm day and the sun shone brightly. Normally a prisoner would be kept outside, tied to a stake, not given the luxury or comfort of a lodge. But Sandrine knew why Little Bear had kept the Crow inside the lodge. Many of her people were still angry about the Blackfoot hunters who had been killed by the Crows. It would be foolish for Little Bear to leave the Crow outside so that everyone could be reminded of their hatred.

Sandrine ducked her head and went inside. Little Bear spoke to the guard who sat across from the Crow. The man nodded, stood up, and left the lodge. Sandrine walked closer, staring at the man. He was young, his skin and hair dark, and he wore only buckskin pants and moccasins. His hands were tied behind his back. He sat very straight, his eyes meeting no one's. His nose was straight, and his cheekbones were quite prominent. Sandrine thought he looked like many of their young warriors.

"Sit down, Bright Star," Little Bear said, motioning for his cousin to sit across from the Crow.

Slowly Sandrine sat down, folding her legs beneath her. She kept staring at the Crow until he finally turned his head to look at her. *His eyes are fearless,* she thought. "You wanted to speak to me," she said in halting Crow. When the man did not answer, she repeated her question. She looked at Little Bear. "I don't think he understood me. It has been awhile since I've spoken the Crow tongue."

"You spoke clearly enough, cousin. He is just making you wait."

Sandrine understood what Little Bear meant. The man had come into the camp of his enemy unarmed, to speak to her, and now he was being treated as a captive. His pride would not permit him to speak to her just yet.

Sandrine waited for some time, but when the Crow said nothing, she spoke to him again. "My name is Bright Star. Do you bring me news of Gray Wolf?" When he still did not answer, Sandrine got up and walked behind him, taking out her knife.

"What are you doing?" Little Bear demanded.

"I am cutting him loose. You can protect me, can't you, cousin?" Before waiting for Little Bear to respond, Sandrine put the blade between the Crow's hands and pulled the sharp knife upward, cutting the rope. She went back to the place where she had sat before and looked at the man. He was rubbing his wrists. "Now will you tell me why you are here?"

The man looked at her for a moment, then nodded slightly. "I have been sent by Shining Bird."

"Shining Bird? She is not ill, is she?"

"No, she is well, but she is worried about her father."

"Is something wrong with Gray Wolf?" Sandrine couldn't hide the concern in her voice.

The Crow hesitated for a moment before continuing. "His wife, Red Bird, died many moons ago. Since then, it is as if the life has gone out of Gray Wolf. Shining Bird thinks he is trying to die so that he can be with Red Bird."

Sandrine clasped her hands together tightly. Red Bird had been so kind to her. When Bear Killer had taken Sandrine into the renegade camp, she was dying. But Gray Wolf had bought her from Bear Killer and taken her into his lodge, and Red Bird had tended to her as if she were her own daughter. They were enemies and spoke little of each other's language, but they communicated like mother and daughter. Red Bird had reminded

Sandrine of her own mother; she didn't try to hide the tears that quickly formed in her eyes as she thought of the Crow woman's kind face. "What happened to Red Bird?"

"It was a sickness. She died quickly. She did not suffer."

Sandrine shook her head. "My heart is heavy. Red Bird was a good and kind woman."

"Yes, she was," the man agreed. "Shining Bird said that you and Gray Wolf were close. She said that you were like a daughter to him."

"He saved my life. I would do anything for him."

"Then you will come to our camp to try to help him."

"No!" Little Bear said adamantly. "It is not possible. Gray Wolf is a great man, but I will not allow my cousin to put herself in such danger."

"She will be in no danger if she is with me."

Little Bear laughed harshly. "You expect me to let my cousin ride with you, Crow?" His voice was bitter.

"Little Bear, don't," Sandrine said. She looked back at the Crow. "I can do nothing for Gray Wolf," she said as gently as she could.

"Shining Bird thinks otherwise."

Sandrine shook her head. "But she is his daughter. She should be with him, not I."

"She says you are special to him. She does not dislike you for this. She speaks highly of you. She thinks you can help her father."

Sandrine looked over at Little Bear again. "No, I can't go. I'm sorry."

"You said that Gray Wolf saved your life. Do you not owe him, Bright Star?"

"She owes him nothing," Little Bear said angrily. "She is the one who found Shining Bird and brought her to him. If it had not been for my cousin, Gray Wolf and Red Bird would never have seen their daughter again."

The Crow nodded. "It was a good thing you did for Gray Wolf, but is it the same as saving a life?"

"Enough!" Little Bear said, holding up his hand. "I will hear no more of this foolish talk. My cousin will not ride into Crow territory. It is too dangerous, especially now."

"I will guarantee her safety," the Crow replied calmly.

"Why is this of such importance to you?" Little Bear asked, his eyes never leaving the Crow's face.

The warrior's dark eyes met Sandrine's. "Gray Wolf is my father," he said simply.

"Your father?" Sandrine repeated. She shook her head. "We knew only of Shining Bird."

"I am his son. My name is Lone Wind."

"Why didn't your father tell us about you?" Sandrine asked.

"Perhaps it is because we had not spoken for many winters, since before he and my mother left the camp. He told you of my sister's husband?"

"Yes." Sandrine quickly recalled the story of Shining Bird's violent husband and how Gray Wolf had had to kill him in order to save his daughter's life.

"Her husband was my best friend. When my father killed him, I sided with my sister. I hated my father for what he had done. My sister refused to speak to our father, but I could not even stand the sight of his face. I left our village, and I did not return for a long while. When I did, my parents were gone. I still missed my friend, but I began to realize that my father had done the right thing. If he had not, my sister might be dead."

"It still does not explain why Gray Wolf never spoke of you. Many times he told us about Shining Bird, but never of you," Little Bear said, eyeing Lone Wind suspiciously.

"I cannot say why he never spoke of me. Perhaps it was easier for him. My father and I always argued. He would not let me find my own way."

"And how do you feel about him now?" Sandrine asked.

"I think he is a good man."

"He is more than a good man," Sandrine said defensively. "You should be proud to have a father like Gray Wolf. He is honorable and true of heart."

"This I am beginning to learn," Lone Wind said, his voice steady.

"How could you not know this about your father before?" Little Bear demanded. "This is a man unlike any other." Little Bear's eyes narrowed as he glared at Lone Wind. "Your people were responsible for the deaths of my wife and child, but Gray Wolf taught me that not all Crows are my enemies. I learned many things from him."

"As I am beginning to," Lone Wind said curtly. "So, Bright Star, will you come to our camp? You and your cousin speak of what a fine man my father is, yet you have shown no interest in helping him."

Sandrine held up her hand to quiet Little Bear when he started to speak. "I have no need to prove myself to you, Lone Wind. Gray Wolf knows what is in my heart." Her eyes narrowed as she glared at him. "If you believed Gray Wolf to kill for no reason, then you did not know him," she said, standing up. "You are free to go, Lone Wind." Sandrine walked across the lodge and had her hand on the flap when Lone Wind spoke, his deep voice filling the lodge.

"He has asked for you."

Sandrine hesitated, clutching the hide. If this was true, if Gray Wolf had asked for her, how could she say no? After all he had done for her, how could she leave him alone in his sorrow? She turned and walked back to Lone Wind. "What did Gray Wolf say?"

"He said he wished he could see you again." Lone Wind shook his head. "He speaks as if he is dying, Bright Star."

Sandrine looked at Lone Wind, then at her cousin. Slowly

she nodded her head. "I will go with you, Lone Wind. I cannot stay long, but I will do what I can for your father."

"Thank you, Bright Star."

"No!" Little Bear said angrily, following Sandrine out of the lodge. "Have you lost your senses? You cannot ride into a Crow camp."

Sandrine stood her ground with Little Bear, her hands on her hips. "Why not? I did it before when I went to search for Shining Bird." Sandrine touched Little Bear's arm. "I owe him this, Little Bear. I would not be here if it was not for Gray Wolf, you know that. If I can help him in some way . . ." She thought of her grandfather and the emptiness she felt without him. She knew how Gray Wolf's children would feel if he were to die.

"Do not be foolish, cousin. We are at war with the Crows again. They will not want you in their camp. They will resent you. This is too dangerous. And what about Colter? What will you tell him?"

"I'll write him," Sandrine said quickly, turning away. What would she tell Wade, she wondered, and would he even mind if she were gone that much longer?

"You cannot do this, Bright Star. I do not trust this man. We do not even know for sure if he is Gray Wolf's son."

"Why would he lie? Why would he come into our village just to talk to me if he wasn't Gray Wolf's son?" Sandrine hesitated. "I know you are only concerned for my safety, Little Bear, but I have made up my mind. I am going."

Wade stopped hammering and wiped his hand across his forehead. He set down the hammer and took a drink of water. The dry wind blew through the valley unrelentingly. He looked up at the clear sky; not a cloud to be seen. He still wasn't used to this kind of heat.

He took another drink and sat down on the front porch, looking down at the valley and the small cabin where he and Sandrine now lived. This really was a beautiful place. He thought of Sandrine, and he felt a tangible ache in his gut. . . . He loved her so much it almost frightened him. When he thought of what his life might be like without her, he couldn't envision being happy. She was everything he had ever wanted or dreamed of in a woman. There was no doubt—she was his happiness.

Wade looked around him. The house was coming along. He and Jim had almost finished building the forms for the adobe blocks. And he'd decided to surprise Sandrine—he was going to build an upstairs bedroom for her. From their bed they would be able to see the mountains in the distance and the entire valley. They would also have two bedrooms downstairs. There was going to be a large living area with a stone fireplace, and a separate room for cooking. In it, Sandrine would have everything she needed. Without her knowledge, he had already ordered a modern new cookstove from St. Louis. He couldn't wait to see her face when it arrived. He knew she'd protest, say they couldn't afford it. But he still had most of the money he'd earned scouting, as well as the large sum he'd been paid for saving a snowbound wagon train. Wade grinned. Sandrine was really going to object to his ordering the big mahogany fourposter bed, too. But she would love it.

Wade stood up and sighed deeply. But there was so much to do. Many of the cattle would soon be dropping their calves, and he would have to brand them. There were fences to be built, and he needed another barn. Then there were the daily chores: there was the garden, and the cows and goats to be milked, wood to be chopped and water to be fetched. Eventually he wanted to build an ice house like the ones he had seen in Missouri and Kansas. . . . Wade shook his head. He'd never get the house done at this rate.

He picked up his hammer and some more nails. He at least wanted to get the porch finished before Sandrine came home.

He drove a few nails into the wood when the sound of hoofbeats made Wade look up. He recognized Jim's big bay gelding and straightened up. It looked like he wasn't going to get anything done. He put down the hammer and nails, and waited for Jim to dismount and tether his horse to one of the big beams that would eventually support the roof.

"What brings you out here?" Wade said. "Don't you have more than enough to do with that niece of yours?" It had been several days since Wade had found Emily and brought her to Jim and Rose's.

Jim took the handkerchief from his back pocket and wiped his face. "You don't have to tell me about Emily. I've had just about as much of her as I can take."

"Wearing on you, is she?" Wade grinned as he gestured for Jim to sit down on the partially built plank porch.

"Jesus, Wade, you weren't exaggerating. I've been telling myself that she's been through a terrible ordeal, that she's not used to the way things are out here, but that's not it at all. She's just a spoiled brat and willful as hell. I can't believe my sister would raise someone like her."

"Yep, I'd say she's definitely used to having things her own way."

"Poor Rose," Jim said, shaking his head.

"Rose can take care of herself. She's the person to put Emily in her place."

"Well, right now she's trying everything in her power to make Emily feel at home, including making pastries the way Emily likes them and letting Emily sleep late and take naps. She doesn't do a thing to help Rose."

"And of course you won't say anything," Wade said.

"Well, she is my niece, after all. If I was to send you or Danny back East to stay with my sister, she'd extend you both every hospitality."

"That doesn't mean you have to let Emily run your household. Put your foot down, Jim."

Jim grimaced then cleared his throat. "I want you to do me a favor."

"What?" Wade asked, raising an eyebrow.

"Come to dinner tonight."

Wade shook his head. "I don't think so, Jim. I want to do some more work on the house, and I still have chores."

"I'll help you around here," Jim said. "Come to dinner, Wade. Rose could use the distraction."

"I think it'd be best if I stayed here, Jim. I don't think your niece would be too happy to see me."

"Dammit, Wade. Do you want me to beg?" Jim said angrily, standing up.

Wade grinned broadly. The only time he'd seen Jim this discomfited was when he'd talked to Wade about proposing to Rose. "All right, I'll come, but don't expect me to put up with your niece." When Wade saw Jim's slight grin, he nodded his head. "You want me to start a fight with her, don't you? That way, she can't blame it on you."

"I can't help it if she gets on your nerves," Jim said lightly, walking to his horse.

"Wait a minute," Wade said, standing up. "We had a deal. I come to dinner, and you help with the chores."

Jim hesitated, then shook his head. "All right, a deal's a deal, but I don't know if this is worth it."

Wade shrugged. "Well, if you'd rather go back and face your niece alone . . ."

"Where's the wood you want chopped?"

Wade grinned at Jim over his shoulder and led the way down the hill.

* * *

It was almost dark when Wade and Jim rode up to Jim's ranch house. They dismounted, and Jim quickly took Wade's reins from his hand.

"Why don't you go on in? I'll see to the horses."

Wade started to protest, then decided against it. Jim was going to kill as much time as he could in the barn. He was counting on Wade to help make the evening go smoother. Wade shrugged and headed for the front door, entering the house without knocking. "Smells good in here, Rose," he called, ignoring Emily, who was sitting in a chair by the hearth, her hands folded primly in her lap. Rose stood at the stove, her apron tied neatly at her waist. Wade walked up and hugged her from behind.

Rose straightened, feigning surprise. She twisted in his arms and kissed his cheek.

Wade heard Emily's tongue click in disapproval, but he ignored her, holding on to Rose a moment longer than he might have. "God, you're a pretty woman, Rose. If Jim hadn't found you first—"

"He didn't," Rose interrupted, laughing. "You were just too young and too shy."

"Too stupid is more like it." Wade kissed Rose on the cheek and stepped back.

"I'm glad you're here. I wasn't sure you'd come," she said.

Wade glanced past her at Emily, who still sat rigidly, obviously uncomfortable with Wade's open display of affection toward Rose. Wade wondered what else she had disapproved of here. He looked at Rose. She was probably as fed up with Emily as Jim was, only Rose was too kind to say so.

Wade looked around suddenly. "Where's my boy? Where's Danny?"

"He's over at the Foster place for a few days. He and Jeremy like to play."

It was easy for Wade to read the meaning behind Rose's words. Danny's noise had gotten on Miss Emily's nerves. "Too bad, I was looking forward to seeing him. It's not the same around here without him. Too quiet."

Rose brushed past Wade and turned toward Emily. "Emily dear, you've been so still, I don't think Wade even realized you were there."

Wade pressed his lips together to keep from grinning. As always, Rose was careful not to tread on anyone's feelings. He walked across the room and stood next to Emily's chair. "Good evening, ma'am. You look better than the last time I saw you."

Emily lifted her chin, looking straight into Wade's eyes. "I never thanked you properly for helping me, Mr. Colter."

"I'd do anything for Jim." Wade saw Emily's face tighten, and he was immediately sorry. "I'm glad you're all right, Emily. It must have been very frightening for you."

Emily's eyes flashed. "You have no idea how frightening something like that is for a woman."

Wade tightened his hands into fists, willing himself to control his anger. This girl had no idea what women like Rose and Sandrine had had to endure. He felt Rose's hand on his arm as she came to stand next to him. He looked at her. Even though she did not speak, he knew exactly what she was thinking. She did not want him to provoke an argument with Emily. People from back East never understood the harsh realities of the West, and there was no sense in trying to explain them. Emily would either stay long enough to find out for herself, or she would never know.

"I still have a bottle of wine that Frank Lauter gave me. Why don't we open it now?" Rose said, walking back to the kitchen.

Wade followed Rose to the sideboard. She stood tensely, digging at the cork in the wine bottle with a knife. Wade took the knife from her hand and leaned to whisper in her ear, "What's the matter?"

"Where the hell is Jim?" She glanced across the room at

Emily, smiling as though Wade had said something funny to her.

"I'll go check on him." He handed the open wine bottle to Rose and headed toward the door. But before he got there, it opened and Jim came in, smiling broadly. "Had to wait until the horses cooled off before I could water them," he said too quickly.

"Well, at least you're here now. We were just going to have a glass of wine." Rose poured the wine and handed everyone a glass. Then she sat down on the settee opposite Emily, leaving the two men to stand awkwardly.

Wade looked at his glass. "Here's to the rest of your stay, Emily. I hope that it's pleasant."

Emily nodded briskly, holding the glass to her lips, but she didn't answer. The silence lasted so long that Jim finally cleared his throat and spoke, looking at his wife.

"You should see the house, Rose. At the rate Wade is going, he'll have that place finished in no time."

"Sandrine will be so surprised when she gets back. Has the bed come yet?"

"No, not yet. Neither has the stove."

"Who is Sandrine?" Emily's voice was polite, correct.

"She's my wife," Wade said evenly.

"She's the prettiest thing in this valley," Jim said proudly.

Rose nodded, and Wade felt a rush of affection for both of them. But Emily's voice cut it short: "She's a local girl then?"

Wade started to answer but Jim was already speaking. "No, she's from Montana. Her father has a trading post up in Blackfoot country. In fact, she's part Blackfoot herself."

Emily caught her breath, one hand involuntarily rising to her lips. "Really? She's . . . part Indian? I'm sorry, I don't mean to be rude. That just surprises me."

"It's hardly a surprise; her mother is a full-blooded Blackfoot," Wade said tersely.

"Well, it's just that we read so much about Indians. They don't seem civilized."

"That's funny, the people in Paris didn't seem to think Sandrine was uncivilized. In fact, they were intrigued by her."

"Paris? Your wife was in Paris?" Emily couldn't contain the shock in her voice.

"She went to school there. That's where her father's parents live." Wade took a long drink from the wineglass. "Sandrine was quite taken with Paris at first. She even became engaged to a count. But she missed her home and her parents. I don't think she'd go back to Paris and all of those civilized people now, even if you made her."

"If you don't mind my asking, where is your wife now, Mr. Colter?" Emily asked, her eyes challenging Wade's.

"She's with her family. Her grandfather is very ill. But I'm sure she'll be back as soon as she can." Wade drank the rest of the wine and set his glass on the sideboard.

"Well, are you all ready to eat?" Rose asked, looking around at everyone.

"I'm starved," Jim said, putting his arm around his wife.

"I wasn't asking you. What about you, Emily? Are you hungry? I've made a roast and vegetables, and baked some loaves of bread. And I made a peach pie for dessert."

Emily hesitated, tugging at the cuff on her sleeve. "You people out here certainly have healthy appetites. Back home we don't eat quite so much."

Wade couldn't take it anymore. He walked over to Emily and grabbed her upper arm, yanking her to her feet.

"I demand that you take your hands off me immediately," she sputtered.

"Not until we've had a little talk," Wade said angrily, ignoring Rose and Jim as he pulled Emily through the house to the porch. Once outside, he closed the door and turned to face her. "Just what the hell is the matter with you, lady?"

BRIGHT STAR'S PROMISE 49

"What're you talking about?"

"These are two of the finest people you'll ever meet, and you're treating them as if they're your personal servants."

"I'm a guest," Emily replied indignantly.

"So what the hell does that mean? Do you think that entitles you to treat Rose and Jim like dirt?"

"I didn't say that. It's just—"

"Listen to me," Wade said, tightly gripping Emily's shoulders. "These people are my friends, and you're taking advantage of them. I won't have it, do you understand? They're doing you a favor by letting you stay here. I won't allow you to abuse their hospitality." Wade dropped his hands and turned away from Emily, trying to control his anger.

"I'm sorry," she said softly, standing next to Wade. "It was never my intent to take advantage of Rose and Jim. I just feel so out of place here. I'm not quite sure what to do or how to act."

Wade looked at Emily, surprised by the sincerity in her voice. "Why did you come here, Emily? It's obvious you don't like it much."

"My mother thought it would be good for me to see the West. She said I needed some excitement in my life." She shrugged her shoulders. "At least I've had some of that lately."

Wade had to smile. So she had a sense of humor, after all. "I am sorry about what happened on the stage."

"And I want to thank you for risking your life to help me."

Wade leaned on the railing, looking out into the clear twilight sky. "It's not so bad, you know."

"What isn't?"

"The West. I've traveled to lots of cities myself. I've even been to Boston." Wade shook his head. "But there's no place like the West. It's wild and untamed, and a man can do anything he wants out here."

"I don't mean any offense by this, Mr. Colter, but it does

seem primitive. It's quite frightening to be so far removed from everything, don't you think?"

Wade didn't get angry this time. "I don't know any other life. I couldn't imagine living in a city, not even Santa Fe."

"But what if your wife got ill? What would you do?"

"I know a few remedies, and Rose is close by. And there is a doctor in town if we need one."

"But it's not the same. It's not just the doctor. You don't have access to things like the theater, the opera, a library, or even a good restaurant. I mean, what do you do with your days?"

Wade wanted to laugh. If Emily only knew what his days were like . . . He shook his head. "I have so much to keep me busy, I barely have time to sit down during the day. And if you've observed Rose at all, you can see how busy she is."

"I guess I haven't paid much attention."

Wade glanced over at her, shaking his head. He had never met such a self-absorbed individual in his life. He watched her as she looked up at the sky. He noticed that she had a long, graceful neck.

"I think the stars are bigger here." Her voice sounded small, like a child's.

"Everything's bigger out here," Wade said. Wade had a sudden idea. "Would you like to come over to my ranch tomorrow?"

"What for?"

"Well, you want to know what I do with my days, so I'll show you. Maybe you can even help with some of the chores. I'm sure you're not as weak as you appear."

"I'm not weak at all," Emily said indignantly. "Once I helped my mother polish all of the floors and railings in our house, and we live in a very large house."

"Well, this won't be quite the same," Wade said in an amused voice. "You might get dirty. Why don't you ask Rose for some old work clothes. You wouldn't want to ruin any of yours."

"Just what is it we're going to be doing?" Emily asked, her hand nervously fidgeting with her collar.

"I'm going to show you what a day consists of out here, but you have to be willing to get up early and spend the day with me. Can you do that?" Wade's voice was challenging.

"I suppose I could. . . . I just—"

"Look, Emily, if you're going to be here for awhile, you might as well get used to the fact that you're not living in a mansion anymore. There are no servants here. It's not Rose's job to wait on you. You're her guest, and it's your job to help her out."

"All right," Emily said, her voice short. "I'll have Jim bring me over to your ranch in the morning."

"Better yet, why don't you ride over with Jim? You're in New Mexico now, you best learn how to ride a horse." Before Emily could respond, Wade gently cupped her elbow. "I believe they're waiting dinner on us. Shall we?" As Wade guided Emily toward the door, he wondered just what he'd gotten himself into.

Three

Sandrine moved nervously in the saddle. She knew they had been watched since they had entered Crow territory. She glanced back at Little Bear, who wasn't far behind her. Her cousin rode as always, his back straight and his head still, but his eyes scanned the horizon incessantly. He, too, knew that they were being watched. She almost wished Little Bear hadn't come with her; she feared for his safety. But she knew he would never have permitted her to go alone.

She turned back in the saddle and looked at Lone Wind riding ahead of her. He rode at a steady pace, but not so fast that it would tire the horses. They had been riding for over three days and he had not said a word to either her or Little Bear. Clearly his intention was just to act as a guide and nothing more.

Sandrine took a drink from her water bag and hung it back over her saddle horn. She wasn't as tired or sore as she thought she'd be. She was getting used to being in the saddle again, and she liked it. She had forgotten how much she had always enjoyed riding, especially the small hunting trips she had often taken with Little Bear and their grandfather.

By late afternoon Lone Wind had slowed his pace and turned his horse eastward. They followed a stream that led them over some rocky terrain, but soon Sandrine could see stands of cottonwood. She ducked her head as they rode underneath the low-hanging branches. Again she looked at Lone Wind; she wished that he were not so silent. It made the miles seem much longer than they were. Even Little Bear's naturally high spirits were dampened, and he was as quiet as Lone Wind. As the day wore on, Sandrine could not help but wonder why she had insisted on coming.

As the sun moved lower in the sky, Sandrine's delight in riding quickly faded. Her muscles ached, and she would've given anything to have been able to get off her horse and walk around. They were in the foothills now and had to ride carefully. Twice her horse nearly lost its footing as they picked their way across broad expanses of scree. Both times Lone Wind glanced back at her but did not slow the pace. He seemed determined to ride all night even though it was obvious that the horses needed to rest.

Sandrine closed her eyes and straightened her back, trying to force herself to ignore how sore she felt. They rode until the sun was below the horizon and the sky was ashen gray. Suddenly Lone Wind reined in, quickly dismounting. As they entered a stand of aspen, they were in the cover of boulders and trees, and it made for a good camp. Sandrine dismounted and turned toward Little Bear, but she could see by his expression that he was as weary as she was and not in the mood for conversation. She sighed deeply and took her bedroll from her horse. Then she gathered deadwood and made a small fire while the two men unpacked their horses. She watched Little Bear and Lone Wind and noticed that they were careful to keep a proper distance between themselves, avoiding anything that might cause them to have to speak to each other. Sandrine found herself fighting an urge to scream, just to break the tension and the silence.

Sandrine took a handful of dried berries from her rawhide pouch. The two men ate food from their own packs as well, avoiding each other's eyes. Little Bear kept glancing up at Lone Wind, the old, crazy hatred darkening his eyes, and it frightened Sandrine. It had been a long time since she had seen it, but she knew that Little Bear's grief for his family had never dimmed. His young wife and son had been killed by Crow warriors, and he had never remarried, had never started another family. Even though she knew that his affection and respect for Gray Wolf were real, so was his hatred for the Crows, the ancient enemies of his people. Sandrine drew in a breath then hesitated. Nothing she could say would change the way Little Bear felt. Determined not to make the situation worse by interfering, she finished eating and laid out her bedroll. She feigned sleep, but she was soon overcome by her own weariness.

They were back on the trail before sunrise. As they got deeper into Crow territory, Sandrine could feel Little Bear's nervousness. She dropped back to ride beside him. More than once, she wanted to speak to him, to try to help him see that Lone Wind had had nothing to do with the death of his family. She ached for her cousin, but she knew that his pain would be with him until he died.

As they rode, Sandrine said a silent prayer to Napi that there would be no trouble, that the old hatreds would not flare. Slowly the aspens gave way to cottonwoods and willows as they descended into a wide valley. Sandrine noticed Lone Wind's horse nodding its head and pulling at the reins. A few minutes later, she smelled wood smoke and she knew that they were close. She felt the eyes of the Crow sentries on them as they rode past the perimeter of the village.

Dismounting, they walked on, leading their horses. Sandrine watched Lone Wind as he acknowledged the greetings of many people with barely perceptible nods of his head. She searched the faces of the village people, looking for Shining Bird, as she tried to ignore the hostile stares she received in return. She felt like an intruder, and she found it difficult to look into the eyes of the people she'd been taught to hate since childhood.

"Gray Wolf's lodge is there," Lone Wind said, stopping abruptly.

Sandrine stopped, glancing at Little Bear.

"Leave your horse here," Lone Wind said.

"I will not leave my horse with you," Little Bear said harshly.

"You have not been invited into the lodge of Gray Wolf. You will stay here."

"Stop it," Sandrine said angrily, looking from one man to the other. "Remember where we are, Little Bear," she said, staring into her cousin's eyes. "This is not a Blackfoot camp; it is a Crow village. Please remember why we are here." Then she turned to Lone Wind. "Little Bear will come with me into the lodge, or I will not go. Gray Wolf has great respect for my cousin." She stood tall and straight, challenging Lone Wind with her eyes.

"All right," Lone Wind said begrudgingly, "he can go in with you. I will take care of your horses."

Before Little Bear could say anything, Sandrine took the reins from his hands and handed them to Lone Wind, leading Little Bear toward Gray Wolf's lodge. It was customary to ask for permission to enter another person's lodge, but Sandrine ignored the custom this time. The lodge flap was tied to the side, and without speaking, she ducked inside. Sunlight filtered through the smoke hole and brightened the lodge. She could see Gray Wolf sitting against his backrest on the other side. She hesitated, reaching for Little Bear's hand. She suddenly felt frightened. What would she say to Gray Wolf?

"Just remember what you once told me when I had no will to live, cousin," Little Bear said softly.

Sandrine nodded and silently thanked Little Bear. She took a deep breath and walked across the lodge, standing in front of Gray Wolf. She wasn't even sure if he saw her. "Gray Wolf," she said gently, waiting for him to acknowledge her, "it is Bright Star." She knelt in front of him. "Do you remember me?"

"Of course I remember you, Bright Star," he said, his eyes staring blankly ahead. "Why are you here?"

"I am here to see you."

"Ah, you have heard of Red Bird, is that it?"

"Yes," Sandrine said, moving closer to her friend. She sat down next to him, crossing her legs beneath her. "I am sorry, Gray Wolf. My heart is heavy. Red Bird was a fine woman."

"Yes, she was that," Gray Wolf said, nodding his head, still staring toward the lodge door. "I see the sun is shining brightly today."

"Yes, why don't you come outside and see for yourself."

"I like it in here. This was the lodge that Red Bird and I shared for many, many winters. When I am in here, her memory is strong."

Sandrine pulled in a deep breath. "But you carry Red Bird with you, do you not? Is her memory not strong no matter where you go?"

"Why did you come here, Bright Star? You are a long way from home, are you not?"

"Yes, I am, Gray Wolf, but I wanted to see you. I wanted to know that you are well before I go back home."

"Why should it trouble you so? I am just an old man."

"You saved my life, and I will never forget that. I would be dead now if it weren't for you, and I would have no life at all. So does it surprise you that I care much for you?" Sandrine's voice shook with emotion.

"Where is Colter?"

"I did not come here with Colter. I came with Little Bear."

Gray Wolf tilted his head to one side. "Is that you, Little Bear? Come here."

Little Bear walked across the lodge and sat down next to Sandrine. "It is good to see you, Gray Wolf."

"You traveled through Crow country to see me? Why, Little Bear?"

"Like my cousin, I have great respect and admiration for you, Gray Wolf. You and Red Bird saved Bright Star's life, and you

BRIGHT STAR'S PROMISE

took all of us into your lodge without question. I cannot forget that."

Gray Wolf was silent for a time, and he seemed to be studying Little Bear's face. "I see hatred in your eyes, Little Bear. It is not easy for you to be in a Crow village."

"No, Gray Wolf, it is not easy. I am often reminded of what happened to my wife and son. I had them for so short a time . . ." Little Bear's voice broke.

Sandrine looked at Gray Wolf's face. She wasn't sure if he was even listening to Little Bear. His face betrayed no sign of emotion. "You had many, many winters in this lodge with Red Bird," Sandrine said slowly, her voice even, "but Little Bear had only one winter with his wife. You and Red Bird lived to see your children grow up. You even lived to see your grandchildren. You must be thankful for the time you had with her, Gray Wolf. Red Bird would not want it otherwise."

Gray Wolf didn't acknowledge that Sandrine had spoken, and she exchanged looks with Little Bear. She felt like a fool. What could she say to a man like Gray Wolf, a man whose grief was so overwhelming that nothing else mattered?

"You think me a foolish old man, Bright Star?"

"Never," Sandrine replied, taking Gray Wolf's hand. "To have such a love as yours and Red Bird's . . ." Sandrine choked back tears when she thought of Red Bird's sweet and gentle face.

"You have such a love, Bright Star. That is why I am moved that you are here. But you can do nothing to help me if it is my time to go."

"How do you know it is your time to go, Gray Wolf?" Sandrine held his hand tightly.

"A man knows these things."

"Are you ill? Are you wounded?" Sandrine demanded.

"I am wounded in a way you will never understand," Gray Wolf said, "and it is inside here." He took his hand from hers and placed it over his heart.

"What about your children?"

"My children are grown."

"What about your grandchildren? They are young and need your guidance."

"There are others to guide them."

"You are making me angry, Gray Wolf," Sandrine said suddenly, her voice curt. "You are talking like a spoiled child who has had something taken away from him and wants to punish all those around him because of it."

"You have a sharp tongue, Bright Star. I do not remember this about you."

"Her tongue has always been sharp, Gray Wolf," Little Bear said. "Especially when she is angry."

"You cannot sit in this lodge and simply die," Sandrine said angrily, ignoring Little Bear. "You have too much to teach those around you. It would be wrong of you to give up like this." Sandrine leaned closer to Gray Wolf, taking his hands. "You did not let me give up, even when my shame was so great that I wanted to die." Sandrine bit her bottom lip, but she couldn't keep the tears from streaming down her cheeks. "You are like my blood, Gray Wolf. Do not do this to the people who love you." Sandrine's eyes met Gray Wolf's, and she began to cry aloud. She lowered her head, unable to stop the tears.

"Come here, child," Gray Wolf said, putting his arm around Sandrine.

Sandrine laid her head on Gray Wolf's shoulder. She had already lost her grandfather; she didn't want to lose Gray Wolf, too. She felt Gray Wolf stroke her hair, and she closed her eyes.

"Bright Star," Gray Wolf said in a gentle and soothing voice, "how is it that a girl of the Blackfoot tribe, a tribe that has always been my enemy, should come into my life and change it so? There is so much goodness in you, Bright Star, and so much love. I told you once that you are like a daughter to me. Now I think perhaps I was wrong. I think you *are* my daughter.

You and I are connected in a way that is unexplainable. It is as if my blood runs through your veins. Red Bird said this once, and I believe that she was right."

Sandrine sat up, looking at Gray Wolf. He was so handsome and regal, his face so proud. "I became your daughter when you saved my life, Gray Wolf."

"No," Gray Wolf demurred, reaching out to wipe the tears from Sandrine's cheeks. "You became my daughter when you brought Shining Bird to us."

"Gray Wolf," Sandrine said softly, picking her words carefully, "you know that it is not your time to leave this place. You have too much to teach others, and you know that Red Bird will wait for you. She will always wait for you." For the first time, Sandrine saw Gray Wolf's eyes glisten with tears.

"She was a good woman," Gray Wolf said simply. "She was my wife, but she was also my friend. When we were young, we desired each other all the time. Then, as we got older, our desires became different. We wanted to talk to each other, to lie together on our robes and look up at the stars, to speak of our grandchildren. I could say anything to Red Bird. It was as if she could see into my heart."

"She probably could," Sandrine said softly. "Will you walk with me, Gray Wolf?"

"Walk?" Gray Wolf looked at her, puzzled.

"I want to see you out in the sunlight. I want to see the face of the man who is responsible for my life, who took it upon himself to save me when I did not want to be saved."

"I do not feel like walking," Gray Wolf said abruptly, staring straight ahead.

"Then I will stay here."

"And she will not leave," Little Bear said. "I know my cousin, Gray Wolf. She is very stubborn. After I lost my wife and child, I was eaten up by hatred and sorrow. But Bright Star came to me and would not leave me alone. She would not permit me to give in to my sorrow." He looked at Sandrine and shook his head. "She will not give up on you, Gray Wolf. Better for you to walk with her."

Gray Wolf looked at Sandrine and Little Bear, then shook his head, turning his face to the sky and holding out his hands. "How is this, Great Spirit? Do you not find it strange that a man like me, a Crow warrior, is being kept from my path by two Blackfeet? Stranger yet, these Blackfeet are not my enemies but my friends. And one of them," he looked at Sandrine, "has the face of an innocent child but the heart of a mountain lion. If I did not know better, I would think that Red Bird had sent her."

"Perhaps she did," Sandrine said, putting her hand on Gray Wolf's arm. "Come, walk with me." Sandrine waited, hoping that Gray Wolf would not refuse. He sat silent, his eyes closed. Sandrine glanced at Little Bear, not knowing what to say or do next.

"You and Little Bear have come a long way to see me, Bright Star. I suppose I can walk with you," Gray Wolf said, his face less stern.

Sandrine quickly stood. She and Little Bear held out their hands to help Gray Wolf, but he waved them both away and stood up on his own. Sandrine followed his long strides across the lodge until they were outside. She smiled when she saw Gray Wolf look up at the sky and nod. It was a clear cloudless day, and the sky was a deep blue. Gray Wolf began walking away from his lodge, and Sandrine and Little Bear followed.

"I will leave you two alone," Little Bear whispered.

"No, do not leave, Little Bear. Gray Wolf is fond of you."

"Yes, but he thinks of you as his daughter. It is all right, cousin. I will wait in his lodge."

"Promise me you will not get into trouble."

"I will admit that I have sometimes had bad judgment in my

life, cousin, but I am not stupid. Do you not recall that we are in a Crow village, surrounded by Crows?"

Sandrine grinned as Little Bear walked back toward Gray Wolf's lodge. She then quickened her step until she caught up with Gray Wolf. She didn't speak; she didn't really know what to say anymore. She had said all that could be said. Now it was up to Gray Wolf.

"Look there," Gray Wolf said suddenly, pointing to the sky.

Sandrine looked up. A hawk soared gracefully, its wings outstretched, catching the wind and gliding in long, wide circles. "It's beautiful."

"It is a redtail hawk. Red Bird was named after this animal."

The hawk screeched loudly, circled above them, then flapped its wings and flew off toward the mountains. "Perhaps it was Red Bird checking to see if you have gotten out of your lodge today," Sandrine said with a smile.

"Yes, it is possible," Gray Wolf said, watching the hawk until it was a mere speck in the sky. When they left the village, Gray Wolf turned onto a path that had been worn into the meadow grass by the village women as they made their way back and forth from the woods on their never-ending daily chores. Gray Wolf led Sandrine to a cottonwood that had been struck by lightning long ago. It had fallen, but it had not died. For almost fifty feet, it grew horizontally, its enormous trunk grayed from the sun. "Let us sit here. We can sit for awhile, can we not?" he asked, raising an eyebrow as he looked at Sandrine.

"Yes," Sandrine said, nodding. She sat next to Gray Wolf, breathing in the fresh air. She could hear the sounds coming from the people of the village and the birds who called to each other in the trees. If she closed her eyes, she could imagine that she was in her own village. Somehow, the differences of their two people didn't seem so great.

"How is Colter?"

Sandrine hesitated. "He is wonderful." She felt her cheeks

flush crimson, and she looked away from Gray Wolf. She hadn't allowed herself to think about Wade.

"Yes, I believe that marriage agrees with you. Your eyes are bright and your cheeks have much color. You are more beautiful than I remember."

"You are far too kind, Gray Wolf."

"It is true, Bright Star. But you should not be away from your husband for too long. Many things could happen."

"I'm not going to be away long. I just want to make sure that you're going to be all right."

"It was good of you to come," Gray Wolf said suddenly.

"It was Shining Bird's idea. She sent Lone Wind to find me." Sandrine saw Gray Wolf's body tense when she mentioned his son's name. "Why did you never tell me about him?"

"I did not think it was important to speak of him."

"But he is your son."

"He does not consider himself my son. I am not sure that he ever has."

"Forgive me if I go too far, Gray Wolf, but what happened to you and your son to create such a distance between you?"

Gray Wolf tore a piece of bark from the trunk of the tree and began to toy with it, breaking off small pieces and tossing them to the ground. "There was always a distance between us, even from the time he was a young boy. I tried to teach him, I tried to be patient with him, but I managed to drive him away. It was always easier for me with Shining Bird, at least until . . . until I killed her husband."

"She understands why you did that, Gray Wolf, and she has forgiven you."

"But Lone Wind has not. Shining Bird's husband was his best friend."

"He also has forgiven you," Sandrine said. When Gray Wolf looked at her, she continued, "When he came to my village to find me, Little Bear did not believe he was your son. Lone Wind told us how he hated you for what you had done to Shining Bird's husband. He said that he left the village because of his hatred for you. But after a time, he realized that you had done the right thing."

"He said that?"

"Yes, hasn't he told you?"

"We have not spoken much since Red Bird's death. I think he blames me."

"He cannot blame you for an illness."

"He told Shining Bird that I should never have taken Red Bird from this village. He says that we traveled so many places that Red Bird could have caught many white man's sicknesses, or she could have even gotten the sickness from one of the other tribes." Gray Wolf crushed the remaining bark in his hand and let it drop to the ground. "Maybe he is right."

"No, he isn't right," Sandrine said angrily. "Even if you had told Red Bird to stay here when you left, she would have followed you. She loved you. She knew there was nothing more she could do for her children. She also knew that you were right."

Gray Wolf looked over at Sandrine. He reached out and put his large hand on her cheek. "You are a gift, Bright Star."

Sandrine felt tears sting her eyes as she looked at Gray Wolf's sad face. She covered his hand with her own. "I just want to help you the way you helped me. Please, let me do that, Gray Wolf."

Gray Wolf took his hand away and stood up. "Let us walk some more. The air feels good in my lungs, and I like the feel of the warm sun on my skin." When they reached the stand of cottonwoods at the edge of the meadow, Gray Wolf stopped. "You may stay here for no more than one moon, then you must go back to Colter. Your life is with him, not with an old Crow warrior."

* * *

Sandrine followed Shining Bird as she walked through the village. Sandrine tried to ignore the angry stares of some of the women, but she found it hard to do. They resented the fact that a Blackfoot woman was being treated with such respect by such a powerful and honored man as Gray Wolf.

"We will stop here, at the lodge of Buffalo Woman," Shining Bird said. "She always has fresh vegetables. I will trade some of our meat for her vegetables and we will have a fine dinner tonight." When Buffalo Woman came out of the lodge, she eyed Sandrine curiously for a moment, then ignored her as she spoke animatedly with Shining Bird. As the two women talked, Sandrine walked around, looking at the men who sat in front of their lodges and the women who never seemed to stop working. She smiled at a group of children who ran by, howling like a pack of coyotes.

"So you got my father out of his lodge. You must be a witch."

Sandrine jerked around at the sound of Lone Wind's voice. He had come out of nowhere, it seemed. "I am no witch."

"Then how could you do what my sister could not? Did you cast a spell over my father?"

"I told you, I am not a witch." Sandrine avoided Lone Wind's dark, piercing eyes, and she continued walking.

"You do not like me very much, do you?"

"I don't even know you." Sandrine stopped, meeting Lone Wind's gaze.

"But you judge me to be a dishonorable son to my father. I can see it in your eyes."

"If you can see that, then perhaps you are the witch." Sandrine looked past Lone Wind toward Buffalo Woman's lodge. Buffalo Woman and Shining Bird were sitting down now.

"If you are waiting for my sister, do not. She and Buffalo Woman are talking, and those two are like crows jabbering. They will not stop until darkness forces them to sleep."

Sandrine couldn't resist a small smile.

"I have finally made you smile. Good."

Sandrine reached up and pushed some loose strands of hair back from her face. "Will you walk with Gray Wolf and me today?"

Lone Wind shook his head. "I do not think that would be wise." Lone Wind turned away, heading toward the meadow.

Sandrine walked with Lone Wind, determined to find out what had caused the trouble between him and his father. "Do you have a wife and children?"

"No." Lone Wind's voice was hard.

"What about Shining Bird? Are you close to her?"

Lone Wind stopped, glaring at Sandrine. "If I had known you would ask so many questions, I would not have brought you here." He shook his head as if thinking, then he started walking again. "Come with me. I do not like talking here. Someone is always listening."

Sandrine followed Lone Wind on the path away from the village. He stopped near the place where she had walked with Gray Wolf the day before. She studied him when he stopped to pick up a rock. He was tall and muscular, his hair long and black. His cheekbones were high, his nose straight, his eyes dark and intense. If she had faced him as an enemy, she would have been afraid of him. But as the son of Gray Wolf, she found him intriguing. She watched as he drew his arm back and threw the rock far across the meadow and into the trees. He nodded slightly when the rock hit.

"How long will you stay with us, Bright Star?" he asked suddenly.

Sandrine shrugged. "I will stay for two or three weeks, and then I must return home."

"To your husband?"

"Yes, to my husband."

"Shining Bird tells me you are married to a white man. How does he treat you?"

"What do you mean?"

"Does he treat you as his slave?"

Sandrine laughed and shook her head. "No. I am his wife. He treats me well."

"I have traveled. I have seen the way white men treat their Indian wives." Lone Wind walked farther into the meadow, reaching down and pulling a thatch of long grass from the ground.

"My husband does not treat me like a slave because I do not allow it," Sandrine said, starting to get impatient. "But perhaps that is the way you are used to treating women, so you think all men are like you."

"It is clear to me, Bright Star, that you and I are not going to be the best of friends," Lone Wind said, breaking the grass into small pieces and letting it drop through his fingers.

Sandrine could see by the look in Lone Wind's eyes that he was not serious, that he was trying to make a joke. "Anything is possible, Lone Wind. We could try to get along for your father's sake."

"Yes, I owe him that, at least."

"What about Shining Bird? Are you close to your sister?"

"I suppose I am closer to my sister than I am to anyone," Lone Wind said. He looked past Sandrine, his eyes focused somewhere in the distance. "I was close to my mother. She was a woman of great heart."

"Yes, she was." Sandrine recalled how many times Red Bird had stroked her head or had held her in her arms when she had awakened crying in the night with nightmares of Bear Killer. "When your father bought me from the Blood Indian, Bear Killer, I was near death. Your mother watched after me every minute of the day. She never left me alone. I could not speak the Crow tongue then, and she spoke no Blackfoot, but we communicated as if we spoke the same language." Sandrine smiled, remembering the look on Red Bird's face when Sandrine had given her a blouse she had beaded for her. "She and your father gave me hope when there was none. I will miss her."

"Yes, I, too, will miss her," Lone Wind said, his voice low.

"Why don't you visit your father?"

"Because I do not wish to visit my father," Lone Wind said angrily. "Besides, you are here now. It is your job to make him well." Abruptly Lone Wind turned and walked across the meadow, disappearing into the trees without another word.

Sandrine shook her head, angry that she had even started talking to him. As far as Lone Wind was concerned, he had done his duty—he had brought her to the camp to help his father. And it appeared that was all he was going to do.

"I can't do this!" Emily stood up, backing away from the cow. "I don't even like milk."

"Yes, but I'm sure you like butter. It's not that hard to milk a cow, Emily," Wade said, barely able to keep from laughing. "Sit back down on the stool."

"I don't like being that close to the cow. I'm afraid it's going to kick me."

"She'll only kick you if you hurt her," Wade said, putting his hands on Emily's shoulders to keep her seated. "Now grasp the teats high up, right where they join the udder." Emily reached out, then recoiled when she felt the cow's warm flesh. Wade tightened his grip on her shoulders. "Just try. If you can at least learn to milk, you can help Rose out a little."

"I should've never left Boston." Emily's words came on a sigh so deep that Wade again had to fight back laughter.

"Try."

Emily reached forward again, and this time she managed to loosely grasp the cow's teats.

"Now squeeze your thumb and forefinger like I told you, so the milk won't run back up inside." Wade smiled at Emily's perfectly manicured hands. "Now tighten your middle finger and then the rest. Squeeze out the milk you have trapped in the teat." Beneath his hands, Wade could feel Emily lowering her shoulders, and he could imagine her face set in girlish concentration. After a moment, a thin stream of milk squirted into the pail. Emily squealed in delight.

"I did it," she said, twisting around to look up at him, a smile on her face.

Wade straightened, suddenly uneasy. When Emily smiled, her prim face was transformed. She was always pretty; smiling, she was almost beautiful. "Now all you have to do is fill the bucket."

Emily's smile faded, and she turned back to face the cow. Slowly at first, then faster, she forced little streams of milk into the bucket. The milk foamed as the level rose. Wade lifted his hands from her shoulders and stepped back. "When the pail's full, pour it in here," he said, gesturing toward a tall container.

"But I . . ."

"You'll do fine," Wade assured her. "I have other things to do." Before Emily could protest, Wade walked out into the sunlight. He turned resolutely toward the new house, shaking his head and lecturing himself as he walked. It had been stupid to bring Emily here. No matter how badly Rose and Jim needed a break from their willful niece, he didn't need to spend time with her. She was exasperating, but she was also attractive. He didn't know which would be worse; he could get angry enough to tell her how lazy and spoiled she was, or he might spend the whole time fighting the urge to kiss her. Either way, Miss Emily was a thorn in his side. For the hundredth time, he wished that Sandrine had not had to leave.

Wade pulled in a deep breath and started up the hill. When he got to the porch, he picked up his hammer but then sat down on the steps overlooking the valley. He missed Sandrine so much that it made him ache. He missed making love to her. She was a passionate woman, and their married life was all any man could ever want. But even more than that, he missed waking up with her, talking about the day's chores, working side by side with her, and laughing with her. He tried to imagine what she was doing at that very instant. Had her grandfather already died? Wade tightened his hand on the hammer. Night Sun had been a great warrior and a wise man. Wade knew how much Sandrine would miss him.

"Wade!"

Wade saw Emily walking toward him, voluminous skirts gathered in one hand and the milk pail in the other. Even at this distance, he could see that she was beaming like a schoolchild. When she reached the porch, she set the nearly full pail down next to Wade. "I thought you'd probably want to check it."

Wade nodded. "Not bad."

"I thought that's what you'd say." Emily smoothed her hair, looking past Wade. "So this is the house you're building. It's . . . interesting."

"You don't have to like it, Emily. I'm not building it for you."

"But I do like it," she said, walking back and forth. "I like the design. You're going to have two stories?"

"I'm going to build our bedroom upstairs."

"You should put more than one room upstairs," Emily said thoughtfully.

Wade got up and stood next to her, looking at the house. "Why do I need more than one room upstairs? I've already decided we'll have two downstairs."

"Well, you can't have your bedroom the same size as your entire downstairs, can you? And if you make it any smaller, it will throw off the symmetry of the house. It would look rather silly to have half of your roof flat, and the other half a second story."

Wade stared at the house for a minute. Already he had built the wide wooden porch, and he had made the arched entryway into the house out of smaller adobe blocks. He had envisioned the separate kitchen, the large living area, and two bedrooms downstairs. What he hadn't thought about was the bedroom upstairs. He had never even considered what Emily had said. "You're right. I never gave it a thought."

"Well, it shouldn't be that difficult to figure out. You'll have a staircase leading to the second story, and your room can be on this side so that you can take advantage of the view. You can build two smaller rooms on the other side. Then you can make a larger living area downstairs, and you can build a large pantry for your wife."

Wade shook his head in disbelief. "Thank you, Emily."

"You're welcome," she said, smiling.

Wade thought again how pretty she was, and he forced himself to look away. "You did a good job milking the cow. It takes most people awhile to get the hang of it."

"It was a challenge, I must admit." She looked at the house again. "So what are you going to do now?"

"I'm going to work here awhile, then I've got to ride out and check on some of my cows. They're pretty close to dropping their calves." Wade watched Emily's face and he grinned. "You can go back to Jim's now, Emily. I won't make you stay the rest of the day."

"No, I wanted to find out what you do, and I intend to. So what's next? Can I help you here around the house?"

Wade started to object, but he stopped himself. Emily had already proven herself fairly knowledgeable about building houses; maybe she could help him. "I don't suppose you can use a hammer? Have you ever pounded a nail before?"

Emily walked to the porch and picked up the hammer. "Where are the nails?"

Wade motioned to the nail keg that was on one side of the porch. Emily reached in, took some nails, and stood up.

BRIGHT STAR'S PROMISE

"There're some planks that need to be nailed down over there and—"

Before he could finish, Emily had squatted down, dropping the nails into her skirts. She put a few nails into her mouth and began to drive another into a plank. She drove the nail expertly and cleanly. Wade was astonished. He watched as Emily nailed down the plank and moved on to the next one, hesitating only once or twice. When she ran out of nails and walked back over to get some more, Wade realized he was staring at her. "Where did you learn to do that?"

Emily reached into the nail keg. "Didn't I tell you? My father was an architect and a builder. From the time I was a little girl, he would take me to houses with him and let me use a hammer. I loved it. When he died . . ." Emily stopped for a moment, staring at the hammer. "When he died, my mother decided it was time for me to become more of a lady. She said my father had almost ruined me, almost turned me into the boy he never had." Emily shrugged. "But those were wonderful times that he and I spent together." She walked across the porch and began nailing planks again.

Wade watched Emily as she worked, unable to believe that this was the same young woman who was afraid to get up on a horse or too lazy to do anything to help Rose. He was beginning to think he had misjudged her. He was also beginning to wonder what her real reason was for coming west.

Sandrine smiled across the fire at Gray Wolf. He winked, and she shook the bowlful of numbered bones. She had predicted she would throw twenty. When she threw the bones onto the ground, she quickly counted them and looked over at the man next to her. "That's nineteen, Swift Raven. Can you do better?"

"I do not like gambling with women," Swift Raven mumbled, putting the bones back into the bowl.

"If you are afraid, Swift Raven, I am sure we can find someone to take her place," Gray Wolf said, his eyes twinkling.

Swift Raven ignored Gray Wolf's jibe and shook the bones around in the bowl. "I will throw fifteen," he said, glaring over at Sandrine. When the bones were thrown, Sandrine quickly counted eleven. She had come closer than anyone in this game. She tried to conceal her glee, not wanting to make Swift Raven or the other men angry.

"You have done well, Bright Star," Gray Wolf said, nodding for her to take her winnings. She had won beads, a bone necklace, a pipe, a flute, and Swift Raven's knife. She held the large knife in her hands, knowing that it was his hunting knife and that he had probably made it himself. "I am sorry, Swift Raven, I cannot take this," Sandrine said, handing the knife to the Crow warrior.

"What do you mean? It is a fine knife. There is none better."

"I am sure it is a fine knife, but my hands are much too small to grasp it. I cannot take it."

Swift Raven looked perplexed. "I must give you something."

Sandrine looked at Swift Raven, knowing she mustn't dishonor him. "I have been admiring your belt all night. The beadwork is very pleasing to my eye."

Swift Raven seemed to consider the offer, then nodded his head, untying the belt and handing it to Sandrine. "It is a good belt, Bright Star."

"Yes, I can see that. I am satisfied."

"I am done," Gray Wolf said, slowly getting to his feet. "I have already lost too much tonight."

"It is good to see you out, Gray Wolf," one of the men in the circle said.

"Yes, I think Bright Star has been good for you," Swift Raven said, nodding his head. "Join us tomorrow night, Bright Star. Perhaps you will not be the lucky one then."

"We shall see, Swift Raven," she said, nodding her head to

the men as she stood up and went to Gray Wolf. She took his arm as they walked away from the group of men.

"I think you have charmed Swift Raven. That was a wise thing you did, Bright Star. He loves that knife."

"Yes, it was easy to tell. He should be careful not to bet things he is capable of losing."

"He will lose the knife eventually," Gray Wolf said. "Where is Little Bear?"

"He stays by your lodge. He thinks it best."

Gray Wolf shook his head. "There are some of my own people, people in this very village, who I do not trust as much as I trust Little Bear. Yet he is supposed to be my enemy."

"And I care for you as if you are my own father, and you are supposed to be my enemy. Yet one of my own, one I was supposed to trust, kidnapped me and subjected me to such cruelties . . ." Sandrine held tightly onto Gray Wolf's arm. "It is all so strange, Gray Wolf. It is as if the things we have been taught no longer hold true."

"That is good for us, is it not?"

"I suppose it is," Sandrine said, smiling. Before they reached Gray Wolf's lodge, they could hear Shining Bird's laughter. Gray Wolf stopped.

"Look there," he gestured. "Little Bear and Shining Bird are sitting together, and she is laughing. I have not seen a man make my daughter laugh in a long time. And look at the way my grandchildren sit around him. They do not know that he is supposed to be the enemy."

Sandrine watched as Shining Bird and Little Bear talked. She could see Little Bear's hands gesturing wildly, and she could imagine what he was telling her. "I would like to see my cousin happy again."

"And I would like to see my daughter happy again."

Sandrine glanced at Gray Wolf, her eyes narrowed. "Do you think . . . is it possible that they are interested in each other?"

"Look at the way they laugh with each other. I think they are good together."

Sandrine felt her stomach tighten. "But your people would never accept Little Bear, and my people would never accept Shining Bird. They would have to live on their own, away from their tribes, as you and Red Bird did for so long."

Gray Wolf shook his head. "I do not think so. I think they are both strong enough to make their people accept each other. Look at you and Colter. He is white, you are Blackfoot."

"That's different, Gray Wolf. My father is white."

"But you look Indian. There must be times when you and Colter go to a white man's village and people stare at you. It must be difficult."

Sandrine nodded absently, recalling the many times they had ridden into town and the many times that cowboys or women had made disparaging comments about her. But she also remembered how Wade had put his arm around her and had made her hold her head up high. "It is sometimes difficult," she said, watching Little Bear and Shining Bird.

"But you would have it no other way."

"No," Sandrine agreed. As they started forward, Gray Wolf's grandchildren spotted them and came running. There were two boys and one girl. Gray Wolf reached down and picked up his granddaughter while the boys walked on either side of him.

"Did you win at the game, grandfather?" Running Fox, the eldest boy, asked.

"I won a few times, Running Fox, but Bright Star won the most. She is good at the game of bones."

"What did you win, Bright Star?" Tall Horse, the younger boy, asked.

"I won many things—a pipe, a flute, many colored beads, and this belt."

"I like the belt," Spotted Deer, the little girl said. "It is pretty."

Sandrine reached out and rubbed Spotted Deer's cheek. "Then you may wear it sometime." When they reached the lodge, Little Bear and Shining Bird had already gotten up.

"Do not stand for us," Gray Wolf said, setting his granddaughter on the ground. "We did not mean to interrupt you two."

"You did not interrupt anything," Little Bear said almost too quickly.

"No," Shining Bird agreed. "We were just talking about you, father, and how much better you look."

"It pleases me that I give you two a reason to speak to each other. I would not want you to be enemies."

Sandrine looked at Shining Bird and she saw her blush. Little Bear shuffled his feet nervously. "Well, I suppose you won everything there is to win," he said, refusing to look at Shining Bird or Gray Wolf.

"I did well enough," Sandrine said, handing the flute to Little Bear. "Here, you can use this to play music to the woman you love." Before Little Bear could say anything, she turned and walked away from the lodge, smiling to herself. She stopped at the edge of the meadow, where it was quiet and where she could be alone. She sat down on the ground, crossing her legs beneath her. She looked up at the star-filled sky and sighed, allowing herself to think about Wade. She missed him and she longed to go home. Gray Wolf was doing well enough; she wouldn't need to stay here much longer.

"You should not be out here alone." Lone Wind came out of the darkness to stand next to Sandrine.

Again, Sandrine had not heard him, and she flinched at the sudden sound of his voice. "I like it here."

"It is dangerous."

"I am not afraid," she said stubbornly, looking back up at the sky.

"You should be afraid. Two moons ago, a woman and her daughter were kidnapped at this very spot by Blackfoot raiders."

"I am sorry for the people who were kidnapped, but the same thing will not happen to me. I will not be kidnapped by one of my own." Sandrine tried to make her voice sound steady and fearless.

Lone Wind squatted next to Sandrine. "But you were kidnapped by one of your own, Bright Star."

"It does not matter, Lone Wind," she replied angrily. She wished that he hadn't found out about Bear Killer. "I'm not worried."

"You should be worried. The two women who were taken by the Blackfoot were killed and left on the prairie like butchered buffalo."

Sandrine fell silent, unable to think of anything to say.

"When will you return to your home?" Lone Wind asked, his voice less harsh.

"Soon," she said. "I don't think your father needs me anymore. I'm not sure he ever did."

"He is a strong man, it is true. But you helped him, Bright Star, of that I have no doubt."

Sandrine looked at Lone Wind in the dim light from the village campfires. "Your father is a good man, Lone Wind. I am not sure you know that."

"It does not matter what I think."

"Of course it matters. You are his son."

"I am grateful that you came all this way to help my father, Bright Star. It was a good thing to do. But do not try to get involved in things of which you have no understanding."

"I understand more than you know," Sandrine said, getting to her feet and starting toward the village. Before she could get very far, she felt Lone Wind's hand on her arm. She turned, met his eyes, and stopped. "Let go of my arm," she said, her words carefully measured.

Lone Wind looked at her a moment, then took his hand from her arm. "What did you mean?"

"I know that you love your father, Lone Wind. If you did not, you would never have looked for me."

"I did not want him to die."

"Say what you will," Sandrine said, shrugging. "I know only that there are two men who need each other, but neither will admit it."

"You know nothing about me."

"I know what I see."

"And what do you see, Bright Star?"

"I see a man who is being eaten away by hatred and bitterness, a man who pretends not to care."

"You say strange things," Lone Wind said. "You look like an Indian, but you speak like a white woman. It is troubling."

Sandrine almost smiled. "Why is it troubling? Because I speak the truth?"

"I will admit to no truth of yours, Bright Star," Lone Wind said angrily.

"Is there any truth that you will admit to?"

"If your tongue was any sharper, you could cut hides with it."

"My cousin has said similar things to me many times." Sandrine realized that she was enjoying taunting Lone Wind. "But I always ignore him." She turned and stared up at the sky. "I believe that Red Bird is up there now. I think she is probably one of the brightest stars that shines."

"Like you?"

Sandrine glanced at Lone Wind, then looked quickly away. She was glad it was night so that he couldn't see the quick flush that had spread over her cheeks. "I should go back. They will be worried," she said, heading toward the village. Lone Wind didn't move, but she could feel him staring at her as she walked away. It was only when she had reached some of the outlying lodges of the village that she allowed herself to breathe. She touched her own cheek, then let her fingertips trail over the smooth skin of her throat. Lone Wind had a dangerous effect on her—there was no point in denying it. She would have to be careful.

Four

He had been watching the woman since she had watered her horse in the stream. She was riding a large bay gelding and she handled the horse well. He had not intended to follow her, but something about her fascinated him. Pulling up, he was careful to stay out of sight in the shadows of the trees. He watched her as she cantered across the open prairie; she looked like a young girl on her first ride.

He peered back through the trees; still there was no one. She was not being followed. He dug his heels into his horse's flanks and the animal leapt forward. Long moments passed before the woman turned and saw him, her eyes going wide with fear. He whipped his horse into a gallop and bore down upon her, screaming a war cry to spook her mount. When the animal faltered, he leaned forward and slashed downward with his whip. The woman cried out as she felt her horse stumble in pain and fear. Seeing his chance, the warrior urged his horse forward, whipping it mercilessly. Sandrine's mount stumbled again, then plunged to a trembling stop. The Blackfoot grabbed the reins and jerked them from Sandrine's hands before she had time to react.

"I am Blackfoot," she said, her voice angry.

He stared at her and said nothing. She spoke the Blackfoot tongue well, but it made no sense. She did not look Blackfoot, and she was dressed in Crow clothing.

"I am Bright Star of the Northern Blackfoot," she repeated stubbornly.

He looked around him, making sure no one had followed her. Then he leaned across his horse, reaching for the woman. He grasped her wrist and jerked her off her horse, smiling when she cried out. Once she was steady on her feet, he gripped her arm harder—hard enough so that tears flooded her eyes. He loosened his grip, and the moment he did, she surprised him by wrenching free and starting to run. He smiled again; this one had spirit. He rode after her, leaning down to grab at her arm.

"Let me go!" she yelled angrily as he dragged her up onto the horse in front of him, her chest barely on the horse's withers, her legs kicking wildly.

He held tightly onto her blouse, but the cloth tore and she fell to the ground. She began to run again and he watched her, knowing there was no place she could go. When exhaustion slowed her pace, he kicked his horse and started after her, this time turning in front of her and cutting her off. When she tried to go another direction, he cut her off again. This time she spun, running back in the direction she had come. It took a moment longer for him to wheel his horse around, but once he had, she was no match for him. He nearly ran her down, sliding his mount to a stop in front of her.

She looked wild-eyed into his face, her breath coming hard. Then once more, she surprised him and ran again, heading desperately toward the cover of the trees. He reined in and let her believe for a moment that she would escape. When he saw hope lift her stride, he let his mount have its head and he overtook her, laughing aloud at the cry of anguish as she heard the hoofbeats behind her. He watched her as she fell to her knees, taking in great gulps of air. He waited until she looked at him.

"Are you ready to come with me now?" he asked. Slowly he watched as the animal look left her eyes and reason returned.

BRIGHT STAR'S PROMISE

"I will never be ready to go with you." She stood up, standing close to his horse. To his disbelief, she stared defiantly at him, then drew her arm back as if she had a weapon. An instant too late, he saw the rock clasped tightly in her hand. He tried to dodge it, but she managed to graze the side of his head. By the time he looked back, she was running again.

"You will be sorry for that, woman," he said whispering, his teeth clenched. He kicked his horse into a run until he was beside her. Pulling out his war club, for an instant he contemplated killing her, but he knew it would be foolish. There was a chance she would turn out to be a good slave. Sometimes the spirited ones were the best. If not, her looks would make her valuable for trade. Instead of a killing blow, he lowered his war club carefully, almost gently, and struck her in the middle of her back so that she sprawled onto her face. Within seconds he had jumped from the horse and had slipped a rope around her waist. "You will come with me now," he said, mounting up again.

Immediately she struggled against the rope, but he urged his horse forward so there was not enough slack for her to loosen it. He glanced back. She was still trying to get free, clawing at the rope with both hands, but her movements were weak. It wouldn't be long before the fight went out of her.

He nodded to himself, glad that he had controlled his rage. If he decided not to keep the woman for himself, she would certainly be worth a lot in trade. Early that morning, he had come across a small herd of buffalo. He had been eager to return to his village to tell the people about it. Now the day had become even luckier.

Lone Wind walked around the corral, checking on the horses that he and some of the other men had just rounded up. There were some mares and two colts that would add to their herd.

There was also a pinto stallion that they had separated and put into another corral. The stud was nervous and had tried several times to jump the railing, but the rope held him.

"What do you think?" Black Buck asked, standing next to Lone Wind. "He is spirited."

Lone Wind nodded. "Yes, but he can be broken." Lone Wind leaned on the railing and looked at the stallion as he pounded the length of the corral then wheeled and followed the railing back, his eyes rimmed with white. Lone Wind decided that he would take him down to the water and tire him out. He didn't want to risk injury to this animal.

"Lone Wind, look there," Black Buck said, pointing across the meadow.

Lone Wind looked up and saw Bright Star's bay gelding running into the meadow where the other horses grazed. He walked to the horse, patting him on the neck. The animal was breathing heavily and was covered in sweat. The gelding's return made him uneasy. Where was Bright Star? he wondered. He knew that she was an experienced rider. Perhaps something had spooked the horse and he had thrown her.

Quickly he took one of the hackamores hanging from the top rail of the corral. He spotted his sorrel stallion grazing in the pasture and whistled. The horse lifted its head and moved toward him. He patted its neck as he slipped the hackamore over its muzzle. Then he mounted. It was easy to pick out the tracks of Bright Star's horse. It was the only one that wore the white man's iron shoes.

Lone Wind rode slowly out of camp, his eyes on the ground. The bay had taken a meandering course—the kind of course a riderless horse will always take. It had stopped to graze many times and had taken a drink at a stream. Impatiently Lone Wind followed the trail, dreading what he might find at the end of it. After a long time, the bay's tracks deepened and became erratic, indicating that the horse had been running and frightened. Lone

Wind kneed his sorrel into a canter, easily following the trail of uprooted meadow grass and dislodged pebbles. When the tracks veered abruptly to one side, he pulled up and leaned to examine them more closely. For anyone who could read the tracks, the story was clear. Sandrine had not had an accident but had been taken captive.

He urged his horse a little faster, careful not to lose Bright Star's trail. A false start would cost him more time than he could afford to lose. He knew it was possible that whoever had taken her would kill her outright, but it was even more likely that she would be enslaved, perhaps even sold and taken far from home. Lone Wind shook his head. Bright Star had already had to survive one cruel captor. It was not right that she should have to suffer again. He urged his horse faster.

Sandrine's legs were trembling with fatigue. The Blackfoot warrior jerked on the rope, and she stumbled forward, trying desperately to keep her footing. She was terrified that she would fall and that he would drag her. They had been heading toward the foothills for what seemed like hours, and the constant upgrade had become sheer torture. Still, she refused to cry out. She could feel herself hardening, her emotions, even her pride, closing down. She knew what it would take for her to live through this, and she could only pray that she could summon the strength to do it once again. As she fought to keep her balance, and to keep from crying out where the rope had badly chafed her skin, she frantically tried to think of a way to convince the warrior that she was Blackfoot. It might not make any difference to him, she knew, but it was her only hope.

Sandrine felt a hopelessness settle over her, a hopelessness so profound that she did not hear the hoofbeats behind them until the Blackfoot jerked his horse around. Sandrine stumbled as the rope slackened, then tightened again. Turning, she saw

Lone Wind galloping toward them, his lean body low against his horse's neck, his bow held steady with an arrow already nocked. An instant later, she watched as the Blackfoot clutched at the shaft of the arrow that had entered his chest. He slumped sideways and fell from his horse, not moving once he hit the ground. Sandrine stared at him, swaying with exhaustion. It took her a moment even to hear Lone Wind's voice, and even longer to understand his words. Weak with relief, she could only stand still as he dismounted and gently loosened the rope from around her.

"Are you all right? Did he hurt you?"

Sandrine looked into Lone Wind's dark eyes, knowing what he was trying to ask, and grateful that he cared. If Lone Wind had not found her, the Blackfoot would almost certainly have raped her. The thought took the last of her strength, and she involuntarily leaned into Lone Wind. His arm went around her shoulders, and he supported her gently, bending to look into her eyes.

"Did he hurt you, Bright Star?"

"Thanks to you, he did not."

Without speaking, Lone Wind picked her up and carried her to his horse. He lifted her onto the animal's back, then swung up behind her. Sandrine leaned back against him, unable to stop her trembling.

Lone Wind rode slowly, and Sandrine was grateful that he did not try to talk to her. Her emotions were complicated, and she felt more gratitude than she would ever be able to express. Lone Wind had saved her, and now he had the gentleness and the understanding to let her recover herself in silence.

She closed her eyes for a moment, suddenly very troubled. She couldn't believe that one of her own people had tried to kidnap her. Again. Two times she had been kidnapped by men of her own tribe, and her rage was mingled with shame. When the horse stopped, she opened her eyes. Lone Wind had brought her to a small pond. He dismounted and held out his arms to Sandrine.

"I thought you would want to drink and wash."

Sandrine nodded, letting Lone Wind help her from the horse. Her legs still felt shaky, and she wobbled slightly when she stood. Lone Wind put his arm around her and helped her to the water.

"Thank you," Sandrine said, kneeling in the damp soil at the edge of the pond. She cupped her hands together and drank until her thirst was quenched, then she sat back on her heels, untucking her blouse from her skirt. She grimaced as she touched her waist.

"Let me see," Lone Wind said, sitting down next to her. He lifted her blouse away. "The rope has cut you and you are still bleeding. You must clean it."

Sandrine nodded, trying to hold the blouse up as she dabbed water on the cuts with her other hand.

"I will help you if you do not mind," Lone Wind said.

"No, I don't mind," Sandrine said wearily, holding the blouse away from her bare skin. She knew she should have been embarrassed, but she wasn't. She was too tired to care. She watched as Lone Wind tore a strip of cloth from the hem of her skirt and wet it in the water. Then he carefully put it against her skin. Sandrine flinched at the cold and the stinging pain she felt, but she didn't say anything. She let Lone Wind tend to her wounds, and then she leaned back on her hands, letting her blouse fall loosely down around her. "Thank you," she said, looking at Lone Wind. His dark eyes were hard to read, but she thought the expression in them had softened.

"Give me your hands," Lone Wind said as he gently washed each one. "They have been burned by the ropes. You should not have fought so hard. He might have killed you."

"He might have killed me if I hadn't," Sandrine said, closing her eyes as Lone Wind tended to her.

"I am sorry, Bright Star. We should have kept closer watch."

Sandrine opened her eyes. "Why are you sorry, Lone Wind? I was taken by one of my own people." She shook her head. "I don't know what to think anymore. It makes me ashamed of the men of my tribe, and it makes me understand more clearly why your people hate mine."

"You are a strange one, Bright Star," Lone Wind said, reaching up to wipe the dirt from her face. "I do not know many women who would speak as you do."

Sandrine drew back. "You think it strange that I tell the truth? Should I make excuses for that man? Should I say that I know he would not have hurt me just because he was Blackfoot?" Sandrine's voice had grown shrill. "I have been hurt by one of my own kind before . . ." She stopped, not wanting to relive the past yet again. She looked away, tears stinging her eyes.

Lone Wind finished cleaning Sandrine's face and sat down next to her. "It is not just your people, Bright Star. There are men like that in every tribe."

"I know that." She squirmed slightly, trying to find a comfortable position.

"Perhaps it is time for you to return to your home, to your husband."

Sandrine looked over at Lone Wind. His voice was gentle and his eyes were kind. It would be easy to let her feelings for him overcome her good sense. She nodded her head. "Yes, I think I should return soon."

"I would not have let my woman go so far away from me."

Sandrine caught her breath and looked away, not wanting him to see the effect his words had on her. "Will you ever forgive your father?"

"It is not necessary for me to forgive him for anything."

"But you seem so determined to make him suffer. I don't understand that."

"Just because I do not show my feelings like a woman does

not mean I hate my father." Lone Wind stood up. "We should go now, or your cousin will think that I kidnapped you."

Sandrine smiled. "You and my cousin are very much alike, you know."

"We are nothing alike." Lone Wind walked toward his horse.

Sandrine struggled slowly to her feet. "You are both stubborn, and you both hold your anger deep inside of you."

"Do not compare me to your Blackfoot cousin," Lone Wind said shortly, lifting Sandrine up onto the back of the horse. He swung up behind her, taking the reins in his hand.

Sandrine tried to find a comfortable position, but she could not. She gave up and leaned against Lone Wind, feeling his muscular chest against her back. She thought of how long the journey would be to go home, and it exhausted her to think about it. She closed her eyes. Lone Wind's arm tightened around her, keeping her against him. She liked the feel of him, his strength. It made her feel safe, and she needed that right now.

Wade downed the glass and slammed it on the table, making a loud, rasping sound. "Nothing like a good shot of whiskey."

"That's what I always say," Jim agreed, filling their glasses again.

They had been sitting in the saloon since they'd finished Rose's shopping, which had been about three hours ago. Neither one was in a hurry to leave.

"Well, what should we drink to?" Jim said, holding up his glass.

"Let's drink to women." Wade started to drink then stopped. "No, let's not drink to women. They cause too much confusion. I love my wife, but I haven't seen her in almost a month. Then there's your wife, the best darn woman I've ever known, but, boy, can she cut you down to size. And there's your niece."

"Ah, Emily," Jim said. "Emily's different altogether. I'm not even sure we should classify her with the others."

"She sure is pretty though," Wade said, thinking of Emily's green eyes and auburn hair.

"You're a married man, Wade, and don't you forget it."

"I haven't forgotten; I just said that Emily is pretty. I know you've never noticed another woman since you've been married to Rose," Wade said, holding his glass lower. "Except for Mary over at the telegraph office and Martha at the General Store. Oh, and don't let me forget about Lucy. You remember Lucy, don't you, Jim? She's the one who throws her arms around your neck every time you come in here and gives you a big kiss on the mouth. Have I left anyone out?"

"All right, so I admire a few women. I've never done anything about it."

"And neither will I with Emily." Wade picked up his glass. "So let's drink."

Jim lifted his glass, staring into the amber-colored liquid. "How about if we play it safe and just drink to whiskey. It's a damned fine brew."

Wade nodded and downed the glass, closing his eyes until the burning in his throat had passed. He hadn't had this much to drink in a long time, and it felt kind of good. He liked Jim's company and he liked the saloon. Being here helped him forget how much he missed Sandrine.

"Well, well, fancy meeting you two gents here." Frank Lauter came up to the table, dressed like a gambler, with ruffles peeking from beneath his expensive black jacket and a diamond ring on the little finger of his left hand.

Wade looked up at Frank, no longer wary. Even though this man had gambled with Sandrine—and could have taken her virtue and Jim's ranch when he had won—he had ultimately proved he was a gentleman. Wade had hated Frank at first, but over time, he had come to like this smooth-talking cattle baron.

He was a good man in a card game, always honoring his debts, never hotheaded when he lost. He was a man of his word, too. He had promised Rose that he would never gamble with Jim again, and he had not. "Join us, Frank?" Wade pulled out a chair.

Jim motioned to the bartender as Frank sat down.

Wade touched the brim of his hat. "What brings you into town, Frank? Got a game going in the back room or just stopping by to see Sal?"

Frank smiled. "I still don't know what she sees in me, but I'm grateful. She's the finest woman I've ever known."

Jim banged his glass on the table. "We were discussing that earlier. Women, I mean. Once one gets ahold of you, life is never a simple thing again."

"I'm just glad to be gotten ahold of." Frank laughed and set down his empty glass. "I won a horse just now you boys ought to come look at. A real beauty."

"Looks aren't everything in a horse," Wade said.

Frank nodded. "That's a fact. This one's supposed to be almost impossible to ride." He stood up and scraped back his chair. "Come on. It's obvious that you two don't have anything better to do."

The three men went out the doors of the saloon and into the bright sunlight. Frank led the way, past the dry goods store, then across the street to the livery. He showed the stableman a piece of paper and explained what had happened. A moment later, the man led a tall black stallion out to the livery yard. The animal pranced nervously, pulling at the lead rope.

Wade whistled in appreciation. "He is a beauty, Frank."

The stableman ran his hand through his graying hair and shook his head. "He's a killer, is what he is."

Wade shook his head. "You're handling him all right."

The stableman nodded grimly. "Yeah, he's all right like this with just a halter, but if you try to put anything on his back, he goes crazy. He tried to throw Clem Simsom yesterday."

Wade shook his head. "Clem Simsom can't stick on a horse to save his life."

The stableman shook his head. "Nobody could stay on this one."

Wade felt Frank and Jim watching him. The whiskey was still warm in his belly, and as he watched the beautiful stallion paw the ground, he shook his head again. The stallion just didn't look that mean. Nervous, but not mean. Wade stepped forward and took the halter rope from the stableman's hand. "You going to ride him now, Frank?" Wade said over his shoulder.

Frank shook his head. "If he's a killer, I'll probably sell him." Frank laughed again. "Or maybe I'll go lose him in a card game to another sucker."

Wade turned to face Frank. "Don't do that. If you feel like gambling, I'll make you a bet right here. I can ride him. In fact, I'll ride him to a standstill." Wade felt Jim's hand on his arm, but he shook it off. The horse really was magnificent, exactly the kind of stallion he'd been hoping to buy in another year or two. Even if he was never a reliable saddle horse, he would be a valuable stud. All Wade had to do was ride him once. It had been a long time since a horse had managed to throw him, and even though the stallion was tall and strong, he didn't show any of the usual signs of a killer. As Wade watched, the stableman reached out to rub the horse's forehead. Impulsively Wade turned to look at Frank. "I'll try to ride him right now. If I do, he's mine."

"I think that whiskey's gone to your head, Wade. Any damn fool can see that this animal's loco."

Wade looked at the stallion again. "He doesn't look crazy to me. What about it, Frank, is it a bet?"

Frank shrugged his shoulders. "I don't mind losing the horse if you can ride him, but what's in it for me if you can't?"

"How about my silver belt buckle? I know you've always admired it."

Frank hesitated.

"It's real silver," Wade told him, trying not to sound too eager.

"Wade . . ." Jim tried to interrupt, but Wade shook him off again.

"The hell with it," Wade said, stepping forward. "Help me get him saddled."

The stableman went into the livery barn and came back a moment later carrying a saddle and bridle. The stallion stood, alert and uneasy, but it accepted the tack without fighting. Wade motioned for the other three to stand back. He took a deep breath, then slid his foot into the stirrup and swung up onto the stallion's back. From long practice, he sat the horse easily, his weight balanced precisely. For an instant he thought that the horse was not even going to buck. Then all hell broke loose. The stallion screamed and lifted his front feet off the ground, rearing and striking. Then he twisted and leapt, jarring Wade's bones with the force of his stiff-legged landing. The moment his hooves touched the ground, he launched himself again. This time, kicking at the sky with his hind feet and lowering his muzzle until it almost touched the ground, he managed to unbalance Wade. Feeling the advantage he had gained, the stallion screamed again and reared. Wade tried to regain control over the animal, tried to regain his own balance, but the stallion almost seemed to know his thoughts.

Instead of coming back to the ground, the stallion arched his back and threw his head higher. Wade could hear Jim and Frank yelling at him, but he could not understand what they were saying. The stallion rose higher and higher until Wade was forced to lean forward, afraid that his weight would pull the horse over backward. The stallion was doing what very few horses will do—he was trying to fall, to crush his rider. Panicked, Wade beat at the animal's face and neck with his fists, trying to force him back to the ground. As the horse began to go over backward, Wade tried to disengage his feet from the stirrups, but his own weight made it impossible. The stallion was falling, and there was nothing Wade could do except to lean sideways and hope that the stallion wouldn't crush him.

Wade felt as if he was falling in slow motion. Wade was aware of the black tangle of the horse's mane so close to his face and the animal's frantic screams. He could hear Jim and Frank shouting. He could feel the sun on his back and the reins caught between his fingers. Then, as suddenly as summer lightning, he was pinned between the thrashing stallion and the ground. A sharp pain ignited in his back, then spread to his skull. Wade tried to drag in a breath, but the weight of the squealing stallion was crushing him, pinning him helplessly on his back. Then the sky went black and Wade couldn't feel anything at all.

It had been a week since Wade had ridden the stallion, and he'd been in and out of consciousness. Immediately after the horse had fallen on him, Jim and Frank had taken Wade to the doctor. He'd examined Wade, but he couldn't say what was really wrong with him.

"Seen lots of people thrown from horses," he'd said. "Some lose the ability to walk, some lose their sight, others never even wake up. Hard to tell what will happen with this young man."

So Jim had taken him to his house and put him in Emily's room. Rose had doted over him, hardly leaving his side, hoping he'd awaken at any second. But he hadn't, not really. Occasionally he'd open his eyes, look up at Rose, then close his eyes again.

Jim was sitting at the kitchen table, going over bills, when he heard Rose's frantic voice.

"Jim, I think you'd better come in here."

Jim stood up and walked to the front door and looked outside to make sure Danny was all right. Emily was pushing Danny on the rope swing, and he was laughing loudly. Jim hurried to Wade's room and stood next to the bed. Rose was sitting on the bed next to Wade, holding his hand. Wade's eyes were open. "Well, it's about time," Jim said, grinning at Wade. "We were wondering when you'd decide to join us." Wade didn't say anything. Jim glanced at Rose. "What's wrong? You can see me, can't you, Wade?" He leaned over the bed, his face close to Wade's. "Can you hear me?"

"I can hear you," Wade replied slowly.

"Jesus, boy, you had me scared," Jim said, straightening.

"Where am I?" Wade asked.

"You're at our ranch, Wade," Rose said gently, still holding Wade's hand.

"Have I been here before?"

Jim exchanged worried looks with Rose. "Of course you've been here before. You first came here when you were sixteen years old. We're like your family, Rose and me."

"I don't remember you," Wade said, looking from Rose to Jim. "I don't remember anything."

"You just need to rest, that's all," Jim said, trying to calm himself as he spoke. "You had a nasty fall off that stallion. It'll just take you awhile to get back to sorts."

Wade closed his eyes, slowly shaking his head back and forth. "I don't even know my name."

Jim felt a stabbing pain in his gut. Wade sounded like he had when he was a kid and had lost his parents. "Your name is Wade Colter, and we're Jim and Rose Everett. I raised you after you lost your folks. You're like my son." He watched Wade as he spoke, but he showed no signs of recognition.

"It's all right, Wade," Rose said, reaching up and pushing the damp hair back from his face. "It'll just take you some time to recover. You just rest and get strong."

"You're a nice lady. Thanks."

Rose nodded, obviously barely able to control her emotions.

"So I don't have any family?" Wade asked, looking up at Jim.

Jim looked at Rose again, feeling as if he'd just been hit across the back of the head. "You have a wife, Wade. Her name is Sandrine."

"Is she the girl who was in here before?"

"No, that's Emily," Rose replied. "She's Jim's niece."

"Where's my wife? Does she know about this?"

"No, she doesn't know. She's visiting her family. She should be back real soon." Jim paused. "How's the head? Still feeling pain?"

"Some," Wade replied, looking at Rose. "Your wife has been taking real good care of me."

"That's because you're like a son to me," Rose said, dipping a cloth into the bowl next to the bed and wringing it out. She folded it neatly and laid it across Wade's forehead. "It's awfully hot today. That should help some."

"Thank you, ma'am."

"Please don't call me ma'am. Call me Rose."

Wade nodded and closed his eyes. "Do you all mind if I sleep some now?"

"No, you go right on ahead. I'll be in the next room if you need me," Rose said, standing up.

Jim led the way out of the room and walked to the front door, looking outside again. He shook his head. How was it possible? How was it possible for Wade to forget everything about his past?

"What're we going to do?" Rose asked, putting her arm through Jim's.

Jim shook his head and put his arm around Rose. "I don't know, darlin'. He's young and strong. He'll probably be fine."

"You heard him in there, Jim. He doesn't know who we are.

He doesn't even know who Sandrine is. My God," Rose said, shaking her head, "it's like having a stranger in my house."

"Wade will never be a stranger to us," Jim said angrily, pulling away from Rose and walking back to the table. He sat down, thumbing through the bills from town, but he quickly slapped the pile back down on the table and stood up again. He walked to the cabinet and took a drink from the bottle of whiskey.

"That won't help," Rose said. "That's what got Wade into this mess in the first place."

"I know," Jim said contritely, jamming the cork back into the bottle and putting the whiskey back in the cupboard. "I should've never let him ride that damned beast. I had a bad feeling about it from the beginning."

"There's nothing you can do about it now," Rose said, wrapping her arms around Jim's waist. "The only thing we can do is help Wade get back to the way he used to be."

"And what if that's not possible? What if he never gets his memory back?"

"Then we'll have to tell him what kind of man he was."

"And what about Sandrine? Just what is she supposed to do?" Jim pounded his fist against the wall. "Sonofabitch! Why did this have to happen?"

"I don't know, Jim."

Jim looked at Rose's face, then he pulled her into his arms, holding her tightly. Nothing had ever frightened him so much before. It had never occurred to him that anything would happen to Wade. He was so young and strong, it was hard to believe that anything *could* happen to him. He shook his head, wishing they'd never gone into town that day.

Sandrine let Shining Bird lift up her blouse and look at her cuts.

"They are almost healed. Let me put some more of this on," Shining Bird said without hesitating.

Sandrine turned her face away from the familiar odor of bear grease and sage. It was a horrible smell, but it helped to soothe the pain.

"You are finished," Shining Bird said, rubbing the rest of the grease into Sandrine's hands. "Lone Wind will be happy to know that you are healing well."

"Why should Lone Wind care?"

"He was concerned for you, Bright Star. He did not wish for you to be hurt."

"Your brother is a strange man, Shining Bird. I do not understand him."

"I do not think that anyone does," Shining Bird said. "Lone Wind's name fits him. Even when we were children, he was always off by himself."

"Has he ever married?"

"There was a woman once, but she ran off with a Piegan. Lone Wind never talked about her after that."

"Where did he go when he left your people for so long?" Sandrine hoped that her voice did not betray the depth of her curiosity.

Shining Bird stood up, putting the bowl of bear grease back on the ledge that held all of her healing medicines. "I do not know for sure. He said that he traveled many places and saw many people. He told me that he even went to a place called Mexico, a land of brown-skinned people. Do you know of this place?"

"I've heard people talk about it. Our ranch is less than a week's ride."

"I have heard stories of this place," Shining Bird said in a knowing voice. "I have heard that the Indians there are much different from us. I have heard that they practice strange customs."

Sandrine could barely keep from smiling. Shining Bird was speaking in a whisper. "Did Lone Wind live in Mexico?"

"He says that he lived there for a time. He says that he lived with the Comanches for a time." Shining Bird shook her head. "Who knows? He told me no more than that." Shining Bird picked up two baskets from the ledge. "Let us go outside. It is a beautiful day. I thought we could go to the meadow and pick berries. Soon we will be leaving for the buffalo hunt. I will need them to make pemmican."

Sandrine stood up and followed Shining Bird out of her small lodge. It had been the lodge Shining Bird had shared with her husband, and she had continued to live in it even after her parents had returned to the village. As Sandrine and Shining Bird walked through the camp, Sandrine smiled when she heard the voices of the children as they played. In this, their people were the same: their children were still carefree enough to laugh. A few of the women spoke to Sandrine, and she nodded and greeted them in Crow. They were beginning to grow less wary of her, and they had begun to accept the fact that she was not their enemy.

As they neared Gray Wolf's lodge, she saw that Shining Bird's mood had grown lighter, and Sandrine knew why. Little Bear was standing outside of Gray Wolf's lodge, and he smiled broadly at Shining Bird. Shining Bird smiled back and swung the basket as if she was a young girl.

"Hello, cousin," Little Bear said absently. He looked at Shining Bird, his eyes intently focused on her. "Hello, Shining Bird. Where are you off to today?"

"Bright Star and I are going to pick berries."

"Perhaps I should accompany you. It could be dangerous for you out there alone."

"Don't worry about me," Sandrine said dryly, winking at Gray Wolf. "I'll be fine on my own." She continued on through the village, nodding to people she recognized. It would be hard to leave this place, she realized. She was getting to like it here. The people had finally accepted her, and she enjoyed spending time with Gray Wolf and Shining Bird. As happy as she was in New Mexico with Wade, there was a freedom, a simplicity of life with Indians that she never quite felt in the white man's world.

She hesitated as she walked toward the corral. Lone Wind was working with a horse. It was a high-spirited pinto that he'd captured on a raid. She had noticed him working with the horse before but had never stopped to watch him. She stopped now, knowing that he was too intent on his work to see her.

Lone Wind was speaking in a low voice to the nervous animal. As he tried to touch the horse's neck, the pinto half-reared, shying away. Lone Wind did not slacken the lead rope, and Sandrine could see the taut muscles in his back. The horse jerked its head upward, trying to loosen the constraint of the lead rope. Lone Wind held him steadily, skillfully, loosening the lead rope just enough to allow the horse to move his head, then tightening it again. Sandrine smiled: the pinto had met his match. There was a steadiness in Lone Wind's movements that spoke of tremendous strength and assurance. Sandrine watched the pinto try to pull away once more. The muscles in Lone Wind's back knotted, and his legs tensed. Sandrine followed the hard, curving line of his thigh. A sudden rush of guilt flushed her cheeks. She quickly looked away and headed toward the meadow, trying to put Lone Wind from her mind.

"Where are you going in such a hurry, Bright Star?" Lone Wind called out.

Sandrine heard his deep voice and was so startled that she stumbled and almost fell. She had been so sure that he hadn't seen her. She turned around slowly, hoping he was too far away to see how pink her cheeks were. "I am going to pick berries for Shining Bird."

She thought Lone Wind would turn back to the corral, but

instead he slid the hackamore off the animal's head, swung it over his arm, and walked toward her. As she watched him approach, Sandrine realized that *he* was the reason she wasn't ready to go home. Unconsciously she stepped backward, stumbling on a rock.

"It would be wise to look where you are walking, Bright Star."

Sandrine felt herself flush again, and she knew that she could not hide it from him this time. He smiled slightly, and she looked down, no longer able to meet his eyes.

"How odd that you should be going to pick berries. I have been wishing I had some all morning."

Sandrine forced herself to look up. He was smiling.

"I will go with you," he said.

"You don't have to do that. I'll be fine on my own." She turned away again, wishing that he weren't so close.

"I do not mind. I have been working with that stubborn horse since the sun rose."

Sandrine didn't know what to say. She couldn't tell him to go back. She walked across the meadow and absently kicked at the long blades of meadow grass. Once they crossed the pasture, Sandrine walked through the trees and made her way to the thickets that grew close to the stream. The branches were heavy with dark red berries, and Sandrine began to pick the ripe fruit, dropping them into the basket. Occasionally she would pop one into her mouth, savoring the sweetness. She forced herself not to look at Lone Wind, but she could hear him moving.

"This is a good year for berries," he said. "There have been years when the women in the village fought over each bush."

Sandrine looked at him finally. He stood with one of his hands full of berries, eating them with great relish.

"My mother told me that the berries were so scarce one spring, one of the old women of the village had to go out and count an equal amount for each woman. It's hard to imagine such a thing when you see so many," Sandrine said as she picked more berries, filling the basket halfway. She stopped when she saw a particularly plump and large one, and she plucked it from the bush and put it into her mouth. She closed her eyes as she ate it.

"You look like a child, with juice spattered on your face like that."

Sandrine opened her eyes as she felt Lone Wind gently wipe the juice from her chin with his fingers. He brushed his hand across her cheek, pushing back tendrils of hair.

"I have never seen a woman with eyes such as yours, Bright Star," he said, his eyes staring into hers.

Sandrine watched, transfixed, as he leaned toward her, his face close to hers.

"I ask you again, are you a witch?"

"No," Sandrine said, still unable to look away from his dark hypnotic eyes.

"But I feel as if you have cast a spell over me and I do not know how to break it."

Sandrine felt her heart pounding in her chest. She knew she should leave, but still she could not. "I have cast no spell, Lone Wind."

"I do not believe you," Lone Wind said, his voice deep and low. He put both hands on Sandrine's face, staring into her eyes. "I will miss you when you go."

Sandrine couldn't move. She felt as if she was the one under a spell. But she knew she could not allow herself to feel anything for Lone Wind. "I should go back now." She forced herself to turn away from him, and she started back through the bushes.

"You do not have to be afraid of me, Bright Star. I will not hurt you."

Sandrine stopped, slowly turning to face Lone Wind. "This cannot be, Lone Wind. I am married. You know that."

"Yes, I know that you are a married woman." Again he stood

close to her, his eyes burning into hers. "If you had been a Crow, or I a Blackfoot . . ." He reached out and touched her cheek again.

Sandrine closed her eyes, enjoying his gentle touch for a moment. She was afraid to open her eyes, afraid to look at him. She saw things in his eyes which frightened her, things she didn't want to see. Suddenly she dropped the basket on the ground and ran toward the village, knowing that she had to leave as soon as possible.

Five

Wade sat on the porch watching Emily as she pushed Danny on the swing. She was a pretty young woman. He liked her. She'd been real nice to him.

"You all right?" Rose asked, leaning against the open door.

Wade looked up at Rose. Jim had been trying to give Wade back his memories by telling him about himself. But he didn't need to be told anything about Rose. Even though he didn't remember her, he felt a bond with her. Jim had told him the story of how he had helped deliver Danny on the wagon train when he was only sixteen years old, and that ever since he and Rose had been very close. It didn't surprise Wade at all.

"You didn't answer me," Rose said. "It's awfully hot today. Maybe you should go back inside. It's a little cooler in there."

"I'm fine, Rose. Thanks."

"Lunch will be ready soon. Are you hungry?"

Wade shrugged his shoulders. "I guess."

"You have to eat, Wade. You're practically wasting away to nothing."

Wade looked down at himself. He had to admit, he did look pretty thin. He wondered what he had looked like before. "What're we having?"

"Grown particular?" Rose's voice was tinged with sarcasm.

Wade shook his head. "I'll eat whatever you make."

"Good."

"Rose," he said thoughtfully. "I was thinking of riding over to my ranch today."

Rose came onto the porch, sitting in the chair next to Wade. "I don't think that's a good idea, Wade. It hasn't been that long since you got hurt. Riding a horse could be the worst thing for you."

"Well, you never know. I could get thrown again and get my memory back." Wade grinned broadly, and he was pleased to see Rose smile.

"Well, that sounded like the old Wade. Pretty soon you'll be asking me to have a nip with you."

"A drink does sound pretty good. Whiskey."

"So you can remember some things, can't you?"

Wade nodded, his smile fading. "Doc says it's like that. I can remember how to take care of myself, how to eat, how to ride. Hell, I even remember how to read." He rubbed his hand over his eyes. "But the rest is gone, Rose. Everything that made me Wade Colter is gone." He shook his head, feeling scared.

"Sandrine will be home soon. Why don't you wait until she gets here, and you both can go out to the house together."

Wade felt his fear deepen. He was married, they told him, to a beautiful woman. But he couldn't even remember her face. If they met on a street, he'd walk past her and never even know it.

Rose squeezed his arm. "You just take it easy and remember what Doc said: the more rest you get the better." She stood up. "I'll go get you that lunch now."

Wade stood up and leaned on the porch railing. He waited until he could hear the sound of Rose's footsteps fading, then he ducked under the rail and started toward the barn. With every step he expected her to call out to him, but she didn't. He hesitated at the barn door, then went inside. He was going crazy sitting around. Even his thoughts felt strange, as though his mind had become so empty that they echoed endlessly.

He walked into the barn. No matter what Rose thought, he had to ride; he had to do something to occupy his time. He hesitated, realizing that he did not know which horse was his. He walked to the second stall and opened it. The horse moved toward him, wickering. Either it was his, or it was simply a calm and friendly animal. He patted it, then turned to the saddle rack. Within a few minutes, he was ready to go.

Wade looked out the barn door, hoping that Rose was still inside. She was. He led the horse into the yard and swung up into the saddle. In one smooth motion, he leaned forward, urging the horse into a canter. The animal responded immediately, and for a few seconds Wade felt exhilarated and free. Then he stiffened in the saddle, suddenly fighting a cold-sweat terror that seemed to appear out of nowhere. Even though the horse's hoofbeats were loud, he could hear his own heart. A tiny pain began at his temples, and it seemed to command his entire attention.

Without realizing that he was doing it, he pulled up on the reins, slowing the horse to a walk. He looked down at his hands. They looked tense, clammy, and rigid, and suddenly they began to shake. His heart pounded so loudly, he thought it was going to burst.

He pulled back sharply on the reins until the horse stopped. Quickly he dismounted, his legs shaky. He walked, taking deep breaths, trying to calm himself. Maybe it was his head, maybe there was something else wrong with it. Doc said anything could happen. He sat down, closing his eyes. The pounding in his chest had lessened, and he was able to breathe more deeply. Whatever had happened to him was passing. He was going to be all right—this time.

"Wade!"

The sound of Emily's voice startled him. He wiped his forehead on his sleeve and turned to face her, forcing himself to stand up. As he took the first few steps toward Emily, he felt his strength returning. He watched as she lifted her skirts and ran toward him.

"Rose said to catch you if I could and to tell you that you're not supposed to be riding at all."

Wade was glad to see Emily, glad for a friendly face. He was much weaker than he realized. She strode up to him, linking her arm through his. "You look pale."

Wade shook his head in irritation. "I don't need a mother, Emily."

Emily frowned. "You could've used one the day you decided to get on that stallion. If I had been there, I would've tried to talk you out of it."

Wade couldn't help but smile at the genuine concern on her face. "I doubt if it would've done any good. From what I hear, I've always been pretty stubborn."

Emily smiled. "So, have you remembered anything yet?"

Wade felt the fear again, distant this time, but still there. He shook his head. "No, not a thing. I remember the past three weeks since the accident, but that's all. The only people I know are you, Rose, Jim, and Danny. I can't even remember my own wife."

Emily nodded in sympathy. "I'm sure it will all come back to you, Wade. Just be patient and take care of yourself."

Wade looked at Emily. Her auburn hair seemed burnished in the sunlight, and her fine, clear skin was lovely. She was dainty and feminine enough for any man. Before he realized he was staring at her, she had frowned, thrusting out her lower lip in a little-girl pout. She reached up to brush her hair back from her forehead, and he noticed again how pretty she was.

"How much longer will you be staying?" he asked.

She shrugged, smiling slightly. "I thought I'd be home by now, but I'm going to stay on a little longer, I think. Now you might not remember this, but I was impossible when I first got here. It's just that everything was so new to me." She looked around her, then at Wade. "But the longer I stay, the more I like it. I might even decide to live here someday."

Wade held his tongue, not knowing how to respond. He liked Emily; he liked her a lot. But he was married. Rose and Jim both told him how much he had loved his wife. The problem was that he couldn't remember her or their life together. "It's pretty country, and Jim and Rose are nice people. I can see why you like it here."

"Are you all right? You look pale."

"Just wondering what I used to be like. I feel like I'm walking around in the dark and I can't see a thing."

"It'll come back to you, Wade. Just give it time."

"Time is one thing I have a lot of." He walked to the horse, taking the reins in his hand. "I guess we'd better get back, or Rose will be having a fit." When they entered the yard, Rose was sitting on the porch steps, Danny on the step in front of her. Danny ran to greet them, and even from this distance, Wade could see that Rose was angry.

"Did you fall again, Wade?" Danny asked, walking alongside.

"No, I didn't fall, Danny. But I should've listened to your ma. I'm not ready to be riding yet."

"How about if Danny and I take the horse to the barn?" Emily said, taking the reins from Wade, trying desperately not to show her fear of the animal.

"Not like that, Emily," Danny said impatiently, taking the reins in his small hand and leading the animal toward the barn.

Wade smiled as he watched Danny and Emily walk away. As strange as it felt not to remember anything about his past, he enjoyed all of these people. They helped to dull the edge of uncertainty that was constantly plaguing him.

"Well, that showed a lot of intelligence." Rose walked up to him, shaking her head.

Wade felt like a little boy who had just gotten caught doing something wrong. "Look, Rose, I know you are trying to look out for me, but I'm not sixteen years old anymore. I'm a grown man."

"But you have to be careful, Wade. If something else happened—"

"What, Rose? What could possibly happen that could be worse than this?" he asked, his voice full of anger. He kicked at the ground, clenching and unclenching his fists, then looked at Rose. She wasn't the cause of his frustration, and he had no right to take it out on her. "I'm sorry, Rose, I've just got to get out of here," Wade said, heading toward the barn.

"Wade, don't!" Rose yelled after him.

Wade ignored Rose's plea and went into the barn, taking the reins from Emily's hand.

"What're you doing, Wade?"

Wade ignored her, swinging up on the horse and riding toward the wagon road with his back straight and his shoulders squared, anxiety hitting him in waves. He was tired of being surrounded by people who thought they knew what was best for him. He knew what he wanted right now. He couldn't remember much, but he remembered how good the slow burn of a shot of whiskey felt. If he got lucky, he could get drunk enough to forget that he couldn't remember what his life had been like before.

Sandrine stamped her foot. "You promised. You said you'd take me home when I was ready."

Little Bear's face was impassive. "I will take you home soon; I just do not wish to leave yet."

"But we have to leave now."

Little Bear shook his head gravely. "You are like my sister, Bright Star. I would do anything for you. I think I have proven that. But you, of all people, should understand why I wish to stay here longer."

Sandrine studied his face. "And why is that?" Little Bear averted his eyes. Suddenly Sandrine understood. "It's Shining Bird."

Little Bear nodded almost imperceptibly.

"How am I supposed to get home then? You're the one who made me come here."

"No, I made you go to our village. You are the one who decided to come here."

"But you hate the Crows." She narrowed her eyes. "At least you used to."

"I will take you home when the time is right."

Sandrine looked past Little Bear at the lodges of the Crow village. She knew Little Bear could never be happy living here. No matter what he felt for Shining Bird and Gray Wolf, she knew he still hated the Crow people. And would Shining Bird ever be happy living with the Blackfoot? She looked back at her cousin, fighting to keep the pity out of her eyes. Little Bear needed and deserved love in his life and had for so long. Why did he have to fall in love with someone who was going to bring him so much pain? Shining Bird was a beautiful woman with a kind heart, but she was still the enemy.

"You live with an enemy of our people," Little Bear said as if reading her thoughts.

Sandrine met Little Bear's eyes. "Wade has been a friend of our people since he was a boy."

"Perhaps, but his skin is white and our people hate his people."

"But where will you live?"

"Do not worry about me so much, cousin."

Sandrine reached out to touch his cheek. "I worry about you because I love you. I have no intention of stopping." She tried to smile. "Don't argue with me. You know how stubborn I can be." Little Bear nodded, an exaggerated groan escaping his lips. Impulsively Sandrine hugged him. When she released him and stepped back, he was smiling. "How much longer will you want to stay?"

"I know you miss Colter, but he will wait for you because your love is already strong. Give me just a little more time."

Sandrine nodded, unable to refuse Little Bear's request. "All right," she said, lowering her eyes in mock submission, "I will be a good Blackfoot woman and go about my work." She turned on her heel and could hear Little Bear laughing as she walked away.

Sandrine quickened her step, knowing that she could not hide her uneasiness from Little Bear forever. It was wonderful that he was in love with Shining Bird, but she was afraid of what might happen if she stayed in the Crow village much longer.

The high boisterous voices of children brought her out of her thoughts. Shining Bird's eldest son, Running Fox, was pretending he was a horse, and he was pulling his younger brother and sister in circles on a makeshift travois they had made using deerhide and sticks. Sandrine stopped to watch them. Squealing, Spotted Deer urged her brother to go even faster. Tall Horse sat behind her, one arm around her waist, the other raised in the air like a cowboy riding a bronco.

Sandrine laughed when Running Fox turned too sharply and dumped his sister and brother unceremoniously onto the ground. Her laughter faded when she saw that Spotted Deer was hurt. Blood trickled from a cut on the girl's knee, and although she was doing her best not to cry, her little face was flushed pink and her eyes were flooded with tears. Sandrine started forward and was about to scoop the child up into her arms when a strong hand on her shoulder made her stop. Startled, Sandrine turned to see Lone Wind standing behind her. He stepped past her and swept his crying niece into his arms.

"You are fine, Spotted Deer. It is just a small cut." He wiped the tears from her face.

"But it hurts," Spotted Deer said, looking at her knee.

Lone Wind nodded. "Yes, perhaps you need something to cover it, something to show the others that you are not afraid to fall." Lone Wind set Spotted Deer on the ground and took his knife from the thong on his thigh. He quickly cut a piece of leather from the flap on his moccasin and tied it around his niece's knee. "There. You look like a warrior who has just returned from battle."

"Thank you, uncle," Spotted Deer said, hugging Lone Wind's legs. Then without another word, she was off to play again with her brothers.

Sandrine looked at Lone Wind. He had never looked more handsome than when he had been comforting Spotted Deer. When he looked at Sandrine, she felt as if he could see inside of her. She quickly glanced away, turning to walk back toward Gray Wolf's lodge.

"Bright Star."

Sandrine stopped, but she didn't turn around. "Yes?"

"Would you like to ride? I have finally broken the pinto."

"No, I don't think so," she stammered, wishing he were not so close. "I have many things to do."

"Why do you feel it necessary to avoid me?"

Letting out a silent sigh, Sandrine turned to face him, looking around her as she did. "I am not avoiding you," she said in a low voice.

"Then ride with me. You will enjoy it."

"No, I—"

"It is a good day for riding. Look at the sky. Do you not feel the breeze?"

Sandrine looked at Lone Wind, determined to stand her ground. "No, I cannot." She spun on her heels and headed back toward Gray Wolf's lodge. She didn't turn around again, but she knew that Lone Wind would not follow her. When she reached the lodge, she saw Gray Wolf sitting in front, carving on his new bow. She sat down next to him. "Where is Shining Bird? I was to help her dig roots."

"Ah, it seems that my daughter has better things to do than dig for roots," he said, carving into the wood with small delicate strokes of the knife.

"The bow is beautiful, Gray Wolf."

"It will be a marriage gift to Little Bear."

"They are to be married?" Sandrine was unable to contain her surprise.

"They have not said as much, but I believe it will happen soon enough."

Sandrine watched Gray Wolf as he worked on the brittle cherrywood. "Does the thought of a marriage between Shining Bird and Little Bear not bother you, Gray Wolf?"

Gray Wolf put the knife down next to him and blew the loose chips of wood away. Then he rubbed the area with his fingers. "I am not so troubled as you, Bright Star."

"I am only worried because I know this will not be an easy marriage for them, Gray Wolf. Will your people accept the marriage? Will mine?"

"I do not know." Gray Wolf picked up his knife and began carving again. "I only know that there is love between them and Little Bear is a good man. It is of no matter to me that he is Blackfoot," he said gently, his wise eyes meeting Sandrine's. "Just as it is no matter to me that *you* are Blackfoot. They will find their own place, just as you and Colter have."

Sandrine nodded. She knew that Gray Wolf spoke from experience. After Shining Bird had asked her father to leave the village, he and Red Bird had stayed away for many years. They had traveled from village to village until they eventually found their home in the renegade camp. And she had seen no two people who were more in love than Red Bird and Gray Wolf. "It is their choice, of course."

"Yes, it is."

"Can I ask you something, Gray Wolf?" Sandrine lowered her voice to barely a whisper. "Something personal."

Gray Wolf stopped working and looked at Sandrine. "You may ask me anything, Bright Star."

Sandrine hesitated, trying to find the right words. "Was there ever a time during your marriage to Red Bird that you desired another woman?" As soon as she asked the question, Sandrine regretted it. "Never mind. It doesn't matter." She started to get up, but Gray Wolf held onto her arm.

"Sit," he said, his voice firm but gentle. He laid the bow and the knife on a piece of rawhide, and he rubbed his hands together. "This is hard on the fingers. My father could carve all day and night without stopping. I could never understand that kind of discipline." Gray Wolf looked at Sandrine. "Red Bird was my life," he replied.

"I know that. I'm sorry. It was a stupid question."

"It is a question that is worthy of an answer." Gray Wolf said, patting Sandrine's hand.

"But you already answered it," Sandrine said. She shook her head. "I'm sorry, Gray Wolf. I didn't mean to bother you."

"When have you ever bothered me?" he asked. "If you ask such a question, then it is important for you to know the answer." He smiled slightly. "Red Bird was a good wife, a good mother, and a good companion. She was a skilled hunter and rider, and she had a fine sense of humor. But," Gray Wolf said, staring straight ahead and shaking his head, "there was a young woman in our tribe who was so beautiful, she made me ache inside. Every time I saw her, I wanted to talk to her, to be with her."

"Were you ever 'with' her?" Sandrine asked, her voice still low.

"Not in the way that you mean, but I found ways to be near her, and she found ways to be near me."

"Did Red Bird know of your feelings for this woman?"

Gray Wolf shook his head. "She knew nothing until I told her. Then she told me to take the woman for my wife so I would not spend all of my time desiring her."

"I couldn't do that," Sandrine said. "I'm not such a generous person."

"Red Bird was not being generous, she was being smart. Once she gave me the permission to be with the woman, I no longer wanted her. I realized that Red Bird was the only woman I wanted in my lodge."

"It's hard to be so far away from home," Sandrine said, making circles in the dirt with her finger.

"You miss Colter?"

"Yes, very much."

"But you are troubled. You worry about your feelings for another man."

"No," Sandrine said almost too quickly.

"I am not accusing you of anything, Bright Star. You are far from home, and it is easy to depend on others when your husband is not here. But remember that you will soon be home with him and you do not want anything to come between you."

Sandrine nodded, reaching out and running her fingers along the fine wood of the bow. "Sometimes I feel strange in the white world, Gray Wolf. It is different from our world. I do not know if I will ever feel accustomed to the stares of people."

"Do these people matter to you? Are they important in your life? I think not," he said, taking her hand. "The only thing that is important is your life with Colter. He does not make you feel uncomfortable, does he?"

"No," Sandrine said, thinking about how defensive Wade was of her. "It is just me, or the Indian in me. Sometimes I just want to be with my own people."

"That is good. You will never forget your people. When you have children, you will tell them about the Blackfoot and you will tell them the stories your grandfather told you."

Children. Sandrine still couldn't imagine what it would be like to have children with Wade. She wanted to have a family, but she knew that they needed more time together, especially now that she'd been gone for so long.

"Are you all right, Bright Star?"

"Yes, thank you, Gray Wolf. My mind is full of thoughts." She stood up. "I will let you work on your bow."

"I am never too busy to talk to you."

Sandrine looked down at Gray Wolf, feeling a warm rush of affection for the man. She felt as close to him as she did to her own father. "I know that. Thank you."

Sandrine left Gray Wolf's lodge and walked through the village toward the horse corral. She wanted to ride. It was the only thing that would let her be at peace with her thoughts.

When she reached the corral, she leaned on the top railing, looking at the horses. Like her village, the most valuable horses, the ones that were used for war, were staked close to the lodges or kept in the corrals. The others were left free to graze in the pastures. She grabbed a hackamore from the corral railing and walked through the long-bladed meadow grass. She saw her horse grazing on the far side of the pasture. When she called to him, he lifted his head and wickered. Sandrine smiled and walked up to the animal, rubbing its nose. "We haven't been for a ride in a long time," she said, patting his neck. "I wish we could just ride home."

She stroked the bay's neck for a few seconds and then slipped the hackamore over his muzzle. She grabbed a handful of mane and swung up onto his back.

Sandrine guided her horse from the pasture, ducking as they rode through the branches of the aspens. They rode along the bank of the stream, and Sandrine delighted in the sights and smells of early summer. The ground was awash in colorful wildflowers, and the water was still running hard from the winter runoff. She could hear a hawk screeching in the distance and the rhythmic sound of a woodpecker looking for food. The breeze felt warm on her skin, and she took in a deep breath. Everything felt new and clean.

She kneed her horse and guided him across the river, kicking him into a canter and then a gallop. She rode hard, feeling the animal beneath her and the wind in her face. She had never known anything like riding. Nothing had ever given her the kind of freedom that it had. She rode hard, pushing her horse until they were both breathing hard. Then she pulled back on the reins, slowing the bay to a walk. She looked around her. The prairie seemed endless, except for the mountains looming on the horizon. She felt as if she were the only person alive. She felt like a little girl again, riding without a care in the world and no one to bother her.

The shape of a rider on the horizon startled her out of her carefree daydreaming. The rider was coming from the direction of the Crow village, but it was impossible to tell whether he was a friend or an enemy. She had nothing with which to protect herself except her knife, the one Lone Wind had given her. She pulled it from inside her moccasin and held it hidden beneath her skirt. But as the rider drew closer, she could see that it was no enemy. It was Lone Wind. He reined his horse in next to hers, eyeing the knife in her hand with a raised eyebrow.

"I followed you to make sure that no harm would come to you. It appears my concern was unnecessary."

Sandrine replaced the knife and looked at Lone Wind. He was riding the pinto. "Does he ride well?"

"He is not as swift as many, but he could go on for days. He has the strength of two horses."

Sandrine nodded. "My grandfather said that was much more important in a horse. He always said, 'What is so good about riding swiftly away from your pursuers if they will eventually catch up with you?' "

"I think I would have liked your grandfather." Lone Wind looked past Sandrine. "It is a good time on the prairie. The sun has not yet burned everything brown, and the breeze that blows is warm. Soon we will leave for the hunt." His eyes met hers. "But you will probably be gone by then."

Sandrine spoke without meeting his eyes. "No, I won't be leaving for a time."

"Why?"

Sandrine hesitated, wondering if Lone Wind knew about Little Bear and Shining Bird. If he did not, he might get angry hearing the news from her. Still, she might be able to calm him down enough so that he didn't try to kill Little Bear. "It seems my cousin and your sister have grown quite close."

"A Crow and a Blackfoot," he said, staring past her again. His voice held no hostility.

"Will it anger you if they marry?"

"My sister will do as she pleases. I cannot stop her. I am only her brother."

"But can you accept my cousin?"

"If your cousin possesses any of your qualities, I suppose I can learn to accept him."

Sandrine held his eyes for a moment, then looked away. "You are very good with your niece."

"She is lovely, is she not? She will have too many marriage offers when she is of age."

"But I am sure you will be there to protect her." Sandrine didn't look away this time. Lone Wind's eyes were dark, but they had light flecks in them, making them appear lighter. He was a handsome man, there was no doubt of that. She could well imagine the Crow women who yearned for him.

"What is it you see, Bright Star?"

"Your eyes do not reveal very much, Lone Wind."

"But yours do," Lone Wind replied, his gaze never leaving her face.

Sandrine felt her cheeks burn, and she urged her horse forward. She couldn't stay this close to Lone Wind and try to hide anything from him. When he reined in beside her, she steadfastly avoided his gaze.

"So, Bright Star, how will you get home if your cousin stays here? Will you return to your people and have one of them take you home?"

"I don't know," Sandrine replied, not really knowing what she was going to do.

"Will you stay long enough to see them married?"

"I don't know," she repeated. She turned, looking south. "I can't wait forever."

"Will your husband come for you?"

"He doesn't know where I am."

"If I were your husband, I would find you no matter where you were."

Sandrine pulled up on her horse. She wanted to defend Wade, but she could not. There was a part of her that couldn't forget the way he had let her go without seeming to care. It had been two months. Two long months.

"I will take you to your home."

Sandrine had been so lost in her own thoughts that she hadn't understood what Lone Wind had said.

"Did you not hear me, Bright Star? I will take you home."

She looked at him. Although this meant she wouldn't have to wait until Little Bear and Shining Bird got married, she knew it was an unrealistic solution. She wanted to be back with Wade, but it would be unwise for her to travel such a long distance alone with Lone Wind. "No, thank you, but I will wait for Little Bear to take me. I must be here for his marriage anyway."

She lifted the reins and leaned forward, but before her horse could move, Lone Wind reached across and covered her hands with one of his. "Why do I frighten you so, Bright Star? Have I ever done anything to harm you?"

Sandrine lowered her eyes, shaking her head. How could she tell Lone Wind that what she was feeling was another kind of fear? She forced herself to be calm, and she met his eyes. "You have never harmed me, Lone Wind."

"But I do frighten you, do I not?"

Sandrine nodded slightly.

"Is it because I am Crow, because I am your enemy?"

"No," Sandrine replied quickly. "I do not think of you as my enemy." She shook her head, knowing she couldn't explain her feelings to him.

"Walk with me. Please." Lone Wind dismounted and stood next to Sandrine's horse, his hand outstretched.

Sandrine found herself unable to refuse. She dismounted, taking Lone Wind's hand. He took her reins and led the horses as they walked in a companionable silence. Sandrine stopped to pick some wildflowers, and she gave one to Lone Wind, smiling as he held the tiny flower in his large hand. "It is sad that something so beautiful must die," she said, staring at the flower.

"But it gave pleasure to some while it was here. It did not bloom for nothing." He twirled the small flower around in his fingers. "Now whenever I see this flower, I will think of you, Bright Star."

"Please don't," she said, her voice strained.

"What?"

Sandrine stopped, facing him. "You know exactly what you're doing. You're saying kind things to me so that I will weaken . . ." Sandrine suddenly felt like a fool.

"I have upset you again."

"It isn't you, it's me," she said angrily, walking ahead, trying to put some distance between them. She felt like she didn't know herself anymore, and it scared her.

"Bright Star!"

Lone Wind said her name so firmly that Sandrine turned sharply. "What is it?"

"Quickly. Get on your horse."

It was an order given by a man who was used to being obeyed when danger threatened. Sandrine quickly mounted up.

"Do you hear them?" Lone Wind said after he had swung onto his horse.

"Hear what?"

"Buffalo."

Sandrine's stomach tightened. She had been so lost in her own thoughts that she hadn't even noticed the low drumming rumble. She had seen a stampede once when she was a little girl. Two warriors had been trampled to death. Involuntarily she looked over at Lone Wind. "What do we do?" Her voice sounded shaky, childlike, but she could not stop remembering how the two bodies had looked.

"We will not try to outrun them," he said calmly. "The horses might panic, and a fall would mean death. Instead, we will ride in a circle around the herd. You must stay on your horse, Bright Star. Even if the herd comes close to you. Do you understand?"

Sandrine turned in the direction of the sound; for the first time she saw the billowing clouds of dust. As she watched, transfixed, murky shapes began to appear. An instant later, the monstrously large animals were pounding toward them. She looked back when she heard Lone Wind screaming her name.

"Ride, Bright Star!"

Sandrine knew he was right. She knew that she had to urge her horse into a gallop, that she had to overcome the paralysis of her remembered terror. But all she could see inside her mind were the mangled bodies of the two Blackfoot hunters. This was the nightmare of her childhood, the dream so terrible it had awakened her countless times. Now it had come true. She could not move.

"Bright Star." Lone Wind's face was rigid, impassive. "If you do not ride, we will both die."

Sandrine glanced back at the herd. He was right. Her fear would kill them both. She kicked her horse into a gallop, wrenching herself free from her memories. Lone Wind held his horse back, staying behind her, and Sandrine knew what he was doing. If her horse stumbled, or if she were thrown, he wanted to be able to help her. She felt her horse falter as they changed direction to avoid rocky ground. Sandrine tried to relax enough to think clearly. In a few moments they would not be able to see anything as the dust clouds thickened around them. Her horse had never been used to hunt buffalo and it ran wildly, fighting her attempts to control it. Sandrine screamed as a buffalo bull materialized out of the roiling clouds of dust. Her horse stumbled, its head thrown back. For a terrible instant, Sandrine was sure that she was going to die beneath the murderous hooves. Then she felt herself being lifted, pulled off her plunging, panic-stricken horse. Another terrible instant passed as Lone Wind managed to drag her onto his horse and steady her, his strong arms tightly around her. Sandrine shut her eyes, trying to close out the horrible noise and the choking dust. It seemed like an eternity had passed before she heard Lone Wind's voice again, this time repeating her name softly, over and over. The horse had slowed to a weary canter, and the deafening sound of hooves was diminishing.

Sandrine let her body relax, and she leaned her head back, resting it on Lone Wind's shoulder. His arm was still tight around her waist, and she welcomed the feel of it. She felt the heat of his chest against her back, and his other arm encircled her. She closed her eyes, feeling a terrible ache inside. He had saved her yet again. Now she knew it would be impossible for her to deny her feelings for him. She felt his hand go up to her chin, turning her face toward his.

"Are you all right?"

"Yes," she said, her voice trembling. She could see the tiny gold flecks in his eyes. "I don't know what happened. I don't know why I couldn't . . ."

"There was nothing you could do."

"If you hadn't followed me out here . . ." She shook her head. "You must think that trouble follows me around."

"I do not think that."

Sandrine lowered her eyes as he brushed some hair from her face. His hand was large, but it was very gentle. "I would never have had the courage to do what you did."

She sat up straighter, but he kept his arms around her, holding her close to him. She closed her eyes, sighing deeply. It was time to tell him there could be nothing between them. But when she looked at him, saw the intensity in his eyes, felt the strength in his arms, no words would come to her. Even as he moved his mouth close to hers, she could find no words to stop him. And finally, when he pressed his lips to hers, she wanted nothing more than to be kissed by him.

She felt his arms tighten around her, and for a brief moment, she was lost in time. But suddenly Lone Wind pulled away from her, and she looked up at him. He had already taken the reins in one hand and had begun to guide the horse back to the camp. His other arm, while still around her, barely touched her waist. Sandrine faced forward, suddenly embarrassed. She had acted like a foolish young girl, not able to control her impulses or her desires.

When they reached the horse pasture outside of the village, Lone Wind swung off the horse, holding out his hand to Sandrine. Without making eye contact, she took his hand and dismounted. She didn't know what to say to him. He, not she, had had the strength to pull away, and she felt ashamed. She started toward the village, wishing she had never come here, wishing she had never met Lone Wind.

"Bright Star."

Lone Wind's voice almost caressed her name, and she stopped, her back still to him, clenching her hands at her sides.

"You are a part of me now, Bright Star. We are part of each other."

Sandrine caught her breath and started running, trying to put the sound of Lone Wind's voice from her mind and the meaning of his words from her heart.

Six

Wade lifted his head, then with a loud groan, he buried his face in the pillow again. He hadn't been in this much pain since the accident. Sun shone brightly into the room, and he tried without success to cover his head. He only wanted to sleep.

"You look like hell."

Slowly Wade focused his eyes. There was a woman standing next to the bed. She had a head of flaming red hair and a feisty look on her face. Even behind the dowdy apron, he could see that she had a fine figure.

"I've heard from Jim that you can't remember a lot of things. My name is Sally. You used to call me Sal. I own the restaurant down below, the Half Moon."

Wade started to sit up, then realized he wasn't wearing a shirt. He pulled the sheet halfway up his chest and sat against the backboard. "What am I doing here?"

"You got into a little bit of trouble in the saloon last night, so I had you brought to my place."

"Why?"

Sally grinned and sat on the edge of the bed. "I like knowing things that you don't, Wade. Gives me a real advantage."

"Look, lady, don't play games with me. Just tell me what I'm doing here."

"Well, I see you haven't lost that nasty temper of yours." Sally shook her head. "I don't owe you an explanation. I saved your ass last night, Mr. Colter." She stood up. "If the sheriff had come in and found you busting the place up like you were, you would've woken up over there in that stinking hole of a jail, instead of in my place." Sally walked over to the table and sat down. She picked up a newspaper.

Wade shook his head, forcing himself to forget about his headache. He couldn't remember a thing about the saloon or the night before. He looked at his hands. His knuckles were bruised. So he'd been in a fight. "I'm sorry," he said, trying to sound contrite. The paper didn't move. Sally wasn't going to forgive him that easily. "What exactly did I do last night, if you wouldn't mind telling me." He waited, hoping that she would give in. Finally she lowered the paper.

"What didn't you do would be more like it," Sally said, unable to conceal the impatience in her voice.

"Do I have to beg?" Wade asked.

"Maybe," Sally said, smiling slightly. "All right," she said, folding the paper and putting it on the table. "You came into the saloon and started drinking. You went through three-quarters of a bottle when you decked the first man. Then you got into a card game and you made the mistake of winning. A couple of the fellas accused you of cheating, and you pulled a gun on them. Fred, the bartender, knew you, so he sent one of his girls to fetch me before someone went for the sheriff. I got you out of there as quick as I could after I made sure the men were nice and calmed down, of course."

"I didn't shoot anyone, did I?"

"No, you just shot a few holes in the floor and the wall. I told Fred you'd pay for the damages later."

Wade ran his hand over his face. "I don't know what to say, Sally."

"Thanks would be a start."

Wade grinned. "Thanks."

"You're welcome."

"Did I do this kind of thing often?"

Sally narrowed her eyes. "No, and that's what worries me. It's one thing to lose your memory but something else entirely to change your character."

"What was my character? Jim and Rose make me sound like a Sunday saint."

Sally threw back her head and laughed. "You were a good man, Wade, but I wouldn't go that far."

Wade watched Sally laugh and wondered how well they had known each other. She was a very attractive woman, and he liked her already. He especially liked her honesty. "We must've been pretty good friends if you know so much about me."

"Good enough for me to know about that birthmark way down low on your belly."

Wade actually felt his cheeks burn beneath Sally's direct gaze. When he couldn't outstare her, he looked away.

Sally laughed. "As much as I like that birthmark, I haven't seen it since you married Sandrine, and I don't ever expect to see it again."

Wade rubbed one hand over his face. "Jim and Rose have told me about her. Do you know her?"

"Yes, I know her. She's sweet, good-hearted, and beautiful. Probably way too good for you."

"She doesn't seem to be in any hurry to get back to me."

Sally frowned. "Maybe you did hit your head hard enough to knock most of the sense out of it. You must still have some idea how dangerous and uncertain the trail is from here to Montana. Anything could happen. Besides, she'd wanted to spend time with her parents. She has no way of knowing you got hurt." Sally shook her head. "I still can't believe you didn't go with her. The Wade Colter I knew would've done anything to be with his wife."

"Well, I'm not the Wade Colter you used to know." Wade put his feet on the floor, dragging the sheet across his middle. "Are my clothes anywhere around here?"

"Didn't think you'd wake up this soon. I sent them out to get washed."

"Why the hell would you do that?"

"Because they stunk."

Wade started to stand up and realized he couldn't, not unless he wanted to leave Sally's wearing only a sheet.

Sally pressed her lips together, obviously trying not to laugh. "You're free to leave anytime you want," Sally said, drumming her fingers on the table. "Just return the sheet as soon as you can."

Wade shook his head. "Were you always this ornery?"

Sally grinned and shrugged. "I can't see where you have much room to talk. At least I haven't single-handedly closed down the best saloon in town." Sally stood up and poured a cup of coffee, handing it to Wade. "Your clothes should be here soon, then you can go back to the ranch."

"I'm not going back to the ranch."

"Where the hell are you going, then?"

"I'm not sure yet, all I know is I can't take one more day out there."

Sally narrowed her eyes. "What're you thinking of doing, Wade? I don't like that look in your eye."

Wade didn't answer, suddenly angry. He was sick and tired of everyone telling him what he should and shouldn't do. He wasn't going to tell Sally anything. He didn't owe her or anyone else an explanation. It was, after all, his life.

Sandrine smiled as Gray Wolf stood between Shining Bird and Little Bear, proclaiming them husband and wife. She recalled the day Gray Wolf had married her and Wade. He had said similar words. For an instant, she pictured Wade's face clearly, then the details began to fade. When she tried to picture him again, she found that she couldn't. A stab of guilt ran through her.

She looked across the large fire at the faces of the people who had come to celebrate this marriage between Crow and Blackfoot. They had all seemed to accept it. She laughed as she watched Little Bear describe in great, broad gestures the way that Shining Bird had trapped him into the marriage. The people around him were laughing, calling out across the circle. Then she saw Lone Wind. He was standing so close that she might've reached out and touched him. The memory of their kiss was still fresh in her mind, and she found herself staring at his finely carved mouth. She watched as he stepped toward her, his eyes never leaving hers.

"You are pleased?" he asked, bending so that he could be heard above the voices of the others.

"Yes," she nodded. "I think it will be a good marriage. And you? Have you accepted my cousin into your family?"

"I have nothing to say about it. My father is still the head of this family."

"He would welcome your opinion, I am sure of it," Sandrine said, turning back to the fire. Little Bear and Gray Wolf were now telling the people how they had met.

"They are more like father and son," Lone Wind said.

Sandrine looked at him as he watched Little Bear and Gray Wolf. There was no anger in his voice, only a distinct sadness in his eyes. "You are Gray Wolf's son, Lone Wind. No one will ever take your place."

"You have a good heart, Bright Star, and your intentions are fine, but you really know nothing of me and my father. You know nothing."

"I know enough," she said angrily, walking away from the circle toward Gray Wolf's lodge. Her heart pounded, and she fought back angry tears.

"Wait," Lone Wind said behind her.

Sandrine didn't stop this time. She hurried to Gray Wolf's lodge, pushing aside the flap and going inside. She sat down on one of the robes, trying her best to ignore Lone Wind when he followed her inside.

"You are a stubborn woman." He sat down close to her.

"I am stubborn?" she said, her anger flaring. She shook her head. "You don't know me, just as you say I don't know you." She crossed her arms in front of her and looked away, avoiding Lone Wind's eyes.

"Then tell me what you feel, Bright Star. Tell me."

"I will not. Why should I tell you what is inside me when you will not let me see into your heart?" She shook her head. "No."

"Your eyes grow dark when you are angry," Lone Wind said, touching her chin and trying to force her to look at him. "All right," he said softly. "I will show you what is in my heart if you will do the same. Can you do that?"

Sandrine met Lone Wind's eyes, feeling herself being drawn into them. "Yes," she replied. She watched him as he squared his shoulders, staring into the small fire that was burning in the pit.

"Gray Wolf is not my real father," Lone Wind said, his voice even, conveying no emotion.

Sandrine folded her hands together, forcing herself to remain silent.

"My mother, Shining Bird, and I are Cheyenne."

Sandrine glanced up sharply. Red Bird spoke the Crow tongue perfectly—Sandrine had never doubted that she was a true Crow.

Lone Wind did not look at her, but he continued speaking in a low, even voice. "Gray Wolf captured us on a raid when I was almost thirteen summers old. I was young enough so that he could make me into a Crow warrior, but old enough to remember my father. I tried many times to escape, but Gray Wolf always brought me back. Eventually he tied me up like a dog. He wouldn't feed me until I promised not to run away again. He told me it was for my own good, so I would not run away or hurt myself.

"So I began to pretend. I did anything he told me to do, even learning the Crow tongue. But while my mother and Shining Bird began to accept the Crows as their people, I never forgot that my true people were Cheyenne or that my father was a Cheyenne warrior. I made sure never to let Gray Wolf know of my hatred for him. I kept it hidden and became a Crow warrior. I made Gray Wolf proud." Lone Wind became silent, still staring into the flames of the fire.

"I made a friend, a good friend. His name was Running Horse. We hunted and fished together, and we played the games that boys play. We shared many secrets with each other, and I even told him of my secret hatred for Gray Wolf. He understood how I felt. He had tried to court Shining Bird for a long time, but since Gray Wolf had never given his permission, they met in secret. Finally when Shining Bird threatened to run away with Running Horse, Gray Wolf gave in and said that they could marry.

"I thought it would be a good marriage. I only believed what I wanted to believe. It was not long before Running Horse began to beat Shining Bird. I saw the bruises on her arms and legs, yet I said nothing. She was my sister, but I did nothing to help her." Lone Wind shook his head. "It was as if Running Horse hated Shining Bird. He punished her for everything. She could do nothing right in his eyes. Many times I would see her crying, but I told her it was her duty to stay with her husband. And she did. I asked Running Horse why he hit my sister, but he never said why. He said she was his wife and she needed to be dutiful to him. He said if I interfered, he would accuse her of adultery and have her banished from the tribe. So once again, I did nothing." Lone Wind's voice was hard and cold. "I watched my own sister suffer, and I did nothing."

Sandrine watched Lone Wind as he spoke, and she saw the pain that was there. "He was your friend. You wanted to believe that he was good."

"That is no excuse. My sister was my blood; he was not." He shook his head. "The night Running Horse almost killed Shining Bird, I was gambling. Shining Bird told me later that if Gray Wolf had not come into the lodge so quickly, she would have died. Running Horse was ready to kill her. Gray Wolf saved her life, and I was not there to help.

"I was too consumed by my hatred for Gray Wolf to see correctly. When I found out he had killed Running Horse, I told him I hated him. But I did not." Lone Wind shook his head. "I hated myself. So I rode away. I knew where I wanted to go, where I needed to go."

Impulsively Sandrine reached out and touched Lone Wind's arm.

"I went in search of my father. It took me a long time to find him." Lone Wind hesitated. "He was not happy to see that his son had become a Crow warrior. He said that I could rejoin the tribe, but I would have to renounce all of my ties to the Crow people." Lone Wind paused. "As angry as I had been at Gray Wolf, I could not do that. He had been a good father to me and Shining Bird, and he had loved my mother well. But my Cheyenne father said that either I was a Cheyenne or I was a Crow. I could not be both.

"I began to think of how Gray Wolf had treated me all of this time, as if I was his son, his blood. He was always proud of me, and when he taught me something and I learned it quickly, he would tell the whole village." Lone Wind smiled slightly. "I remember when I shot my first buffalo bull. That night, after the day's hunt, he stood up and talked about my bravery and courage. He said a man could have no better son." He narrowed his eyes. "I do not remember my blood father speaking of me that way. I do not know if he was ever proud of me."

He shrugged his shoulders. "So I knew that I was not Cheyenne. I left there, and I traveled for a time. I went south into Mexico, and I even rode with the Comanches. But I never stayed any place long. I knew the only place I truly belonged was with my family, my Crow family." He looked at Sandrine. "I came back here to talk to Gray Wolf, to tell him that it would be different between us now, but he and my mother were gone. I could not believe it. I searched for them, but I did not find them. I did not see them again until they returned last spring. By then my heart had hardened and I could not say the things that I had wanted to say to Gray Wolf."

"Did Red Bird know how you really felt?"

"Yes, I told my mother. It gave her great comfort to know that I did not hate Gray Wolf. I promised her that I would find a way to become his son again."

"You haven't kept your promise," Sandrine said gently. "You must let go of your anger, Lone Wind."

"Perhaps it is not just my anger, Bright Star. Perhaps Gray Wolf has some anger of his own." He looked at Sandrine, his eyes reflecting the fire's flames. "Now it is your turn."

Sandrine looked away, not wanting to meet Lone Wind's eyes. "There is nothing to tell about my life. You know everything."

"How did you meet your husband?"

"He rode on a wagon train that stopped at my parents' trading post every spring. We have known each other since we were very young."

"And you have always known that he would be your husband?"

Sandrine thought for a moment. She hadn't always known how she felt about Wade. For a brief time in her life, she had even considered marrying another man. "No."

"Tell me about your husband, Bright Star. What is he like?"

Sandrine stared down at her hands, nervously rubbing them together. "He's a good man, he's fair, and . . ." Sandrine thought about the way Wade made love to her, and she felt her cheeks flush.

"You love this man."

Sandrine looked at Lone Wind, meeting his eyes. "Yes," she said, her voice breaking.

"Will you answer another question for me, Bright Star?"

"What?"

"What are your feelings for me?"

Sandrine locked her fingers together, barely able to control the slight trembling of her body. She looked away from Lone Wind, unable to withstand his piercing gaze.

"Can you not answer this question, Bright Star?"

Sandrine squeezed her fingers together tightly. "I owe you my life, Lone Wind."

"And that is all? You feel nothing more for me?"

"I *cannot* feel anything more for you," she said, her voice barely above a whisper. "I cannot." She closed her eyes, afraid to look at him again. She heard him move closer to her, and she felt his hand on her arm.

"I believe what you say, Bright Star," he said, his mouth close to her ear. "I believe that you love your husband. I believe that he is a good man, for I cannot imagine you with any other kind of man. But I also know that your husband is not here, and I am." He cupped the nape of her neck in his palm, turning her face toward his.

Sandrine tried to pull away, but Lone Wind held her. He was so close that she felt his warm breath on her cheek. "This is not right."

"We have done nothing wrong, Bright Star."

Sandrine closed her eyes as Lone Wind leaned his head next to hers. She felt his other arm wrap around her so that she was leaning against him, completely encircled in his arms. His mouth moved along her cheek, and Sandrine held her breath. "If we do this, I cannot go home," she said, her voice filled with pain.

"Then do not go home. Stay here with me. I will be your husband. I will take care of you."

Sandrine was entranced by the sound of his voice and the feel of his arms around her. He made her feel safe and, more than that, desired. She relaxed her body and leaned back against him, letting him hold her.

"You are trembling, Bright Star. Do I frighten you?"

"Yes," Sandrine said, feeling the heat of his body against hers. "I am afraid to be alone with you. Whenever I am with you, I lose my senses."

"That is not so bad, is it?"

She felt Lone Wind's mouth on her neck, and she rested her head on his shoulder. Suddenly the image of Bear Killer's face came into her mind. Had he changed her so much? Had he used her in so many ways that now it did not matter that she was even faithful to her own husband? Her body stiffened and she sat upright, trying to pull away from Lone Wind.

"What is it?"

Sandrine felt tears stream down her face. She was frightened and confused. She didn't know herself anymore. "I cannot stay here."

"I will not let you go, Bright Star."

"I cannot do this thing with you, Lone Wind," she cried, her tears turning to sobs. But even as she cried, she felt Lone Wind pull her down to the robe with him. He held her as she cried, and she buried her face in his chest, reveling in the strength she felt in his arms. If she stayed with him much longer, she knew, it would be that much more difficult for her to go home. It would be too easy for her to stay with Lone Wind forever.

Wade held the cigar clenched between his teeth, squinting through the haze of smoke at the man across the poker table. He was bluffing, Wade knew, and all Wade would have to do was wait him out. He looked at the pile of money in the middle of the table and tried to keep from smiling. It was the biggest pot he'd seen all night, and if he was patient, it would soon be his.

"Would you hurry up, Carr," Lyle Roberts said. "Christ, you can make a man crazy."

Carr finally looked up from his cards. "I'll see the one hundred and raise two hundred." He looked across the table at Wade as he spoke.

The betting continued around the table until it got to Wade. He hesitated for a moment, then spoke. "I'll see your two hundred and raise you two hundred more." He pushed his money stacks into the middle of the table. The crowd of people who had been watching the high-stakes game all night moved in tightly around the table. The smell of whiskey, perfume, and trail dust was overwhelming.

"I'm out," Otis Gentry said.

"Me, too," Mills Reilly said, throwing his cards face down on the table.

When it was Carr's turn, he smiled and threw two hundred more dollars onto the table. "I'm in." He looked at Roberts. "How about you, Lyle?"

"You crazy?" He shook his head. "Can't afford to lose it. I'm out."

"Guess that leaves you and me, mister," Carr said, smiling at Wade.

"I guess you're right," Wade said. He glanced at his hand once more—full house, queens high. It was a good hand. Still, Carr might have kings or aces, but Wade didn't think so. "I call," Wade said, taking the cigar from his mouth and blowing out a big puff of smoke. He watched as Carr slowly turned over his hand and fanned out his cards. Wade saw two kings, and for a moment he felt his heart pound in his chest. But as Carr got past the second king and Wade saw the ten, he knew he only had two pair. Remaining outwardly calm, Wade watched as Carr showed his cards.

"Two pair, kings high," he said confidently.

"That is a good hand," Wade agreed, nodding his head. "But this one's better," he said, slowly showing his cards. He heard the sighs of the crowd as he laid down his hand. "Sorry, Carr. Guess it was just my night." Wade reached into the middle of the table and drew the large pile of money toward him.

"You're a sonofabitch, Colter," Carr said angrily, standing up so suddenly his chair crashed to the floor.

"I expect I've been called worse," Wade replied, grinning at one of the pretty saloon girls who stood nearby. "Drinks on the house," he announced loudly, putting the paper and coins in stacks.

"Would you like a bag for that, Mr. Colter?" Fred asked, coming up to the table.

"That would be handy, Fred, thank you," Wade said, smiling as he watched Fred disappear behind the bar. Since that night a few weeks ago when Sally had rescued him, Wade had paid Fred back for all of the damages plus extra. They'd established an understanding that if Wade got into any kind of trouble, he would always pay for the damages. So Fred figured he had a good customer and a poker player who brought other players into the saloon. The more men in the saloon, the more money spent on liquor and women. Wade even had a room there now.

"Here you go," Fred said, handing Wade a cloth bag.

"Would you mind holding onto this for me until tomorrow morning, Fred? I wouldn't want anyone getting any ideas. I believe there's about six thousand dollars in there. And this, of course," Wade said, handing Fred one hundred dollars, "is for you."

"Thank you, Mr. Colter. I'll make sure the money gets right into the safe."

"Thanks, Fred." Wade took another puff on his cigar, then

stuck it in the ashtray. He downed the rest of his glass of whiskey and stood up, looking around the room. That pretty saloon girl was looking at him. She had curly blond hair and big blue eyes, and her low-cut dress left nothing to the imagination. She was new to the saloon, and she seemed very young.

She walked up to him, a hand on one hip. "You interested in having a good time tonight, Mr. Colter?"

"What's your name?"

"Rachel," she said, smiling sweetly.

"That's a pretty name. Why're you working in a place like this, Rachel? Can't you find some other kind of job?"

Rachel looked discomfited, and she shifted nervously. "I don't know what else to do. I'm not very good at anything else. I don't have much learning. When my folks died . . ." Rachel folded her hands together. "This isn't that bad of a job, Mr. Colter. At least I ain't robbing banks."

Wade grinned. "Damned right, you're not. But how about something else, something less . . ." Wade measured his words, "something less demanding." It was obvious from the look on Rachel's face that she understood what he meant. She blushed and looked past Wade to the men who were standing at the bar. "Some of my customers are real good to me. They like me."

Wade touched her shoulder. "Of course they do. You're a very pretty girl, and you're kind-hearted." He reached into his pocket and took out some bills. "You save this. Save it for the day you decide to open a hat shop."

Rachel's smile was radiant, and she giggled. "Hat shop? Me?"

Wade shrugged. "You always have ribbons in your hair, or flowers. I'll bet you could make up some real nice hats." Wade lowered his head and whispered into Rachel's ear, "Lord knows the women in this town can use all the help they can get."

Rachel kissed his cheek. "You're a fine man, Mr. Colter."

"Let's just keep that between you and me." He watched her

as she smoothed her skirt and touched her hair, still smiling at him. Then Fred called to her, and she turned away. She really was a pretty girl, and he hoped she was smart enough not to use the money for lace petticoats and French perfume.

Wade shook his head and decided to take his own advice. Sometimes it was smarter to quit while you were ahead. He glanced at the stairway that led to the rooms upstairs. He didn't want to go up there now; it'd be far too noisy. And besides, he didn't want to be alone.

He nodded to Fred as he left the saloon. The night was warm, and the stars glittered brightly. As he got farther from the saloon, the noise of the player piano faded along with the sounds of rough laughter. Wade became conscious of his own footsteps on the planked sidewalk. The dry goods store was dark and locked down tight as were all the businesses on Main Street. As Wade passed the jailhouse, he could hear the low melodic singing of Simon, the old man who haunted Main Street like a drunken ghost. If the cell was empty, the sheriff brought him in so that he could sleep safe and warm.

At the far end of the street, amber light spilled out of the windows of Sally's restaurant. As he got closer, he could hear the voices from inside. He looked through the window and saw Sally talking to some of her customers. As usual the restaurant was full of people, and the smell of steaks almost lured Wade inside. But he hesitated. He really wasn't hungry. What he wanted was to talk to Sally and he knew she was too busy. He walked behind the restaurant and up the stairs to Sally's room. He reached for the hidden key and let himself in. Sally had told him that in the old days, he would've waited for her, stretched out across her bed. Now he eased himself onto her sofa. Sally was an honest woman, a one-man woman, and he knew he was no longer the man.

He looked around the room that was becoming familiar again. It was strange to think that Sally had been his lover. It was such a crazy feeling not to remember people who claimed to love him. He sighed.

Rose and Jim disapproved of him living over the saloon. At first Jim had tried to talk him into coming back home, then he had given up. Wade was grateful for Jim's help in taking care of the ranch while he was gone, and he knew that he should be grateful for his friendship as well. But he wasn't. Both Jim and Rose lectured him too much. They treated him like a child. And he was sick of hearing about how Sandrine would be coming home soon.

Sometimes, lying alone in his room, he felt like Sandrine, his other life, even his friendship with Jim and Rose, belonged in a dream. It was hard for him to believe that he had a wife. It was hard for him to even care. Where was she? And even if she did come back, would he still love her?

And then there was Emily. She'd been to town several times, using Rose's errands as an excuse to see him. He smiled. The last time she'd come to his room. His smile widened, remembering how she had sat primly on the edge of his bed, her hands folded in her lap. But she had laughed prettily, and she had stayed for almost an hour. And when he had kissed her goodbye, she had pressed herself against him and kissed him back.

Wade's reverie was interrupted by the sound of boot heels on the stairs outside. He rested his hand lightly on the butt of his gun, but he didn't bother to stand up. An instant before the door opened, he knew who it was. The scent of expensive cologne was not that common in Santa Fe.

"Hello, Frank," Wade said, touching the brim of his hat.

Frank stood in the doorway, trying not to look surprised. "Heard you won big tonight, Wade. Thought you'd be out celebrating with some pretty young thing."

Wade shrugged his shoulders. "Is there a woman around here who compares to Sally?"

"Yeah, your wife."

Wade watched Frank as he walked to the small sideboard and poured himself a drink. "How is Sandrine anyway?"

"Don't know," Wade replied tersely.

"Shouldn't she be back soon?"

"Don't know that either," Wade replied stubbornly.

"Don't you even care about her, Wade?" Frank shook his head. "If you only knew."

"If I only knew what?"

Frank sat down in one of the chairs next to the sofa. "If you only knew how beautiful Sandrine is, you wouldn't be acting this way. Hell, most men I know would give anything to have a woman like her."

Wade pulled his hat down over his eyes and crossed his arms over his chest. "Well, as far as I'm concerned, any man can have her. I'm not interested in being married. The only thing that interests me right now is taking a nap."

"You're a stubborn bastard," Frank said.

"Maybe, but at least I'm honest." Wade lifted up his hat. "How can I love a woman I don't even know, Frank?"

"You don't remember Sally, yet you don't seem to have a problem caring about her. In fact, now that I think about it, you're here all the time."

"You're right, I do care for Sally, but I don't love her. Love is something else."

"But what about Sandrine? What're you going to do when she gets back and expects to go on with your marriage? Are you willing to hurt her like that, Wade?"

Wade pushed his hat back farther on his head and let out a long low sigh. "I guess I'll have to, Frank, 'cause I'm not going to be married. I don't think I'm the marrying kind. I'm beginning to think the fall from that horse of yours was the best thing that ever happened to me. Brought me to my senses."

"We've never talked about that, Wade. I'm real sorry you got hurt. If there's any way I can make it up to you—"

Wade held up his hand. "As a matter of fact, you can make it up to me, Frank. You can start setting up some high-stakes games. I'm tired of living in that room over the saloon, and when Sandrine comes back, I suppose I'll have to give her some money so she can get on with her life. I don't want to scrape by like Jim and Rose. I want more than that."

"You're making a mistake, Wade. Jim and Rose have what most people strive for. You always wanted what they have."

"That was before. Are you going to help me or not?"

Frank nodded. "I'll help you. But there might be other ways to make some money."

"What other ways?" Wade sat up straighter.

"Running guns to the Indians."

"Is it illegal?"

"Of course it's illegal. If it was legal, I wouldn't be making money at it."

"What kind of money are we talking?"

"Five hundred a wagonload."

"Are you crazy? I made six thousand tonight. Why would I risk my neck riding into Indian country for five hundred?"

Frank shrugged. "It was worth a try."

"I lost my memory, Frank. I didn't become stupid."

"That's debatable," Frank said, sipping at his drink.

"Do you have anything else, anything I could make some real money at?"

"I still can't believe this is you talking, Wade."

Wade leaned forward. "Well, it's not me, or at least the old me. It's the new me, and you damn well better get used to it, Frank," he said angrily. "I'm tired of everyone telling me what a great guy I was, that I was happily married, that I like my ranch . . ." Wade shook his head. "I'm the person who has to live inside this body without any memories of my past, and I'm the person who's going to decide how I'm going to live my life."

"Now that we've got that clear," Frank said, "I'll get you in some high-stake games, if that's what you want." He finished his whiskey, set the glass on the table, and leaned back in the chair. "But you better be prepared to win, 'cause if you lose, you'll lose big, Wade. You also better be prepared to take people's homes and businesses from them, because that's what happens. Hell, it almost happened to your friend Jim."

"Jim lost his ranch?"

"He owed me a large sum of money. I always fancied Rose, and I told her maybe we could swing a deal of some kind. But that spunky little wife of yours pulled a gun on me and said she'd play me for the land." Frank smiled, shaking his head. "Can you imagine? She bet herself, just so Jim and Rose wouldn't lose their ranch. Takes some kind of guts," Frank said in an admiring tone. "Never seen anything like that."

"I take it she won."

"She lost," Frank said, grinning broadly.

"So you . . ." Wade narrowed his eyes. "From what Rose said about her, she didn't seem like the type who would—"

"I didn't take her up on it. I gave the land back to Jim, and I promised Sandrine that I'd never let Jim into one of my games again."

"If she's as pretty as you say, why didn't you take her up on it, Frank?"

"Because she's got class, Wade, real class. Sandrine's the kind of woman you want to come to you willingly. Too bad your memory is gone."

Wade shook his head impatiently. "I want to make money, Frank, lots of money."

"Why, Wade? Why are you suddenly so interested in being rich?"

"Because I can make my own rules."

Frank stared at Wade. "I would've never figured you for the

kind of man who was interested in power." He quickly held up his hands. "Sorry, I forget this is the *new* Wade Colter."

"So when are we going to play some poker?"

"Soon enough, and I won't bail you out."

"I won't need you to bail me out, Frank." Wade shoved his hat back on his head. "Before long, I'll own your ranch and you'll be coming to me for money."

"You talk big, but let's see if you can back it up." Frank stood up and walked over to the sideboard again, pouring himself another drink. He took a sip and turned to Wade. "There's a game tomorrow at my ranch. Five thousand dollar buy-in, no limit table stakes. Just remember, if you lose, I don't want to hear about it."

Wade stood up and walked to the sideboard. He poured himself some whiskey, finishing half the glass before he spoke. "The only thing you're going to hear from me is the sound of jubilation, Frank."

"We'll see."

"I guess we will," Wade said, finishing his drink and setting the glass down firmly on the sideboard. "Tell Sally I stopped by," he said, walking to the door. He turned and grinned at Frank, setting his hat firmly on his head. "Say goodbye to that money of yours, Frank. After tomorrow night, it's going to belong to me."

Wade moved his head around, trying to relax his shoulders. The evening hadn't gone quite as he'd planned. He'd started out with five thousand, and he was now down to six hundred. He'd misjudged a few hands, but worse than that he'd played foolishly. With no limit on the raises, he'd stayed in a few too many times.

He forced himself to relax as Jeb Anderson dealt the cards. He took a deep breath before he picked them up off the table, one by one. The first ace raised his hopes; the second one startled him; the third almost made him stop breathing. He set his face carefully, hiding his excitement. He had to play this well. Frank had been hot all evening. If Wade gave any early indication that he had good cards, Frank and the others would simply drop out.

He reached out and took his whiskey glass, downing the contents. With any luck, Frank would think he was scared. He looked up, caught Frank looking at him, and he quickly averted his eyes.

"How many cards, Mr. Colter?" Jeb asked politely.

Wade picked up his cards again, studying them as if he might see something he hadn't seen before.

"Hurry up, Wade. The rest of us want to play sometime tonight," Frank said.

"I'll take two," Wade said, placing two cards down on the table. Jeb slid the new cards to him, but Wade didn't immediately pick them up.

"What's the matter, Wade? That six hundred dollars looking a little small to you right now?" Frank said, laughing loudly.

Wade ignored Frank and picked up the cards. He fanned out the three aces and the two new cards. A three of hearts—and the fourth ace. Four aces. Wade stared at his cards, trying to keep the expression on his face impassive. This was the hand to bet it all on. But he had to do it carefully.

"Your bet, Rocky," Frank prompted.

"A hundred."

"Well, well," Frank said, tapping his fingers on the smooth mahogany table. "My turn." He put his fingers on his chin, then he very carefully pushed two stacks of coin into the pot. "I'll see your one hundred and raise you two."

Wade watched as Wayne raised it another one hundred dollars. Jeb saw that and raised it one hundred more. By the time it was Wade's turn, he could barely control his breathing.

"That's five hundred to you, Wade." Frank shook his head. "You in or out?"

Wade looked at his cards once more, then at his pile of money. "I'll see it," he said quietly.

"Why, I think that's real brave of you, Wade. And that leaves you all of one hundred dollars to play with by the time it's your turn again."

Wade ignored the laughter of the men at the table and watched as the betting continued. Rocky raised it another one hundred dollars. By the time it was to Frank again, it was obvious he could barely contain himself.

"Let's see, that's six hundred to me," Frank said, pushing the money into the center of the table, "and I'm going to raise two hundred more. That's eight hundred to you, Wayne."

Wayne shook his head. "That's pretty steep for me," he said, staring at his cards.

"Hell, even old Wade stayed in, and he's practically down to nothing. Either you have a good hand or you don't," Frank said, drumming his fingers on the table.

Thank you, Frank, Wade thought. You're getting people to stay in the game—doing my work for me.

"Oh, hell," Wayne said, pushing eight hundred dollars forward. "I'm in."

"That's eight hundred to me," Jeb said, pushing his money forward. "And I believe I'll raise that another hundred." He looked at Wade. "Sorry, kid, but I think you're out of the game."

"That's nine hundred to me, right?" Wade asked.

Frank looked around the table. "Yeah, but it doesn't make any difference now. You're finished."

"It makes plenty of difference," Wade said, bending down and taking some bills out of his shoe. "I'll see the nine hundred and raise two hundred." He put the money in the middle of the table and stared at Frank. Rocky threw down his cards. Wade looked across the table at Frank. "You in, Frank?"

Frank shook his head and laughed. "I swear, you got guts, kid. Not too smart, but you got guts." Frank took a sip of whiskey, took a puff of his cigar, and looked back at Wade. "I'll see your eleven hundred," he said, putting the money on the table. "And I'll do you the favor of not raising."

"I've never known you to do anybody a favor, Frank," Wayne said, throwing his cards on the table.

"Too high for me," Jeb said, folding.

Wade stared across the table at Frank. "I call."

"Feeling confident, are you, Wade?" Frank said.

"Confident enough."

"Well, you've been sure of yourself all night, and you've been losing."

"Let's see 'em, Frank."

Wade watched as Frank laid out his cards—three kings and two tens. A full house.

"Sorry, kid," Frank said. "Didn't mean to take that last thousand. Didn't know you had it." He leaned forward, reaching for the pot.

"Don't you want to see my cards, Frank?" Before Frank could respond, Wade laid his cards face down, then slowly turned each one over—ace, ace, ace, ace, three. He heard the sighs from the men and the loud thud of Frank's fist on the table.

"Four aces? I haven't seen that very often."

"You accusing me of cheating, Frank?" Wade said, his voice hard.

"What else did you take out of your boot besides money?" Frank asked angrily.

Wade started to react, then stopped. Frank was trying to bait him. He'd worked hard for this money, and he wasn't going to lose it now. "Check the deck if you don't trust me." Wade turned to Jeb. "Better yet, you check the cards, Mr. Anderson. See if they're all there."

Wade kept his hands on the table where everyone could see them as Jeb counted, then checked the suits of the cards.

"They're all here, Frank."

"What about him? You didn't check him."

"I don't think that's neces—" Jeb started to say.

"Why isn't it? He's not a regular. For all we know, he's got cards stashed all over the place."

"It's all right," Wade said, standing up. "Go ahead and check me out, Jeb. I don't mind." Wade waited patiently as Jeb examined him.

"Nothing, Frank. Mr. Colter didn't cheat. I think you owe him an apology."

Frank shook his head. "I still don't believe it—"

"Ah, let it go, Frank. The kid won fair and square," Rocky said. "Let him have his money. There's no rule that says you have to win every hand."

Wade didn't wait for Frank's okay. He pulled the stack of bills and coin toward him.

"You still feeling lucky, Wade?" Frank asked.

"I guess I am."

"Good. We're upping the ante in this game. It's five hundred just to play."

"Come on, Frank. I hate it when you get like this," Rocky said.

"It's high-stakes poker, gentlemen. Either you're in or you're not." Frank was staring at Wade as he spoke.

Wade pushed five hundred dollars into the middle and waited for the others to ante up and the cards to be dealt. He felt relaxed suddenly, in his element. As he looked around Frank's immaculately decorated cardroom, he decided he was going to own this house. He would enjoy taking it away from Frank.

Wade played a smart game into the early hours. He lost some hands, but he won some very large ones. By early the next morning, the half-drunk players staggered out of Frank's house and the game was over. Wade had won back his five thousand dollars and had won seventy-three hundred more. He now had twelve thousand dollars and change. He put the money into a leather saddlebag, then he poured himself another drink as Frank saw the others out. When Frank returned, Wade was walking around the room, admiring the fine wood paneling and the collection of rifles.

"You like this room, Wade?" Frank asked, pouring himself a brandy.

Wade, nodded. "I could get used to it."

"Well, don't," Frank said. "This is my home, and not you or anybody else is going to take it away from me."

"What makes you think I want to take it away from you, Frank?" Wade asked nonchalantly as he looked hungrily at the rich furnishings in the room.

"I see that look in your eyes, Wade. I know that look. I had it once."

"You mean before you owned all this?" Wade said, gesturing widely. "Just how did you get this house, Frank? Did you build it yourself?"

"I had it built. Why?"

"What about the land? Was it yours?"

"Of course it was; do you think I'd build on someone else's?"

"Did you win it in a poker game, Frank? And what about the things in this house? Did you win some of them in a game, too?" Wade pointed to a painting on the wall. "Somehow I don't see that as something you'd pick out, Frank. Looks like something a woman would've chosen."

Frank barely glanced at the painting and downed his drink. "So I won the land in a game: it's still mine. The painting and many of the furnishings in the house I won in games. But I never stole anything from anyone. All the men I played with knew what they were getting into when they played with me."

"Just like Jim did," Wade said, setting his glass down on the card table.

"It's a little late for you to be defending Jim Everett, isn't it?"

Wade shrugged. "Doesn't really matter to me. I just wonder if he and the others knew that you're a cheat. Good, too. Real good. Took me the whole damned evening to figure it out," Wade said, pulling out a chair and sitting down. He propped his boots up on the card table, watching as Frank walked toward him, sitting down across from him.

"I don't cheat. I don't need to."

"Maybe you can lie to the men around here, Frank, but don't lie to me. Jim said he taught me how to play cards on the wagon train, and I ought to thank him the next time I see him, because he taught me real good." Wade picked up the deck. "I noticed the cards getting scuffed right after I got my four aces. See here, right in the corner. There's a little mark. I know you did it with your ring. I'll bet if I look at all the aces and face cards, I'll find marks on all of them. Hell, I bet I'll even find them on the tens." Wade reached for some more cards, but Frank slapped them from Wade's hand, scattering them all over the table.

"All right," he said, his voice low. "What do you want? Money? How much?"

Wade shook his foot, propping his hands behind his head. "I told you before, Frank, I don't just want money, I want a lot of money."

"You're still not saying what you want, Wade."

"Then I'll make it clear for you, Frank. You'll be sitting out some of your games for awhile. I want your seat. I want a chance to win some big money."

"You won some big money tonight. Don't get greedy."

"You're not one to be lecturing me on greed, Frank." Wade narrowed his eyes. "As I see it, you don't have much of a choice."

"What does that mean?"

"You wouldn't want all of those men that you've been playing with for so long to find out that you're a cheat, would you, Frank? Wouldn't do much for your reputation—and maybe not for your health."

"You bastard," Frank said, his teeth clenched.

"You're lucky I was the one who found out, Frank. If it had been someone else, they might have shot you in the back and taken all your money. All I'm asking you to do is give me your seat in some high-stakes games for awhile. You could probably use the rest anyway."

"I don't like being blackmailed."

"I'm not blackmailing you. I'm simply making you a business proposition. Hell, I don't even care if you play in the same game with me as long as I get a chance at some real money. You know rich people all over the territory, Frank. I'm sure there're plenty of them who would like to lose their money."

"Then what? What happens when you win all the money you want?"

Wade shrugged. "I pack up and take off. There's nothing to keep me around here anyway. So what do you say?"

Frank sighed. "What can I say?"

"Good, it's a deal then. Oh, by the way, Frank. I do want this house. I'll give you one week to find another place to live."

"What?" Frank yelled, standing up and coming around the table. "I thought you said there's nothing to keep you here."

"There's not now, but who knows?" Wade stood up, standing a good six inches taller than Frank. "Everyone keeps telling me how attractive my wife is. Hell, I might decide I like her when she comes back."

"I feel sorry for her," Frank said disgustedly. He shook his head. "All right. Take the house, you bastard."

Wade watched Frank as he left the room. Wade walked over to the fine mahogany bar and poured himself a brandy. He leaned against the wood, looking around. Funny how things changed so quickly. A few months ago he was a simple rancher with a simple life. A couple hours ago he was close to losing his shirt. Now he had seven thousand more dollars to add to the six he'd won the night before and the ten he had in the bank. Before long he'd be as wealthy as Frank.

For a brief instant he thought of Rose and Jim, and then of Sally, and he wondered what they'd say when they found out what he'd done. All of them would be disappointed in him, he knew. But he didn't care. He turned around and slammed his glass down on the bar. He didn't care what any of them thought.

Seven

Sandrine sat next to Gray Wolf in front of his lodge. The evening fire was growing dim and the camp was quieting. It had been two weeks since the marriage of Little Bear and Shining Bird. Sandrine and Gray Wolf had built their marriage lodge for them. As was the custom, the newly married couple would take time apart from the others in the village. Sandrine had no idea when they would return, and she was finding it more and more difficult to be so near Lone Wind.

"I have a favor to ask of you, Gray Wolf."

"What is it, Bright Star?"

"Can you take me back to my people?"

"You know it is too dangerous to travel right now, Bright Star."

Sandrine nodded slowly. He was right and she knew it. She picked up a stick and poked it into the fire, then tapped it against the round stones of the fire ring. "I do not like life sometimes," she muttered, thrusting at the red-hot embers again.

"Life is always preferable, Bright Star. Remember that."

Sandrine looked over at Gray Wolf. He was staring into the fire, his face impassive, but she could see the sadness in his eyes. "I am sorry, Gray Wolf. I did not mean to be cruel. I know that you miss Red Bird." She touched his arm.

"Red Bird is at peace now. It is I who am restless."

"You would not do anything to harm yourself?" Sandrine tightened her hold on Gray Wolf's arm.

Gray Wolf smiled slightly and looked at Sandrine. "Do not worry so, Bright Star. I know I am needed here."

Sandrine nodded, taking her hand away. "I will miss your village," she said, staring into the flames.

"I thought you were impatient to go home. What is it that keeps you here, Bright Star?"

"You know that it is you, Gray Wolf," she replied, almost too quickly.

"I know that it was I who brought you here, but it is not I who keeps you here. Talk to me, Bright Star."

"I cannot," Sandrine replied, trying to hide the emotion in her voice.

"You do not have to say it, for I can see it in your eyes."

Slowly Sandrine looked up.

"It is Lone Wind."

Sandrine closed her eyes for the briefest moment. Even the sound of his name was unsettling to her. "We have become friends."

"Close friends?"

Sandrine hesitated. How could she tell Gray Wolf what she had been feeling for his son? She longed to tell someone. She looked into her old friend's kind, forgiving eyes, and she knew she could tell him anything. "Yes, we have become close. I am troubled by this, Gray Wolf."

"Do you question your feelings for Colter? Have your feelings for him changed?"

"No, they have not but . . ." She shook her head, smoothing her skirt in a nervous gesture. "My feelings for Wade are the same, but my feelings for Lone Wind have grown stronger. It frightens me."

"Does Lone Wind feel the same?"

"I think so," Sandrine said. She shook her head, hugging herself. "I feel foolish, Gray Wolf, like a young girl who cannot make up her mind about the boy with whom she wishes to dance."

Gray Wolf took Sandrine's hand. "There is no reason to feel foolish, Bright Star. If you possess a true affection for Lone Wind, then it must come from somewhere deep inside. You are not the kind of woman who possesses false feelings. I know this about you."

"Do you think less of me for this, Gray Wolf?" she asked, lowering her eyes.

Gray Wolf pressed Sandrine's hand between both of his. "How could I think of you with anything but overwhelming love, Bright Star? You are like my daughter. Indeed, without you I would have never seen Shining Bird again. Without you I might be dead myself now." He shook his head. "I would never seek to judge you. I have made too many mistakes in my own lifetime."

"But I am scared and confused, Gray Wolf. When I am with Lone Wind . . ." She didn't finish. What she wanted to say was when she was with Lone Wind she never wanted to leave him. It was almost as if Wade was a distant memory.

"You are with Lone Wind much of the time now, so it is natural that you would think about him. But is it not the same way with Colter?"

"But what's the matter with me, Gray Wolf? How is it possible for me to care for two men in the same way?" Sandrine was startled when Gray Wolf laughed loudly and took her hand to his mouth, kissing it gently.

"There is nothing wrong with you, girl."

"Don't laugh at me."

"I am not laughing at you, Bright Star. I am merely charmed by your manner."

"How can you be charmed by a woman who betrays her husband?" she asked, tears in her eyes.

"Have you betrayed Colter?" Gray Wolf asked.

"No, but—"

Gray Wolf held up his hand. "Thoughts are not deeds, Bright Star. They grow and die in the mind."

"But what if my feelings for Lone Wind grow stronger?"

"I cannot help you with that. You must decide where you belong and which man you wish to be with." He picked up Sandrine's stick and poked the fire. "I will take you to your parents if you feel you must go. But it would be safer to go directly south than to cross Blackfoot land."

Sandrine nodded and stood up. "Thank you, Gray Wolf."

Gray Wolf nodded. "Lone Wind is with the horses. Perhaps it is time that you two talked."

Sandrine kissed Gray Wolf on the cheek. "Thank you," she said, hugging him tightly. She walked through the village, barely acknowledging the quiet greetings of some of the women. When she reached the edge of the pasture, she hesitated, looking toward the corral. She wasn't sure if she was ready to confront Lone Wind. A cool breeze blew against her face, and impulsively she unbraided her hair and shook it out, feeling the breeze lift it from her shoulders. She pulled in a heavy breath, then went toward the corral. She heard the nicker of some of the horses and heard Lone Wind's soothing voice as he talked to them. She was barely able to see his face from the faint light of the village.

"I must go home," she said, her voice tremulous.

"Bright Star." Lone Wind turned to face her.

"I can stay here no longer, Lone Wind. I'm afraid that if I do, I will betray my husband. I don't want to do that."

"Go if you must," Lone Wind replied, his voice low.

Sandrine's eyes filled with tears. "I have no wish to hurt you."

"I know that, Bright Star. Do not be troubled. You have made your decision."

"Yes," Sandrine said, uncertainty softening her voice.

"I will miss you."

"And I you." Sandrine felt her resolve begin to crumble as Lone Wind reached out to touch her cheek.

"You are so very beautiful, Bright Star." Lone Wind stepped closer, a hand on either side of Sandrine's face.

Sandrine closed her eyes, enjoying his touch. "You *have* cast a spell over me, Lone Wind. I cannot get you out of my mind. How will I ever forget you?"

"I hope that you will not," Lone Wind said, pulling Sandrine closer to him. He tilted her face up. "I hope that I will always be in your thoughts, Bright Star." He brushed his lips against hers. "I hope that when you go to sleep at night, you think of me."

Sandrine felt Lone Wind's lips press against hers and his arms encircle her. Her whole body trembled, and tears streaked her cheeks. She felt him gently wipe the tears away.

"Do not cry."

Sandrine felt his arms tighten around her, and she pressed her cheek against his bare chest.

"Will you lie with me this night, Bright Star?"

Sandrine's body stiffened. She tried to pull away from Lone Wind, but he held her tightly. "No, I cannot. You know that I cannot." She finally managed to free herself from his hold, and she ran into the pasture. She ran until her breath came so hard that it hurt. She heard Lone Wind behind her, but she was afraid to face him.

"Are you all right?" He stood close, but he didn't touch her.

Sandrine looked upward. She nodded slowly, finally giving in to her feelings. "I will lie with you this night, Lone Wind," she said calmly. "But I cannot stay here. I want to go home."

"I will take you home if that is what you wish." Lone Wind pulled her into the circle of his arms and stroked her long dark hair.

She took his hand. "I am tired. Let us go to your lodge."

Sandrine tried not to think as they walked. She kept remembering what Gray Wolf had said—but this was no longer in her mind, this was about to become real.

When they reached his lodge, Sandrine ducked inside, waiting for Lone Wind. The lodge was dark; there was no fire. She held his hand as he led her to his robe. She sat next to him on the soft fur, suddenly feeling weak with excitement. She felt his hand move up her arm to her shoulder, and slowly his fingers traced the line of her neck. Then he was touching her lips, gently caressing them. Her heart pounded wildly in her chest.

"Bright Star of the Northern Blackfoot tribe, I want you to be my wife." Lone Wind's voice was solemn.

"I cannot be your wife, Lone Wind. I can never be your wife."

"Then be my wife for this night," Lone Wind said, touching his lips to Sandrine's.

Sandrine felt the gentle pressure of his kiss, and she kissed him back, aware of the urgency in his body and her own. She wanted Lone Wind, just as she had always wanted Wade, and it frightened her. How was it possible to feel the same way about two men? "I am afraid I will never forget you, Lone Wind. Never." She touched his face and leaned forward, pressing her lips to his. Lone Wind covered her mouth with his own. For an instant, she held herself away from him, but her own passion rose so quickly that she could not control it. She trembled as Lone Wind held her back from him, then slowly lifted her dress over her head. She knelt before him, naked, frightened, but anticipating what they would share together. Sandrine sat back on her heels, her eyes closed, transfixed by his touch. She could feel his bare chest against her breasts as he ran his hands from her shoulders down to the small of her back, and back up to her waist. He rested his hands there for a moment, then gently stroked her belly.

"You are so beautiful," he said, kissing her passionately, his mouth soft and warm.

Sandrine shivered as he touched her breasts, then took her hands and guided them over his chest. As she ran her hands over his warm, smooth skin, she was amazed by the quiet strength that he possessed. "Lone Wind. It is a good name," she said softly, pressing her body against his. He held her tightly, and she leaned her head on his shoulder. She didn't know how she could leave him and go back to Wade.

Wade. A clear picture of him came into her mind. She thought of his blond hair and blue-gray eyes—she could see his face clearly. Wade loved her, he had always loved her. Suddenly she was overwhelmed by guilt and shame.

"You are thinking of your husband," Lone Wind said, his voice unsteady.

"How can I not think of him, Lone Wind? He is a part of me. We have loved each other since we were children." Lone Wind released her.

"Perhaps it would be best if you went back to my father's lodge. To have you here . . ." He didn't finish.

"I am sorry," she said, barely able to control her tears. She reached for her dress and pulled it over her head. She stood, intending to leave, but found she couldn't. "Please understand, Lone Wind."

"I understand, and I admire your loyalty to your husband."

Sandrine heard the sadness in his voice, and she knew she couldn't leave. Not like this. She knelt down next to him, taking his hand. "I want you to know that my heart is full of you. I did not think I could feel this way about any man but my husband. You have given me back my life, and for that I will always be grateful." She brought his hand to her mouth, and she kissed it lightly. "I am sorry that we cannot be together, Lone Wind. As you once said, if only I were Crow or you were Blackfoot—"

"That would not matter, Bright Star. The white man is too

much a part of your life. I envy him. I hope he loves you as you should be loved."

"He does," Sandrine said, feeling the overwhelming sadness again. "I am so sorry." She reached for him, gently touching his face, then kissed him, her lips barely brushing his. Then she stood and left the lodge.

Outside, Sandrine covered her mouth with her hand, trying to keep from crying. The camp was quiet. The village fires had dimmed to a faint glow, and the people had retreated to their lodges. She took a deep breath, trying to still the shaking of her body. As she started back toward Gray Wolf's lodge, she stopped. She thought she saw a movement in the darkness. She squinted her eyes, trying to see if someone was there, but she decided it was just her imagination or some of the boys playing a trick on her. She continued on but stopped again when she heard a sound. This time it wasn't her imagination. Someone was in the camp. Quickly she turned on her heel and, without hesitating, ran back toward Lone Wind's lodge. She screamed his name as loudly as she could, praying that the warriors would come quickly. But before she reached his lodge, she felt a heavy blow on her back, knocking her to the ground. She struggled to free herself, but strong hands shoved her face into the dust.

"Bright Star." She heard Lone Wind's voice in the still night.

She wanted to cry out to him, but she could not. All she could do was struggle futilely. When Lone Wind shouted her name again, she found a strength she hadn't known she possessed. She twisted to the side, screaming. Then she heard rifle shots and the shouts of men. She lifted her head and watched as warriors ran from their lodges, armed with rifles. Suddenly the weight of her attacker lifted. It took her a moment to realize that she was free, that he had let go of her and run. She scrambled to her feet and looked around frantically for Lone Wind. He was running toward her when another shot rang out. Sandrine watched helplessly as he stumbled, then collapsed, falling heavily to the ground. She ran to him. His chest was covered with blood, and she suppressed a cry. Without hesitation, she knelt next to him, resting his head on her lap.

"Bright Star," he said, his voice weak.

"I am here, Lone Wind. I am here." Sandrine couldn't stop shaking. She looked up when she saw Gray Wolf running toward them.

Gray Wolf knelt next to them and reached out and touched his son's face. "You will live, my son," he said.

Lone Wind looked at his father and smiled weakly. "You do not lie well, father. You never did." He coughed violently, spasms wracking his body. He looked at Sandrine, reaching up to touch her face. "My wife," he said softly, his voice barely audible. "You will always be my wife."

Sandrine met Gray Wolf's eyes, and she found the strength she needed. "Yes, I will always be your wife. But now you must get well. Please, Lone Wind."

"It is strange, is it not, father?"

"What is that, my son?"

"I have never known where I belong. I was Cheyenne, then I was Crow, and then . . ." he coughed again, "and then I would have become Blackfoot if that is what this woman wanted. I would have done anything to be with her." He closed his eyes and shook his head. "And now I shall never have her."

"You shall always have her, my son. In here," Gray Wolf said, putting his hand over Lone Wind's heart. "And you will meet again on the other side."

"But she will have the white man with her."

"I have not heard of white men on the other side," Gray Wolf said confidently. "Do not worry, my son. She will be there."

Sandrine bent close to Lone Wind, brushing her lips against his forehead. "I am so sorry. It is my fault."

"There is no fault here, Bright Star."

"If I had not called your name—" Lone Wind's hand came up and touched Sandrine's mouth.

"Even if you had not called my name aloud, I would have heard you."

Sandrine closed her eyes and leaned her head against Lone Wind's. "I do not want you to leave me," she sobbed. "Please, Lone Wind. Please." She felt his hand in her hair, and she clutched his head in her lap as she would that of a child.

"Do not be sad for me, Bright Star. I have had a good life."

Her hand shaking, Sandrine wiped the sweat from his brow. Then she watched as he reached up to touch Gray Wolf.

"You have been a good father to me . . ." Lone Wind coughed again.

Gray Wolf moved behind him, helping him to sit up so he could breathe. "Do not talk, my son."

"I must talk now, father." He pulled Gray Wolf's head close to his, whispering words so softly that Sandrine couldn't understand what he was saying. Finally she saw Gray Wolf nod solemnly. Lone Wind closed his eyes and was silent for a moment. "Father . . ."

"I am here, my son," Gray Wolf said, taking Lone Wind's hand.

Lone Wind opened his eyes. "I am sorry for the time that we missed. I did not realize how much I loved you, how good a father you were to me until it was too late. I know now you are my true father, my only father."

"Thank you, my son." Gray Wolf lowered his head until it touched Lone Wind's. "And you are my son, my strong, courageous son."

When Gray Wolf lifted his head, Sandrine could see tears on his cheeks. She looked around as she heard some of the men of the village shouting. She heard shots from the river, but whatever was happening there seemed unreal.

"I want to see your face, Bright Star," Lone Wind said weakly.

Sandrine looked at Gray Wolf. She was already crying, but Gray Wolf, nodded his head slightly, urging her to be strong. She allowed Gray Wolf to cradle Lone Wind's head, and she moved so that Lone Wind could see her face. Gently she stroked his cheek, leaning down to kiss him. "I am sorry I could not give you this one night," she said softly, sobs choking her voice.

"But you gave me many nights, Bright Star. You opened your heart, and you told me your true feelings for me. For that, I am thankful." He reached up and touched her cheek, barely brushing her lips with his fingers before his hand dropped. He closed his eyes. "Live your life, Bright Star, and love fully. Love with all that is inside of you."

"Lone Wind," Sandrine said frantically, looking at Gray Wolf.

Gray Wolf bent over his son, resting his head on his chest. Slowly, wearily, he raised his head. "I can no longer hear his heart."

"No!" Sandrine cried out. She lay across his chest, her body wracked with sobs, until she felt Gray Wolf's arms on her shoulders.

"Come, Bright Star."

"No," she said, closing her eyes. "Please, I want to stay with him. Please."

Gray Wolf shook his head. "He is free now, child. He is at peace. He walks the land where the sun is never too hot and the wind is never too cold. Come, let me prepare him for his journey so it may be complete." Gray Wolf held out his hand to Sandrine.

She kissed Lone Wind's cheek, then took Gray Wolf's hand and stood up. She leaned her head against his arm, feeling as if she would collapse. Gray Wolf led her to his lodge, and he forced her to lie down. He covered her with a robe. "Sleep, child. It will do you good."

"It is my fault," she said, her voice barely above a whisper.

"It is no one's fault, Bright Star. It was meant to be. Neither of us could do anything to change that."

Sandrine heard Gray Wolf as he left the lodge. She stared into the flames of the fire, her head aching. She had never felt such pain in her life. How could this have happened to him? How? Perhaps it was because she had grown to care for him. Perhaps his life had been taken because of her love for him, the love that she should only have had for her husband. She had loved Lone Wind, of that there was no doubt. And because of that he was now dead. How could she ever forgive herself?

Sandrine stood next to the horses, waiting for Gray Wolf. She ran her hands over her saddlebags one last time. It had been hard for her to concentrate on packing for the long journey home. It had been only two days since the attack by the Cheyennes, yet it had felt like months. She sighed, turning her head to look out at the far meadow. Even from this distance, she could see the scaffolding that held Lone Wind's body. She had wanted to see him one last time, but Gray Wolf had forbidden it, had even forbidden her to attend the burial ceremony. He had said it would be best for her to forget Lone Wind and think about her life with Wade. She knew Gray Wolf was right. She also knew she could never forget Lone Wind, not as long as her memories of him were still so clear.

She shook her head as she tightened the cinch on her horse. She still couldn't believe that Lone Wind was gone. It had happened so quickly—one moment they had been together in his lodge, the next moment he was dead. She pulled in a deep breath, closing her eyes. She ached to see him just one more time.

"Are you ready, Bright Star?" Gray Wolf asked, walking up to the horses.

Startled, Sandrine opened her eyes and nodded. "I am ready," she replied, swinging up onto her horse. As they rode out of the pasture, she forced herself not to look back. She gripped the reins tightly, following Gray Wolf as he led them across the stream and onto the prairie. Out here, riding across open country, it was impossible for her not to think of Lone Wind. She didn't try to stop the tears that flowed from her eyes. She had learned it was impossible to stop them. Gray Wolf had told her to forget about Lone Wind and return to her husband. As much as she loved and missed Wade, she knew she would never forget Lone Wind. Never.

One day rolled into the next as Sandrine and Gray Wolf traveled south. Neither of them spoke much; there wasn't much to say. Many times as they rode, she found herself looking behind them. She wasn't just grieving for Lone Wind, she was missing Little Bear. She had not even been able to say goodbye to him because he and Shining Bird had not yet returned. Little Bear, she knew, was the only person who would understand the pain and emptiness that she felt.

As the grass-covered prairie changed to sparse, barren land, Sandrine recognized that they were finally getting close to home. Home. She felt as if she'd been away forever. She had lived in a hide lodge for so long now, it would be strange living in a house again. Wade. How could she tell him about Lone Wind? Yet how could she not?

They camped that night under an outcropping of rocks. Sandrine had barely built the fire when she heard the distant sound of yipping coyotes. She smiled slightly. She liked the sound. She had liked it since she was a girl.

"I am worried about you, Bright Star," Gray Wolf said as he returned from hobbling the horses. He walked to the fire and sat down.

"There is no need to worry about me, Gray Wolf," Sandrine said, handing him some dried meat and some berries that they had picked that day.

"I know that you still blame yourself for Lone Wind's death. Do not."

Sandrine stared down at her clenched fingers. "How can I not blame myself, Gray Wolf? Perhaps he was punished for the love I felt for him."

"Those do not sound like your words, Bright Star. They sound like the words of superstitious old women. You know better."

"I don't know anything anymore, Gray Wolf." Her eyes filled with tears, and she quickly wiped them away, looking up at her old friend. "I am married to Wade and I love him very much. Yet I allowed myself to fall in love with your son. That is not an honorable thing for a woman to do, Gray Wolf. I feel so ashamed." She lowered her head, staring at the ground.

"Bright Star, look at me. Please."

Sandrine hesitated, then looked up to meet Gray Wolf's kind and understanding eyes.

"I am going to ask you a difficult question. You do not have to answer if you do not wish to."

"I will answer," Sandrine said, sitting up straight.

"Were you loyal to Colter?"

Sandrine hesitated, then slowly she shook her head. "No, I was not loyal to him, Gray Wolf. I allowed myself to fall in love with Lone Wind."

"Did you lie with my son?" Gray Wolf's voice was calm and steady.

Sandrine met Gray Wolf's intense gaze. "He held me in his arms. But there was nothing more."

"Then there was no betrayal on your part, Bright Star. The feelings you had for Lone Wind were true and honest, and they should not weigh heavily on your heart."

"But what if I had lain with him, Gray Wolf? Could you have ever forgiven me?" Sandrine looked at the man she respected

BRIGHT STAR'S PROMISE

and admired so greatly, and she knew the answer before he even spoke.

"It would not have been up to me to forgive you, Bright Star. You would have had to forgive yourself."

Sandrine smiled faintly. "You continue to surprise me, Gray Wolf. Just when I think I know you . . ." She shook her head.

"Did you think I would hate you if you had been with Lone Wind? No, I ceased passing judgment on people after I killed Shining Bird's husband. But I must ask you something else."

Sandrine nodded. "Ask me anything."

"If Lone Wind had lived, would you have stayed with him?"

Sandrine closed her eyes, remembering the moments with Lone Wind inside his lodge. "Part of me wanted to stay with him and become his wife, but I knew I could not. I told him I had to go home. I had to go home to Wade."

Gray Wolf nodded, seemingly satisfied. "Yes, it is right that you should be with Colter. He has such a love for you . . ." Gray Wolf stared off into the distance. "It reminds me of the love I felt for Red Bird. And you felt this love, even when you were with Lone Wind. It is good that you follow your heart, Bright Star."

Sandrine pulled the blanket from her bedroll and wrapped it around her shoulders. "I will never forget Lone Wind."

"No, I do not think that you will. It was destined that you two should meet. You brought out the goodness in my son, and he helped to guide you back to your husband. You will not forget him." Gray Wolf sighed deeply. "We should sleep now. I think the sun will be fearsome tomorrow."

"You are not used to this heat. You are not a young man anymore, Gray Wolf."

"Do not say such things to me, Bright Star. You wound me with your words."

Sandrine laughed for the first time. "I will miss you. I love you as I love my own father."

"You know how I feel about you. And like my son, I will never be far from your thoughts. When you are lonely or frightened, picture me in your mind, and I will be with you."

Sandrine nodded and lay down on her bedroll, pulling the blanket over her. She felt better than she had since Lone Wind's death. It had been good to talk with Gray Wolf. His words had helped to ease her heart and mind of the heavy burden she had been carrying.

Sandrine and Gray Wolf had arisen before dawn and had ridden hard until midday. With the sun high overhead, they turned southward onto the trail that led to Santa Fe. Sandrine began to feel an odd, uncomfortable excitement. She wanted so badly to see Wade, but she was afraid. When they stopped to eat and rest under the shade of an old gnarled oak, Sandrine took the thin gold band Wade had given her from her finger. She put it in the palm of her hand and held it out to Gray Wolf. "I want you to take this back to Shining Bird. She has always admired it."

"I cannot do that. I know that is a great symbol in the white man's world. Colter gave it to you."

Sandrine shook her head, pressing it into Gray Wolf's palm. "I want her to have it. Make sure Little Bear puts it on her finger. It is the white man's custom."

Gray Wolf stared at the gold band, then put it into the pouch that was hanging from his belt. "Shining Bird will be angry that she did not give you anything."

"Shining Bird gave me her friendship. I could not ask for more."

Gray Wolf squeezed Sandrine's hand and nodded. "I have something for you, something from Lone Wind."

Sandrine caught her breath and nodded slowly.

Gray Wolf reached into the pouch and took out a silver bracelet. It was fashioned of two thin strips of silver that intertwined and met in the middle. Gray Wolf reached for Sandrine's left arm and put it on her wrist. "He gave this to me."

"You spoke with him?"

"Yes, only briefly. He brought the bracelet to me. He said he knew you would soon be going home. He asked me to give this to you."

Sandrine ran her fingers over the fine silver, and she marveled at the beautifully intricate, yet simple design of the bracelet. "It is so lovely."

"He traded for it when he traveled in Mexico. He said he knew that he would give it to the woman he fell in love with. That woman was you."

Sandrine took a deep breath, trying to keep from crying. "Thank you for this, Gray Wolf. I shall always cherish it."

"I have one more thing," he said, standing up and walking to his horse. He came back carrying a rawhide bundle. He handed it to Sandrine. "Open it."

Sandrine quickly unwrapped the gift and saw the cherrywood bow that Gray Wolf had carved. She looked up at him. "But you were making this for Little Bear."

"I was until I saw how much you admired it. I decided then to make another for Little Bear and give this one to you."

Sandrine ran her fingers along the expertly carved wood. "It is wonderful, Gray Wolf. I do not know what to say." Sandrine stood up, holding the bow in front of her, and slowly drew back the taut gut string. "It has been a long time since I have used one. I have probably lost my aim. I would need to practice."

"If you tire of practicing, it is a gift you may one day give to your son."

Sandrine walked to Gray Wolf and hugged him tightly, closing her eyes for a moment. "Thank you, Gray Wolf. I have had no more special gifts in my life than this bow and this bracelet.

Now I will always have something by which to remember you both."

"You must work the bow, remember, to loosen it up. You may rub it with bear grease sometimes. It will last you a long time."

"I have no doubt of that."

"I also have a quiver of arrows painted with my colors. Should you ever have to use one, your enemy will know that they have been shot by a Crow arrow."

"Not just any Crow arrow, but an arrow made by Gray Wolf of the Crow tribe."

Gray Wolf nodded and smiled. He looked out from under the shelter of the oak branches. "Let us go. We are wasting time."

Sandrine held up her hand. "You will go no farther. I can ride on my own from here."

"No, I will not let you ride alone."

"I will be safe," Sandrine said, holding the bow up high in the air. "Besides, it is too dangerous for you here. Too many white men who do not like Indians. Please, Gray Wolf, go home. Go home to your daughter and your people. I hope to have word that by next spring you have another grandchild."

Gray Wolf grinned broadly. "Yes, that would be good news. All right, I will go." He put his hands on Sandrine's shoulders. "I could not love you more if you were of my own blood, you know that. I would never lie to you. So you must promise me something."

"Anything."

"Promise me that you will no longer blame yourself for Lone Wind's death, and do as he asked you to do. Love with all that is inside of you."

Sandrine nodded, tears filling her eyes. She hugged Gray Wolf fiercely, not wanting to let him go. But finally she stepped back, wiping the tears from her cheeks. "Safe journey, Gray Wolf. You will always be in my heart." Sandrine watched him as he picked up his bag and walked to his horse. He swung easily up onto his horse's back and looked down at her. He held up the first two fingers of his right hand in front of his face and raised them high above his head. Sandrine smiled and signed back to him. Friend. It had been the sign for friend.

When she could barely see Gray Wolf in the distance, she walked to her horse. With an overwhelming sadness, she said goodbye to the life she had lived for the last few months. Now it was time to get back to her old life and to Wade.

Sandrine reined in. This was it. She was home. She looked straight across the valley at the half-finished house. It was hard to see through the trees, but she thought Wade had made progress on it. She smiled. This was a busy time of year for him, but he had still managed to work on their house. Sandrine hesitated, looking down the valley. Something was strange. There was no smoke from the cabin chimney. She glanced around. The instant she thought it, she knew what was wrong. There were no cattle. Wade would have never moved the calves this early in the season.

Sandrine urged her horse into a canter, then a gallop down the hill. When she saw that the corrals in front of the cabin were empty and that there were no fresh footprints in the dust, she kneed her horse up the slope, following the path to the new house. She dismounted quickly, dropping the reins to the ground.

Slowly she walked back and forth in front of the house. The wide porch was finished, and the railing around it was almost completed. The arched doorway was in place, rising above the unfinished walls. She stepped onto the porch and went inside the house. She smiled as she looked around. Although it was far from being finished, she could imagine what it would look like: the kitchen off to the right, the large living area straight ahead, and the two bedrooms to the left.

Sandrine walked around, aware of the soft sound of her moccasins on the rough wood. She stood in the middle of the room and stared upward. Part of the adobe wall went up high, higher than they had planned. Wade had changed something in the design. She walked outside and looked. It appeared that there was going to be another story to the house. Was he going to build her a bedroom upstairs? She turned and looked down at the valley below. Unconsciously she touched her left wrist, running her fingers over the silver bracelet. Deliberately she took her hand away. Her life was here now.

She mounted her horse and rode down the valley to the log house. She looked toward the cabin. There was still no one around. She dismounted and cupped her hands to her mouth. "Wade!" she called loudly.

When there was no response, she shouted his name again. She walked around the house to her garden. All of the vegetables were dried up. Tomatoes, corn, and squash were all rotting in the soil. She walked to the back of the house where she kept her small flower garden. All of the flowers were dead. Something was wrong. Wade knew how much she cared for her gardens. She ran to the front of the house and went inside. Nothing had changed, everything was in place, but there was dust everywhere. It was obvious that no one had been here in a long time.

Sandrine hurried to her horse and mounted. She guided him up the slope to the trail, then kicked him into a gallop. A terrible panic suddenly gripped her as she rode—what if something had happened to Wade while she was gone? She rode hard, forcing herself not to think, but to concentrate on guiding her horse over the rough ground. Whatever had happened, it would only make things worse if she got hurt.

Her horse was covered with sweat and blowing hard when she galloped into Jim and Rose's yard and then reined in sharply, slipping from the horse. She hurried to the porch and knocked on the door. As soon as she saw the expression on Rose's face, she knew that something was wrong, that something had happened to Wade. Before she could steady herself, her legs gave way and she collapsed onto the porch. She heard Rose call her name, but she didn't want to open her eyes. Not this time. She didn't want to face what Rose had to tell her.

Eight

Wade and Emily walked down the sidewalk until they reached the dress shop. He handed Emily some bills. "Here, buy yourself some new dresses. You deserve something pretty."

"Thank you, Wade," Emily replied, standing on her tiptoes to kiss him on the cheek. "Where shall we meet?"

"I'm going to grab a bite at the Half Moon. I'll wait there for you."

Emily smiled, lowering her eyelashes. "I'll see you later then. You won't be disappointed."

"I'm sure I won't," Wade responded, watching her as she delicately lifted her skirts in one hand and walked into the store. He watched her as she walked away, charming all passersby. She had stayed with him last night and had shared his bed. Emily had proven to be a welcome distraction, someone who demanded nothing of him.

Wade headed on down the street, tipping his hat to every lady he passed. He felt good. He'd been in Frank's house for a few weeks now and he liked it. He liked being a wealthy man. He stopped before he reached the Half Moon. This was going to be the hard part though, facing Sally. They had been friends before and they were friends now, at least until he'd blackmailed Frank out of his house. Now maybe Sally wouldn't speak to him at all.

Wade shrugged his shoulders and went inside. Sally was at a table, setting down plates. She glanced at him briefly but made no acknowledgement. Wade went to a table in the corner and sat down. He took off his hat and put it on the chair next to him. This was going to be harder than he thought.

"Coffee?"

Wade looked up. Sally was standing next to the table, coffeepot in hand. "Please."

"Going to eat?"

"Yes, I'd planned on it."

"We've got chicken and potatoes or beef and potatoes. What will it be?"

"Beef."

"I'll be back with your soup."

Wade watched Sally as she walked by another table, refilled some coffee cups, and smiled at the customers. She wasn't going to make this easy for him. She went into the kitchen and came back out carrying a steaming soup bowl on a plate and a small basket. She set them down in front of him. "It's vegetable, and here's some fresh bread."

"Thank you."

"Don't mention it," she said, not attempting to cover the disdain in her voice.

"Sally," Wade said, gently taking her wrist as she moved away. "Will you talk to me?"

Sally turned back, her eyes narrowed. "I don't think we have much to say to each other, Wade. Or are you Wade Colter? Hell, I'm not sure."

He looked down when she walked away and picked up his soup spoon, feeling strange. He tasted the soup but then set down his utensil. He wasn't really hungry. He recalled how angry Jim and Rose had been when he told them that he was moving into Frank's house.

"What about the house you're building? What about Sandrine?" Rose had asked.

Wade shook his head angrily. What right did Rose have to

tell him to build his life around a woman he didn't even know? What right did either of them have to judge him? He'd tried to be a friend, he had even offered Jim a loan so he could buy more cattle. But both he and Rose had steadfastly refused, saying they didn't want his money. He picked up the spoon and idly stirred his soup. Now Sally was turning her back on him, too. Didn't any of them understand? Was there something wrong with being rich? He almost laughed aloud. Emily didn't have any problem helping him spend his money. She openly admitted that she liked money, and she admired his ambition. Wade nodded to himself. Any man in the territory would be proud to have her on his arm.

"The soup not to your liking?" Sally asked.

Wade looked up. "I guess I'm not as hungry as I thought," he said.

"Why don't you hire yourself a cook? Then you can have your food specially made to suit your taste," Sally said, reaching for the bowl.

"Please talk to me, Sally." He saw her hesitate and then shake her head.

"No, Wade, not this time. You used to be able to look at me with those beautiful gray eyes of yours and I would do anything for you. But not now. No more." She took the bowl and went back into the kitchen.

Wade shook his head. He could see this was going to be a waste of time. Sally came back out and slammed the plate of food in front of him, crossing her arms in front of her. "What? What're you staring at?" Wade asked uncomfortably.

"I'm just wondering how a thud on the head can change a person so dramatically. I was thinking that maybe none of us ever really knew you at all. Maybe this is the real Wade Colter."

"Yeah, maybe it is," Wade said angrily, standing up. He reached into his pocket and threw a bill on the table. "The food is fine, but I can't say much for the service." He went to the door, but he felt Sally's hand on his arm.

"I feel sorry for you, Wade. I still think of you as that sixteen-year-old boy who first came to me." She lowered her voice, looking around her. "You were so sweet and so innocent. But even when you grew up, you were decent and good." She shook her head. "I can't stand seeing you like this. And I hope to God that Sandrine never comes back. It would tear her apart to see what you've become."

"You're not worried about Sandrine. You just can't stand the fact that I'm living in your lover's house." Wade saw Sally's eyes widen, then narrow, and he was caught off guard when her hand lashed out and hit him hard across the face.

"You're not welcome in my place anymore, Wade. Don't come back."

Wade went outside, stopping for a moment. He could still feel the sting of Sally's hand on his face, but that was not what was bothering him. It was something more than that. He felt cut off, removed from everything and everyone.

Forcing the confrontation with Sally from his mind, he walked down the street. He saw Emily before he even reached the dress shop. She was carrying some boxes and smiling like a young girl who had just gotten a piece of candy. It was good to see a friendly face, he thought.

"You should see what I bought," Emily said breathlessly, handing her boxes to Wade.

"You can show me when we get to my house."

"I thought I was going back to Jim and Rose's."

"I'll take you back there if that's where you want to go," Wade said impatiently, crossing the dusty street to the wagon. He put the packages in the back and helped Emily up on to the seat, then climbed up after her. He took the reins in his hands and flicked. Wade didn't say anything. As much as he tried not to think of his conversation with Sally, he couldn't get it out of his mind.

"Why don't we dress for dinner tonight? I have something I'd like to wear for you," Emily said sweetly, putting her arm through Wade's and resting her head against his shoulder.

"If you like," he said, still thinking about Sally. He couldn't forget what she'd said about his wife, that it would break her heart to see him like this.

"My Uncle Jim is going to be real mad at you. If I don't come home again tonight, he may come looking for me."

"Let him look," Wade said. He reined in suddenly and turned to Emily. She was wearing a pale green dress and a matching bonnet. He untied the ribbons from underneath her chin and took the bonnet from her head. The sun shone on her auburn hair, and her eyes looked startlingly green. He pulled her into his arms and covered her mouth with his, kissing her passionately. He felt her resist him, but he continued to kiss her, running his hands over her body. Soon she had relaxed in his arms, moaning slightly.

He released her and drove the wagon from the road. He jumped down and held out his arms to Emily, carrying her into a stand of oaks. He laid her on the ground and, without hesitating, removed her undergarments. He loosened his pants as he kissed her again. He had assumed the night before that she was a virgin, but she wasn't and he was glad. Now whatever guilt he might have felt had dissolved. She was a grown woman and she was willing.

Emily ran her hands up and down his buttocks and then along the sides of his thighs until she reached for him, moving her hand back and forth. Wade kissed her breasts and was surprised when he felt Emily guide him into her. He looked at her a moment; her eyes were closed and her cheeks were flushed. She looked lovely. Wade felt her moving underneath him, and without words of love, he drove himself into her, listening to her cries of passion, feeling her body rise up to meet his. When he heard her cry out, he pressed his body against hers, thrusting himself into her again and again until his body was spent.

"Wade," Emily said softly, stroking his hair.

Wade rested a minute, then rolled away from Emily, quickly adjusting his pants. He lay on his back and looked up through the thick oak branches to the sky above. It was strange, he thought. He had just made love to a woman, yet he felt no love. He felt nothing. Would he ever feel any kind of connection to a woman again? Would he feel the way Jim felt about Rose or the way Frank felt about Sally? Or would he always feel like this—empty and hollow.

"Sandrine, would you wake up? Wake up."

Sandrine moved her head slowly, opening her eyes. She blinked until she was able to focus. Danny was standing next to her, his face only inches away.

"You're awake," he said, a grin on his face.

"Yes, I am," she said, smiling. She sat up against the headboard and pulled the sheet up. "Is your mother here, Danny?"

"She's in the kitchen. I was supposed to watch you and tell her if you woke up."

"You can tell her I'm awake now, but first come over here and give me a hug. I've missed you." Sandrine held out her arms and hugged the small boy tightly. She kissed him on the top of the head. "I think you've grown since I've been away."

"I have. I'm bigger now."

"I can tell. Can you get your mother now?"

"Okay," Danny said, throwing open the door and running into the other room, his voice high with excitement. Sandrine smiled to herself as she heard Rose berate her son. Soon after, Rose appeared in the doorway carrying a tray.

"You're up."

"Yes."

"Well, I figured Danny would get around to waking you up." Rose set the tray on the table next to the bed. She put another pillow behind Sandrine and then put the tray on her lap. "You hungry?"

"I'm always hungry for your food, Rose." Sandrine reached out and took her hand. "I've missed you."

"I've missed you, too. More than you'll know," Rose said, leaning down and hugging Sandrine.

"What is it, Rose? Something has happened, I know it." She held onto Rose's hand. "Has something happened to Wade?"

"Why don't you eat first. You must be starving."

"Please," Sandrine said.

Rose sighed deeply and nodded. She set the tray on the nightstand, and she sat down on the edge of the bed. "First of all, Wade is all right."

"He's not hurt? You're sure?"

"Yes," Rose replied. "Actually, he's not all right. He's . . . different."

"What do you mean, Rose? Tell me." Sandrine tried to keep the panic from her voice.

"He had an accident while you were gone. He was trying to break a horse, and he fell and hit his head. He has no memory of the past."

Sandrine stared at Rose, slowly shaking her head. "Wade has lost his memory," she repeated.

Rose nodded, her face bleak.

"He can't have forgotten everything," Sandrine said. "He remembers me, doesn't he? Doesn't he, Rose?" She saw the look of sadness in Rose's eyes.

"He doesn't remember you, Sandrine. He didn't remember us either. I'm so sorry."

"Where is he? He wasn't at the house."

"He hasn't been living at the house," Rose said, sighing deeply. "He's living at Frank's."

"He's living with Frank Lauter?" Sandrine shook her head. "I don't understand."

"I'm not sure I do either, Sandrine," Rose said, taking the cup of coffee from the tray and handing it to Sandrine. "It's as if after the accident, Wade woke up a different person. We've all tried to talk to him, but he won't listen. He just keeps saying he doesn't want to hear about the way he used to be."

Sandrine clutched the cup between her hands, trying to still her trembling. "Did you tell him about me?"

"Yes," Rose said, her voice low.

"What did he say? Doesn't it matter to him that he has a wife?" When Sandrine looked up and saw the look in Rose's eyes, she knew she had her answer. "He doesn't even want to see me, does he, Rose?"

Rose shook her head. "I'm so sorry, Sandrine. I think if we just give him time—"

"Has he seen a doctor?"

"Yes."

"What did he say? Is there a chance Wade will get his memory back?"

"Doc doesn't know. He said he might, he said he might not."

Sandrine moved to the edge of the bed, putting her feet on the floor. "I have to see him. Maybe if he sees me, he'll remember." She stood up, looking down at her dusty, ragged skirt and blouse. She smiled weakly. "I guess I wouldn't be much of a memory looking this way, would I?"

"Why don't we ride out to the house and get some of your clothes? You'll be staying here anyway."

"No, I'll stay at my own house, even if Wade won't."

"We'll talk about that later. Let me get Danny."

Sandrine pulled on her moccasins and walked outside, not waiting for Danny and Rose. By the time they came, Sandrine was mounted. "Don't worry about me, Rose. I can get cleaned up on my own."

Rose walked to the horse, putting her hand on Sandrine's leg. "Don't shut me out, Sandrine. I've already lost Wade; I don't want to lose you, too."

Sandrine tried to nod reassuringly, but Rose's words scared her. Had she lost Wade, too? Slowly she nodded her head. "All right. Come on." She pulled Danny up behind her and waited while Rose saddled a horse. On the ride back to Sandrine's ranch, only Danny felt like talking. His happy chatter rose and fell, and Sandrine tried to nod and smile as he told her about a nest of baby birds he had found. Sandrine tried not to look at the big house as they rode down the slope into the valley past it. She tried not to remember the laughter and late nights as she and Wade had planned their future together.

She reined in and went inside the cabin, steeling herself against the flood of memories. She went to her small wardrobe and found a simple blue skirt and white blouse. She pulled some undergarments and stockings out of a drawer, as well as her worn pair of black boots. Then she got her bar of lavender soap and a towel. Every object she touched brought a stab of pain, and she found herself moving around the cabin like a stranger. She refused to start crying. She refused to despair. Wade hadn't seen her yet, and Doc had said he might get his memory back. Without speaking, she went to the door and walked to the stream, followed by Rose and Danny.

"You go on over there and play," Rose ordered Danny. "And stay where I can see you. And don't climb any trees."

Sandrine smiled as Danny skipped away. After undressing, she stepped into the cool, clear water of the stream, picked a shallow place where she could sit down and bathe. She leaned back to wet her hair and lathered the bar of soap. She scrubbed herself thoroughly, getting rid of all traces of trail dust. When she was finished, she stood up, walked to the grass, and quickly dried off. Rose was off watching Danny, making sure he stayed away until Sandrine was dressed. Sandrine slipped into her undergarments and then put on the blouse and skirt. She sat down to pull on her stockings and boots. She grimaced as she pulled the constricting hard leather onto her feet.

Rose came back and looked her up and down. "You look pretty. Are you ready?"

Sandrine fought a sudden uneasiness. "What about my hair?"

"It's beautiful just like that, loose around your face. That's the way Wade always liked it anyway."

Sandrine pulled in a deep breath. "What're we waiting for? Let's go." She turned on her heel, feeling odd and clumsy in the boots and long skirt. Rose had said that Wade had changed a lot; she had, too. But their love for each other would still be there. Of that much, Sandrine was still sure. She waited until Rose was mounted, then she lifted Danny into his mother's arms. Sandrine mounted, the strange feeling of clumsiness persisting, and she led the way out up the hill.

Sandrine shifted in the saddle, glancing over at Rose. They hadn't spoken more than a few sentences to each other since they'd begun riding. Rose's face was set in an expression of concern. Even as she answered Danny's incessant questions, Sandrine knew Rose was worrying. Sandrine sighed. If Rose was that worried, Wade must have changed a great deal. She forced herself to stop thinking and kicked her heels to her horse's sides, urging the animal into a canter. She wanted to see Wade. She wanted to touch him. She couldn't believe that he wouldn't remember her.

Sandrine did not rein her horse in until they had ridden the length of the tree-lined lane that led to Frank's sprawling, two-story house. She was startled by the size of the house—she had never seen it in the daytime. She was startled a second time when a young man dressed in work clothes appeared out of nowhere and insisted on taking their horses to the stables to water them. Sandrine glanced at Rose as they walked toward the large oak front door. Sandrine lifted the heavy brass knocker, then let it fall. She tried to still the trembling in her body as she waited for Wade to answer. As the door opened, she steeled herself, holding her breath, then nearly cried out when a servant, not Wade, stood on the threshold.

"We'd like to see Mr. Colter," Rose said in a firm voice.

Sandrine silently thanked her, grateful that she had come.

The servant cleared his throat as though deciding whether or not to ask them in. Sandrine felt her face flush.

"You may wait here," the man said with practiced civility.

Rose stepped forward. "We'll wait inside, thank you." Pushing Danny along in front of her, she made her way past the astonished butler.

Sandrine followed. Once they were inside, the butler closed the door and asked them to wait while he informed Mr. Colter that they were here. Rose stood tensely, tapping her foot, mumbling something about the butler. Sandrine reached out to calm her, but froze when she heard the sound of boot heels on the marble floor.

Sandrine looked up, feeling her heart pound. Wade was walking down the hallway, and she caught her breath. He looked even more handsome than she remembered. He was wearing black pants, a snow-white shirt with pearl cufflinks, and shining black boots. Before she could stop herself, she called out his name, but the cool expression on his face told her that Rose had softened the truth. Not only did he not remember her, he didn't want to. She clenched her fists and fought the trembling that resurged in her legs.

"Wade, it's Sandrine. She's back," Rose said.

With cold eyes, Wade glanced from her to Rose. "Why did you bring her here?"

Sandrine felt her eyes flood with tears, and she half-turned to hide them.

"What are you talking about, Wade Colter?" Rose demanded. "She's your wife."

"She shouldn't be here, Rose," Wade said, his voice impatient.

"What's the matter with you?" Rose said angrily.

"Hello, Wade," Danny said uneasily, looking from his mother to Wade.

"Hi, Danny. I've missed you."

"I missed you, too. How come you haven't been to see us?"

Sandrine thought she detected some softness in Wade as he talked to Danny, but before Wade could answer, a woman came down the hall.

"You can't leave me standing there like that, Wade." She stopped when she saw Rose and Sandrine. "Hello, Rose," she stammered.

"Hello, Emily," Rose said icily. Rose looked Emily up and down. "I see you've finally managed to get yourself some new clothes." She waved her arm around. "And a place where you really feel at home."

"That's enough, Rose," Wade said firmly.

"I don't think so," Rose said. "Danny, I want you to wait outside. Go see the nice man who took our horses. I'm sure he'll show you around."

"Okay, ma," Danny said, running toward the front door.

Sandrine studied Emily. She was a pretty girl, small with auburn hair and green eyes. And there was no disguising the fact that she was in love with Wade; it was written all over her face.

"Emily, I'd like you to meet Wade's wife, Sandrine."

Sandrine watched the effect Rose's words had on Emily. Her eyes widened, and she shook her head slowly. She turned to Wade. "Maybe I should wait in the other room. I'm sure you two have things to talk about."

"I think that would be a good idea, Emily," Rose said, taking her arm. "I'll go with you." Before Sandrine or Wade could argue, both women were gone.

Sandrine stood uncomfortably, trying to think of what to say to the man who had known her most intimately, but who now knew nothing about her at all. "So you're living here now. Does Frank mind?"

"He doesn't have anything to say about it anymore. I own it." Wade stepped closer. "Look, I don't know what to say to you. Everyone tells me that we were in love and married but I . . ." Wade shrugged his shoulders. "I can't lie to you. I don't remember anything about you."

"That's fortunate for you, isn't it?" Sandrine said with rancor, thinking of the possessive look on Emily's face. Without saying another word, she turned and walked toward the door.

"Wait," Wade said, following her. "The house and the land, I want you to have them."

Sandrine whirled around and glared at Wade. "You really don't remember anything, do you?" She shook her head, anger and sadness welling up inside her. "I can't believe I came back for this," she said, flinging open the door.

"Would you wait a minute?" Wade said, grabbing her arm. "I want to help you."

"You want to help me?" Sandrine laughed harshly. "How exactly are you going to help me, Wade? Give me some money and send me away? You wouldn't want any reminders of your past, would you?"

"Look," Wade said, "I didn't mean for this to happen. It just happened. I woke up and forgot everything in my past, including you. I'm sorry, but that's the way it is."

Sandrine looked at Wade. For a moment she thought his eyes softened. He was still so handsome it was painful. Everything about him looked the same, but on the inside he was a completely different person. "I don't want anything from you. I'll get my things from the house as soon as I can."

"But I want you to have the house."

Sandrine shook her head and hurried toward the stables. She asked the stable hand to get her horse, and she mounted, kicking the animal into a canter as she rode out of the yard and down the lane. She didn't know where she was going, she just wanted to get away from here.

Wade sat on his bedroom terrace, his bare feet propped up on the railing. He swirled the brandy around in the snifter and then took a sip, slowly letting it wind its way down to his stomach. He'd left Emily in her room after making love to her, and had come to his room. He took another sip of the brandy and thought about what had happened that day. After Sandrine had left, he'd walked into his study only to find Rose and Emily screaming at each other. He'd had to calm them both down, convincing Rose that he would talk to Sandrine again. But he had no intention of doing that. There was nothing he could say to her.

He thought of Emily and what it was like to make love to her. She was eager enough, but she lacked the kind of passion he wanted in a woman, the kind of passion he wondered if he had had with Sandrine. He took another drink. Sandrine was beautiful, there was no denying that. And those eyes. She had incredible blue eyes. He smiled. She had a temper, too. He liked that. He liked the fact that she wasn't afraid to fight back.

He put the glass down on the terrace floor and folded his hands behind his head. Considering everything that had happened to him, he felt pretty lucky. He was living like a rich man and had a pretty woman at his beck and call. He had everything a man could want. He shook his head. Except love. He didn't have the kind of closeness that Jim and Rose had; he knew he could never have that with Emily. Emily was not the kind of woman you could live a lifetime with.

He stood up, leaning against the railing. Tomorrow he'd ride out and talk to Rose; he had to make it right with her and Jim. They'd been good to him after the accident, and he couldn't forget that. And maybe while he was there, he'd even talk to Sandrine. It wouldn't hurt to get to know her a little better.

Sandrine sat at a table in the corner of Sally's restaurant, drinking coffee and eating a piece of pie. She couldn't think of any other place to go but here. She had walked into the restaurant, feeling lost, but Sally had given her a huge hug, then had told her to sit down. Sandrine had sat through two meals and was now waiting for Sally to finish cleaning up. Sally had been a good friend to her and Wade; Sandrine would be able to talk to her.

As Sandrine blankly watched Sally set the tables for the next day, she thought about what had happened with Wade. At first, riding here to town, she had felt sad. But now, thinking about how arrogant Wade had been, she was angry.

"You going to kill that pie or you going to eat it?"

Sandrine glanced up at Sally and then at her piece of pie. Without realizing it, she had been smashing it with her fork. "Sorry, I don't know what I was thinking."

"I do," Sally said, sitting down opposite Sandrine. "Look, the shades are pulled, everyone's gone home, and we're alone. You can talk to me. You saw him, didn't you?"

Sandrine nodded, moving her fork back and forth through the crust of the pie. "I saw him." She shook her head. "He looks so good. I just wanted to run up to him and throw myself in his arms, but . . ." She looked up at Sally.

"It's all right, Sandrine, you can cry if you want." She covered Sandrine's hand with her own.

"I've already done enough of that. Won't do any good anyway." She set down the fork and reached for the coffee cup.

"You should have seen his eyes, Sally. They were so cold. When he looked at me, it was as if he hated me."

"I know the feeling. He looks that way at everybody."

"What happened to him? How could he have changed so much?"

"I don't know, sweetie. I wasn't sure Doc knew enough, so I wrote to a doctor friend of mine in Philadelphia. I told him about Wade. He said pretty much the same thing that Doc said—Wade might get his memory back at any time, or he might not. He said from what he knows of cases like this, people don't normally change like Wade has, but it's not impossible."

Sandrine started to take a sip of coffee, but set the cup down. "So I have a husband who doesn't want me, and I have nowhere to go."

"What about the ranch? He's not living there."

"He offered it to me, but I won't take it from him."

"Don't be so damned stubborn, Sandrine. Part of that ranch is yours."

"I don't want to live on a ranch by myself, Sally. Do you know how much work it takes to keep it up?" She shook her head. "Besides, I don't want anything from him."

"Don't give up so easily, Sandrine. If you're around him enough, you might make him remember."

"I'm not going to him again. It was humiliating enough the first time. Besides, have you seen the woman who's living at his house?"

Sally nodded and rolled her eyes. "Yeah, Miss Prim-and-Proper from Boston. Can't believe Jim would ever be related to someone like that."

"Tell me one thing, Sally. Does he love her?"

"Are you kidding? I'm not sure he even likes her. She's pretty enough, and I'm sure she's more than willing, but love . . ." Sally shook her head. "I'm not sure Wade even knows what that is anymore."

Sandrine rested her elbows on the table, rubbing her face with her hands. "Maybe I should just go home to my parents. There's nothing to keep me here now."

"Is that what you really want, Sandrine? Do you want to live in a trading post the rest of your life?

"It wasn't a bad life. It's where I met Wade."

"Why don't you just go join your Blackfoot people? If you're going to run away, that would be the place to go."

Sandrine's hand went to the bracelet on her left wrist. She glanced down at it, smiling sadly. "I almost didn't come back, Sally, that's what makes this so hard to take." She looked at Sally, her eyes brimming with tears. "I almost stayed to be with a Crow warrior named Lone Wind," she said, staring at the bracelet. "But as much as I cared for him, my love for Wade was stronger. So I came back here." She laughed harshly. "Our love is so strong that he asked me to leave his house today." She quickly wiped the tears from her eyes.

"I'm sorry, Sandrine, really I am. But I want you to listen to me." Sally took her hand. "I truly believe that somewhere inside of that callous shell of a man, there's the real Wade Colter. When I told him I didn't want him in here anymore he looked like a little boy who'd just been scolded. And he was upset about hurting Jim and Rose. Give him some time. It hasn't been easy for him, either. He woke up one day and he didn't remember who the hell he was or anything about his past. So all of us stepped right in and told him everything we thought he needed to know. I think he's just tired of hearing about the kind of man he used to be. All he knows is the kind of man he is now."

"From what I can see, that's not much of a man."

"It'll take time. He's like a child who has to learn all over again between good and bad, right and wrong. Think about it. It must be a horrible thing not to have a yesterday."

Sandrine nodded slightly, grateful that Sally was here. "Thank you. I could always count on you for the truth." She sat up straight, pulling in a deep breath. "I should get back to the ranch and let Rose know I'm all right. She's probably worried sick."

"Yeah, and she's probably made Jim pay the price." Sally stood up. "Why don't you stay here with me? I know it's not the ranch, but—"

"What about Frank? Wade's already done enough to come between you two."

"Wade hasn't come between us, Sandrine. Frank has a room over at the hotel. A nice room, I might add." She shrugged, smiling. "Besides, I'd like the company. I'd like to talk about something besides card games and business deals."

"Tell me something, Sally. Just how did Wade wind up living in Frank's house?"

Sally sat back down, shaking her head. "Cards, how else? Frank really hates Wade right now, but I think he'll eventually cool down."

"Did Wade cheat?"

"Wade? No. He caught Frank cheating and said if he didn't give him the house, he'd tell all the men he's ever played with. Pretty clever if you ask me."

"I think that's pretty dirty. I can't believe Wade would do something like that."

"He didn't cheat, Sandrine. He just used a little blackmail."

"What else has he done?"

"He's won a lot of money, that's all I know. Right now your husband is a wealthy man. Unless, of course, Miss Boston spends all of it."

Sandrine nodded, pushing her hair back from her face. "All right, I'll stay with you for awhile." She looked around. "But I'm going to need money. I don't suppose you could use some help around here?"

"I can't pay you much."

"I'll work for food and lodging."

"You've got yourself a job."

"I need to let Rose know I'm all right. I don't want her to worry."

"What about the ranch? Are you just going to let it fall to ruin?"

Sandrine shrugged. "Right now, I don't know what I'm going to do, Sally. I'm not even sure I should have come back."

Three days had passed since Rose and Sandrine had been to see Wade, and he had made a firm decision—he was sending Emily back to live with Jim and Rose. As he rode toward the Everett ranch, Wade knew that it would be hard to face his friends. He knew they were both angry with him, and he wouldn't be surprised if Jim took a swing at him. But he had to try to get through to them; they were his only friends.

He had waited until dusk, knowing that Jim would be at the ranch. Wade followed the line of the ridge and guided his horse down the slope. He looked across the valley, thinking about his own small ranch, wondering if Sandrine was there now. He had to make sure she was taken care of.

He reined in by the corral and tied his horse to one of the railings. The amber glow of the house spilled onto the porch as he stepped on to the worn planks. He could hear Danny's rambunctious voice, rambling on about something, and he could hear Jim and Rose, calm and reassuring. He took a deep breath and knocked twice on the door. When Jim opened it, Wade took off his hat, nodding slightly.

"Hello, Jim. I wonder if I could come inside for awhile."

"Who is it, Jim?" Rose called from inside.

"It's Wade," Jim replied, his voice hard. He looked at Wade, his gaze never varying. "I don't know that we have that much to say to each other, Wade."

"I have a lot to say to you two, if you'll let me." Suddenly

BRIGHT STAR'S PROMISE

the door flew all the way open and Danny ran out, holding on to Wade's legs. Wade picked him up and rumpled his hair. "How you been, Danny?"

"That's sure a big house you live in, Wade. Don't you get lost in it sometimes?"

"Sometimes I do," Wade said. He looked over Danny's head to Jim. "Can I come in?"

Jim nodded silently and closed the door behind Wade. "Danny, you finish your dinner."

"Why don't you eat dinner with us, Wade?" Danny asked, climbing up into his chair.

"No, thanks," Wade said, standing uncomfortably as Rose steadfastly ignored him.

"You might as well sit down and join us," Jim said, glancing over at Rose. "We have enough, don't we, hon?"

Before she could answer, Wade held up his hand. "It's all right, I'm not hungry. Look, I just wanted to apologize," Wade said quickly, clutching the edge of his hat.

"Danny, why don't you take your dinner into your room and finish it there," Rose said gently, taking his plate from the table.

"Eat in my room? Why, ma? I want to see Wade."

"I'll be here, Danny. I just want to talk to your folks for a bit. You don't mind, do you?"

"No, I guess not. Will you say goodbye to me before you leave?"

"Yeah, I'll say goodbye." Wade waited until Danny was out of the room, then he looked at Jim and Rose. They were standing side by side, grim expressions on their faces. "I owe you both an apology. You were real good to me after the accident, and I'm not sure I ever thanked you for taking care of me." Wade looked down at his hat. "I know I'm not the man I used to be. Hell, I'm not even sure what that was. It's a strange feeling not remembering anything about yourself and then having everyone tell you what you used to be like, where you used to live, who your friends were, and who you used to love. I guess I just got tired of hearing what a good guy Wade Colter was; it's as if he was someone else to me. Maybe I'm even a little jealous of him because I can't be him anymore."

Rose stepped forward, tentatively touching Wade's arm. "But you are him, Wade."

"I don't know who I am or what I want, Rose."

"It seems to me you're taking what you want."

Rose put her hand on her husband's arm. "Jim . . ."

Wade shook his head. "It's all right, Rose. I know what he means." Wade looked at Jim. "Emily's not a child, Jim."

Jim let out an exasperated sigh. "Maybe not, but you've taken advantage of her. She's a proper young lady, and you've ruined her."

For an instant Wade thought about telling Jim that he hadn't been the first man to be with Emily, then he decided not to. There was no point in disillusioning Jim about his niece. "I came to tell you that she'll be back here tomorrow," he said aloud.

"Well that's real generous of you, Wade," Jim said angrily. "Now that you've taken what you wanted from her, you're just going to throw her away."

"I'm not throwing her away, Jim. This is where she belongs. I know that now."

"And what about Sandrine? Where does she belong?"

"I offered to give her the ranch, but she won't take it."

Jim pounded his fist on the table. "Just how in hell do you expect a woman to run that place on her own?"

"I plan to send some of Frank's hands over to help her out." Wade knew it sounded hollow, and he hated the look of disgust in Jim's eyes, but there was nothing he could do about it. For the hundredth time, he tried to remember—he tried to remember himself as a scared boy and Jim as the kindly wagon master who had adopted him. But there was nothing. The memories were gone. Wade shifted his weight, suddenly so uncomfortable that he could hardly wait to leave. "I guess I better be getting—"

"Yeah, I think you'd better be leaving."

"Are you sure you won't stay to dinner, Wade? We have plenty."

In spite of his uneasiness, Wade could not help but smile at Rose. He couldn't remember the friendship that they'd had before his accident, but he didn't need to; he had a special fondness for Rose that was based on the present, not the past. Impulsively he stepped forward and bent to kiss her on the cheek. "Thanks, Rose."

Out of the corner of his eye, he saw Jim stiffen, but Wade didn't care. As he straightened up, he glanced at Jim, then back at Rose. "There's a little bay colt I'd like to give to Danny on his next birthday. He won't be able to ride him for awhile, but he can work with him. It'll be his horse." Wade heard Jim draw in a sharp breath, but before Jim could speak, Wade turned and headed for the door. He settled his hat on his head, pausing just long enough to thank Rose for the invitation to dinner. He started out the front door and across the porch.

When he got to the corral, he untied his horse and swung up. Kicking the animal into a gallop, he headed toward town. He wasn't sure what he had expected, but it sure hadn't gone the way he had hoped it would. He tightened his hand on the reins. With any luck, he'd do better with Sally.

Wade walked around to the back of the Half Moon and lightly knocked on the door. When there was no answer, he slowly opened the door. Sally was cleaning off the large wooden table and covering pies for the next day. "Sally," he said softly, not wanting to frighten her. When she looked at him, he held up his hand. "I know you told me not to come in here anymore, but I had to talk to you." He saw her hesitate, then nod toward the swinging door.

"Wait in the dining room. I'll be in after I clean up here."

Wade nodded and pushed the door with his shoulder, listening to it swing back and forth behind him. He started forward but stopped when he saw Sandrine. She had her back to him and was setting a table. She was wearing the same blue skirt and white blouse that she'd had on the day she came to see him, but they looked as if she'd just washed and pressed them. Her lustrous black hair was pulled back in a blue ribbon and hung down the middle of her back. He watched her as she moved from table to table, meticulously setting each napkin and each piece of silverware. When she turned around and saw him, she couldn't hide her look of surprise. Again, he was amazed by her startling blue eyes. Jim, Rose, and Sally had not lied about one thing—Sandrine was a stunningly beautiful woman. When she saw that he was staring at her, she quickly moved on to the next table.

"Sandrine." He said her name as if for the first time.

"What're you doing here, Wade?"

"I came to talk to Sally. She told me to wait in here." Sandrine barely nodded and continued with her work. "Why aren't you at the ranch?"

"I told you before, I don't want the ranch."

"But it's yours. I want you to have it."

Sandrine stopped, clutching a handful of silverware. "I don't want it. I don't want anything from you."

"What're you going to do, live here in town and work for Sally?"

"That's none of your business," she said, pushing by him to the next table.

"So you're just going to let the ranch sit. It'll fall apart."

"I suppose you should've thought of that before you moved into the mansion on the hill."

"I'll sell it to you if you don't want to take it from me," Wade said, following her around the room.

"I don't have that kind of money."

"But your things are there. Aren't you at least going to take them with you?"

Sandrine looked at him, narrowing her eyes. "I'll take what belongs to me and nothing more."

"God, you're a stubborn woman," Wade mumbled.

"But at least I'm honest," she said coldly, pushing by him again.

Wade took her arm. "What does that mean?"

Sandrine shook her arm free. "That means I'm going to work hard for everything. You can be damned sure I won't take someone's house just because I caught him cheating in a poker game." She started toward the kitchen, but Wade grabbed her arm tightly.

"I didn't do anything wrong. I didn't cheat; Frank did."

"Yes, but you chose to blackmail him with that knowledge."

"You honestly think Frank wouldn't have done the same thing to me? Hell, from what I hear, he did the same thing to Jim, only he was willing to take Rose to pay off the debt. If you hadn't stepped in and played cards with him, who knows what would've happened."

Sandrine pulled her arm away from Wade's grasp, putting a hand on her hip. "So you're telling me that you had no choice but to sink to Frank's level?"

Wade couldn't get over the color of Sandrine's eyes as she stood staring at him. Her gaze never wavered, and he was impressed by the strength he saw there. He was surprised he hadn't noticed before how tall she was. Tall, slim, and quite lovely.

"Aren't you going to answer me?" she demanded.

Wade tried to recall the question. The look of disdain in her eyes made him angry. "I don't owe you any explanations, do I? I've offered to help you: there's nothing else I can do. If you don't agree with the way I live, I can't help that. I can't live my life trying to earn your approval."

"I didn't expect that you would," Sandrine said quietly, walking into the kitchen.

Wade watched her as she left, feeling foolish as he stared at the swinging door. The hell with her, he thought. She didn't know him anyway. He shook his head. Hell, she probably knew him better than anyone else. The problem was, he didn't know himself.

Nine

Emily glanced over at Rose, then looked at the road ahead of them. The creaking of the wagon wheels was monotonous, irritating. It had been over a week since Wade had brought her home. At first she'd been angry with him, but now she realized that he'd only been trying to save her reputation. She put her hand up to her throat and sighed. She couldn't stop thinking about Wade—the way he looked, the feel of his lips on hers, and the way he made love to her. She felt herself blush, and she turned so that Rose would not see. Sometimes she was tempted to tell Jim and Rose how she felt about Wade, but she was afraid they would send her home.

Rose had barely spoken to her since she'd been back, and her uncle had been as civil as he could be considering the circumstances. She knew what they thought of her, but it didn't matter. She loved Wade Colter, and she knew he loved her. Or at least she thought he did.

Emily watched Rose flick the reins over the horse's back as they neared the outskirts of town. They passed ramshackle adobe houses with dirty-faced children playing in the yards. She sat primly as the wagon rolled by the livery and the blacksmith shop, then the dry goods store. Near the center of town, there were more wagons. It was always obvious which of the families had come to town most recently. Faces and clothing darkened with trail dust, they looked hollow-eyed and weary. As Rose and Emily came close to the open-air market, the smell of freshly cooked tortillas hung in the air. Colorfully dressed women tended the small fires of their outdoor cocinas. Emily was uneasy, as always, hearing a language she could not understand.

Rose stopped the wagon in front of a hitching rail. She climbed down, looping the reins over the brake handle. She looked up at Emily. "You can either come with me or go back to the dry goods store. I need some needles and white thread."

Emily hesitated. She didn't really want to be with Rose; she didn't want to hear the lecture she knew was coming. "I saw something in the milliner's window last week. How about if I meet you at the dry goods store in an hour?"

Rose nodded silently and walked away, lifting her skirts to keep them out of the dust.

Emily sighed heavily and climbed down from the wagon. She knew that people were looking at her. Her clothes were much more fashionable than any woman's around here. At least that was what the women looked at, the men looked at her for another reason entirely. She started toward the milliner's, walking daintily through the dirt and dust. On the other side of the street, she stepped up onto the sidewalk, gracefully accepting the proffered arm of an older gentleman. She smiled and thanked him, feeling his eyes on her as she walked away. She looked into the milliner's window and grimaced. Everything here was at least a year old. Impulsively she started up the planked sidewalk, careful not to catch a heel in the cracks. Already bored, she barely glanced into Tilly's Dress Shop. Wade had already bought her everything in here that was worth buying. There was nothing in this town she wanted.

She walked along the sidewalk, nodding to strangers, smiling as if she cared. She came to the Half Moon and stopped. The smell of coffee and frying sausage made her realize how hungry she was. She put her hand on the door but hesitated. She wasn't the kind of woman who went unescorted into restaurants. Still, this was the West. Things were different here.

Slowly she opened the door and went inside. Much to her surprise, Emily found the restaurant to be quite quaint. Square tables were placed along the walls and in the middle of the room. Some tables served four people, some served two, and they were all covered with tablecloths of blue and white linen. She could even see that the china was embossed with blue flowers and the linen napkins were a snowy white. The utensils were a fine quality silver, and even the salt and pepper shakers were white bone china.

Emily stood by the door waiting for someone to help her. Finally a woman with red hair came out of the kitchen carrying some plates of food. When she was finished, she walked over to Emily.

"Would you like to sit down?"

Emily nodded politely and followed the woman to a small table that was against the wall opposite the door. She sat down, taking off her gloves and bonnet and setting them on the chair next to her.

"Would you like some coffee?"

Emily looked up at the woman. "My name is Emily Dodd. I'm Jim Everett's niece."

"Yes, I know. Would you like some coffee?"

There was no mistaking the curtness in the woman's tone, and Emily simply nodded. For some reason, this woman didn't like her, and Emily didn't know why. She waited while the woman made her way around the restaurant, chatting pleasantly with her customers. Emily noticed that there was an odd assortment of people: cowboys dusty from the trail; women, like Rose, who worked hard and were enjoying a few hours respite; and couples just out for a day together. Yet they all seemed to be enjoying themselves, and the woman who had waited on her was obviously the one who made them feel that way. When the woman came back to the table, Emily smiled at her. "Might I ask you your name?"

"My name is Sally," she said, pouring Emily a cup of coffee. "Are you going to be having lunch?"

"What do you recommend?"

"We have some real nice stew, and we also have some roasted chicken."

"I think I'll have the chicken," Emily replied, studying Sally. "Pardon me, but you look very familiar. Have we met before?"

"Frank Lauter is a good friend of mine."

"Oh," Emily replied, quickly looking away from Sally. Now she remembered. Sally had been with Frank when he had come out to talk to Wade. He and Wade had gotten into a fight, and Sally had stepped between them. From what she had heard, it sounded like Sally had known Wade, too.

Emily reached for the sugar bowl and spooned a generous amount into her coffee, then brought the china cup to her mouth. She sipped slowly, surprised at how good it tasted. The swinging door to the kitchen opened again, and she glanced over, expecting to see Sally. Instead she saw Sandrine. Emily steadied the coffee cup between her hands as she watched Sandrine balance three platefuls of food and carefully set them down on a table. She smiled at the people, and when she looked up, she saw Emily. Impulsively Emily put up a hand, waving Sandrine toward the table.

"Did you need something?" Sandrine asked, wiping her hands on her apron.

"No, I just wanted to say hello. Do you remember me? I was at Wade's house the day you . . . Well, we met briefly."

"Do you need anything?" Sandrine repeated impatiently.

Emily shook her head, fascinated by this half-Indian woman. "Have you spoken to Wade since that day?"

Sandrine smiled, but her eyes showed no warmth. "As a matter of fact, I have spoken to him. Now, if you don't need anything, I have customers."

Emily started to say something else, but Sandrine had already moved across the room to another table. She was pretty. In fact, in the right clothes, with her hair done, she would be stunning. But it didn't matter how pretty she was or that she was Wade's wife; Wade didn't remember anything about her. The only woman he had any memories of was her. She smiled to herself, feeling a warm blush spread over her cheeks. She was startled when a plate was set down heavily on the table in front of her.

"Here's your lunch," Sandrine said, quickly turning away from the table.

"Wait," Emily said. "I want to ask you a question." She watched Sandrine's face as she stood by the table. "Do you still love Wade?"

"Even if I did, you would be the last person I'd tell," Sandrine said coldly, walking away from the table.

Emily felt her own anger rise, but she calmed herself. This was not the place to make a scene; if she had learned one thing from her mother, it was never to make a scene in public. She quietly ate her lunch, all the while watching Sandrine as she worked. The woman moved with a quiet grace that Emily admired, but there was no mistaking the Indian blood in her. No matter what Rose had said, Sandrine would never pass in polite society.

When she had finished her lunch, Emily sat patiently, waiting for Sandrine to come to her table again. When she did, Emily smiled at her, holding up her cup. "I'd like another cup of coffee, please. And dessert. What kind of dessert do you have?"

"We have apple and peach pies."

"Hmmm," Emily twisted her mouth for a moment. "I think I'll have a piece of peach, if you don't mind. And don't forget that coffee." Emily couldn't contain a smile as she watched Sandrine walk away, a scowl on her face. When she returned, she was carrying a coffeepot and a plate. Silently she refilled Emily's cup and set down the plate.

"I feel sorry for you, you know," Emily said. "I can't imagine what it would be like to be in love with a man like Wade and then have him forget everything you ever shared." Emily made her voice sound sweet, but her tone and her words were vicious. "Thank you, that'll be all. I'll just have my dessert now," she said, dismissing Sandrine as if she were her personal servant.

Emily put a forkful of pie in her mouth and was amazed that it tasted so good. Sally's restaurant served good food, and Emily knew she would enjoy coming here often, especially if she could undermine Sandrine's interest in Wade. She looked up when she heard Sally talking to a customer. Sally said something, and the table full of cowboys dissolved into laughter. Sally seemed perfectly at ease with any type of person. As she neared her table, Emily smiled, dabbing the corners of her mouth with her napkin. "This is wonderful pie, Sally."

"May I sit down for a moment, Emily?" Sally asked politely.

"Yes, please join me." Emily waited until Sally was seated. "You have a wonderful place here." Emily looked around the room. "I'm really quite surprised."

"Why is that, Emily? Because I'm not from Boston? You'd be shocked to know that even people in the West have manners."

"I think you misunderstood me, I—"

"No, I didn't misunderstand you, Emily. I'm going to tell you what I told Wade," Sally said slowly, her voice low. "I don't want you coming into my place again. I don't like you, and I don't want you here."

"You can't talk to me like that," Emily said, her anger rising.

"I can and I will if you ever come in here again."

"What did I do?"

"Don't act so innocent, Emily. You may fool your uncle, but you don't fool me. I've seen your type a hundred times before."

Emily neatly folded her napkin and laid it on the table next

BRIGHT STAR'S PROMISE

to her plate. She straightened her shoulders and met Sally's intense gaze. "And just what type is that, Sally?"

Sally nodded her head and smiled slightly. "You're good, Emily. You're very good. I can see how a man like Wade would fall for you, a man who has no memory of how much he loved and adored his wife."

"But he has no memory of her now, does he?" Emily said, her voice hard.

"Don't count on it." Sally hesitated. "He was in here just the other day talking to her. Guess he's a little curious about their past together."

"I don't think it's unusual that Wade would come in here," Emily said, trying to remain calm.

"That's good, because he'll be back. He couldn't take his eyes off Sandrine. He even asked me what they used to be like when they were together."

"I don't believe you," Emily said. "You're just trying to upset me."

"I don't need to try to upset you, Emily. I can already see that I have." Sally stood up, her hands on the table. "Remember what I said, don't come back into my place again."

Emily felt her cheeks burn, and she quickly composed herself, straightening her skirts. She put on her bonnet and gloves, took some money for the lunch from her purse, and put it on the table. Then she stood up, walking across the restaurant and out the door. She didn't look to see if Sally and Sandrine were watching her. She held her head high and walked toward the dry goods store, trying to push Sally's words from her mind. Maybe Wade did go into the restaurant, but it probably wasn't to see Sandrine. She'd seen him with her at his house, and he'd shown absolutely no affection for her then. Sally had just been sticking up for her friend.

Emily sighed heavily, dreading the ride home with Rose. But she knew she just had to be patient. It wouldn't be long until

Wade came for her, and then she'd never have to go back to the Everett ranch again.

Wade reined in at the top of the ridge. He could see the house from here. Slowly he let his horse pick its way down the hill. In front of the house, he sat still for a moment, staring, then he dismounted. The view from here was incredible. Not only could he see the entire valley, he could see the distant mountains. He could understand why he had chosen this spot to build a home. He looked at the mountains once more, then went inside. The adobe walls were halfway finished, and he could see where he'd begun to build a staircase to the second floor. It was eerie looking at something that he had done but couldn't remember doing. The fact that the house was unfinished and might never be finished bothered him.

He walked back out to the porch and sat down, stretching out his long legs. He looked down the valley at the small log house he'd built. Jim had said he'd taken great pride in it. He leaned back on his hands, taking in the breathtaking scenery. It would be easy to live here. As he sat up, he ran his hand over a rough spot in the planking. He turned and looked down. *Wade Loves Sandrine* was carved into the wood. Wade shook his head. It seemed like a childish thing to do; he couldn't imagine himself ever doing something like that. He took his hat off and ran his hand through his hair. That Wade, the man he had been, had obviously been too in love to care what anyone thought. For an instant Wade felt a sharp envy for the man he had been and the man he could never be again.

He looked up when he heard the sound of hoofbeats. He recognized Jim's horse from a distance and waited until he rode into the yard. Wade stood up while his friend dismounted. "Howdy, Jim."

Jim nodded his head. "Never expected to see you here. Was

riding up on the ridge and saw fresh tracks leading down. Thought I'd better check it out."

"Thanks."

Jim shook his head. "It's a nice piece of land. It's a shame to let it go to waste."

"I never said I was going to let it go to waste."

"Well, you have no use for it now that you're living in the house on the hill."

Wade tried to ignore the jibe.

"I thought I might make you an offer. What do you say, Wade?"

"No," Wade snapped, surprised at the quickness of his own reply.

"Why not? You don't intend to live here."

"I want to build the house," Wade said, staring up at the half-finished adobe walls.

"Why?"

"I want to finish it for Sandrine. I want her to have someplace nice to live."

"Oh," Jim said, nodding.

"It's not what you think, Jim."

"I wasn't thinking a thing," Jim said, hitching his horse to the rail and sitting down on the planked porch.

"Yes, you were. You were thinking that I care for Sandrine."

"Well, don't you?"

Wade shrugged. "I care because I'm supposed to, I guess. But I still don't remember a damn thing about her."

"Then why are you willing to put the work into this place?" Jim gestured to the house.

Wade sat down next to Jim. "I want her to have something. She deserves it."

"She won't take it from you, you know. She's about as stubborn as they come."

"Yeah, I know." Wade recalled the look of defiance in Sandrine's fine blue eyes when he had talked to her in Sally's restaurant.

Jim stretched out his legs in front of him. "If I didn't know better, I'd swear you were beginning to change, Wade. Just when I thought you were the biggest bastard around these parts."

Wade grinned. "I guess a man can't be a bastard all the time."

"Guess not," Jim agreed.

Wade looked away. "I am sorry about Emily, Jim. I never meant to hurt her in any way." He shrugged. "I guess I thought she was a woman who knew her own mind."

"I don't think Emily knows what she wants. She's been pampered her entire life. Being with you was like an adventure to her. I don't think it would've lasted long between you two anyway. She's a lot different from you, Wade." Jim shifted uncomfortably. "So have you told Sandrine you're going to finish building the house?"

"I just decided myself," Wade said. "Besides, if I told her . . ." Wade shook his head.

"You'll have to approach her slowly on it. Rose and I could help. We could tell her that if she doesn't take the land and the house, you're going to sell it to some greedy bastard that we don't want for a neighbor. I'm sure we can persuade her."

"I really want her to have it, Jim. I get the feeling that . . ." Wade stopped, staring down the valley. "I just get the feeling that she liked it here."

"She loves it here. So do you. Or at least you did before you decided to go and get your skull cracked."

Wade grinned ruefully. "That decision affected a lot of people. But there's not a hell of a lot I can do about it now." Wade stood up. Anger coursed through him. He had been married, happy, content with his life. Or so they all told him. Now he was . . . Without thinking, he doubled his right hand into a fist and swung at one of the porch timbers. An instant later, the pain in his hand forced the anger back down.

"That's not going to help anything," Jim said.

"What the hell do you know about it?"

"Take it easy." Jim stood up next to him.

"How would you take it if you couldn't remember Rose or Danny? If they meant nothing to you?"

Jim shrugged, his face clouding.

Wade stepped toward him. "You can't even imagine it, can you? You can't imagine what it's like to wonder whether or not you like apple pie or blueberry, or whether you like your coffee black or with cream. Everything," Wade slammed his fist into the adobe bricks again, "everything is a question. It's like being a stranger in your own body."

"This won't do any good, Wade. You've got to calm down. Give it time. It'll all come back eventually."

"But what if it doesn't, Jim? Doc doesn't know everything." Wade looked down at his bloody knuckles. "Maybe you better go on home now. Rose will be wondering what happened to you."

"Since you're out this way, why don't you come to dinner? Rose would love to have you."

Wade shook his head. "Don't think I'd be good company, but thanks anyway." He could feel Jim looking at him, but he did not meet his friend's eyes. He turned and busied himself picking up scrap lumber until Jim had ridden away. Only then did he raise his right hand and grimace. The knuckles were split, and rivulets of blood ran down his fingers. He could see sand from the adobe bricks along the edges of the cuts. There was probably some grit down inside. He untied his horse and swung up. Kicking the animal into an easy lope, he rode downhill toward the creek.

Sandrine smiled at the woman in the lavender dress. Her gentleman companion was putting away his wallet, and they were leaving. Sandrine breathed a silent sigh of relief. She liked working at Sally's and enjoyed talking to the people, but sometimes she couldn't wait to get outside. The heavy smells of cooking and the constant sound of human voices were grating on her nerves right now. She looked around and caught Sally's eye.

"Go when you're ready," Sally called across the dining room. "Betty's here now."

Sandrine quickly cleaned off the table, then headed for the kitchen. She reached up and took down one of the wicker baskets that Sally kept on the top shelf. She packed some cold roast beef, rolls and cheese, and half of a day-old apple pie. Untying her apron, she picked up her basket and headed for the door. She wasn't sure where she was going until she had her horse saddled. By the time she was a mile out of town, she was singing. She kicked her horse into a gallop and pounded along the road, her hair streaming in the wind. She turned up the ranch road without slowing her horse, intoxicated with the sheer freedom of riding fast. Still, as she topped the ridge, the sight of the stark and jagged adobe walls brought an almost physical pain.

She veered away from the new house and let her horse have its head. When she finally pulled up, her horse was blowing hard, its shoulders and neck flecked with sweat. She turned the animal toward the creek, glad there was water nearby. It wasn't until she had dismounted and her horse was sucking in great drafts of the cool, clear water that she noticed the fresh hoofprints on the bank. Glancing around, she fought the desire to remount and gallop away. This was still her land, and no one was going to make her afraid here. Impatient to find the trespasser, she led her horse along the edge of the stream, scanning the tracks as she walked. She had not gone far before she noticed the drops of thickened blood. Worried, she increased her pace.

When she saw Wade lying bare-chested in the tall grass, an involuntary cry escaped her lips. She ran, dropping to her knees beside him. Frantic with fear, her hands trembling, she pushed his hair back from his face. He opened his eyes, and in the instant that it took him to recognize her, she remembered herself at sixteen, staring into those same clear gray eyes. And the truth was she loved him now even more than she had loved him then.

"Sandrine."

Startled, she pulled her hands back and folded them in her lap. "I . . . I was just . . ." She gestured helplessly. "I saw the blood . . ." Wade sat up and she inched back, suddenly aware of him. "I thought someone was hurt."

Silently he held up his hand for her to see.

She caught her breath. "What happened?"

Wade hesitated. "Do you care?"

Flustered by the intensity of his gaze, Sandrine reached up to smooth her hair, then dropped her hands in irritation. "Of course I care. You're the one who's lost his memory, not I."

Wade looked away, but not before she saw the pain in his eyes. Sandrine shook her head. "I'm sorry. I know it must be awful for you."

Wade nodded slowly, but he wouldn't speak, and she knew he would never admit to her how frightening it must have been to simply wake up without a past.

Sandrine picked a stem of grass and rolled it between her fingers. "What're you doing out here anyway?"

"Just came out to check on the place. I wanted to make sure no drifters moved on in. I can ask you the same question, you know."

Sandrine nodded, not sure what she should say. "I was just riding—"

"And you just happened to wind up here?"

Feeling defensive, she nodded. "What difference does it

make?" Quickly she stood up. "Since you're all right, I'll just be getting back." She turned to walk to her horse.

"Where? To Sally's? You like living in town? The noise getting to you yet?" Wade stood up.

Sandrine spun around, her cheeks flushed with anger. "I like living with Sally. She doesn't bother me, and she doesn't ask me questions all the time. I can come and go as I please."

"You didn't answer the question. Do you like it in town, Sandrine?"

Sandrine shuffled uncomfortably when he said her name. "I like it well enough."

"Damn, you're a stubborn woman." Wade shook his head.

"Why, because I won't do what you want?"

"And what is that?"

"You want me to take this land so you can ease your conscience."

"No, I want you to take this land because if you don't, I'm going to sell it. Do you honestly want someone else living here?"

Sandrine made her way through the tall grass, trying to ignore Wade behind her. She could feel him looking at her. She stopped when she got to her horse. "You can do what you want with the land. After all, it is yours." She gathered up the reins and started to mount up, but Wade took the reins from her.

"Don't go yet."

Angrily Sandrine reached for the reins.

"Please," Wade said, his voice softening.

"Why?"

"I'd like to talk to you." Gently Wade placed the reins in her hands. "I want to know more about the way I used to be. Besides Jim and Rose, you knew me better than anyone."

Sandrine looked into his eyes, and she could see that Wade was sincere. She dropped the reins to the ground and let her horse graze. "What do you want to know?"

Wade looked toward her horse. "Is that a picnic basket you have there?"

"It's my lunch," Sandrine replied.

"Were you planning to eat out here all alone?"

"This isn't so far out, Wade," Sandrine laughed. "I guess you don't remember much about my background, do you?"

"I know some."

Sandrine reached up for the basket. Gathering her skirts in one hand, she pushed her way through the tall grass until she found a suitable spot near the stream. As Wade sat down next to her, she reached into the basket and got two rolls. She handed one to him. "Did Rose and Jim tell you anything about me?"

"They told me you were Blackfoot, or half. Your father is French?"

Sandrine nodded. "I grew up at a trading post that my father built not too far from my grandfather's village. If I wasn't helping out at the trading post, I was always at the village. I loved it there; I loved the freedom I had. I could shoot arrows, ride horses, swim in the river, and play with my friends all day long."

"You couldn't do that at the trading post?"

"There weren't any kids there. Besides, my father wanted me to act like a lady." She smiled slyly. "It didn't work though. I'd play cards with the cook, Josiah, and some of the other men. I'd find ways of having fun anyway."

"What are your parents' names?"

"My father's name is Luc. My mother's name is Running Tears."

"Running Tears." Wade repeated the name several times. "It's a good name." He looked at Sandrine. "Did she and I get along?"

"My mother adores you," Sandrine said, watching his face. "After all, you saved my life. You could never do anything wrong in her eyes."

"I wonder what she'd think of me now," Wade said.

"I don't know," Sandrine replied, shaking her head. "But she wouldn't judge you. She's not that way. She has the kindest heart of anyone I've ever known."

"What about brothers and sisters? Do you have any?"

"No, but I have a cousin who is like a brother to me. His name is Little Bear."

"Little Bear," Wade repeated, squinting his eyes as if forcing himself to remember. "Did he and I get along?"

"You are good friends. You've known each other since you were boys. You and Little Bear rode together for months to find me when I was kidnapped by a Blood Indian named Bear Killer. I would've died if you two hadn't found me."

Wade smiled weakly. "So no matter how much I want to think otherwise, I was a decent man."

"You were more than decent," Sandrine replied honestly. "When you were barely sixteen years old, you delivered Danny all by yourself. You saved Rose's life, I'm sure. And you were very protective of her when her husband died."

"That's why she feels so comfortable chewing me out all the time."

Sandrine smiled. "I suppose so. Did Jim tell you about the time you tried to lead five wagons west in the dead of winter?"

"That doesn't sound too smart."

"They'd gone on their own without a guide, and the father of one of the women hired you to get them safely to Oregon."

"Did we make it?"

"No, you ran into a blizzard and you were stranded for days. One of the children on the wagons was deathly ill, and you decided to ride to the trading post for help. But you didn't make it. You almost froze to death yourself. Thank God, Little Bear found you and took you to our village."

"Doesn't sound like I was a very good guide."

"You were one of the best," Sandrine said without hesitation, "but there wasn't much even you could do. These people had undertaken a difficult trip during the worst time of the year. If you hadn't gotten them as far as you had, they would've all died."

Wade put the rest of the roll into his mouth and chewed. He leaned back on his elbows. "I like hearing stories about myself. I sound almost heroic."

Sandrine brushed her hands on her skirt. "You weren't perfect, that's for sure."

"What about us, Sandrine? Tell me about us."

Sandrine met Wade's eyes, and she felt her cheeks burn. How could she tell him all that they had shared—all of the experiences, all of the laughter and tears, all of the love. There was no way she could make him understand the way it had been between them.

"Sandrine."

Sandrine shook her head, staring out at the stream. "What we had is over now, Wade. Talking about it won't bring it back."

"But maybe it will help me understand."

"Understand what?" Sandrine said angrily. "You keep saying how terrible this is for you, but do you know what it's been like for me? I've loved you since I was a girl. I thought we would be together forever." Tears welled up in her eyes, and she turned her head, quickly wiping them away.

"I'm sorry," Wade said, covering Sandrine's hand with his own. "You're right. I've been selfish. I've only been thinking about me. I haven't thought about you at all."

Sandrine felt the pressure of Wade's hand on hers, and she closed her eyes, thinking for a minute that he had come back to her. But when she opened her eyes and looked at him, she saw the expression in his eyes—he felt sorry for her, nothing more. She pulled her hand away from his. "I'm fine. I don't need you to feel sorry for me." She clasped her right hand over her left, and she ran her fingers along the fine silver of the bracelet that Lone Wind had given her.

"That's a beautiful bracelet."

"Thank you." Her voice was short.

"Did I give it to you?"

"No." She studiously avoided his eyes.

"Did someone in your family give it to you?"

"Why?" she snapped.

"Because it's unusual. It doesn't look like something that your people would make."

"How do you know what my people would make?"

"I don't know," Wade said, shaking his head. "But the design of the bracelet looks familiar. Like it's from around here."

Sandrine looked down at the sparkling silver on her wrist, and she thought of Lone Wind. If only she had stayed with him . . .

"Did another man give it to you?"

"What does it matter, Wade?" Sandrine turned away and gathered her skirts in one hand, preparing to stand.

"Will you talk to me, please?"

She hesitated, then settled herself again. "Why is it so important that you know about this bracelet?"

"And why is it so important that you not tell me?" Wade said, his voice even.

Sandrine emitted a deep sigh. "It was given to me by a Crow warrior. His name was Lone Wind." She couldn't control the trembling in her voice as she said his name.

"I know enough to know that the Crows are enemies of your people, aren't they?"

Sandrine nodded. "It's a long story, and it doesn't matter. Are you still hungry? I have more food in here." She reached into the basket, but she felt Wade's fingers around her wrist.

"Tell me about him, Sandrine."

Sandrine nodded absently, almost relieved. Whether or not Wade still loved her, he was her oldest friend and she trusted him. She began talking. She found herself telling him how he and Little Bear had rescued her—how they had finally found her in the care of Gray Wolf and Red Bird. She told him how fond she had grown of the old man and his wife. She stopped, self-conscious at how long the story was taking, but he nodded his encouragement, and she continued. Then she told him of Red Bird's death and her trip to the Crow village with Lone Wind and Little Bear.

"What about Lone Wind? You haven't said anything about him," Wade finally interrupted her.

"He and I didn't get along at first. I felt he treated his father badly, and I didn't like it. We argued about everything, but like you," Sandrine looked at Wade, "he watched out for me. I couldn't help but grow fond of him."

"Did you love him?"

Sandrine closed her eyes. It seemed like Wade had shouted the words. "I didn't mean for it to happen," she said, her voice barely audible. Her eyes filled with tears again, but she didn't make any effort to wipe them away. She looked up at Wade. "He wanted me to be his wife. He wanted me to stay with him." She covered her face with her hands. "I should've stayed with him. There's nothing for me here . . ." She tried to control her sobs, but she couldn't. She felt Wade's hand on her shoulder, but she shook it off, looking at him. "If I hadn't wanted to come back here to be with you, he'd be alive now. He died saving my life." Her voice sounded shrill and loud, but she couldn't control it.

"Sandrine, I'm sorry. I never meant to hurt you."

Sandrine laughed harshly. "I don't think you care about anyone but yourself, so stop pretending like you do." She started to stand, but Wade wrapped his fingers around her wrist.

"Sandrine," he said, pulling her to him. "I am sorry."

"Leave me alone," Sandrine said, unable to control her tears. She struggled to pull away, but Wade held her tightly, and the familiarity of his arms was too overwhelming. She pressed her face against his bare chest, unable to keep herself from crying.

"Let me help you," Wade said, stroking her hair.

Reluctantly Sandrine sat up, wiping the tears from her face. She looked at Wade, smiling sadly. "You can't do anything to help me."

"Yes, I can. I can fix this place up for you, and I can send some hands over here to help you with the work. You don't have to work for Sally, and you don't have to live in town. This is your place as much as it's mine."

Sandrine tried to hide her disappointment. The one thing that Wade could do to help her he wasn't able to do. He couldn't give her his love. She tightened her fists, forcing herself to remain calm. She didn't want to dissolve into tears again. "Thank you anyway, but I don't think so." She stood up. "I should be getting back. It'll be dark soon, and Sally will worry if I'm late."

"Yes, you don't want to upset Sally."

There was no mistaking the bitterness in Wade's voice, but Sandrine ignored him. She repacked the basket, then walked back to her horse. She hooked the handle of the basket over the saddle horn and then mounted up. Without looking back, she rode up the hill, away from the house and Wade.

Sandrine smiled and waved to Danny. She was sitting on the porch, and he was playing with his dog in the yard. She winced, trying to ignore the angry voices of Jim and Rose that came from inside the house. Rose had invited her to dinner, knowing that Emily would be staying with neighbors for a few days. Now Sandrine wished she hadn't accepted the invitation. She had heard similar arguments before—they didn't have enough money to buy new stock, or feed, or supplies for the ranch. Years ago Jim had tried to gamble to make extra money, and he had almost lost the ranch doing it. Now he had another idea, an idea which made Rose furious. He had an offer to take over a large wagon train that was on its way to California. The wagon master had come down with cholera and Jim had been recommended for the job. At first he had refused, but when the people on the train had joined together and offered him a sizable amount of money, he had agreed. He had just broken the news to Rose.

Sandrine tried not to listen, but Rose's voice was shrill and it carried.

"I can't believe you could be so stupid," Rose shouted. "How could you be so thoughtless? What are Danny and I supposed to do while you're off playing cowboy? I can't take care of this ranch by myself.'

Sandrine wriggled uncomfortably, feeling badly for both of her friends.

"I don't see that we have much of a choice, Rose. We need more stock in order to produce more, but we don't have the money to buy it. It's the same with everything around here. We just don't have the money."

"We'll get by somehow, Jim," Rose said, her voice softening. "Please, don't go. If something happens to you . . ."

Sandrine could hear Rose crying, and she closed her eyes, wishing there was something she could do for them.

"I don't have a choice, Rose. Listen to me. I'm not like your first husband. I know my way around; I've been doing this since I was a boy. Nothing's going to happen to me."

"You don't know that," Rose sobbed. "Why don't you just ask Wade for the money, Jim. He's rich now. He'd give it to you, I know he would."

"No!" Jim shouted. "I won't take anything from Wade."

"Why not? Does it bother you so much that Wade is doing well? My Lord, Jim, he's like your son. You should be happy for him."

"Don't tell me how I should feel about Wade, Rose. I raised him, not you."

"It could just be a loan, until we're back on our feet. Please. If you don't want to ask him, I will. I don't mind."

"If you ask Wade for that money, Rose, so help me . . ."

Sandrine couldn't hear the rest of Jim's words. They were cut short by Danny's happy shouts as he ran toward the porch steps. Sandrine stood up and stopped him before he was able to climb the stairs. "Why don't we find Scout? I saw him run over toward the corral."

"But I'm hungry. I want to eat."

Sandrine put her hands on Danny's shoulders and steered him toward the corral. "I bet Scout is playing a trick on you. He thinks you can't find him."

"I can find him!" Danny shouted as he ran toward the corral. "I'm coming after you, Scout."

Sandrine smiled for a moment, her thoughts quickly going back to Rose and Jim. Even if Jim led the wagon train and came back all right, things might never be the same between them again. She pursed her lips together and went inside the barn. She got her tack and brought it outside to the corral, quickly saddling her horse. When Danny came running around the side of the barn, he stopped short when he saw her.

"Are we going for a ride? Where are we going? Are we going to stay out till after dark?"

Sandrine reached down and lifted him onto the top rail of the corral. She tousled his dark hair. "I need your help, Danny. I need you to keep a secret for me."

"A secret?" Danny lowered his voice and looked around. "What is it?"

"I have to go someplace very important right now, but I don't want your parents to worry. So I want you to tell them I've ridden back into town. Tell them I've gone back to Sally's."

"That's not a secret. That's a lie." Danny shook his head. "I can't tell Ma a lie. She'll get real mad at me."

"I want to do something very special for your mother and father, Danny. If I tell them where I'm going, they'll know what it is."

"Oh," Danny said, kicking his heels against the wood.

"You don't even have to lie. Just tell them you don't know where I went. That way it won't be a lie."

"Okay," Danny readily agreed. "Are you going now?"

"Yes, and you stay out here until your folks call you to dinner. They're having a talk."

"They're arguing, you mean," Danny said, twisting his face in an unreadable expression.

"Well, sometimes grownups argue. Everyone argues. It doesn't mean your mother and father don't love each other." Sandrine looked up at the sky. The sun was quickly fading, and the sky was growing dark. "I better go, Danny." Sandrine kissed him on the cheek and lifted him back down to the ground. "I'll see you soon."

"Bye, Sandrine. I won't say anything."

"Thank you," she said as she led her horse out of the yard and mounted up. She headed toward Wade's ranch. She was going to ask him to loan Jim and Rose the money they needed. She hated the thought of asking Wade for anything, but it would be easier for her to do it than it would be for Jim. She took a deep breath and kicked her horse into a run.

Ten

Wade ignored Emily as she prattled on. He finished the wine in his glass and then poured some more. Emily had shown up on his doorstep the night before, begging him to let her stay, saying that she'd gotten in a horrible fight with Rose. He'd tried to reason with her, but she'd only gotten more upset. He had let her stay in the guest bedroom, and he'd been sure to lock his bedroom door. Even when he heard her knock lightly on his door later that night, he had ignored her. Whatever had once been between him and Emily was now in the past.

"You haven't said a word, Wade."

Wade glanced up at Emily. Her cheeks were flushed from the wine, and she was smiling. She was pretty, but she held no attraction for him. He still couldn't understand what had made him make love to her in the first place. Maybe it was because she had been there and had comforted him after the accident. He had felt some affection for her at the time. Now . . . Wade shook his head, trying to ignore Emily's monologue.

He moved his fork around on his plate, but he wasn't interested in eating. The only thing, the only person, who interested him right now was Sandrine. He couldn't forget the look of pain in her eyes as she told him about Lone Wind, and he couldn't forget how she had felt in his arms. And when he had looked into her eyes, he had seen the love she still felt for him.

"Are you finished, Señor Colter?"

Wade looked up absently at Rialta. "Yes, I'm sorry." The

woman was kind, and she worked hard. "Let the dishes go until tomorrow, Rialta. Go home to your family."

"But señor, there is so much to do. I cannot—"

"Don't argue with me." Wade took the plate from her hands. "Go home and take some of this food with you."

"*Gracias,* señor." She nodded and smiled.

"Why did you do that? I hope you don't expect me to clean up this mess," Emily said.

Wade stood up. "I don't expect anything from you, Emily," he said, heading toward the study. He went inside the large room and walked to the felt-covered game table, chalking a cue and setting the balls. Then he leaned down and broke, scattering the multicolored balls all around the table.

"Are you angry with me, Wade?" Emily said as she stood next to him.

Wade shot a solid green ball into a side pocket and straightened, chalking his stick again. "I'm not angry with you, Emily. I just don't want you staying here. It doesn't look right."

"You didn't care how it looked before," Emily said, putting her arms around him from behind.

Wade put down the cue and took Emily's hands away. He turned around to face her. "You're an attractive woman, Emily, and I appreciate the time we got to spend together, but that's all there is to it. I don't have any feelings for you. We're too different, you and I."

Emily's expression quickly changed. "It's her, isn't it?" she asked angrily, pursing her lips together.

"Who?"

"Sandrine. You've been seeing her, haven't you?"

"No," Wade said impatiently. "I've talked to her once or twice, that's all. I don't even know the woman."

"That's not what I heard."

"Emily, look—"

"You used me, Wade. You were lonely and scared, and you

used me to ease your fear. Well, you can't do that." Emily stomped her foot and began to cry.

Wade put his hands on her shoulders. "Calm down, Emily. It'll be all right."

"No, it won't be all right. I love you."

"You don't love me. I'm just a cowboy with no manners. You're a proper lady. You'd be sick of me in no time."

"No, I wouldn't. Just give me a chance, Wade. Please." Emily clutched his shirt front.

"It won't work, Emily. You'll be going back to Boston soon. That's where you belong."

"How do you know where I belong? You can't do this to me, Wade."

He put his arms around Emily as she cried, patting her on the back. "After you're back in Boston for a few months, you won't even remember my name."

Emily pulled away, and for an instant Wade saw something in her eyes that unsettled him. But before he could react, it was gone.

"Don't patronize me, Wade. I'm not a child. I know what I want." She reached up and touched his face. "I want you."

"But I don't know what I want, Emily," Wade said, taking her hand away. "I'm just trying to get used to my life." Wade looked up when he saw the butler. "What is it, Walters?"

"There's someone to see you, sir."

"Who is it?"

Walters looked from Wade to Emily, then back to Wade, unable to hide the look of disapproval. "She says she's your wife, sir."

"My wife?" Wade repeated the words, then looked at Emily. If Sandrine had come here, something must be wrong. "Tell her I'll be right there, Walters."

"Very well, sir."

Wade took Emily's hands in his. "You're welcome to stay

here tonight, Emily, but I want you to go back to Jim and Rose's tomorrow."

"I knew it was her. You still love her, don't you?" Emily's eyes narrowed and her voice sounded hard.

"I told you I don't even remember her, Emily. We have to talk business, that's all. Now will you please go up to your room and give me some privacy," he said impatiently.

"All right," Emily said, leaving the study. "But it's not over yet," she said angrily.

Wade followed her to the staircase and waited until she was at the top, then he walked to the entryway. Sandrine was staring up at a painting, her hands locked behind her like a little girl. Her hair was pulled back loosely in a ribbon, and she wore a gray dress. When she turned and looked at him, Wade felt a strange sensation. He didn't know if it was memory or if he was just pleased to see her, but it wasn't like anything he'd felt with Emily. Slowly he walked forward. "This is a surprise," he said, his voice sounding strange in his own ears. He watched her as she stepped toward him, her hands twisting together. She was obviously nervous.

"I need your help," she said, her voice slightly tremulous.

"Why don't you come inside," Wade said, guiding her through the entryway, down the wide hall, and to the study. He motioned to the sofa in front of the fireplace. After they were seated, he said, "What do you need, Sandrine?"

"It's not for me. It's for Rose and Jim." She lowered her eyes for a moment and then looked back at Wade. "They're in trouble."

"What kind of trouble?"

"They need money to buy stock and supplies, and if they don't get it . . ." Sandrine reached up and pushed the hair back from her face, shaking her head. "If Jim knew I was here . . ."

"He'd probably kill you," Wade finished the sentence. "How much do they need?"

"I don't know. I just heard them arguing tonight. Jim said he got a job on a wagon train. All he has to do is lead them from here to California."

"He can't do that."

Sandrine nodded. "Rose is so upset. She's afraid something will happen to him. She lost one husband; she doesn't want to lose another."

Wade caught the look of sadness in Sandrine's eyes as she spoke, and he wondered if she was talking about Rose or herself. "We can ride over there right now if you like."

"I don't think that'll work, Wade. Jim will never accept the money from you. He's too proud."

"He would've accepted it from me before, wouldn't he?" When Sandrine hesitated, Wade nodded. "It's only now that I've won most of this money gambling that he won't take it from me. It's not like I stole the money, Sandrine, or even this house. Frank was the one who was cheating at cards. I just happened to be the one who caught him."

"You didn't have to take his house, Wade."

"Frank Lauter is still worth more than most people ever will be in a lifetime," Wade said shortly. "Besides, if he'd really wanted to stay here, he would've found a way. He'll build another house if he wants to."

Sandrine shook her head. "Well, I'm not worried about Frank right now, I'm worried about Jim and Rose. If Jim takes that job as wagon master, I'm afraid Rose won't be here when he comes back." She looked at Wade, her eyes round. "We have to find a way to help them, Wade. They're like family to both of us."

Without thinking, Wade touched Sandrine's face. "Don't worry, we'll think of something." Her cheeks flooded with color and she lowered her eyes, but Wade raised her chin. "Look at me, please." When Sandrine's eyes met his, he held her gaze.

The Publishers of Zebra Books
Make This Special Offer
to Zebra Romance Readers…

AFTER YOU HAVE READ THIS
BOOK WE'D LIKE TO SEND YOU
**4 MORE FOR *FREE*
AN $18.00 VALUE**

NO OBLIGATION!

ONLY ZEBRA HISTORICAL ROMANCES
"BURN WITH THE FIRE OF HISTORY"
(SEE INSIDE FOR MONEY SAVING DETAILS.)

MORE PASSION AND ADVENTURE AWAIT... YOUR TRIP TO A BIG ADVENTUROUS WORLD BEGINS WHEN YOU ACCEPT YOUR FIRST 4 NOVELS ABSOLUTELY *FREE* (AN $18.00 VALUE)

Accept your Free gift and start to experience more of the passion and adventure you like in a historical romance novel. Each Zebra novel is filled with proud men, spirited women and tempestuous love that you'll remember long after you turn the last page.

Zebra Historical Romances are the finest novels of their kind. They are written by authors who really know how to weave tales of romance and adventure in the historical settings you love. You'll feel like you've actually gone back in time with the thrilling stories that each Zebra novel offers.

GET YOUR FREE GIFT WITH THE START OF YOUR HOME SUBSCRIPTION

Our readers tell us that these books sell out very fast in book stores and often they miss the newest titles. So Zebra has made arrangements for you to receive the four newest novels published each month.

You'll be guaranteed that you'll never miss a title, and home delivery is so convenient. And to show you just how easy it is to get Zebra Historical Romances, we'll send you your first 4 books absolutely FREE! Our gift to you just for trying our home subscription service.

BIG SAVINGS AND FREE HOME DELIVERY

Each month, you'll receive the four newest titles as soon as they are published. You'll probably receive them even before the bookstores do. What's more, you may preview these exciting novels free for 10 days. If you like them as much as we think you will, just pay the low preferred subscriber's price of just $3.75 each. *You'll save $3.00 each month off the publisher's price.* AND, your savings are even greater because there are never any shipping, handling or other hidden charges—FREE Home Delivery. Of course you can return any shipment within 10 days for full credit, no questions asked. There is no minimum number of books you must buy.

4 FREE BOOKS

TO GET YOUR 4 FREE BOOKS WORTH $18.00 — MAIL IN THE FREE BOOK CERTIFICATE TODAY

Fill in the Free Book Certificate below, and we'll send your FREE BOOKS to you as soon as we receive it.

If the certificate is missing below, write to: Zebra Home Subscription Service, Inc., P.O. Box 5214, 120 Brighton Road, Clifton, New Jersey 07015-5214.

FREE BOOK CERTIFICATE
4 FREE BOOKS
ZEBRA HOME SUBSCRIPTION SERVICE, INC.

YES! Please start my subscription to Zebra Historical Romances and send me my first 4 books absolutely FREE. I understand that each month I may preview four new Zebra Historical Romances free for 10 days. If I'm not satisfied with them, I may return the four books within 10 days and owe nothing. Otherwise, I will pay the low preferred subscriber's price of just $3.75 each; a total of $15.00, *a savings off the publisher's price of $3.00*. I may return any shipment and I may cancel this subscription at any time. There is no obligation to buy any shipment and there are no shipping, handling or other hidden charges. Regardless of what I decide, the four free books are mine to keep.

NAME _____

ADDRESS _____ APT _____

CITY _____ STATE _____ ZIP _____

TELEPHONE ( ) _____

SIGNATURE _____ (if under 18, parent or guardian must sign)

Terms, offer and prices subject to change without notice. Subscription subject to acceptance by Zebra Books. Zebra Books reserves the right to reject any order or cancel any subscription.

ZB0794

GET FOUR FREE BOOKS
(AN $18.00 VALUE)

ZEBRA HOME SUBSCRIPTION
SERVICE, INC.
120 BRIGHTON ROAD
P.O. BOX 5214
CLIFTON, NEW JERSEY 07015-5214

AFFIX
STAMP
HERE

He didn't know what his feelings were toward her other than a strong attraction. "I'm glad you came to me for help."

"I didn't know where else to go."

"You can always come to me," Wade said, putting his arms around her. When Sandrine let him hold her, Wade rested his chin on her head, breathing in the fresh smell of her hair. It felt good to hold her, he thought. It felt right. Finally Sandrine pushed away, nervously straightening her blouse.

"We should think of a way we can get Jim to accept the money."

Wade sat back, nodding. "He's a proud man, and he's worked hard. He shouldn't have to worry about this now." He stood up and went to his desk. He pulled a key from his pocket and unlocked a drawer, then he took out a metal box. He reached in and took out two stacks of bundled bills. He turned to Sandrine. "Let's go."

Sandrine stood up. "We can't just go there with the money. He'll never take it."

"He'll take it," Wade said, cupping Sandrine's elbow as they walked toward the door. They had made it to the stairway when he saw Emily coming down the stairs. He glanced at Sandrine and saw her stiffen. He waited until Emily reached the landing, and he stood between the two women. "We're going to Jim's. Would you like to come?"

Emily glared at Sandrine and then looked at Wade. "Why would I want to go there? I've been trying to get away from Jim's ever since I arrived in this godforsaken place." She took a step closer to Sandrine. "So you've come to check on your husband, have you?"

"No," Sandrine said coolly.

"Then why are you here?"

"It's none of your business," Sandrine said, her head held high.

Emily pressed her lips together and looked at Wade. "What is she doing here, Wade? Tell me."

"Don't, Emily," Wade said calmly, trying to steer her back to the stairs. "We'll talk later when I get back."

"No, we'll talk now."

"Go up to your room, Emily," Wade said, trying to keep his anger in check.

"I knew she'd do this," Emily spat. "She acts so innocent, but she wants you back. I know she does."

"Stop it, Emily." Wade guided Sandrine toward the entryway, hoping that Emily was finished. But the sound of her boot heels on the marble floor warned him that she was not yet done.

"Tell me something, Sandrine," she said too loudly. "What was it like when you were with that Indian? Rose told me he kept you captive for a long time. It must have changed you. I couldn't imagine how any decent woman could survive such a thing."

Sandrine stopped abruptly, whirling to face Emily. Wade looked at her and saw the anger in her eyes and the flush in her cheeks.

"I'm assuming you're upset and you don't know what you're saying, Emily. But I will tell you something; no woman should have to endure what I did." She stepped so close to Emily that their faces almost touched. "I was kept a captive for months. I was a slave. I had to fetch wood, cook meals, and I had to submit to my captor every night. Every night, Emily. He was disgusting. His breath stank and so did he. When I tried to fight him, he beat me severely. It got to the point where I wanted to die, and I almost did."

Wade watched Sandrine as she spoke, and for the first time, he hurt for her. He had heard the stories from Rose and Jim, but he had never been affected by them until now.

"Well, I'm not sorry," Emily said defiantly. "You're an Indian."

Wade started to step between the two women, but he wasn't

BRIGHT STAR'S PROMISE

quick enough. Before he could, Sandrine drew back her arm and slapped Emily hard across the cheek, knocking her backward. Emily stumbled, trying to regain her balance, and when she stood up, her eyes were filled with tears of rage.

"You're an animal!" she screamed.

"And you're pathetic," Sandrine said, turning and heading toward the door.

Wade looked at Emily, shook his head, and followed Sandrine out the door. He quickly saddled his horse and led the way out of the yard. They rode in silence, and Wade shook his head, remembering the anger on Sandrine's face. He couldn't help but smile slightly. She had no problem sticking up for herself.

For the rest of the ride, he found himself thinking about Sandrine. It was easy to see how he had loved her; any man could love her. So why couldn't he? He forced his thoughts away from Sandrine as they rode into Jim's yard. They hitched their horses to the railing and walked toward the porch. Before Wade could step up, he felt Sandrine's hand on his arm.

"What are we going to say?"

He squeezed her hand in the darkness. "I've been told I have some charm. I guess we'll just see how much." He waited for Sandrine to climb the stairs, and he followed, knocking on the door. When Jim opened it and when he saw the two of them together, his face seemed to darken.

"Aren't you going to ask us in?" Wade said, pushing his way past Jim.

"Yeah, come on in." Jim looked at Sandrine. "Where the hell did you go? We were worried about you."

"I went for a ride."

"And you just managed to wind up over at Wade's spread."

"Stop it, Jim," Rose said, smiling halfheartedly.

Wade noticed that her eyes were red from crying. He went to her and gave her a hug.

"What was that for?"

"Just felt like it," he said. "I don't suppose we could impose on you for pie and coffee, Rose."

"Of course you can. Sit down."

"What do you want, Wade?"

"I'll help Rose," Sandrine said, leaving the two men alone.

Wade pulled out a chair and sat down, taking off his hat. "Just what do you figure you spent on me over the years, Jim?"

"What in the hell are you talking about?" Jim sat down across from Wade. "Have you been drinking?"

"Just a couple glasses of wine with dinner. My mind is real clear. I was thinking that you spent a lot of money on me over the years. You raised me from the time I was a kid—you bought me clothes, a horse, a saddle, boots, and books. Hell, Rose even told me you paid for tutors. That was all money you could've spent on yourself. That's not to mention the time and energy you put into raising me. It couldn't have been easy."

"It was always easy with you, Wade."

Wade saw Jim's eyes soften, and he was genuinely touched by the warmth of his words. "I think you're lying some. You're a good man, Jim."

"So are you, even though you're trying to disguise it right now."

"Well, I'm here to pay my debt."

"What debt?"

Wade stood up and reached into his pockets, taking out the stacks of bills and putting them on the table. "Here's eight thousand dollars. It's probably not half what I owe you but—"

"What is this? Is this a handout? Dammit, Wade," Jim said angrily, pounding his fist on the table. "I don't want or need your money."

"But you do need it, Jim," Wade said gently, sitting back down, "and you'd be a fool not to take it."

"Well, it wouldn't be the first time," Jim said angrily, shooting a look toward Rose.

"Listen to me. This is honest money: I didn't cheat anyone for it, and I didn't hold up any banks. I played poker and I won, fair and square. Don't pretend you never played before, Jim." Wade saw Jim's face contort in anger, but he didn't say anything. "Even though I don't remember the past, I know what you and Rose have done for me in these last months. You've been my family. When I felt lost, you were both there for me. Please take the money, Jim. You and Rose deserve it. So does Danny."

Jim shook his head. "I never took anything from anyone before, especially not from you."

"Why not from me? You raised me, Jim. Without you I might even be dead by now. I want to help you. I need to." Wade lowered his eyes. "I need to feel good about myself for a change."

"Is that an apology?"

Wade looked up to see Jim smiling slightly. Wade shrugged. "I guess I'm not too happy with my life right now. I admit it. But I'm trying to make some changes."

"What about Emily? Is she with you?"

Wade sighed. "She's at the house, but we haven't been together. I told her to come back here, but she wouldn't listen. I swear, Jim, I don't want to hurt her anymore than she's been hurt."

Jim nodded. "And Sandrine?"

Wade looked across his shoulder at Sandrine and Rose, who were talking with great animation about something. "I don't know. I can't seem to get her off my mind."

"That's a start."

"Don't," Wade said, holding up a hand. "I didn't say I love her, I just said I think about her a lot. That doesn't mean anything."

"It means a lot, boy."

Wade stared at Jim, his eyes widening. He'd never called him boy before, yet it sounded so familiar, like he'd heard it a hundred other times.

"Here's your pie," Rose said, placing a plate in front of Wade. "Peach."

"I swear, Rose, a man would kill for one of your peach pies."

"Stop it, Wade Colter. I used to be charmed by you, but I'm too old for that rubbish now." Rose sat down and poured coffee. "I must say, it was quite a surprise seeing you and Sandrine together."

"I was a little surprised myself to see her tonight," Wade said, catching Sandrine's eye from across the table. "But I'm glad she came to me." He smiled at Rose. "I've offered Jim some money, and he's agreed to take it."

"I never agreed to anything."

"But you will," Wade said, grinning. "If you don't take it and you go off and leave this woman all alone, you're plumb crazy, Jim."

Jim reached out and took Rose's hand. "I guess you're right, Wade. It's not worth taking a chance on losing her."

"We'll pay you back, Wade. I promise," Rose said.

"It's not a loan, Rose. It's money I owed Jim. Consider it a gift." He caught Sandrine looking at him, a smile on her face, and he smiled back. He couldn't stop staring at her incredible eyes.

"Did you hear a word, Wade?" Rose said, nudging his arm.

"What?" He looked at Rose. "Sorry. What did you say?"

"I asked if you're still going to sell the ranch."

"No," Wade said, looking back at Sandrine. "I'm going to finish building the house."

"Why bother if you're not going to live there?"

"I might move back. Frank's house is a little too big for me, I think." Again he glanced at Sandrine, but this time she avoided his eyes.

"Well, I'm glad you're not going to sell. I was afraid we'd have some greedy neighbor."

"I'm trying to talk Sandrine into moving back out here, but she won't listen to me. Maybe you two can convince her."

"Why don't you, Sandrine? You can't say you don't miss it."

"I don't want to live out here alone, Rose," Sandrine said.

Wade was hoping that she would look at him, but she steadfastly ignored him.

She stood up. "I should be getting back to town." She took her plate and cup to the wash basin.

"Why don't you stay the night," Rose pleaded. "I miss you. Besides, Emily's room is empty. You can stay there."

"No, thank you," Sandrine replied curtly.

Wade stood up. "Thanks for the pie, Rose. We should be going. Don't worry, I'll make sure Sandrine gets back safely." Wade handed his plate and cup to Rose and kissed her on the cheek.

"Thank you, Wade," Rose said, putting an arm around him. "I knew you hadn't left us."

Wade smiled and shook Jim's hand. "Let me know if you want to look at some of Frank's stock. He's got some prize steers you might be interested in."

Jim nodded. "I'll let you know. Thank you, Wade. I won't forget this."

Wade gripped Jim's hand tightly, then followed Sandrine out the door. They mounted up, waved goodbye to Jim and Rose, and headed up the trail to the ridge. The night was still and quiet, except for an occasional owl and the distant yipping of coyotes. There was a half moon that shed some light as they rode, and Wade looked back often to see if Sandrine was all right. She followed him along the ridge without talking. When they dropped down from the ridge to the main road, Wade pulled up slightly, waiting for Sandrine to catch up with him. He liked having her close to him.

"That was a nice thing you did for Jim and Rose," Sandrine said, and her soft voice almost startled him.

"I'm just glad you told me they were in trouble."

"You never hesitated to help them."

"Why would I?"

"A few weeks ago, I'm not sure you would've cared enough to help them. I think you're changing, Wade, as much as you might not want to believe it."

Wade considered what Sandrine had said, and he knew that she was right. Immediately after the accident, he didn't care about anything or anyone. He didn't care what he did or who he hurt. He was plain scared. "It never felt quite right, you know."

"What didn't?"

"The gambling and the drinking. I'm not saying I've never done it before—I probably have. It's just that . . . I don't know, I didn't feel comfortable acting like Frank."

"You're not like Frank, that's why. Can I ask you something, Wade?"

"Sure."

"Are you in love with Emily?"

Her voice was steady, but he could hear her effort to control her emotion. "What do you think?"

"I asked you."

"I don't love Emily. Hell, I don't even know why I got involved with her in the first place."

"Because she was here after the accident, and I wasn't."

"Maybe, or maybe I was just so scared . . ." Wade shrugged. He didn't know what to say. How could he explain to Sandrine that he had made love to another woman simply because he needed to feel alive. He looked over at Sandrine in the moonlight, wondering what it had been like to make love to her. He felt a sudden ache in his stomach when he thought of her with

Lone Wind. Did she feel the same kind of pain when she thought about him being with Emily?

"You don't have to ride with me all the way," Sandrine said, reining in at the edge of town. "I'll be fine from here."

"This time of night, who knows what kind of people are out walking the streets. I won't let you go alone."

"I'm not a little girl, Wade. I can take care of myself."

"Yes, I noticed that today with Emily."

Sandrine urged her horse into a walk. "I'm sorry I did that."

"She deserved it. She was being cruel."

"She just doesn't understand, that's all. Women like Emily have been sheltered all of their lives."

"Women like Emily have been spoiled and pampered all of their lives. If she had endured what you had, she wouldn't have made it."

"You don't know that. Some people prove their strength only when they need to."

"Why are you suddenly defending her?"

"Because I feel sorry for her. She's desperately in love with you."

"I didn't mean for that to happen," Wade said defensively.

"But it has, Wade. You need to talk to her."

"I have talked to her, and she won't listen. No matter what I say, she keeps telling me she loves me. I don't know what to do."

"Maybe you should go away for awhile."

"I'm not going to let a woman chase me away."

"Stop acting like a little boy, Wade. If you don't do something soon, Emily will do something."

"What do you mean?"

"She had a frantic look tonight. Didn't you see it?"

Wade nodded slightly, remembering the strange look in Emily's eyes. "I guess you're right. I'll talk to her when I get home tonight." Before he realized it, they had reached the stables. Wade hitched his horse out in front and took Sandrine's inside. He took her arm and walked her down the street, past the general store, the millinery, and the boardinghouse. When they reached the Half Moon, Sandrine stopped.

"You don't have to walk me any farther. I'm fine."

"I'd just as soon make sure you're up the stairs and safe, if you don't mind."

"Suit yourself," Sandrine said, picking her skirt up as she stepped down from the sidewalk and walked to the dirt alley. Wade followed her into the shadows behind the restaurant. She went to the stairway that led to Sally's room, walked up two steps, and turned. "I'll be fine now. Thank you, Wade."

"My pleasure," Wade said, feeling like a boy. The rowdy laughter and raucous singing echoed from the saloon, and Wade smiled. "Sounds like they're having fun over there."

"They always have fun over there. Sometimes I wish they'd stop."

"Is it hard for you to get to sleep?"

"Sometimes." Sandrine looked down, obviously uncomfortable.

"Sandrine," Wade said her name softly, almost tenderly. When she looked up, he lightly touched her cheek. "I don't know what's happening here. I just know that I'm feeling something for you. It's not an old feeling, not something I remember, but it's real. I like being around you. You're honest and you're good. Maybe I need to be reminded what that's like."

"I don't think you need to be reminded," Sandrine said. She leaned toward Wade, and slowly, tentatively, she hugged him.

Wade felt the pressure of Sandrine's body against his, and he closed his eyes, enjoying the sheer pleasure of having her so close to him. He could feel her body trembling slightly. "You're cold," he said softly, looking at her in the dim light from Sally's window.

"No, I'm not cold."

Wade studied her face but was unable to read her expression.

He put his hand on her cheek, feeling the warmth of her skin, then he moved his fingers to her mouth and lightly touched her lips. "You could make a man lose his senses, Sandrine," he said, pressing his mouth to hers so that their lips barely touched. He wanted to take her into his arms and kiss her passionately, but he sensed she wasn't ready. Reluctantly he moved his mouth away. "Why don't you go on in now."

Hesitating, she nodded silently and went up the stairs and into Sally's room. Wade waited until she was inside, then he walked back to his horse. It wasn't until he had mounted up and ridden out of town that he realized he felt happy. Suddenly and without restraint, he whooped loudly, kicking his horse into a gallop. He felt like a young boy in love for the very first time. And to him, it was the first time.

Emily heard Wade as he walked to his room, and she waited. She had already decided she was going to his room. Wade was a passionate man, and she was sure she could arouse him. She had been so angry, she had actually thought about shooting him, but she knew she could never harm him. It would be easier to seduce him. She waited until she was sure he was in bed, and then she took off her robe. Dressed only in a thin satin nightgown, she walked down the hall. Quietly turning the doorknob, she tried to go into Wade's room, but she couldn't. She tried again, but the door wouldn't open; it was locked. She knocked lightly and put her mouth against it. "Wade, it's Emily. Please let me in." When there was no response, she knocked again. "I know you're in there, Wade. Let me in. I want to talk."

"Go to bed, Emily." Wade's voice sounded harsh and distant from inside the room.

Emily pounded on the door. "If you don't let me in, I'll scream," she said, her voice shrill. She leaned against the door, listening for any response from Wade. She almost fell forward when the door suddenly opened and Wade stood in the doorway. He reached out and grasped one of her arms tightly.

"What're you doing?" she asked.

"I'm taking you back to your room," he said, easily pulling her down the hall. He took her inside and pushed her on the bed. "I want you to stay in here. Don't come out again tonight. If you do, so help me, I'll tie you to the bed."

"No," Emily cried, jumping up and reaching for Wade's shirt. "Why are you doing this to me?"

Wade turned and took Emily's hands in his. "Listen to me, Emily. You have to stop this. I don't love you. I want you to go back to Jim and Rose's tomorrow. You don't belong here."

Emily wrapped her arms around Wade's waist, burying her head in his chest. "But you love me, I know you do."

"I care for you, but I don't love you. Why don't you just go home, back to Boston."

"How do you know where I belong? Maybe I belong right here, with you."

"No, you don't," Wade said, his voice hard. He took Emily's hands in a firm grip and held them in front of her. "I want you to leave here in the morning, Emily, and I don't want you to come back."

Emily tried to reach out to Wade, but he pushed her away. Before she could say anything, he left her room, slamming the door. She ran after him, trying to open his door, but it was locked. She pounded on it, yelling his name, until she finally gave up. She leaned against the door, sobbing. It wasn't fair. He had used her, and now he was throwing her away. It was just like before.

Emily straightened up and walked back to her room. She went to the window and opened it slightly, taking in a deep breath. She covered her mouth with her hand, trying to stifle her sobs. When she had regained her composure, she stood at the window, staring out at the darkness. She tasted her own blood as she bit her lip, staring motionless into the night. Finally she shook her head and went to her bed, sitting on the edge. How could this have happened to her again? She had come to New Mexico hoping that her life would be better, but it hadn't changed at all.

She lay down on the bed, staring up at the dark ceiling of her room. From the deepest part of her heart, she took out a secret, a secret that no one here knew. Wade wanted her to go back to Boston? She had had to leave because another man had used her, used her just like Wade had. She hadn't let him get away with it, and Wade wasn't going to get away with it either. But this time she would be more careful. No one would ever know that she had gotten even.

Wade stood at the door, knocking, waiting for a response.

"Who is it?"

"It's Wade. I want to talk to you, Frank."

There was silence and then footsteps as Frank opened the door. "What do you want, Wade?"

"Can I come in?"

"I don't know why I should let you."

"Quit it," Wade said, pushing past him as he walked into the room. Wade looked around him. It was the largest room in the hotel, and it was decorated like a brothel, with red brocade wallpaper, red velvet curtains, and crystal chandeliers. There was a small sofa against one wall, and Wade sat down on it, taking off his hat. "Well, I can't say much for the decor."

Frank shrugged his shoulders. "It's not bad if you like red."

Wade grinned. "I have a proposition for you, Frank."

"Oh, no, not another one of your propositions. I don't think so."

"Just listen to me." Wade leaned forward. "You can have your house back."

"What?" Frank stared at Wade a minute, then dragged a chair over in front of him. "I think you better say that again. I'm not sure I heard you right the first time."

"I said you can have your house back."

"Why? What's the catch?"

"I don't want it anymore. It's too big for me."

Frank shook his head. "That's too easy, Wade. There must be something more to it. How much do you want for it?"

"I think we can come to a fair price, but that's not all."

"That's what I figured."

"I want you to lend me some men to help me finish building my house. I want it done before fall."

"I don't get it, Wade. Just a couple months ago you were prepared to do almost anything for money. Why the big change?"

Wade shrugged. "I told you: the big house doesn't fit me. Besides, Walters makes me feel uncomfortable."

Frank smiled. "Nice touch, don't you think? How many people around here have English butlers?"

"How many people around here even have butlers, Frank? Jesus," Wade muttered.

"So what's the price?"

"Twenty thousand," Wade said.

"Twenty thousand! That's highway robbery."

"That's a fair price, and you know it."

"I have to pay you twenty thousand for my own house?"

"I saved your life. If someone else had found out you cheated at cards instead of me, you'd probably be dead by now. I want twenty thousand, some of your prime stock, and some men to help me build my house. That's it."

Frank drummed his fingers on the edge of the chair. "You ought to go into business, Wade. You're ruthless."

"I'm fair. I happen to know you're worth more than ten times that amount."

"And how would you know that?"

"You know Duncan McCrory can't keep his mouth shut once he's had a few drinks. I'm surprised he's been a banker this long."

Frank held up his hand. "All right, it's a deal. You can have the money, you can pick out your own stock, and I'll lend you all the hands you need. Just tell me the truth—why the sudden change of heart?"

"I told you. Your house is too big for me. I don't feel comfortable there."

"It's Sandrine, isn't it? She's gotten to you." Frank smiled. "I knew it was only a matter of time. I told you she was beautiful, didn't I? And those eyes . . ." Frank shook his head and whistled. "If only you had a memory, you could tell me a thing or two about what it's like to make love to a woman like that."

"There's no reason for you to be thinking about Sandrine that way," Wade said angrily. He stood up and put on his hat.

"Oh, you got it bad, boy," Frank said, laughing.

"I want the money today," Wade said impatiently. "I'm not going back to the house. I've already moved my things out."

Frank stood up and offered his hand to Wade. "We can go to the bank right now and get the money. When do you want the men?"

"I'll let you know." Wade walked to the door. "I'll be waiting for you at the bank." When he closed the door behind him, Wade could hear Frank's laughter. He shook his head, wondering himself just what the hell he was doing.

Sandrine stood by the kitchen window, absent-mindedly wiping her hands on her apron. It had been two days since she'd seen Wade, but she couldn't stop thinking about him or the way he had kissed her.

"Sandrine, are you listening to me?"

Sandrine jerked around when she heard Sally's voice. "I'm sorry. Just daydreaming."

"So I've noticed. Why don't you take the rest of the day off. You're of no use to me this way."

"No, I'll be fine, Sally. I'm sorry."

"Don't be sorry," Sally said, her voice softening. "Why don't you go see him."

"Who?"

"Don't play coy, Sandrine; it doesn't become you. I know you're thinking about Wade. Go see him."

"I don't think so," Sandrine said, shaking her head. "I don't want him to think—"

"What? You don't want him to think you're in love with him? Lordsakes, woman, you are in love with him. You're his wife."

"I know, but—"

Sally put her hands on Sandrine's shoulders. "Be with him, Sandrine. I've seen the way he looks at you. The man is crazy in love with you, he just doesn't know it yet. You need to give him a little nudge."

Sandrine grinned. "I like you, Sally. I wish I was more like you."

"No, you don't. You're fine just the way you are." Sally untied Sandrine's apron and gave her a gentle shove. "Now git."

Sandrine didn't even change. She went straight to the stables and had her horse saddled, then she rode out of town. When she reached the road that led to Frank's house, she reined in. Maybe she shouldn't have listened to Sally. She wasn't really sure how Wade felt about her, and she didn't want to throw herself at him the way Emily had. What she really needed was to be alone in a place where she could think. She turned her horse and headed back up the road, hoping that Wade hadn't seen her. She knew where she wanted to go.

As she rode, Sandrine thought about what her life might be like with Wade. It wouldn't be the same, she knew that. He

BRIGHT STAR'S PROMISE 241

wasn't the same man. Tears stung her eyes as she thought of Lone Wind's words: "Live your life, Bright Star, and love fully. Love with all that is inside of you." She nodded slightly, wondering if she would ever love and be loved again.

She reined in as she reached the ridge, letting her horse find its way down the trail. She barely glanced at the big house as she continued down into the valley to the cabin where she and Wade had lived together. She rode into the pasture and unsaddled the horse, letting him graze. She picked up her saddle, her water bag, and the rest of the tack, and headed toward the house. She set the saddle on the small wooden porch and sat down on one of the two chairs that Wade had built for them. She took a drink from the water bag and stretched out her legs, pulling up her skirts. Impulsively she untied her boots and slipped them off, along with her stockings. She wriggled her bare toes in the sun. She looked around, even though she knew no one else was there. Then she unbuttoned her blouse and draped it over the empty chair. She sat in her camisole, with her skirt pulled up to her thighs, and leaned her head back against the chair. She closed her eyes, enjoying the peace and quiet, and the feel of the sunshine on her skin. She glanced at the cabin door. She didn't want to go in yet: there were too many memories behind that door.

She closed her eyes again, trying not to think. The sun was hot on her bare skin, and she could feel the tension and strain she'd felt for so long seeping from her. She let her thoughts drift, let random images float through her mind. Scenes from the Blackfoot camp were superseded by intense memories of her father's trading post. She could see the blue glass beads that her mother treasured, and she could almost smell the imported perfumes that brought tears to the eyes of the trail-weary women on the wagon trains. Then, unbidden, came an image of Lone Wind's face, so vivid, so real that she opened her eyes to let the sunlight erase it. After a moment she closed them again, but this time she let the memories flow freely. The sunlight pressed against her eyelids, and she let herself relax completely, not fighting the drowsiness that overcame her.

She did not know how much time had passed when she became aware that she wasn't alone. She knew, before she opened her eyes, that someone was looking at her, that someone was close. Instinctively she tensed, then opened her eyes. There was no danger. At least not the kind she'd expected. Wade was leaning against the railing, and the expression on his face made her catch her breath and tumble back into time. If only she had never left, if only he had never gotten hurt. He would be sweeping her up into his arms and carrying her inside now. Sandrine pushed her hair back from her face, furious with herself. This wasn't the past, this was a stranger staring at her, his lips curving into a smile. Quickly she pulled down her skirt. He was grinning now.

"Don't hurry on my account."

Suddenly angry, Sandrine snatched her blouse off the chair and turned her back on him. She managed the buttons with trembling fingers, then whirled around to face Wade. "How dare you just stand there and look at me like that."

"How should I look at you?"

She stood. Involuntarily she combed her fingers through her loose hair, then realized what she was doing. Confused and angry, she stomped her foot, bruising her toes on the rough planking. Embarrassed, she felt her face burn, and she tried to meet his eyes. "What are you doing here?"

"I own the place, remember? I think maybe you're the trespasser." Wade took off his hat and rubbed his forehead with his forearm, quickly replacing the hat. "I thought you weren't interested in this place."

"I'm not. I just came out here because . . ." Sandrine shrugged. "Because it's quiet and peaceful."

"You could be here all the time, you know."

BRIGHT STAR'S PROMISE

"I told you before: I don't want anything from you."

"I wouldn't be giving it to you. I propose we strike a deal."

"What kind of deal?" Sandrine asked, narrowing her eyes.

Wade walked forward, and Sandrine stiffened. She backed up slightly, watching him. He leaned down and picked up her water bag. He held it to his lips and drank. Some of the water dripped down his chin and onto his chest. She couldn't keep from staring at him, even as he finished drinking and dragged the back of his hand across his mouth.

"You know I'm going to finish the big house."

"Yes, but I still don't understand why."

Wade turned and looked up the valley toward the rise where the beginnings of the house stood. "I like it here. I'm glad I was smart enough to pick a place like this."

Sandrine followed his gaze. "It is beautiful up there."

Wade looked at Sandrine. "So, you interested in hearing my deal?"

"I don't know."

Wade looked around them. "You busy or something?"

"All right, I'll listen."

"Why don't we go in and get out of this sun." Wade started toward the door.

"No, I like it out here. It's not that hot."

"Suit yourself," Wade said, brushing past Sandrine as he walked to the door and opened it.

Sandrine hesitated as she heard Wade's footsteps from inside. She watched as he pulled the curtains aside.

"It's pretty dusty in here," he yelled.

Sandrine took in a deep breath, knowing she wasn't ready to confront the memories that they had had together. She stood stubbornly on the porch, her arms wrapped around herself.

"You coming in or not?" Wade asked from behind her.

"I don't know," she said, her voice quavering. She heard Wade's footsteps behind her, and she refused to look at him.

"What's wrong, Sandrine?"

"Nothing is wrong." She felt his hands on her shoulders, turning her to face him.

"Talk to me."

"Why should I talk to you, Wade? Give me one good reason."

"Because I care about you."

Sandrine looked into his eyes, but she couldn't see anything there. She turned away from him and stepped off the porch, staring up at the house on the hill. She should never have come out here. She should've known better.

"I'm not a complete fool, you know."

She heard the sincerity in Wade's voice, and she turned to look at him as he stepped off the porch beside her. "What do you mean?"

"I know this was our home. I know we shared things here, the most intimate things a man and woman can share."

Sandrine looked away, feeling her cheeks burn. She didn't want to be reminded of what they had shared together, least of all by him. "You don't have any idea of what we shared here, Wade," she said, her voice hard.

"I know what people tell me, Sandrine, and all our friends have told me that we loved each other very much."

Sandrine turned, trying to conceal the depth of her emotions. "Yes, we did love each other. But that's over now. There's nothing left. So why don't you just leave me alone?" Sandrine reached for the bracelet, feeling the smooth, cool metal under her fingertips.

"No matter how many times you touch that thing, you won't bring him back, you know."

Sandrine's eyes burned, but she refused to cry. "You're a hateful person."

"I didn't mean to be. I was just stating a fact. He's gone and I'm here."

"And that's supposed to comfort me?" Sandrine wrapped her fingers around the bracelet. "He'll always be with me. Always."

"I'm sorry, I didn't mean to insult you in any way." He moved closer, reaching out to touch her, but Sandrine stepped backward.

"Don't."

"Look, can't we just talk? Inside."

"Why do we have to talk in there?"

"Because it's hot out here. Jesus, Sandrine, you act like I'm going to carry you into the bedroom and have my way with you or something."

In spite of her anger, Sandrine could barely suppress a smile. It seemed like such an irony that her own husband would say such a thing. She nodded slowly. "All right," she said, stepping up onto the porch and going into the small house. She hadn't been inside since the first day she'd gotten back—it held far too many memories for her. She looked around. The house was dusty, and it smelled of old air and fire coals. She looked up at the beautiful red and blue blanket her mother had made for them. She walked to the wall, running her fingers over the woven cloth.

"Did your people make it?" Wade asked.

"My mother made it for us. It was a wedding gift," she said, her voice strained. She felt him behind her.

"The colors are incredible," he said, his voice filled with emotion.

Sandrine turned to look at him as he studied the blanket. He looked like a young boy, his long blond hair hanging to his collar, his eyes bright and full of curiosity.

"What is this?" he asked, pointing to two men on horses.

"This one is you," Sandrine said, pointing to one figure, "and this one is my cousin, Little Bear. This is when you two were searching for me."

"And this is you?" Wade pointed to a small figure being held by a larger figure.

"Yes, that is my father holding me up to the heavens when I was born. My father named me Sandrine, but my grandfather named me Bright Star because he said that the stars shined more brightly on the night that I was born."

"Bright Star," Wade repeated. "It fits you." He pointed to the bottom of the blanket. "What about these figures? Who are they?"

Sandrine hesitated a moment, trying to maintain her composure. "They are you and I as we entered our life together."

Wade nodded as if contemplating what she had just said, then he pointed to the left side of the blanket. "Why is this blank?"

Sandrine looked down, feeling embarrassed. "It means nothing."

"There must be some significance to it. Please, tell me."

Sandrine nodded slightly, trying to keep her emotions in check. "It is for the children we were going to have. My mother was going to fill in the space when they were born." Abruptly she turned away and walked to the sideboard, taking out a cloth and dusting the table and chairs as she had done so many times before. Then she sat down, suddenly irritated by all of Wade's questions and the way he was looking at everything in the cabin. "You wanted to talk, let's talk."

"All right," he said, walking to the table and sitting down. "I'm going to finish the house up there before autumn. I'll live here while I'm building, but I'm going to need someone to cook for me, someone who will—"

"No!" Sandrine said angrily, standing up and pounding her hands on the table. "I can't believe you'd even ask something like that of me."

"What? I was going to offer you a job. I need someone to cook and clean for me. You can have the bedroom, and I'll sleep on the couch. As soon as the house up there is walled in, I'll move in there. Then you can have this place. You will have earned it." Wade shook his head. "Look, Sandrine, I know I haven't exactly been the same man you used to know, but I would never ask you to do what you were thinking. Even though we're still married, I know that we're like strangers."

"I'm sorry," Sandrine said, slowly sitting back down. "I don't know what I was thinking."

"It's all right; I probably deserved it. I didn't make myself too clear."

"You'd give me this place just for cooking and cleaning for you?"

"It's already yours, but you won't take it. For some reason, you need to feel like you've earned it. So there'd probably be some laundry duties, too."

Sandrine smiled slightly. "Anything else I need to know?"

"I'm picking out some stock, and I'll probably need some help with them, and I wouldn't mind getting a garden started up there. Now, if that all seems like too much, we can—"

"No, it seems just fine," Sandrine said, surprised that she hadn't even hesitated. As much as she liked Sally, she had quickly grown tired of living in town, and she relished the chance to live here again. "Are you sure you're going to want me for a neighbor once you've moved in up there? You might change your mind."

"I don't think so. I can't imagine a better neighbor for a man than his own wife."

Sandrine laughed this time. "What happens if you get another wife?"

"I don't think that will be happening," Wade said, his voice serious. "I like the one I have now just fine."

Sandrine looked away, unable to resist the look of boyish charm in Wade's gray eyes. "Well, when do we move in?"

"I'll be moving some of my things back in here today. If you could move in sometime in the next few days—"

"I'll be here tomorrow."

"Sally will be sorry to lose you."

"Sally is a big girl. She'll be fine without me." Sandrine

folded her hands together in front of her, nervously touching her thumbs together. "One more thing, Wade. You sleep in the bed. I'll sleep on the couch."

"No, I couldn't let you do that."

"Please, it would be easier for me, at least right now."

Wade nodded. "All right, if that's what you want." Sandrine stood up. "I'd better go round up my horse and get him saddled," she said, trying to sound nonchalant. She walked outside and bent down to pick up her saddle, but before she could get very far, Wade had taken it from her.

"Where is he?"

"In the pasture over there," she said, pointing. She walked alongside Wade. She still couldn't believe that she had agreed to live in the same house with him. She closed her eyes for a brief moment, unable to believe her own stupidity. Just what had she gotten herself into?

When they reached the pasture, Sandrine slipped the bridle over her horse's head and led him to Wade. She watched while Wade saddled him, and she took a drink from her bag. She looked up on the ridge and shielded her eyes. "Wade, there's someone up there."

Wade finished cinching the saddle and looked up the hill. "It looks like Jim's horse."

Sandrine followed Wade as he led her horse to the house, and they waited for Jim to come down the hill. As soon as Jim reined in, Sandrine knew that something was wrong.

"What're you doing out here, Jim?" Wade asked.

Jim looked at them both and shook his head, his voice breaking as he spoke. "Danny's been kidnapped."

Eleven

"Come into the cabin," Wade said, glancing back at Sandrine as he guided Jim inside. He pulled out a chair for him and told him to sit down. "Now tell me what happened."

Jim shook his head. "I don't know. Emily took Danny into town early this morning. He'd been looking forward to it. Some kind of traveling carnival or something. Anyway, a couple of hours ago, a kid rides up to the ranch and hands Rose a letter. He said it was given to him by a man, and he was paid to bring it to either me or Rose. The letter said that Danny and Emily had been kidnapped."

"That's all it said?" Sandrine asked, glancing at Wade.

"It said if we kept our mouths shut and cooperated, Danny and Emily wouldn't get hurt."

"What about a ransom?"

"Didn't ask for one."

"Strange," Wade muttered, "that the kidnappers didn't ask for something, don't you think?"

"I know, I can't figure it out myself." Jim looked at Sandrine. "Will you come and stay with us for a few days, Sandrine? Rose is all upset. I don't want her staying alone if I'm off trying to find Danny."

"I'd be glad to, Jim."

"How's Emily been the last few days?" Wade asked suddenly.

"Emily?" Jim shrugged. "She's been fine, I guess. Haven't paid much attention. Why?"

"Just wondered."

"You never just wonder anything," Jim said. "What is it, Wade?"

"Emily was real upset when I sent her back to your place. She said I'd regret hurting her."

"Emily may have done some stupid things, but she'd never be involved in anything like this. Besides, the note said she's been kidnapped, too."

"Sorry, it was just a thought."

"Do you know for sure that they went into town?" Sandrine asked.

Jim looked at her. "No, I just assumed that they had."

"But maybe they didn't. Maybe they never made it," Wade agreed, looking at Sandrine. "It's easy enough to check. Lots of people know Danny."

"What if they didn't?"

"Then we can assume they're somewhere in the country. Someplace well-hidden."

"I don't even know where to begin," Jim said, his voice sounding weary.

"Why don't I start looking and you go back to the ranch with Sandrine. Rose needs you there." Wade stood up.

"You don't know where to start looking anymore than I do," Jim said angrily, standing up next to him.

Sandrine walked to Jim, hooking her arm through his. "Please, Jim, come back to the ranch. Let's check on Rose. You can always meet Wade later."

Jim nodded silently, letting Sandrine lead him outside.

Wade followed, shutting the door behind them. "I have to go round up my horse. You two go on."

"I've already checked the wagon tracks leading into town," Jim said. "Couldn't find any that veered off the trail."

"Where was the wagon?"

"Wasn't found."

"Then there should be tracks somewhere. Whoever took Danny and Emily took the wagon." Wade waited until Sandrine and Jim were mounted and on their way, then he walked to the pasture to get his horse. He had a gut feeling that Emily was somehow involved and this was her way of paying him back.

Emily made sure Danny was asleep, then she closed and locked the door and went back into the next room. She sat down in a chair, trying to read the newspaper, but put it down, unable to concentrate. They'd probably gotten the letter by now, and she knew they'd be worried sick. It wouldn't be long before Wade found out about it, and then she would send the next letter. She looked up when she heard footsteps outside the house. When the door opened, she smiled.

"You all right?"

"I'm fine," she said, standing up. "You're sure no one knows about this place?"

"No one knows." The man shut the door behind him.

"Are you sure you haven't told Sally about it? I wouldn't want her to suddenly remember that you have a little cabin that you go to sometimes."

"The only person who knows about this place is Walters, and he wouldn't talk if someone put a gun to his head."

"Thank you, Frank," Emily said, putting her arms around him. "I don't know what I would've done without you."

"Is the boy all right?"

"Yes, he's sleeping."

"I told you I'd help you, Emily, but you never really explained why you're doing this. Is the kid in trouble?"

"My uncle is not the person you think he is," Emily said, taking Frank's hand and leading him to the sofa. She sat, pulling him down next to her.

"What about Rose?"

"What about Rose?" Emily asked impatiently.

"Does Jim mistreat her, too?"

Emily hesitated, then nodded. "Sometimes he beats her terribly, and right now he's worried about money, so things are worse. I just didn't think it was a good idea for Danny to be there." She leaned close to Frank, kissing him lightly. "I don't want to talk anymore, Frank."

"Come on, Emily, there are some things I need to know."

"I'll tell you everything you want to know later," she said, lying back and pulling her skirts up high. She saw the look on Frank's face, and she smiled as he quickly pulled her underwear down. She felt his hands on her bare thighs, and she closed her eyes. She wasn't particularly attracted to Frank, but he was going to be very useful to her. She would just pretend it was Wade who was making love to her.

Frank kissed her passionately, and she kissed him back, letting him believe that she desired him. She felt him move on top of her, and she felt his hands on her thighs, moving them apart. Then she felt him push himself into her with a slight grunt, and she moaned deeply, letting him believe that she was enjoying it. As Frank drove himself into her, Emily thought of Wade and of how she was going to pay him back. Then she thought of Sandrine. She couldn't wait to see the look of fear on her face before she died.

As Frank moved faster and faster, Emily realized the power she had over him. With his help, she would be able to do anything she wanted to Sandrine. Without realizing it, she moaned softly, and it was too much for Frank. He cried out, grabbing onto her. Emily lay motionless as he finished, then she pulled her skirts down to cover herself.

"You're wonderful," he said, brushing her cheek with his fingers.

Emily opened her eyes, smiling sweetly. "Thank you, Frank. I . . . I don't know what to say. I've never experienced anything like that before," she said, blushing. "I'm sure you find it much more exciting with an experienced woman like Sally."

"There's nothing quite like innocence," Frank murmured, nibbling Emily's ear.

Emily endured it for a few seconds, then turned her head away. "You should probably be going, Frank. I don't want Danny to wake up and see you here. Did you bring all of the supplies?"

"I brought them."

"Good," Emily said, sitting up. "I don't know how I'll ever thank you for this, Frank." She put her arms around his neck and kissed him again.

"I don't need any payment, Emily." Frank put his arms around her, holding her tightly. "You should hear Sally talk about you," he said, smiling.

"What does she say?"

"She says you're as stiff and rigid as a shirt that's just come back starched from the laundry."

"Well, obviously Sally doesn't know me very well," Emily said, playfully biting Frank's lower lip. "Women tend to be jealous of me. Even poor Sandrine. She's so afraid I'm going to take Wade away from her."

"I don't think Sandrine needs to worry about that," Frank said.

Emily bristled slightly, lowering her arms. "What do you mean?"

"Wade is crazy about her, always has been, and she knows it. All she has to do is say she's ready, and Wade will go back to her in a second."

"Really?" Emily said. "That's not what he told me."

"And just what did he tell you?"

"It doesn't matter." Emily straightened her hair and smoothed her skirts.

"Don't play coy with me, Emily. What did Wade say?"

"He said as soon as he gets Sandrine into bed, he's going to leave her. He said he doesn't feel any kind of love for her."

"I don't know—"

"I'm just repeating what Wade said. He thinks she's a challenge, that's all. Once he beds her, he'll be through with her. He doesn't want to be tied down to any woman, he said. But I could be wrong. You know him better than I do."

"Fact is, I don't know him at all. Thought I did, but . . ." Frank shook his head.

"I can't help but feel sorry for Sandrine. Wade is going to make her think he cares for her, then he'll use her and leave her. I wouldn't be surprised if she just up and went back to her own people."

"I didn't know you cared so much about Sandrine. From what Sally told me—"

Emily put her fingers on Frank's mouth. "Are you going to believe everything that Sally tells you?" She leaned forward and kissed him again, this time running her hand up his inner thigh. "It's wonderful with you, Frank," she whispered, brushing her lips against his. "Make love to me again."

"But what about Danny?"

"He's still asleep," Emily said, lying back down on the couch, her skirts raised, her body ready. She could see the look of desire in Frank's face as he buried his face in her breasts, and she smiled. She could make him do anything she wanted. And she would.

Wade had ridden into town and talked to several people. All of them, including Sally, had seen Emily and Danny together. Even Sally said Danny had looked like he was having a good time. So, Wade had to admit to himself, he'd been wrong about Emily. Now he had to find out who would want to kidnap her and Danny and why.

He had checked all over town for the wagon, but no one had seen Danny and Emily leave. When he was finished in town, he rode west, the opposite direction from the Everett ranch. There were hundreds of tracks leading into and out of town—shod and unshod horses, wagons, and the stagecoach. It was hard to get a clear read on any of them, but Wade was looking for something specific. One of the wheels on Jim's wagon had a deep groove in it, and it was easy to spot. He remembered it from all of the rides that Rose had taken him on when he was recovering from the accident.

Wade rode for the better part of the day, following wagon tracks that looked similar to Jim's. He had made a complete circle and was starting back toward town when he spotted another set of wagon tracks, ones that left the trail. He dismounted and examined them, nodding slowly. This was Jim's wagon, all right. No doubt about it. He swung back onto his horse and followed the ruts. They headed southwest, away from town and away from Jim's. Whoever was driving the wagon was not attempting to cover the tracks, because they were too easy to follow.

Wade kicked his horse into a canter, determined to gain ground on the wagon. He had ridden for over an hour when he saw it in the distance, under an oak tree. He reined in and dismounted. The horses were gone, and so were Emily and Danny. He looked inside the wagon. There was nothing, not even a piece of clothing. He walked around. There weren't even any footprints, but he could see where someone had dragged a bundle of brush to obliterate any tracks. Whoever was driving the wagon was smart enough to know that there was no way to conceal or disguise the wagon tracks, so they hadn't even taken the time to try. But from now on, things would be different. He walked in a slow spiral outward from the wagon, but the ground was rocky and he couldn't spot so much as an impression of a boot heel. Finally when he felt as if he'd looked over every inch of ground, he found the first hoofprint.

Wade squatted down, running his hands over the curved impressions of the shod horse. He shook his head. He stood up and followed the tracks by foot for some distance. He squatted down and examined the ground closely, nodding his head. There were two horses. He walked back to his horse and mounted up. He followed the tracks until they disappeared into a pasture. The grass was so deep he couldn't see anything. He searched for signs that it had been pressed down by horse's hooves, but he didn't see any. He crossed the pasture, but when he came out on the other side, there were no tracks. It was as if the horses had just disappeared in the tall grass. Whoever had taken Danny and Emily was good. Wade lifted his hat, then reset it on his head.

He kicked his horse into a canter, then almost immediately reined the animal in again, chiding himself. Impatience was his worst enemy. Forcing himself to concentrate, he began the slow process of circling the pasture, widening his path slightly each time around. The circle was nearly a mile wide when he finally picked up the tracks again, close to a small stream.

He sat on his horse, looking upstream. The tracks appeared to cross the water and lead on westward, but why, after all the trouble to conceal their tracks, would the riders now forget their caution? Thoughtfully Wade urged his horse into the shallow water and turned him upstream.

Before long he nodded to himself, sure that he'd done the right thing. There was a small cabin set back under the trees. He rode in a wide arc, coming around toward the back of the cabin. He dismounted and tied his horse to a tree. Then slowly he started toward the cabin, his revolver drawn. There was no window in the back, so he made his way forward as silently as he could, pressing himself against the rough wood. He waited patiently, listening for Danny or Emily, but there was only silence. He moved his way around the side of the cabin and carefully made his way onto the porch. Again he listened for voices, but still he heard nothing. Standing next to the door, gun drawn, he kicked it open and rushed inside, every muscle in his body tense, waiting for the sound of gunfire. But the cabin was empty, and it looked as if no one had been here for years. Wade walked around, searching for any sign that Danny or Emily might have been here, but he couldn't find anything. Filled with anger and frustration, he kicked one of the rotted planks and went outside, knowing that he was going to have to begin his search again.

Sandrine opened her eyes. She had been sleeping on the couch, waiting for Wade to get back. When she heard the horse whinny outside in the yard, she stood up and went to the door. Wade was standing there, looking exhausted. He was alone. He walked to the table and pulled out a chair, stretching his legs out in front of him. Sandrine went to the cookstove and poured him a cup of coffee, setting it down on the table.

He looked up and nodded, holding the cup between his large hands. "I thought I'd found them," he said, his voice low.

"You did the best you could," Sandrine said, trying to reassure him.

"That's not good enough right now. I keep thinking about how scared Danny must be . . ." Wade shook his head.

"If you didn't find them, no one could have," Sandrine said quickly.

Wade shrugged. "I don't know how good I am. It's one of those things like riding or playing cards. I think I remember everything I ever knew, but maybe I don't." He shook his head again. "Three separate times I found the tracks and then watched them disappear into thin air. God . . ."

"I trust you, Wade. I know you did the best that you could."

Sandrine lowered her voice and sat down at the table. "Another letter came while you were gone."

"What'd it say?"

"It said Danny was fine and he would remain that way if their demand was met."

"What was it, money?"

"No," Sandrine said, looking down.

"What is it, Sandrine?"

Slowly she met Wade's eyes. "Me. Whoever it is wants me in exchange for Danny."

"What? But that's crazy. Who would want you so badly that they'd . . ." Wade stopped, looking at Sandrine. "Jesus, it must be Emily. She's the only person who hates you enough to do something like this."

"It doesn't matter how much she hates me. If she has Danny, she's capable of hurting him. We have to do what she asks."

"No!" Wade said angrily, slamming his cup down on the table. "I won't allow you to be alone with her. There's no telling what she'll do."

Sandrine looked at Wade, and for the first time since she'd come back, saw concern in his eyes. "I have to go, Wade. We don't have a choice. She might hurt Danny."

Wade leaned across the table, taking Sandrine's hand. "And what about you? We're just starting to get close again, Sandrine."

Sandrine felt the pressure of Wade's hand on hers, and she met his eyes. "I'll be all right. I'm not afraid of Emily."

"No," Wade said, shaking his head.

Sandrine looked up when she heard the bedroom door open and Jim walked out. She touched his arm as he walked to the table.

"Thought I heard voices," he said wearily and sat down. "Did you find anything?"

BRIGHT STAR'S PROMISE 259

"Thought I did. I followed some tracks to an old cabin, but it was abandoned. I'll ride back out again tomorrow."

"Did Sandrine tell you about the other letter we got?"

Wade nodded, glancing at Sandrine. "The kidnappers aren't wasting much time, are they?"

"You need to find those tracks tomorrow, Wade, because I'm not going to let Sandrine take Danny's place."

"Neither am I," Wade agreed. "How much time do we have?"

"Until two hours after sunup. Sandrine is supposed to be by herself at Mill's Pond. They said if they see anyone else but her, Danny will get hurt."

Sandrine cleared her throat. "I have to go. You'll never find the tracks in time, Wade."

"I'll find them."

"You can't do this to Rose," Sandrine said, looking from Wade to Jim. "She's in enough pain. This is her one chance to get Danny back."

"No," Wade said again. "We don't even know the kidnappers will keep their word."

"You don't have a choice," Sandrine said emphatically.

Wade put his hand on her arm. "Just forget it. I won't allow you to do something that foolish."

Sandrine took a deep breath and held it for an instant before she let it out. Wade had changed so much, but he was still as stubborn as he used to be. She knew there was no point in arguing with him, so she didn't even try. She pushed her chair back from the table and stood up, smoothing her skirt. "I'm exhausted. I'm going to go lie down for a little while. When you figure out what you're going to do, let me know." Sandrine turned away from the table and took a few steps toward the couch, then turned back to face the two men. "Would you mind if I use Emily's room, Jim?"

"Of course not, Sandrine. Sleep well now."

Sandrine murmured good night and walked across the living

room and into the bedroom. She closed the door to Emily's room tightly and turned toward the window. Pushing the window sash upward, she took a deep breath of the cool night air. Refusing to feel anything but her resolve to help Danny, she lifted her skirt and swung her leg up over the sill. A moment later, she was outside, running across the yard. It was only a few minutes until her horse was saddled. Leading the animal slowly away from the house, she held her breath, expecting that at any moment the door would bang open and Jim and Wade would see her. But they didn't, and when she was sure that she was out of earshot, she swung up onto her horse and rode off alone into the darkness.

Sally fixed a knowing gaze on Frank's face. There was either something on his mind, or he'd found another woman. They had been up in his room for almost an hour, dawn was breaking, and he hadn't even tried to make love to her. She was starting to wonder why he'd even asked her to come at all. She watched him as he looked past her out the window. She'd known Frank for years, and for most of that time she'd hated him—until the last year or so. Now they were lovers, but she still wasn't sure she completely trusted him. She knew he was a notorious gambler and womanizer. That part didn't bother her. If he had found someone else, she'd know about it soon enough. It wasn't going to break her heart. But she'd rather not lose Frank, as a friend or a lover. She'd come to like and even respect him.

Sally waited quietly until Frank finally looked at her again. He didn't attempt to speak, and she couldn't read anything in his eyes. She'd be damned if she'd act like an insecure young girl and ask him if he'd found someone else. She stood up and walked to the table by the door, picking up her shawl.

"What're you doing?" Frank asked suddenly.

"I think I'd better go. You don't seem much in the mood for company."

Frank shrugged. "Just tired I guess."

"Yes, you seem plumb worn out." Sally tried to keep the sarcasm from her voice. She drew her shawl around her shoulders. "I'll see you tomorrow, Frank."

"Don't go, Sal."

Sally looked at him. "If you want me to stay and watch you stare out that damned window, Frank, I've got better things to do."

"I'm sorry." Frank extended his hand. "Please come over here."

Sally sighed, walking slowly toward Frank. She did have trouble resisting him. In spite of his faults, he was an absolutely charming man. She took his hand. "Just what do you want from me, Frank?"

"The same thing I always want from you," Frank said, pulling Sally down into his lap. He wrapped his arms around her waist and kissed her. "You're a good-looking woman, you know that?"

"On my better days," Sally said with a half-smile. She ran her fingers through Frank's hair when he laid his head on her breasts. She felt his arms tighten around her waist. "What is it, Frank? What's wrong?"

He looked up, gently kissing the hollow of Sally's throat. "You know you've come to mean a lot to me, Sal."

"Are you getting sentimental on me, Frank?"

"I was thinking of asking you to move into my house with me."

Sally raised an eyebrow. She knew how much Frank's house meant to him. As soon as Wade had decided to give it up, Frank had run to the restaurant and told her, lifting her up in front of her customers and twirling her around. She smiled at the memory. She couldn't believe Frank was asking her to move in there with him. "I think things are pretty good the way they are, don't you?"

"They could be better. We could be together all the time."

Frank's voice had a strange sound to it, almost a desperate quality. "Has something happened to upset you, Frank?"

"No, I've just been doing a lot of thinking about us, that's all." He sat up straighter in the chair.

"Is there another woman?" Sally's voice was calm, almost emotionless. When Frank looked at her and then quickly looked away, she knew that she had been right. Slowly she stood up and walked to the chair on the other side of the small table, sitting down and folding her hands in her lap. "I think we better talk honestly, Frank."

"Sally, there's no one else."

"Then why don't you look at me when you say that?" she asked. When Frank did look at her, she held his eyes. "I'm real grown-up, Frank. I've lived life, remember. You didn't make any promises to me. The only thing I'm asking of you right now is a little bit of honesty."

"I am being honest: there's no other woman."

"There's always another woman with you, Frank. You would've slept with Sandrine and Rose if you could've." She reached across the table and took his hand. "I know about your other women. I'm not stupid. I can't even say I ever really minded about them because I know how you feel about me."

"You're special to me, Sal," Frank said, leaning forward and reaching for one of Sally's hands. He brought it to his mouth. "You've brought a lot of happiness to my life this last year. And those other women, they never meant anything to me."

"Then what is it, Frank? Talk to me."

Frank rubbed his face with his hands. "Well, I guess you know that I've been involved in a few shady things in my time."

Sally nodded, waiting.

Frank leaned back in the chair, looking up at the ceiling. "This time I may be in over my head."

"Tell me about it."

Frank nodded wearily. "I think I've been taken."

"Wade again?"

Frank shook his head. "You're not going to like it."

Sally searched his face and waited again. If he wanted to tell her, he would.

"I feel like a fool kid, like I've been duped."

Sally allowed herself a small smile. "You? Who's smart enough to take advantage of you? I thought you learned your lesson with Wade."

Frank avoided her eyes. "This is different."

Sally nodded slowly, understanding. "A woman?"

Frank nodded. "Yes."

"Anybody I know?"

"You know her and you don't like her much."

Sally held her breath. "Emily," she said slowly.

Frank nodded again.

"What have you gotten yourself into, Frank Lauter?"

He shook his head. "I'm not quite sure."

Then as Frank began to speak, Sally held herself still, her disbelief growing as she listened. She forced herself to keep from smiling when Frank said how Emily had talked him into helping her. Sally knew exactly how Emily had talked him into it. She'd been right about her all along. "You're sure Danny is all right?"

Frank started to nod but hesitated. "I never saw him. She told me he was sleeping in the next room."

"And you believed her. It sounds to me like she's gone crazy." Sally slapped the table. "Where are they?"

"You know that cabin I told you about up in the hills? I used to go hunting up there."

Sally nodded. "I remember you telling me about it." She

stood up. "You're coming with me to Jim's right now. It's the least you can do."

Frank hesitated, then nodded and stood up. He walked to Sally, putting his arms around her. "I'm sorry. I feel like a fool."

She squeezed his hand and turned toward the door. "That's because you are one, Frank."

In spite of her fear, Sandrine was almost dozing in the warm early morning sun. The constant babble of the stream and the lazy swaying of the willows in the summer breeze made the danger she was in seem false, unreal. Besides, she had made her decision and she wouldn't back out now. She could only hope that Wade and Jim hadn't noticed that her horse was gone when they went out tracking early that morning and that they would not show up too early.

When she heard a twig snap behind her, she leapt to her feet, whirling to face the sound. She instantly recognized the big dark-haired man who stood staring at her, his gun drawn. He was Nick Boulton, a drifter who worked off and on for different ranches, and drank up his wages every Saturday night. Sally had had to throw him out of the restaurant a couple of times. Sandrine had always avoided him when she'd seen him on the street, even when he looked sober. He had never threatened her in any way, but there was something about him that frightened her.

She straightened her shoulders and tried to keep her voice steady. "Where's Danny?"

Instead of answering her, Nick reached out and grabbed her arm. Jerking her toward him, he pressed his gun against her side. "When I want you to talk, I'll let you know. Now get on your horse." He released her arm and pushed her backward so that she stumbled and almost fell. She fought to keep her composure as she walked toward her horse and mounted up.

"Don't get any ideas. I've never shot a woman before, but it doesn't mean I won't."

Following the terse orders of the man who rode behind her, Sandrine guided her horse up the little valley. For long stretches they rode in the water. It was an old trick, Sandrine knew, but an effective one. Anyone following them would have to search the underbrush carefully to find any tracks. Twice, Nick forced her to turn her horse uphill and ride along the rocky ridge, only to drop back down into the stream a mile farther on. When they finally left the creek bed, they rode over ground so rocky that Sandrine knew it would be almost impossible for anyone to follow them. As the sun rose in the sky, she did exactly as she was told, refusing even to look back at Nick. When they turned toward the foothills, Sandrine tried to keep up her courage. If they had holed up somewhere in the woods, it was going to be that much harder for her to get away.

She saw faint game trails through the brush, but Nick avoided them, choosing instead to keep to hard, rocky ground. Sandrine watched the ground for other tracks, hoping that he'd at least made the mistake of following the same route more than once. But she couldn't see anything. When they rode from the sunlight into the dappled shade of old pine trees, Sandrine was grateful to be out of the intense sun, but she knew that the cushion of pine needles was yet one more effective way to conceal their tracks. She didn't see the cabin until they were almost upon it. It had been built against a wooded slope, tall pines towering over every side. Whoever had built it had been careful to bring the logs from farther up the slope, leaving the trees close to the cabin uncut. They had also been careful not to wear paths. The result was a nearly invisible structure that many people would ride past and never see.

"The corral is in back of the cabin. Swing wide through the trees," Nick ordered.

Sandrine obeyed without answering, then guided her horse

through the trees. Nick didn't give her time to dismount but pulled her sideways off her horse. This time she did fall, and he watched with blank eyes as she stood up, brushing pine needles from her skirt. He walked behind her, and she could feel the light pressure of his gun barrel in the small of her back. This time, she could also smell the whiskey on his breath. When they got to the cabin door, he leaned around her to knock on it. After a moment, a woman's voice called for them to come in. The door swung open, and Sandrine stood facing Emily. She looked as prim and proper as ever, but her eyes looked wild.

"So you're here," she said as calmly as if they were going to have tea.

Sandrine looked around the room. "Where's Danny?"

"He's fine."

"If you've hurt him in any way, Emily, I swear . . ." Sandrine started forward, but she felt Nick's hands on her, holding her back.

"You'll what? Just what will you do, Sandrine?" Emily stepped so close to Sandrine that their faces almost touched. "I hate you, you know."

"You're jealous of me," Sandrine said slowly. "You know that Wade still loves me, and you can't stand the thought." Sandrine saw Emily raise her hand, and she tried to turn away, but Nick held her. She felt the sting of Emily's hand on her face, but Sandrine showed no sign of emotion. She wouldn't give Emily the pleasure.

"Hold her so she can't move," Emily said to Nick.

Sandrine struggled against Nick's iron grip, but she struggled in vain. He held her against him so that she could barely move. Emily took Sandrine's chin in her hand and pressed it so hard, her nails dug into the flesh. "I can do anything I want with you, do you know that? You're my captive. If I tell you to beg, you'll beg. You'll do anything I tell you to do."

Sandrine narrowed her eyes and stared at Emily. "You are a

demon from the bowels of the Earth and soon you will return," she muttered in Blackfoot.

"What did you say?" Emily looked past her to Nick. "What did she say?"

"I dunno. Sounded like Injun to me."

"Tell me what you said, Sandrine."

Sandrine stared into Emily's eyes, her gaze so hard and cold that Emily glanced away for a moment. "I put a curse on you, Emily. It's a curse that the people of my tribe use on their enemies. I've never seen it fail."

"You liar!" Emily screamed, slapping Sandrine again. "Don't lie to me."

"I'm not lying to you. Does it frighten you just a little, Emily?" Sandrine asked, still struggling against Nick's hold.

"You didn't tell me she was an Injun," Nick said.

"What does it matter? You don't believe in those silly things, do you?"

"I heard about a medicine woman from a tribe down in Mexico who placed a curse on the man who killed her daughter. He was found sometime later with his eyes poked out, wandering the desert. Kind of a scary thing."

"Don't be foolish, Nick. She's doing it on purpose to try to frighten us. She probably didn't say anything."

"Where's Danny?" Sandrine repeated.

"I might tell you if you say 'please,' " Emily said, walking around in a circle.

Sandrine forced herself to stay calm. "Please, tell me where Danny is."

Emily stopped walking and looked at Sandrine. "He's on his way home. He should be there by now. I figure once he's home, they'll stop looking for you."

Sandrine thought about the circuitous route she and Nick had taken, and she knew that Wade would never find her. The only person who would have a chance of finding her was Little Bear, and he was too far away.

"What's the matter, Sandrine? It looks like a little of the fight's gone out of you. Are you finally beginning to realize that you're never going to leave this place?" Emily motioned to one of the wooden chairs. "Put her there and tie her hands behind her. Make sure they're tight."

Sandrine stopped struggling and let Nick tie her hands, hoping that he wouldn't tie them too tightly. But he did. She could already feel the rope burning into her skin, and she couldn't move her wrists at all. She watched Emily as the woman pranced around the small cabin as if she was a preening hen, until she stopped and pulled out a chair, sitting directly in front of her. "So tell me. What shall we do with you, Miss Sandrine?"

Sandrine didn't answer, but she felt the anger rising in her. She hated this woman.

"You didn't answer me, Sandrine. What are we going to do with you?"

Sandrine spoke in Blackfoot again, and Emily went wild, slapping Sandrine several times and shaking her shoulders. "Stop that! I hate that. It's a filthy language."

Sandrine spoke in Blackfoot again. But this time, as Emily leaned forward to slap her, Sandrine placed her foot in front of her, then quickly moved it upward. Before Emily could slap her, Sandrine kicked her in the stomach, knocking her and the chair backward to the floor. Emily cried out, and Sandrine couldn't keep from smiling. When Emily stood up, she looked crazed. She ordered Nick to stand Sandrine up and turn her around in the chair so that she was straddling it, her arms and hands over the back of it. She felt Emily's hand on her back.

"Give me your knife," Emily ordered Nick.

Nick hesitated. "I don't know, Miss Emily. I—"

"Just give me the damn knife. You're getting paid to take orders from me, you idiot."

BRIGHT STAR'S PROMISE

Sandrine watched as Nick handed over his large hunting knife, and for the first time, she felt cold fear in the pit of her stomach. She felt the blade on the back of her neck and then as it moved down her back, cutting her blouse and slip. She hugged the back of the chair, trying to cover herself as the blouse hung loosely on her shoulders. She knew what was going to happen.

"Give me your belt, Nick. Hurry, dammit!" Emily yelled impatiently.

Nick took off his thick black leather belt and handed it to Emily.

Sandrine looked up at Nick, and she was surprised to see that he almost looked as if he felt sorry for her. She heard Emily's footsteps on the wooden floor as she walked around to stand behind the chair. She glanced back and saw the end of the belt wrapped around Emily's hand, the buckle loose. Sandrine swallowed.

"Are you just a little bit afraid now, Sandrine?" Emily asked, standing so Sandrine could see her. She waved the belt back and forth in front of Sandrine's face. "You shouldn't have done that, you know. You should've known you'd have to be punished for it."

"You shouldn't use the buckle, Miss Emily. You could really hurt her."

"I don't care if I hurt her, you oaf," Emily said angrily, pushing Nick out of the way.

Sandrine closed her eyes, trying to think of anything but what Emily was about to do to her. The force of the first blow flattened Sandrine's chest against the chair. She barely had time to catch her breath when she felt the cold metal dig into the skin of her back again. The pain was excruciating, and she wanted to cry out, but she wouldn't.

"Anytime you want to beg my forgiveness, I'll stop," Emily said from behind her.

"Go to hell," Sandrine said with all the courage she could muster. When the buckle hit her again, she felt as if the metal had cut through to her spine. Her head fell against the top of the chair, and as the blows continued to come, she thought she heard Nick tell Emily to stop. She wanted to be brave, she wanted to be strong, but all she had been was foolish. She could only hope that Emily's anger would be spent and that she hadn't been lying about sending Danny home.

Twelve

Wade pulled out his pocket watch, sighed, snapped it shut, and headed back toward the spot where he and Jim had arranged to meet. He hadn't had any luck, and they had less than an hour before Sandrine was supposed to be at Mill's Pond. He and Jim still hadn't come up with much of a plan. The only thing he knew for sure was that he wasn't about to let Sandrine sacrifice herself.

Jim was waiting for him at the rock outcropping. "Any luck?" he asked as he rode up and reined in.

"None. I swear, Jim. It's as if they flew out of here. I couldn't find any tracks anywhere."

"Neither could I." Jim climbed down from the rocks. "I guess we best be going."

Wade nodded, waiting until Jim had mounted. It took them less than twenty minutes to get to Mill's Pond. They decided that the only thing they could do was wait and hope that the kidnappers would show. Jim dismounted and waited by the pond while Wade rode back about a half-mile to a small stand of oaks. He grabbed his rifle and found a place where he could lie undetected. He hid in a small stand of willows, his rifle loaded and held in front of him. He sighted Jim easily; he would have no problem shooting someone from here if he had to.

Wade waited patiently, watching Jim as he paced back and forth on the bank of the pond. It seemed like hours until the appointed time, but when he next looked at his watch, he realized it was ten minutes after the hour and there was still no sign of Danny. He looked around him. He was sure he hadn't been seen; there was no place for anyone to hide around here. He watched Jim as he continued to pace, looking in every direction. When a half-hour had passed, and then an hour, Jim held up an arm and waved Wade in. Wade stood up, looked around once more, then walked to the pond.

"They're not coming," Jim said, shaking his head. "They never intended to."

Wade grasped Jim's shoulder. "You don't know that. Maybe they're just making you wait."

"They're not coming, Wade. Let's go back to the ranch."

"But what if they come, Jim? Shouldn't we stay awhile longer?"

"No," Jim answered angrily, mounting up and turning his horse back toward the trail.

Wade walked to his own horse and mounted up. He rode alongside Jim, not knowing what to say to his friend. What could he say? He shook his head, feeling completely helpless. As they rode down the trail that led to Jim's ranch, Wade finally spoke. "I'm sorry, Jim. I should've done more."

"What could you have done, Wade?"

"If I was able to track like I used to . . ."

"It wouldn't have mattered. Whoever kidnapped Danny and Emily is a professional. I've never seen anything like it. I've never seen tracks disappear before. I'm not even sure an Indian could've followed their trail."

"Sandrine's cousin probably could have. She said he was good."

"Maybe he could have, but we'll never know."

Wade heard the disappointment in Jim's voice, and it made him feel even worse. As they rode into the yard, Wade recognized Sally's carriage. They dismounted, hitched the horses, and went inside. When Jim opened the door, Danny slipped from Rose's lap and ran to Jim.

"Danny," Jim said, his voice choked with emotion. He lifted the boy into his arms and hugged him tightly.

Wade walked over to Rose. He bent down and kissed her cheek. "Is Emily here, too?"

"Sit down, Wade," Rose said, her voice strained.

Wade nodded to Frank and Sally, then sat down. "What's wrong? Did something happen to Emily?"

Rose shook her head. "Sandrine's gone."

"What? She can't be. Her horse . . ." Wade hesitated. He hadn't even noticed that her horse was gone when he saddled up that morning. "No," he said, shaking his head. "No."

"That's not all," Sally said, her voice filled with anger. "Frank has something to tell you and Jim."

Rose stood up and went to Jim, taking Danny from his arms. "I'm going to take him to our room for a nap." She kissed Jim on the cheek and went into the bedroom.

"What is it, Frank?" Jim asked, walking to the table and sitting down. "You know something about this?"

Frank held his hat in his lap, nervously crumpling the brim. He glanced at Sally and then at the men, slowly relating his story.

Wade listened as Frank spoke, feeling a rage inside of him so strong that he wanted to reach across the table and put his fingers around Frank's throat. But before he could even think of moving, Jim had gotten up and yanked Frank to his feet.

"I don't think I quite understand you, Frank. You're saying you used Emily, but you're willing to blame the whole thing on her?"

"She said she needed my help. She said she was worried about Danny and she needed a safe place where she could take him."

"And you believed her?" Wade asked, shaking his head.

"I want to know about Emily," Jim persisted.

"I don't think you do, Jim. She's not the Emily you think she is." Frank glanced at Wade. "She hates Sandrine. She never came right out and said it, but she said things that didn't make any sense. Once I got back to town and started thinking, I realized that there was something real wrong. So I told Sally, and she convinced me to come out here."

"That was mighty decent of you, Frank," Wade said, "especially considering you helped plan the whole damn thing."

"I didn't plan anything, Wade. I swear. All I did was give Emily a place to stay and bring her supplies. That's it."

"Is this like one of your poker games, Frank? The hand is dealt but not all the cards are on the table?"

"It's not like that, Wade."

"He's telling the truth, Wade," Sally said.

"How do you know? Hell, he'd tell you anything to keep you in his bed." As soon as Wade had uttered the words, he regretted having said them. He reached for Sally's hand, but she snatched it away. "I'm sorry, Sally. You didn't deserve that."

"No, Wade, I didn't. I've always been a good friend to you, and I'm being a good friend now." She cleared her throat, her eyes moist. "I know Frank can have just about any woman he wants, and he does. But he sleeps in my bed at night because he wants to be there. This may sound strange to you, Wade, but what Frank and I feel for each other is honest. It's a hell of a sight more honest than what you and Sandrine have right now." She leaned forward, her eyes searching his. "Just shut your mouth for once and listen to what Frank has to say."

Wade nodded, looking at Jim. Slowly Jim released Frank, and Wade waited until they both sat down. "Do you think Emily would hurt Sandrine?"

"I don't know. She said she felt sorry for her. She said you were going to use her and then leave her. She said you didn't really care for her. That's when I began to realize something was wrong. I saw the way you were in my hotel room a few days ago. I know how much you love Sandrine, even if you won't admit it to yourself. So I thought Emily might be imagining all of this."

Wade nodded, running his hand over his face. "Emily said those very words to me; she said I was using her and throwing her away."

"How long ago did Sandrine leave?" Jim asked.

"We don't know," Sally said. "Rose went in to wake her up and she was gone."

"How far is it to your cabin, Frank?"

"It's a three, four-hour ride."

Wade stood up. "Then you better get ready to ride, 'cause you're coming with us."

"I'll saddle another horse," Jim said.

"I've already put some food together for you," Sally said, picking up a saddlebag from the floor and handing it to Wade.

Wade nodded his thanks to Sally, then looked at Frank. "Tell me something, Frank. Did you hire the man who made it look like a kidnapping?"

"Yes. Emily said she didn't want Jim coming after them until he had cooled down. She said she wanted to make sure they weren't followed. So I hired an old Army scout. His name is Nick Boulton. He's good."

"He's good, all right. I couldn't find any tracks anywhere. He had me riding around in circles."

"That's what he was supposed to do."

"What kind of man is he?"

Frank shrugged. "He's heavy into the bottle, if that's what you're asking."

"No, that's not what I'm asking. Is he capable of hurting Sandrine?"

"I don't think so," Frank said, looking at Sally. "Mostly he stays to himself. I've never heard he was the violent type."

"Well, let's hope you heard right. 'Cause if he hurts Sandrine at all, I'm holding you responsible," Wade said, his voice hard and cold. He started toward the door but stopped and turned back to Sally. "I owe you for this, Sal. I won't forget it. Let's go, Frank."

Sandrine tried to move, but the pain in her back was almost more than she could bear. Slowly she opened her eyes to orient herself, and soon she remembered where she was. She was still tied to the chair. She lifted her head and looked around, expecting to see Emily standing over her with the belt, but she wasn't in the room. Instead Nick was sitting in a chair not far from her, his dark eyes watching her. As soon as he saw that she was awake, he moved his chair close to hers.

"I'm sorry, miss. I didn't mean for this to happen."

Sandrine wasn't sure she could trust Nick. Still, he was her only hope. "Where is she?" Sandrine asked in a low voice.

Nick gestured toward the other room. "She's in there. She told me to wake her up as soon as you came around."

Sandrine rested her chin on the chair back. Her blouse hung loosely around her shoulders. "Well then, I guess you better wake her." She tried to straighten up, but fiery pains shot up her back, and she cried out, trying to stifle the sound.

"I put some grease on your back. Don't know if it helped much."

"Thank you," Sandrine said, looking at the man. "Why are you helping her, Nick? Does she have some kind of hold over you?"

Nick hesitated a moment, then shrugged his shoulders. "She's offered me a good sum of money, and I need it. I don't seem to be able to hold on to a job."

"I'll give you more money and a job if you help me get away from here, Nick."

He seemed to consider Sandrine's offer, but he shook his head. "I don't think so."

"How much money did she offer you?"

"Five hundred dollars."

"I'll give you two thousand dollars and a job on our ranch. Just help me, Nick. Please." When Sandrine saw the uncertainty on his face, she persisted. "You don't owe her anything. When my husband finally tracks me down, and he will track me down, she'll blame you for the whole thing. You'll be the one who goes to jail, not Emily. Who would believe you over her?" Sandrine saw his eyes dart from the bedroom back to her face, and she continued, "I'm the only person who can clear you. I know what kind of person she is. I can say you saved my life. You won't get in trouble if you help me now." Sandrine watched impatiently as Nick tried to make a decision, and when he finally stood up, she felt a rush of relief flood through her. Then she heard the door to the bedroom open.

"I told you to wake me," Emily snapped at Nick as she walked across the room and stood in front of Sandrine.

"I was going to wake you but—"

"But what?" Emily yelled. "I've never met anyone as stupid as you, Nick. Do I have to explain everything three times to you?"

Sandrine watched Nick as Emily berated him, and she could see the subtle change in his eyes. Instead of looking ashamed, he suddenly looked angry.

"I don't think there's any call for you to talk to me like that, Miss Emily."

"I'm paying you a lot of money," Emily said, poking her finger into his chest, "so I can talk to you however I please. Now get out of my way." Emily picked up the belt again and walked to stand beside Sandrine. "How does that back feel? Are you ready for some more?"

Sandrine looked at Nick, praying that he would help her, but he just stood still, his eyes lowered. She had overestimated him; he was completely cowed by Emily.

"I don't like being ignored, Sandrine," Emily said, her voice getting shrill.

Sandrine had already decided she wasn't going to play Emily's game. She faced forward, ignoring her completely. She started to mutter some of the chants her mother had taught her as a child, chants that would make the evil spirits go away.

"Stop it," Emily screamed. "I told you to quit talking like that." She jerked Sandrine's face upward, holding it in a tight grip. "Everyone says you're so pretty, but when I'm through with you, no one will ever want to look at you again."

Sandrine stared at the large buckle that swung from the end of the belt in Emily's hand, and she knew she couldn't stand being hit in the face with it. "You're going to rot in hell no matter what you do to me, Emily," Sandrine said, dodging the buckle as it came dangerously close to her cheek.

Emily swung the belt again, and Sandrine managed to turn her face just in time, but the buckle caught her on the side of the head, and she could feel the trickle of blood where it had torn her scalp. When Emily raised her hand to swing again, Sandrine tilted the chair forward, purposefully falling sideways to the floor. Emily continued to beat her. Most of the blows fell on her back and shoulders. When Sandrine managed to slip her arms from the back of the chair and cover her head, Emily rained blows down on her arms. As awful as the pain was, Sandrine knew that she had to do something. It was obvious that Nick wasn't going to help her, but she now realized that he probably wasn't going to help Emily either. The next time the belt came down, Sandrine shoved the chair forward into Emily. She stumbled backward to the floor. Then Sandrine was on her, her hands at her throat, squeezing so hard that Emily's face began to turn red.

"That's enough, miss," she heard Nick say, and she felt his arms under hers, lifting her from Emily.

BRIGHT STAR'S PROMISE

Sandrine watched as Emily coughed, turning onto her side, her hands clutching at her throat. Then she sat up, the belt still wrapped around her hand. The look in her eyes was something Sandrine had seen only once before—in Bear Killer's eyes. When Emily stood up, Sandrine refused to move away. She wasn't going to let Emily touch her again. As Emily stepped forward and lifted her hand, Nick reached out and grabbed the belt.

"What are you doing?" Emily yelled, quickly pulling the belt away and snapping it back toward Nick. The buckle hit him across the face. Striking like an enraged animal, Nick lurched forward, snatching the belt from her hands and shoving her to the floor.

"No more," he said, his voice angry. He held the belt up above Emily. "You will hurt this lady no more."

As relief flooded through Sandrine's body, she began to feel the fiery, throbbing pain everywhere. When her knees buckled, Nick caught her, and she fell against his chest. Then she heard a crashing sound as the front door was broken open. She turned her head. Wade, Jim, and Frank were standing there, guns drawn, and Wade was moving forward.

"Let her go," Wade ordered.

"No," Nick said.

Sandrine felt his arms tighten around her. She knew he was trying to keep her from falling to the floor, but before she could explain it to Wade, he lifted his gun and fired, hitting Nick and driving him backward. "No!" she screamed, unable to keep her balance. She dropped to her knees, her entire body shaking.

"Sandrine."

She heard Wade's voice and looked up, tears in her eyes. "He saved my life," she said, her voice choking. "If it weren't for him, Emily would have killed me." Then she fell forward into Wade's arms. She closed her eyes, wanting only to block out the all-encompassing pain.

***

"Jesus," Wade said, rinsing out the blood-soaked rag in the already red bowl. "Can you get me some clean water, Jim?" Wade dabbed at the wound on Sandrine's scalp, trying as best he could to stanch the flow of blood. He took a deep breath and looked down at her back. It was ugly. She'd been beaten badly enough that she'd be scarred. He bent closer, looking at the scars from the beatings that she'd received at the hands of Bear Killer. Her ordeal with him had not seemed real until now.

"Here you go," Jim said, setting down a fresh bowl of water. "How's Nick?"

"He'll be fine. He's as strong as an ox. It's a good thing you're a good shot and hit him in the shoulder instead of the head."

Wade got a fresh cloth and dipped it into the water, dabbing at the blood-streaked lines on Sandrine's back.

"I can't believe Emily was capable of something like this," Jim said. "I feel so responsible."

"It's not your fault, Jim. If anybody drove her over the edge, it was me."

"I think she may have already been over the edge when my sister sent her out here. She just neglected to tell me."

Wade shook his head, rinsing out the rag again. "I can't believe she planned the whole thing just to get back at me. How could I be so stupid?"

"You didn't know. None of us did." He reached for the rag. "Let me do that for awhile."

Wade didn't argue. He sat down in a chair next to the bed, staring at Sandrine as she slept. "I should've known Sandrine would do this."

"How could you have known?"

Wade reached out and gently stroked Sandrine's hair. "She's so damned stubborn and strong-willed, I just should've known."

"I'm afraid she's going to be a long time healing from this," Jim said, rinsing out the rag.

Wade turned and looked through the door to the other room. Emily's hands and feet were bound, and she was gagged. She was lying on a blanket on the floor with Frank standing guard over her, gun in hand.

"I don't know how we're going to get Sandrine back to the ranch. Rose will want to take care of her, of course. Maybe I can ride back and bring the wagon."

"No," Wade said emphatically. "I'll stay here with her. You can bring some supplies and something from Doc for the pain, but I want to take care of her. I can do whatever Rose can."

"Maybe more," Jim said, dropping the rag into the basin and drying his hands on a towel. "The worst time is going to be when she wakes up tomorrow."

Wade nodded. "Do you suppose Nick has some whiskey with him? If I could get her to drink some, it might make her sleep."

"I'll ask. We should probably put something on her back."

"Grease?"

"The only thing I know of. Rose has this godawful ointment that she makes up for burns. Sandrine says it smells a lot like the medicine her mother used to mix up. It's foul stuff, but it helps. I'll bring some of that back, too. Is there anything else you can think of?"

Wade shook his head. Sandrine was lying on her stomach. Her dark hair was spread across the pillow, and her face was turned toward him. He leaned forward and gently kissed her cheek, lingering there for the briefest moment. When he stood up, he saw the glint of silver on her wrist. He lifted her hand and looked at the bracelet.

"It's nice," Jim said.

"Yes, I wish I'd given it to her. If I had, maybe this wouldn't have happened."

"What're you talking about, Wade?"

Wade looked up at Jim. He ran his fingers over the silver bracelet. "She could have had a life with the man who gave her this."

"Looks to me like she chose to come back to you." Jim patted Wade on the shoulder and left the room.

Wade kissed Sandrine once more, then followed Jim, pulling the door shut behind him. Nick was sitting on a chair, his arm in a sling, his head resting against the back of the chair. Wade walked over to him. "Nick," he said, waiting until the man opened his eyes. "I'm sorry. I thought you were hurting my wife."

Nick nodded. "I should have helped her before. She's a nice lady."

"Do you have any whiskey with you? She's going to be in a lot of pain when she wakes up."

"I have a bottle in my saddlebags. Take it."

"Thanks. Can I ask you one thing?"

"Yeah."

"What made you help Sandrine?"

Nick supported his wounded arm and sat up straighter. "She offered me more money and a job. She said I didn't owe Miss Emily anything."

"Is that why you did it, Nick? For the money?"

Nick stared at the floor, and slowly he shook his head. "No, I did it because I could see that she was a fine lady, and a tough one, too. Even when she was in a lot of pain, she fought back. She talked nice to me. She didn't treat me bad like most people do."

Wade nodded. "When my wife is healed and can travel again, I want you to come out to our ranch. I want to hire you on."

"Are you sure you want to do that, mister, after what I did?"

"If my wife offered you a job, that's good enough for me." Wade walked over to the table. He nodded when Jim offered him a cup of coffee, gratefully sipping at the hot bitter liquid. "Has Emily said anything?"

"Besides yelling at me, you mean?" Frank said, then shook his head. "She just kept denying the whole thing." He ran his fingers through his hair. "How could one man be so stupid?"

Wade set his cup down on the table. "Make that four," Wade said, unable to keep from grinning as he looked around at all the men in the room.

Jim sighed loudly. "I'm wondering how I'm going to get her back to Boston. I'll have to take her myself, I expect. I sure as hell can't send her alone, or she'll wind up coming back here trying to kill us all."

"Will your sister do anything, or will she just try to deny there's anything wrong?"

"I'll make sure Emily gets help. If she doesn't, I'll tell my sister that if Emily ever sets foot in this territory again, she'll be thrown in jail."

Wade took another drink of coffee and glanced down at Emily. She was lying on the floor, her eyes open, staring at the wall. He nodded toward her. "Can I talk to her? Alone."

"I don't think that's a good idea, Wade," Jim said, hesitating.

"I'm not going to do anything to her. There are just some things I need to say."

Frank stood up. "I'm going to go outside and have myself a smoke. Join me, Jim?"

Jim looked at Wade, nodded, and followed Frank out the door.

Wade squatted down next to Emily and pulled her up into a sitting position, resting her against the table. Her eyes looked sad, almost childlike. He pulled down the gag. "Are you thirsty?"

"No," Emily said, her voice small.

"Can I talk to you for a few minutes, Emily?" He sat down on the floor in front of her.

"You're angry with me, aren't you? I guess this means I'll have to go home."

"I think that's the best place for you, don't you?"

Emily sighed deeply. "I suppose so. I really don't like it back there. Everyone is so stuffy, and there are so many rules."

"There are rules everywhere you go, Emily."

"Are you going to marry Sandrine now?"

"I'm already married to her, remember?"

Emily nodded, looking past Wade to the bedroom. "I hurt her badly, didn't I?"

"Yes, you did. What made you do it, Emily?"

"She was going to take you away from me."

"Sandrine didn't do anything to you. I was the one who hurt you. Listen to me, Emily," Wade said, taking her chin in his hand and forcing her to look at him. "I'm the one who took you into my bed and then told you I didn't want you anymore. I'm the one to blame."

"No, no, you didn't do anything wrong. It was her," Emily protested, her eyes widening. "She came back and made you love her again. It was her fault."

"No, it wasn't. It was my fault. Are you listening to me? I'm the one who hurt you. I know I can never make it up to you, and I'm sorry for that."

"You could take me back East. Please, Wade. I'm scared. You know what they'll do, don't you? They'll put me in one of those places."

"I can't take you back to your home, Emily. I have to stay here with Sandrine."

"No, you don't!" she shouted, tears streaming down her cheeks. "You see how she controls you."

Wade could see that no matter what he said, it wouldn't make any difference. Emily would still blame Sandrine. "I hope you'll get on with your life and try to get well," he said, his voice sincere.

"Wade, did you ever love me?" Emily asked, her voice soft.

Wade touched her cheek. "I cared for you a great deal. You

helped me at a time when I felt very alone. I'll always be grateful for that."

"I'm tired," she said. "I don't suppose you could loosen these ropes around me?"

Wade reached forward and started to untie the ropes but stopped, thinking about Sandrine's bloody back. Emily was capable of anything, especially lying. "I'm sorry, Emily. I can't untie you."

"You bastard," she hissed, her eyes narrowed. "I should've killed you when I had the chance."

When she started to scream at him, Wade lifted the gag to cover her mouth, then he laid her back on the blanket. When he stood up, Jim and Frank were coming in the door.

"Guess she liked you about as much as she liked me," Frank said.

"I thought I could make her feel better," Wade said. "I was wrong."

"Why don't you get some sleep. We'll be leaving before sunrise. Should be back sometime tomorrow afternoon."

"Thanks," Wade said and walked into the bedroom, closing the door. He sank down in the chair. He felt exhausted, and he rubbed his face with his hands. He leaned forward, resting his elbows on his knees, staring at Sandrine's back. It looked worse than before. Large red and blue welts had formed around the gashes, and her whole back looked swollen. She had turned her head to the other side, and some of her hair had fallen onto her back. Carefully he picked the strands up from the wounds, smoothing her hair to one side. He shook his head, suddenly realizing how tired he was. He untied his bedroll and lay down, feeling as if he could sleep for days. He knew tomorrow was going to be hell for Sandrine, and he hoped that he would have the strength to help her through it.

* * *

Sandrine heard a noise, a sound, but it was from faraway. It was a bird, and she could hear its sweet, cheerful song. As she pulled herself out of the deep comfort of sleep and opened her eyes, she was quickly reminded of the harsh reality of her world. Pain engulfed her as she tried to move, and she took in quick breaths, trying to calm herself. She wanted desperately to sit up, but she didn't have the strength. She lowered her head back to the pillow, feeling the throbbing in her back, head, and shoulders. It felt like every inch of her body was on fire. "God," she muttered, starting to cry. She moved her hands to her sides and tried to push herself up, but the fiery pain made her scream out, and she buried her face in the pillow.

"Sandrine."

She heard Wade's voice, and she felt his hand stroking her hair. She turned her head to one side and finally saw his face. She began to cry harder when she saw him, realizing just how much she needed him. "I can't stand it," she said, closing her eyes and sobbing.

"I want you to drink this," he said gently.

Sandrine opened her eyes again. Wade was holding a glass. "What is it?"

"It's whiskey. It should help you to sleep."

"I don't want to drink it," she said, biting her lower lip.

"Please, Sandrine. Lift your head up high enough so you can drink from the glass. Just try."

Sandrine hated the smell and taste of whiskey; it reminded her of all the trappers and traders who had come to her father's trading post over the years. Still, if it helped with the pain . . .

"Try to drink some, Sandrine."

Slowly Sandrine lifted her head from the pillow. As she arched her back slightly, the pain grew worse, but she made herself sip from the glass. She coughed as the whiskey burned her throat, but she managed to force the rest of it down. Then she dropped her head to the pillow, closing her eyes. She could already feel the alcohol coursing through her veins, making her body feel light.

"A little bit more," Wade urged.

Sandrine didn't argue this time. She lifted her head and drank the whiskey, then lay silently as she felt Wade gently rub her hand. She wanted to open her eyes to thank him, but she couldn't. Instead she lay still, welcoming the sleep that took her into its arms.

Wade heard the horses outside and stood up. Sandrine had been sleeping peacefully ever since he had gotten her to drink the whiskey. He walked outside. Jim and Frank were dismounting, and they were leading a packhorse.

"I only asked for a few things," Wade said.

"You know Rose. She was angry that you didn't want her to come, so she sent everything she could think of instead." Jim untied the packs and saddlebags from the horse.

"Yeah, Sal sent along a few things, too," Frank added.

Wade went inside, pouring both of the men a cup of coffee from the pot he kept on the cookstove. He set the cups on the table, then poured himself one. As soon as Jim and Frank had brought their things inside, they sat down with Wade.

"How's she doing?" Jim asked, looking through one of his saddlebags.

"I got her to drink some whiskey. It put her to sleep." Wade shook his head. "She's in so much pain. I can't do anything for her."

"Rose sent this instead of her usual concoction," Jim said, placing a jar on the table. "She said it'll heal anything. Sandrine showed her how to mix it. She said her mother used it in her tribe."

Wade picked up the jar and opened it, wrinkling his nose at the familiar smell of mint and sage. He remembered it well.

Once he and Little Bear had gone hunting and he'd taken his shirt off. They'd been gone all day long, and by the time they had returned, his back and shoulders were blistered. It felt as if his back was on fire, but Running Tears had put some of her salve on him, and it had relieved the pain.

"You all right, Wade?" Jim asked.

But Wade didn't answer him. Slowly he lifted the jar to his nose again and took in a deep breath. How had he remembered that? Had Sandrine told him the story or had he remembered it on his own? His heart pounded, and he looked up to find Jim and Frank staring at him.

"Are you sure you're all right?" Jim asked again.

"Yeah," Wade said, nodding slowly. "I'm just tired, I guess. So what else did you bring?"

"Sal sent lots of food. She made me bring this whole damned picnic basket just so you'd have an entire peach pie," Frank complained.

"Good for her," Wade said.

"Rose packed some clothes for Sandrine and sent along a brush and soap and other things she thought she might need. I'll let you look." Jim reached into his saddlebag. "I got this bottle of laudanum from Doc. He says to give her a spoonful every four or five hours, or whenever the pain gets too bad. He also said to make sure you keep the wounds clean."

Wade nodded. "Thank you both for coming back out here. I know you must be tired."

"We just want Sandrine to get well," Frank said, his voice low. "I want to tell you again how sorry I am, Wade. If I'd known . . ." Frank shrugged his shoulders.

Wade shook his head. "Like I said before, Frank, it was as much my fault as anyone's. Probably more my fault." He looked at Jim. "Where is Emily anyway?" Wade watched as Jim's expression changed.

"She's in jail until I get back. I figure that's the safest place for her."

Wade took a sip of his coffee. "I'm sorry, Jim, I—"

Jim held up his hand. "I don't want to hear it anymore, Wade. I think maybe you used Emily a little, and I think she used you, too. But what she did to Sandrine was inexcusable. She needs to be put in a place where she won't hurt anyone ever again."

"Well, I don't know about you fellas, but I feel like a piece of peach pie." Frank lifted the lid of the picnic basket and lifted out the pie. "No one makes a peach pie like Sally."

Wade stood up and got some plates, forks, and a knife. He cut pieces for all of them, shoving each plate forward.

"How long you figure to be up here?" Jim asked.

"As long as it takes for Sandrine to recover," Wade said, taking a bite of pie.

"We can bring the wagon up here, you know. We can make her as comfortable as possible in it."

"She'll never make the trip, Jim. Hell, you know what the terrain is like."

"What if you give her some laudanum and knock her out?"

Wade shook his head. "No, I'm going to stay with her until she can ride, and then I'm going to take her back home."

"Which home?" Jim asked.

"The cabin. Looks like I won't be finishing the big house before fall." Wade stood up and walked to the bedroom, checking on Sandrine. She was still sleeping soundly.

"Well, I think we'll be heading on back now," Jim said, standing up.

"So soon? You just got here. I thought you'd spend the night."

"No, we figure we can make it back well before dark. Besides, I've barely seen Rose and Danny."

Frank stood up. "And I need to spend some time with Sally. Actually," Frank said, kicking the floor like a guilty-looking little boy, "I need to get down on my knees and beg her forgiveness."

"You treat her good, Frank. You won't find any lady better than Sally," Wade said sincerely.

"I'll be up in a week to check on you," Jim said, clasping Wade's shoulder. "Is there anything else you need or want?"

"I don't think so," Wade said, walking them to the door. He watched the men as they mounted their horses.

"Take care of Sandrine, Wade," Frank said.

"I will."

"See you soon, boy," Jim said, tipping his hat as he turned his horse. Wade waved to the men and watched them as they rode out of the trees. He suddenly felt anxious. What if Sandrine got worse and he couldn't help her? He took a deep breath, let it out, and walked back inside. Sandrine was his responsibility now. It was because of him that she had gotten hurt, and it was up to him to make her well again.

Thirteen

Little Bear smiled broadly as he watched Shining Bird holding her daughter, Spotted Deer. He couldn't wait until they had a child of their own. It would be soon, he hoped.

"Why do you stare at me so, husband?" Shining Bird asked, smiling.

"I look at you because I have never seen anything so lovely. Indeed, the flowers in the fields pale in comparison to you."

Shining Bird smiled slightly, stroking her daughter's dark silken hair. "What is it you want, Little Bear?"

"Want?"

"Just because I have married you does not mean I have lost my ability to think," Shining Bird said, grinning. "What is it?"

Little Bear shrugged. "I long to see my cousin. I wish to see if all is well with her."

"Will you go alone?"

"I think it best."

"And will you tell her about Lone Wind?"

Little Bear stared at his wife, slowly shaking his head. "How can I tell her that Lone Wind is still alive?"

"She loved my brother. It would bring joy to her heart to know that he lives."

Little Bear sighed, reaching out to touch the little girl's arm. "Her life is with the white man. They are husband and wife."

"She would have stayed with Lone Wind had she not thought

him to be dead," Shining Bird said. "You know this to be true, Little Bear."

Little Bear rubbed his face. He had thought so often of Bright Star lately that it was almost an ache, a kind of need that had grown out of spending all their young years together. He had felt badly that he had not taken her home when she had asked him, and even worse that she had left so abruptly thinking that Lone Wind was dead.

Little Bear sighed, thinking of what Gray Wolf had told him of the night when Lone Wind had been shot. Gray Wolf had thought that Lone Wind was dead, but when he had tended to his son's body and found life still in it, he had been overcome with joy. He had wanted to go to Bright Star, to tell her the good news, but Lone Wind had told him not to. He had said it would be better to let Bright Star believe that he was dead. It would be better for them both that way.

Since Little Bear and Bright Star had been children, they had had a special connection, an ability to sometimes feel what the other felt. Lately he had been feeling her pain and her sadness, and it made him want to go to her.

"You are quiet again, husband. Where are your thoughts now?"

"I am worried about Bright Star. I feel there is something wrong with her."

"Perhaps it is just that you miss her so much," Shining Bird said gently, reaching over her daughter's head to touch Little Bear's arm.

"Perhaps."

"My brother misses her as well," Shining Bird said softly.

Little Bear looked at her, but she quickly glanced down at her daughter. She had made her point about Lone Wind. He had not been the same since Bright Star had gone, becoming even more withdrawn, except with the children. With them he was always kind and generous. Many times Little Bear tried to speak to him about Bright Star but each time Lone Wind changed the subject. But there was one night, after they had gambled and drunk too much, that they had walked out into the pasture and talked of their families, telling stories of their childhoods. When Little Bear told him a story about him and Bright Star, Lone Wind became quiet. When he had finished the story, Lone Wind spoke, his voice barely audible above the night breeze.

"I love your cousin so much I feel as if I'm dying inside," he had said simply.

And Little Bear did not know what to say.

"Tell me about this white man Little Bear," Lone Wind had asked. "Is he a good man?"

"Yes, he is a good man. He is loyal and he loves my cousin very much. They belong together. You did an honorable thing by sending Bright Star back to him, Lone Wind." But Lone Wind was not comforted by his words, only more troubled. And that was the only time he had ever spoken to Little Bear about Bright Star.

"It frightens me for you to go so far into the white man's land alone," Shining Bird said.

"And you think that Lone Wind can protect me?"

"I did not say that."

"I know what you were thinking, Shining Bird. You have seen Bright Star and Colter together. You know the love that they have for each other. What if I take Lone Wind with me and he sees that same love? Do you think that will help him?"

"Perhaps he will be able to resolve his feelings for her if he sees that she is truly happy with another. My brother must find a way to live again."

Little Bear looked at Shining Bird, realizing that she was right. Lone Wind could not live his life because he was still in love with Bright Star, and he believed that she was still in love with him. If he were to see that she was happy in her life with

Colter, perhaps he could finally let the love that he felt for her go. "All right," Little Bear said, his voice low.

"What was that, husband? I did not hear you."

"I said I will take Lone Wind with me. I promise nothing, do you understand me? If he comes back to this village and his heart is more broken still, it will not be my fault."

"I understand, husband, and I thank you," Shining Bird said with a huge grin, leaning forward and putting her cheek next to Little Bear's. "You are a good man."

Little Bear frowned. "I am a man who is ruled by his wife. That is not such a good thing."

Shining Bird laid her sleeping daughter down on the robe and got on her knees, wrapping her arms around Little Bear from behind. "The boys are staying in my father's lodge this night, and Spotted Deer is already asleep," she whispered.

Little Bear took Shining Bird's hands and rubbed his cheek against them. "How is it possible that a man like me has again been smiled upon by Napi?"

"Because you are a good man," Shining Bird said, sitting on the robe and pulling Little Bear to her. "I have missed you, my husband."

Little Bear lay down on the soft robe, putting his arms around Shining Bird and holding her close to him. He did not want to let her go.

Lone Wind sat in front of the small fire in his lodge, staring into the flames. He had smoked the pipe with the old men earlier this evening, and now things seemed clearer to him. He closed his eyes and opened them again as if he was waiting for something or someone to appear. The pain he had felt in his heart since Bright Star had left was beginning again, and he tried to push it away.

BRIGHT STAR'S PROMISE

"Why do you not set me free?" he asked, shaking his head. "I let you go back to your world."

Lone Wind recalled the last time he had seen Bright Star, the night they had been attacked by the Cheyenne. He had thought he was dying, and he had wanted Bright Star to return to her people and to her husband. When he awoke in his father's lodge and his father wanted to bring Bright Star to see him, he made Gray Wolf promise that he would not. Lone Wind knew that it was best if Bright Star returned home.

He closed his eyes again, feeling the chants from the old men begin to work on him. In his mind, he could see Bright Star, and he could see that she was in trouble. He could hear her cries for help.

"I will come to you," he murmured, his eyes still closed. "I will make sure that you are safe."

Sandrine tossed back her hair and closed her eyes. She could feel the warm breeze against her cheeks. There was no sound, not even that of the hawk in the sky above. She was alone, but she was not afraid. She started walking, unable to see but knowing where she was going. Then she heard his voice.

"I am here, Bright Star," he said.

She walked toward the sound of his voice, but she couldn't see him. "Where are you?"

"I am here. Come to me."

"Yes," she said, desperately trying to find him, trying to open her eyes to see.

"Do not be afraid, Bright Star. I am with you."

"But I cannot see you," she cried out, looking around her with unseeing eyes.

"It does not matter. I can see you. I will protect you."

"Please, Lone Wind, do not leave me again." She heard her own voice. It sounded loud as it echoed around her.

"I will be with you, Bright Star. Do not worry."

"Lone Wind!" she shouted loudly, but she knew that he was already gone. She lowered her head and began to cry. She would never see him again.

Wade jerked his head up at the sound of Sandrine's voice. He reached over to take her hand.

"Lone Wind."

He paused when he heard the name, but the need and sadness in Sandrine's voice overcame his hesitation. "It's all right, Sandrine. You were just dreaming," he said softly, stroking her hair.

She didn't open her eyes, but she seemed to calm down. When her breathing was more steady, he sat back in the chair and watched her. She had slept fitfully throughout the day, and now she had a fever. He had tried to get her to drink water, but she barely sipped it. He felt her forehead again. She was still hot. He lifted the sheet and looked at the ugly red gashes that crisscrossed her back and shoulders. Many of them were deep, and the skin surrounding them was ugly and swollen. He filled a bowl with fresh water and cleaned her wounds, dabbing at them as gently as he could, then he reapplied the salve that Rose had sent. He knew she would be waking soon. He went out to the cookstove and set some water to boiling. He put some of a tea mixture that Rose had sent into a cup. According to Sandrine's mother, the herbs could cure anything from a stomach ache to a fever.

When the water was boiling, Wade poured it into the cup. He waited until the steaming liquid had turned dark, then went back into the bedroom, setting the cup on the table next to the bed. As he watched Sandrine, he wondered what would make a woman do what she had done. It was hard for him to understand her. And it wasn't the first time she had done something like this. He had heard all the stories. She had tried to help

Rose and Jim by playing in the poker game with Frank, knowing that she had nothing to wager but herself. What made a person be like that, he wondered? He shook his head. He knew that Sandrine was independent and strong-willed, and he was counting on that will to get her through this.

He wet a fresh cloth and wiped her face. Her cheeks were flushed and her skin seemed even hotter. Somehow, he had to get her to drink the tea. "Sandrine," he said quietly, his mouth next to her ear. "You have to wake up, Sandrine."

She moved her head on the pillow but she didn't open her eyes.

"Wake up, Sandrine," Wade said again.

"No," Sandrine mumbled, turning her head away.

Wade took a deep breath, steeling himself for what he had to do. He reached down and put his arms underneath Sandrine's, pulling her to a sitting position on the edge of the bed. Her moans of pain made him clench his teeth, but he didn't stop.

"No," she said, pushing him away. "Leave me alone."

"Stop it, Sandrine!" Wade said firmly. Finally she looked at him, her blue eyes glazed. "You have a fever. You have to drink this. Do you understand?"

"I can't," she said, falling forward against him, her head on his shoulder.

Wade put his hands on her waist, trying to keep the sheet over her. "I know you're in pain, Sandrine. But you have to drink this. It's your mother's tea. You remember Running Tears, don't you?" Slowly Sandrine lifted her head and looked at him. For the first time, she seemed to understand something he had said.

"Is my mother here?"

"No, she's not, but this is medicine she made for you. She wants you to drink it." Wade held the cup to her mouth. "You have to drink it, Sandrine." When she looked at him and nodded, Wade tipped the cup so that some of the tea went into her mouth.

At first she coughed and spit it up, but quickly she seemed to understand that she needed to drink it. When she had finished the cup, Wade put it on the table. Slowly he started to lay her back down on her stomach, but she resisted.

"Can I sit here for awhile. It hurts less this way," she said, her voice barely above a whisper.

"I wish I could hold you," he said, stroking her hair. He moved closer to her so that her head rested completely on his shoulder.

"Where is Lone Wind?" she asked, her voice small, almost childlike.

Wade's body stiffened, but he didn't move away. She was obviously delirious. She knew that Lone Wind was dead, but in her delirium, she had forgotten. "Don't worry about Lone Wind. He is well. You have to worry about yourself. You have to get strong, Sandrine."

"He said he would come to me," she murmured, lifting her head to look at Wade. "He said he would come."

"Sandrine," Wade said, gently pushing the damp hair away from her face. "I think you were only dreaming. Lone Wind is not here. It's just you and me. I'll take care of you." She was looking at him, but Wade sensed that she was looking past him, to some far-off place where she had been before. "Sandrine," he said, trying to bring her back.

She closed her eyes for a moment, then opened them looking at Wade as if trying to make sense of who he was. She reached up and touched his face, her fingers shaking. "Wade," she said, tears filling her eyes.

"Yes," he said, surprised at the relief he heard in his voice.

"Are you going to leave me?"

He watched as tears streamed down Sandrine's cheeks. He wiped them away and then kissed her face. "I'm not leaving, Sandrine. I'm staying here, with you."

"The pain . . ." she said, unable to finish.

"I know. I can give you something to help the pain, but you have to keep drinking the tea. It's the only way to break your fever."

Sandrine nodded. "Will you help me back into bed?"

Wade lifted Sandrine's legs as she lay on her side. She was sweating profusely, as if the effort had completely exhausted her. When he tried to help her to her stomach, she shook her head.

"No," she said, her voice weak.

"All right," Wade said, covering her with the sheet. He went into the other room to get the bottle of laudanum and a spoon, but by the time he got back, he could hear Sandrine's steady breathing. He sat down, feeling tired and powerless. There wasn't much he could do to help her. There was a time, he was told, when their love would've been enough to make her strong, but that love wasn't there anymore. As much as he cared for her, it was clear that she hadn't yet forgotten Lone Wind. Even though Lone Wind was dead, it seemed that he was still very much alive to Sandrine.

Sandrine opened her eyes, staring up at the unfamiliar crude, wooden ceiling. Somehow she had managed to roll onto her back, and now, with a great deal of effort, she forced herself to roll to her side. Wade was sitting in a chair next to the bed, his feet propped on the edge, his hands folded across his chest. His head was tilted to one side but leaning against the chair back, and she could see that he hadn't shaved in awhile. She wondered how long they had been here, and she wondered why Wade hadn't tried to take her back to Jim and Rose's. But even as she thought it, she knew why he hadn't tried. Even now, probably days after Emily had inflicted the beatings on her, she could barely move without pain. Riding on a horse or in the back of a wagon would have been almost unbearable.

It was strange how things worked out sometimes, she thought. Emily had had her kidnapped and brought here to keep her away from Wade, but all her plan had done was bring them closer together. Her heart ached when she looked at him. It was hard for her to believe that he wasn't the Wade she remembered and that their love wasn't as strong as it used to be. She watched him as he slept, taking in every part of him—his blond hair that brushed his collar, his long, lean body, the strength that was evident in his arms, and the set of his mouth as he slept. When he suddenly opened his eyes, she felt embarrassed, and she quickly averted her eyes.

"You're awake," he said, putting his feet on the floor and sitting up. Quickly he rubbed his hands over his face. "I didn't mean to fall asleep."

"How long have we been here?"

"This is the fourth day," he said, yawning.

"And you've slept in that chair every night?"

"I have a bedroll on the floor, but I didn't want to leave you alone. You had a fever, and you were having some pretty strange dreams." He reached forward and put his hand on her forehead. "Feels like the fever's broke. Good. Must've been your mother's tea."

"My mother's tea?"

"Rose sent it with Jim. She said it was from a bag your mother made up for you."

Sandrine nodded. "It cures everything, according to my mother."

"I guess it does," Wade agreed. "Are you hungry? I've got lots of food."

"Biscuits sound good, or bread."

Wade nodded. "We have both, and Rose sent along some berry preserves." He stood up. "Can you think of anything else you'd like? We need to start building up your strength."

"No, thank you," Sandrine said, watching him as he walked

out of the room. She tucked her hands underneath her head as she lay there, waiting for him to return. She'd had strange dreams, Wade had said, and she knew what they were about. Lone Wind. He'd appeared to her in one dream that had seemed so real that she thought he was next to her. She closed her eyes, trying to blot out the memories of him and the guilt she felt. But the memory of him lying before her, dying, was so vivid that she'd never forget it. She squeezed her eyes tightly, trying to keep from crying, but it didn't do any good. Tears coursed down her cheeks, and she saw Lone Wind clearly; she would never forget his face, no matter how much she tried. He had loved her more than any man had, more even than Wade. It was the kind of love she would never experience again.

"Here you go," Wade said.

Sandrine opened her eyes when she heard Wade's voice and saw him walk into the room carrying a tray. When he looked at her, she reached up and wiped her face.

"Are you all right? Is it the pain?"

"No," Sandrine answered quickly. "Can you help me sit up, please?" She held onto his arm as she put her feet on the floor and sat on the edge of the bed. The sheet fell to her waist, but before she could say anything, Wade lifted it up and tucked it underneath her arms.

"I'm going to slip one of my shirts on you just while you're sitting up. It's nice and loose."

Sandrine smiled as she watched him go through his pack and come out with a blue work shirt. She extended one arm while he slipped a sleeve on, and then the other, grimacing as the fabric touched her back. Quickly Wade buttoned the front. "Thank you," she said, reaching for the cup on the tray, then winced as a searing pain made her catch her breath. Angrily she slammed a hand down on the bed. "I feel like I'll never heal."

"You will," Wade said patiently, handing her the cup.

"Thank you," she said, sighing. "Thank you for everything. I'm sorry you had to stay here with me."

"I wanted to stay. It's my fault that this even happened to you."

"It wasn't your fault, Wade," she said, sipping at the tea. "I should've listened to you, but I tend to be a little stubborn sometimes."

"A little?" Wade asked, cocking his head to one side.

Sandrine grinned. "I never asked you if Danny was all right."

"He's fine. She didn't hurt him."

"Thank God. What about Nick?"

"Nick didn't fare as well as Danny. He got shot."

"How?"

"I shot him. I came in here and saw him standing over you with that belt, and I thought he was the one who had hurt you."

"Is he alive?"

"He's alive and he'll recover. Jim and Frank took him into town, and Doc tended to him."

"I offered him money and a job, Wade. He saved my life."

"Don't worry. I'll see that he gets paid."

"I offered him a lot of money," Sandrine said, staring into her tea cup.

"How much?"

"Two thousand dollars," Sandrine murmured. She looked up, meeting Wade's eyes. "I'll find a way to pay you back, Wade. I promise."

"Two thousand, huh?" Wade said, shaking his head. "That's a lot of money, Sandrine."

"I know, but I was desperate."

"You don't have to pay him, you know."

"Of course I do," Sandrine said indignantly. "If you won't give me the money, I'll borrow it from someone else."

"Sandrine," Wade said gently, touching her hand, "do you honestly think I care about the money? I was just playing with

BRIGHT STAR'S PROMISE 303

you. I wouldn't care if you'd offered him twenty thousand dollars. The most important thing is that you're alive."

Sandrine felt her cheeks burn, and she stared into her cup, swirling the tea around. "I'll pay you back."

"I don't want you to pay me back," Wade said. "I don't want your money. I don't want anything from you, don't you understand that?"

"No, I don't," Sandrine replied, looking up. "I don't know what to think anymore, Wade." Her hand began to shake, and she tried to set the cup on the chair, but she missed. It dropped to the floor and broke. "I'm sorry, I didn't mean to break it . . ." She covered her face with her hands.

"Watch your feet," Wade said gently, lifting them from the floor. "Why don't you lie back down and let me clean this up."

"I'm sorry."

"Don't be," Wade said gently.

Sandrine lay on her side, her knees bent toward her chest. She felt helpless, and her back and head were beginning to throb. She felt as if the pain would never stop. When Wade touched her cheek, she reached for his hand and pressed it to her chest, clutching it tightly.

"I won't leave you, Sandrine," Wade said, his face close to hers.

But Sandrine knew that Wade couldn't make those kinds of promises to her. One thing she had learned was that life was too uncertain.

"I want you to take some of this laudanum."

"No, I don't want to take that."

"It'll help the pain, Sandrine."

"What if I can't learn to live without it? I've heard about women like that."

"That's not going to happen. I'm only giving it to you when the pain is really bad. You're going to have to trust me."

"I do trust you."

"Here," Wade said, pouring some of the medicine into the spoon and holding it to her mouth. "Do you want the shirt off?"

"No," Sandrine said, closing her eyes, feeling the tears come again. She felt Wade's hand on her hair, lightly stroking it.

"It's all right."

"Why do you keep saying that?" She put her hand over her eyes, refusing to look at him. "I want to go home," she said, starting to feel the laudanum work.

"I'll take you to Jim and Rose's as soon as you're able to travel."

"I want to go home," Sandrine said. "I want to go back to my people." She could picture the open prairie. She could see the village with all of the lodges, and the river where she and Little Bear used to play. And she could see the trading post where she had grown up. She didn't belong here anymore; she knew that now.

"You won't be able to travel for awhile, Sandrine, but if you want to see your parents when you're better, I'll take you there."

Sandrine uncovered her eyes and looked at Wade. His expression was sincere, but she knew that he was not the same man she had once known. His eyes were impossibly beautiful, and she saw things there that . . . she sighed. She was tired of being where she wasn't wanted. "I don't want to visit. I want to go home for good."

Rose was hanging up clothes when Danny came running full speed into a sheet, getting himself caught up in it.

"Daniel, stop it," Rose said angrily.

"There're some Indians out there, ma."

Rose hesitated and looked over the clothesline and into the yard. She shook her head. "There's no one out there. You're letting your imagination get the best of you again," Rose said.

"I saw two Indians, ma. They were riding up from the valley."

"If you really did see Indians, I doubt if they're any threat to us."

"But what if they ride in here and scalp us?"

"Stop it, Danny!" Rose finished hanging the wet clothes, then bent down to get the basket. "Come into the house. It's time for you to eat." Rose walked toward the house, holding the basket, listening to Danny and Scout as they played. They had an interesting version of "fetch." Scout had the stick and Danny was chasing him in circles. Rose couldn't resist a smile; Danny had been such a joy to her. She didn't know what she would've done if Emily had harmed him in any way.

"Ma, look! I told you there were Indians."

Rose stopped and looked up on the ridge. She could see two riders, and even from this distance, she could tell that they were Indians. Scout began to bark frantically, and Rose grabbed Danny's hand, dropping the basket and heading toward the house. Once inside, she barred the door and took the shotgun from the rack, loaded it, and placed it on the table. She put more shells into her apron pocket and peered out the window that faced the yard.

"Are they mean-looking, ma?" Danny asked, trying to look out the window.

"Get over to the other side of the room, Danny. Don't move." Rose watched as the Indians reined in and one of them dismounted and approached the house. She didn't know what tribe they were, but she knew from the way they were dressed that they were not Apache. When she heard the footsteps on the porch, she picked up the shotgun from the table and stood to one side of the window. The Indian stood at the door, looking uncertain.

"What do you want?" Rose shouted through the window, not expecting an answer.

"I am looking for my cousin, Bright Star of the Northern Blackfoot," he said, in French-accented English.

Rose hadn't anticipated that he would understand or speak English. She squinted her eyes and looked at the man again, trying to remember Sandrine's description of her cousin. Rose had even seen him once, a long time ago in the stockade, but she couldn't really remember what he looked like. "If you're her cousin, then you'll know her white name."

"Sandrine Renard," he said without hesitation. "She is married to the man Colter."

"What is your name?" Rose asked, watching him as he stood looking at her through the window.

"My name is Little Bear."

Rose lowered the shotgun and unbarred the door, opening it. "Come in, please."

Little Bear glanced back at his friend.

"He may come in also," Rose said politely.

"I do not think he will feel comfortable. Would you mind if he drank some of your water?"

"Of course not," Rose said, going out to the porch and pointing to the pump. She waited while Little Bear spoke to his friend, and then he followed her inside. "Are you hungry?" she asked, placing the shotgun back on the rack.

"No, thank you," Little Bear said, standing with his arms at his sides.

"Nonsense, of course you're hungry." Rose quickly set a bowl of fruit and some slices of bread on the table. "Sit down," she said, pouring Little Bear a glass of water from the pail. When Little Bear still hadn't moved, Rose sat down and motioned to the chair next to her. "Please, you can talk while you're eating."

"Thank you," Little Bear said, finally sitting down. "Where is my cousin?"

"She's not here," Rose said, watching Little Bear, noticing that he seemed acutely uncomfortable.

"She is hurt," he said simply.

"Yes," Rose responded before stopping. "How did you know?"

Little Bear shook his head. "My cousin has been like a sister to me. We share the same blood, and many times we feel the same things. I knew that I had to come here."

"You were right to come," Rose said. "It will do her good to see you."

"Where is she?"

Rose shook her head. "I don't know the way. My husband will have to show you. She and Wade are at a cabin in the mountains. He is trying to make her well."

Little Bear nodded. "It is good that Colter is with her."

"My husband won't return until this evening, and I'm not sure when he'll be able to take you to the cabin."

"We can wait," Little Bear said. He looked past Rose, to Danny, and he smiled slightly. "What is it you are called?"

Danny walked forward, standing next to his mother. "My name's Danny. Are you a real Indian?"

"Daniel Everett!" Rose said.

Little Bear smiled and held up his hand. "Yes, I am a real Indian. I am Little Bear of the Northern Blackfoot. Have you ever heard of the Blackfoot tribe?"

Danny shrugged his small shoulders. "I think Sandrine has told me about them. Are you the one who got her into all that trouble when she was a little girl?"

Little Bear laughed, looking at Rose. "Yes, I got my cousin into much trouble. She was very curious, much like you are."

Rose couldn't resist a smile when Danny moved to stand close to Little Bear. He looked down at the knife that hung from Little Bear's waist.

"Can I see your knife?"

"Danny, no," Rose said. She looked at Little Bear. "I'm sorry."

"Do not be sorry," Little Bear said patiently. Slowly he pulled out the long hunting knife, holding the blade against his palm.

Danny's eyes grew large and round. "Is it sharp?"

"It is very sharp," Little Bear replied, taking Danny's hand and touching one of his fingers to the blade.

Rose stiffened for a moment but realized what Little Bear was trying to do.

"Ouch," Danny said, jerking his hand back.

Little Bear rubbed Danny's fingertip. "This knife is a weapon, and it is a tool. I use it to hunt and skin, I use it to carve weapons, I use it to cut meat, and sometimes I use it to defend myself in a fight. It can be very dangerous. I was much bigger than you before I was allowed to carry my first knife."

"Oh," Danny said, looking wistfully back at his mother.

Rose nodded knowingly. "Why don't you take some of this bread outside to Little Bear's friend. Perhaps he's hungry."

"All right," Danny said, picking up the plate.

"He does not speak English," Little Bear said.

"That's all right," Danny said, hurrying out of the house.

"He is a fine boy," Little Bear said, nodding.

"He's named after Wade. He helped me deliver him on the wagon train."

Little Bear nodded. "You are the one. I heard many stories about it. And you are married to Everett, the wagon master?"

"Yes, we've been married over six years now."

"He is a good man."

"Yes, he is."

Little Bear stood up. "Thank you," he said, holding out his hand.

Rose shook his hand. "You're welcome to stay here as long as you like."

"I will wait outside with my friend. Tell me something, please. What happened to my cousin?"

Rose sighed, walking with Little Bear to the porch. "She was badly beaten. My husband says that she will be scarred." Rose saw Little Bear's face tighten as she spoke, and she reached out and touched his arm. "But she's strong. She'll be all right."

"I hope so," Little Bear said, going down the steps.

"Little Bear," Rose said, waiting for him to stop. "You and your friend should stay close to the house. People in these parts aren't too fond of Indians."

Little Bear nodded.

Rose watched as he walked toward his friend. The man had put Danny on his horse and was leading him around the yard. Rose was glad that Little Bear was here. Sandrine needed all the love and support she could get.

Wade finished shaving the right side of his face and then rinsed off. He'd taken a quick bath at the stream and then come back and decided to shave. When he had toweled off, he put on a clean shirt and tucked it into his pants. He'd already heated water, and he'd even made fresh biscuits. After he set the table, he opened the door to the bedroom and looked in. Sandrine was still asleep. He walked to the bed and looked down. Finally, one week after Emily had inflicted the beatings on Sandrine, she was beginning to show signs of improvement. There was color in her cheeks, and she didn't seem to be in as much pain. The previous night she had even gotten up and walked to the other room with his help.

"Sandrine," he said, sitting down. She was lying on her side, her knees bent, her dark hair spread over the pillow. Her hair was still matted from the bloody gash on her head. Sometimes it made him crazy to think what Emily had done to her. When Sandrine opened her eyes and smiled at him, he couldn't resist touching her cheek. "I haven't seen you smile in a long time."

"Is it time to get up?"

"Only if you feel like it."

"I'd like to try," she said, holding onto his arm as she sat up. "Something smells good."

"I made some biscuits." Wade shrugged. "I'm not the best cook in the world, but if you're hungry, I could throw something together."

"No, biscuits will be fine." Sandrine moved to the edge of the bed. She looked down at herself. "I'm still wearing the same skirt and the shirt you gave me. I must look a sight."

"You look fine."

"I can't wait to take a bath." She looked at him. "You shaved," she said, reaching out to touch his face. "I'm glad."

Wade cleared his throat, feeling uncomfortable. "If you feel up to it, I can take you to the stream for a bath later."

"I'd like that," Sandrine said, slowly getting to her feet.

"If you're not up to this, I can bring the food in here."

"No, I want to start walking. I can't stay in this room forever."

Wade followed Sandrine into the other room, and he grimaced as he looked at the back of her shirt: streaks of dried blood crisscrossed it, and here and there fresh spots of crimson seeped through. Some of the wounds had healed, others had scabbed over and whenever Sandrine moved, they bled again. He was amazed by her strength and will. When she reached the table, she rested her hands on it and eased herself into a chair, making sure she didn't lean against the back.

Wade went to the cookstove and poured two cups of coffee and set them on the table. Then he got the warm biscuits from the top of the stove and sat down next to Sandrine. "There's sugar if you like it. Don't have any milk."

"Sugar is fine," Sandrine said, spooning some into her cup. She reached for one of the biscuits and put it on her plate. She picked up a knife, then hesitated, setting it down. "Thank you, Wade."

"It was nothing," he said lightly.

"No, I mean thank you for everything you've done. You've taken good care of me. You didn't have to stay here with me."

"Yes, I did," he said, reaching out for her hand. "My God, Sandrine, you could've died, and it would've been my fault."

"Would that have mattered to you?"

Wade met her eyes. "You know it would've mattered."

"No, Wade, I don't know that. I used to know . . ." Sandrine stopped and looked down. "I'm sorry," she said, taking her hand away from his.

"Sandrine—"

"It doesn't matter, Wade. I just wanted to thank you."

Wade nodded, not knowing what to say. He couldn't tell her he loved her; he didn't. But he cared deeply for her. They ate breakfast in silence, and when they were finished, Sandrine slowly stood up, walked to the front door, and opened it.

"How far is the stream from here?"

Wade got up. "It's down through the trees," he said, pointing. "I think it'll be too hard for you. Why don't I fill the bowl with water and you can wash up."

"No, I want a real bath," Sandrine said. "Is there soap here?"

"Yes, Rose sent some, and she sent your brush."

"If you don't mind helping me, I'd really like to try to make it to the stream."

"All right." Wade went into the bedroom. He got the soap, brush, a towel, and then as an afterthought, the stack of clean clothes that Rose had sent. When he got out to the other room, Sandrine was already gone. By the time he got outside, she was already making her way down the path. He followed her, holding onto her arm. "If you slip and land on your back . . ."

"I won't," Sandrine said, clinging to Wade's arm as they walked.

By the time they reached the stream, Wade could see that Sandrine was in pain and that she was beginning to bleed again. "Maybe you should wait. The water is cool anyway."

"Please help me, Wade. I feel so dirty. I just want to get clean."

Wade nodded, setting down the things he was carrying. Sandrine struggled to get out of her skirt and slip but could only bend over so far to take them off. Quickly Wade pulled them down over her legs, and she stepped out of them. She stood only in her underwear and his long blue shirt, which she had already unbuttoned. She held onto his arm as she stepped into the water. "Be careful," he said.

"Can you hand me the soap?"

Wade went up to the bank and picked up the bar of lavender soap. When he turned back around, Sandrine was sitting down in the shallow water and the shirt was thrown on the bank. He handed the soap to her and turned away, noticing she was making an extreme effort to cover herself when he was near. "I'll just go back up toward the trees. If you need me, call."

"All right."

Wade stopped at the edge of the trees, staring at a single tall pine for as long as he could stand it. Then he turned around and looked back down toward the stream. Somehow Sandrine had managed to take off her underpants, because he saw them lying next to the shirt on the bank. Even from this distance, he could see the ugly pink welts on her back, and again he felt useless anger rise up in him. Anger at Emily and anger at himself. He kicked at the loose pine needles.

"Wade."

He turned when he heard Sandrine call his name, and by the time he got to the stream, she was already standing. She'd managed to step out and pull on a clean skirt and blouse, but she was shivering. "You're right, it's cold," she said, hugging herself.

Wade quickly picked up the other clothes and the soap and brush, and took Sandrine's arm, guiding her safely through the trees and back to the cabin. Once inside, he led her to a chair by the cookstove. He went to the bedroom and came back with a blanket, draping it around her shoulders. "I'll give you a few minutes to warm up, then I want to put some more salve on your back. You're bleeding again."

Sandrine nodded, rubbing her hands together. "Could you please hand me the brush?"

Wade picked up the brush and stood behind her. "I'll do it," he said, pulling it through Sandrine's long, dark hair. He looked closely at the area around her temple where she'd been hit with the belt. It was finally beginning to heal. As he brushed the hair back away from Sandrine's face, he noticed that her eyes were closed, and he smiled. She actually looked relaxed. Her hair was almost to her waist, and he was amazed how deep the color was. He could even smell the scent of lavender in it.

When he was finished, he put the hairbrush down and moved a chair so that he could sit next to Sandrine. Her eyes were still closed, and he reached over and wiped away the drops of water that rolled down her face. Her lips trembled under his touch, and she opened her eyes. Without thinking, he leaned forward and lightly brushed his lips against hers. He expected her to pull away, and when she didn't, he pressed his mouth more firmly against hers. Her lips felt soft and they tasted so sweet... Wade stopped and leaned back. Sandrine met his eyes for a moment, then looked down, her cheeks flushing crimson. He knew then that she would never fight him. She loved him. She still thought of him as her husband.

Wade stood up. "I'll get that salve now." He went to the bedroom, took a deep breath, and came back with the jar. Sandrine dropped the blanket and slowly unbuttoned her blouse, letting it fall away from her shoulders. Carefully Wade applied the salve to the spots that still hadn't healed. He was beginning to wonder if she needed to see Doc. Even though she tried to hide it, he could tell that she was still in a lot of pain. When he was finished, he started to pull up her blouse, but she shook her head.

"May I have another one of your shirts? They're bigger and looser."

He rummaged through his saddlebag and got another clean shirt, pausing. Why had he kissed her? He didn't want her to think he was in love with her. As much as he wanted her, he didn't want to take advantage of her. "Here," he said, helping her take off the blouse and slip on the shirt. When she stood up and turned around, he took in a sharp breath. Her breasts were barely covered as she buttoned the shirt, and he could see her long legs through the thin white material of her skirt. Her hair was away from her face, and her eyes looked unbelievably large and blue. When her eyes suddenly filled with tears, he couldn't resist her. He pulled her close, letting her rest her head on his chest. He stroked her hair and listened as she cried, her shoulders heaving. "I wish I could get my memory back right now," he said, resting his head on hers.

"Do you?" she asked, looking up at him, tears streaking her cheeks.

"Yes, I do," he said, wiping the tears away and then kissing them away. He put his large hands on her face and kissed her again, more deeply this time, with more urgency. If he could have, he would have carried her into the bedroom and made love to her right then, but he knew he could not. Reluctantly he pulled away, still holding her as gently as he could.

"It frightens me to be around you," she said, her voice shaky.

"Why?" Wade asked, looking at her.

Sandrine shook her head. "In my mind we're still married and I still love you. You look the same to me, and sometimes you even act the same. And when you kiss me . . ." Sandrine looked away for a moment. "It seems like the same, but I know it's not. You might be attracted to me, but you don't love me, and it frightens me that I would do almost anything to be with you." She looked at him a moment longer, then walked into the bedroom and shut the door.

Wade watched her and then went to the table, picking up the lavender soap and smelling it. He was beginning to feel like he'd felt after he woke up from the accident—confused and unsure of himself. He was sure that he didn't love Sandrine, yet when he was around her, all he wanted was to be with her. He shook his head and went outside. As soon as she was able to ride, he'd take her home. Maybe what he needed was to get away from Sandrine, to get away from everyone and everything else that reminded him of his past.

Fourteen

"You have a visitor," the deputy said.

Emily looked up. Rose was standing by the bars to the cell, holding a basket. Emily smoothed her soiled skirt and pushed back her hair. She hadn't bathed in over a week, and she'd barely eaten a thing. She knew she looked terrible, and she hoped that Rose would feel sorry for her.

"Hello, Emily. I've brought you some food and things."

Emily walked toward the bars, looking at the deputy, who was unlocking the door. "You'd better check, deputy."

"I already have." He looked at Rose. "Are you sure you'll be all right in here, ma'am?"

"Yes, I'll be fine."

"Call me if you need me," he said, closing and locking the door behind Rose.

"Well," Emily said, stepping to the side and waving her arm at the cot where she slept. "I'd invite you to tea, but as you see, the accommodations aren't the best."

"Here are some clean clothes and some other things I thought you might need." Rose handed the basket to Emily, but when she refused to take it, Rose set it on the bed.

"Am I supposed to be grateful, Rose?"

"I didn't expect that you would be," Rose said, her voice cold.

"I thought you might be a little grateful. At least I sent Danny home to you."

Rose shook her head. "I'm supposed to be grateful to you for kidnapping my child? You do need help, Emily."

"Don't say that," Emily said angrily.

"How could you kidnap an innocent boy just because you wanted to get back at Wade?"

"Danny was fine. He thought it was an adventure."

"And what about Sandrine? You were going to kill her, weren't you?"

Emily turned around and walked to the edge of the cell, standing on her tiptoes to look out the small barred window that barely gave her a view of the street. "Sandrine is an Indian. That's the only kind of thing she understands."

"What is the matter with you?" Rose said angrily, yanking on Emily's arm until she turned around.

"I've been locked up in this stinking place for over a week, that's what's wrong with me. Why doesn't my uncle get me out of here? He said he was going to take me back home."

"He will as soon as he can leave."

"Why doesn't he just put me on a train?"

Rose shook her head. "How do we know you won't get off somewhere and come right back here?" Rose narrowed her eyes. "You have everyone else fooled, Emily. They all think you're ill up here," Rose said, pointing to her head, "but not me. I just think you're evil, and I want you away from my family and my friends."

"Well, you might not have anything to say about it," Emily said, walking to the cot. She quickly rummaged through the basket until she found what she was looking for. She took out the heavy wooden brush and held it against her chest, still facing the cot. "Thank you for bringing these things, Rose," she said, her voice soft.

"I'd better go," Rose said.

"Wait," Emily said, changing the tone of her voice. "I'm

sorry. I didn't mean to sound so cruel. It's just that . . ." Emily bent her head, pretending to cry.

"Emily, don't," Rose said, coming up behind her.

As soon as Emily felt Rose's hands on her shoulders, she whirled around and hit Rose on the side of the head with the brush, knocking her backward. Before Rose could regain her balance, Emily hit her twice more. Rose collapsed on the floor, unmoving. Emily hid the brush under the folds of her skirt and turned Rose halfway on her back, making it look like she had fainted. Then she called out for help. When the deputy came to the door of the cell, Emily looked up at him, her eyes wide.

"What happened?" he asked.

"I don't know," Emily said, her voice choked with tears. "She just fainted. She's expecting a baby, and I think the trip in here today was too hard on her. Can you please help me get her on the cot?"

The deputy fumbled with his keyring and opened the cell door.

Emily watched tearfully as the deputy lifted Rose into his arms and carried her to the cot. But before he had straightened up completely, Emily smashed the hairbrush into his temple. As he reeled away from her, crying out, she reached for his gun. She took it by the barrel and hit the man on the back of the skull. He fell to his knees, his hands on his head, and Emily hit him once more.

Quickly she slipped out of her clothes, putting on Rose's clean dress. She brushed her hair back and tied it with the ribbon from Rose's hair, then she picked up the gun and put it into the basket. She took the keys to the cell, closed the door, and locked it.

She stood by the heavy corridor door, opening it slightly until she could see that there was no one in the office. Slowly she opened the office door and looked out onto the street. She waited until there was no one on the sidewalk, then she stepped out and walked down the street until she found Rose's wagon. Smiling at a man who tipped his hat as he passed by, she climbed up onto the wagon as if she owned it. She lifted the reins from the brakehandle, released the brake, and flipped the reins until the horse began to walk. When she reached the edge of town, she smiled to herself. She wasn't through with Sandrine yet.

Wade watched Sandrine as she walked along the stream, holding her skirt up around her ankles. She was getting stronger each day, and he knew that it wouldn't be long before they could leave. She hadn't talked to him much since he'd kissed her, and he hadn't said much to her either. It would be easier on them both if he kept his distance, and he was determined to do just that. But it was hard. As he watched her wade through the water, he admired her long, lean legs and the way her hair shone in the sunlight. She was still wearing one of his shirts over her skirt, and he liked it; he imagined that anything would look good on her. She was an incredibly beautiful woman, but he couldn't confuse desire with love. He couldn't do that to her, and he couldn't do that to himself.

He stretched his legs out in front of him. He'd been thinking a lot about his life, and he'd decided that he was going to do some traveling and maybe even go back East. Jim told him that they had traveled constantly when he was young, but Wade didn't remember any of the places he'd been. He wanted to start making a new life for himself. Maybe the way to do that would be to get away from all the people who remembered him the way he was before.

He looked up sharply. He heard a horse's whinny in the distance. Someone was coming to the cabin. He stood up. It was probably only Frank or Jim. Still . . . He rested his hand on his gun, walking closer to the stream. "Sandrine," he said, glancing at her as he watched the trail.

"What?"

"Come here," he said, his voice firm. Sandrine hesitated for a moment but came out of the water. "Stand behind me," he ordered, pushing her close to him with his arm.

"What is it?"

"Probably nothing," Wade said as he watched and listened. He heard the horse again, and when it came out of the trees, he drew his gun. "It's an Indian. I want you to step back toward the trees."

"No," Sandrine said, moving away from him.

"Dammit, Sandrine. Do as I say," he said angrily, shoving her backward.

"No," she said, twisting away from him. "It's my cousin."

Before Wade could stop her, Sandrine was running down the trail toward the horse. He followed her, his gun still drawn. The Indian swung down from his horse and held out his arms. Sandrine ran to him, resting her head on his chest and wrapping her arms around him. He spoke in a language Wade didn't know, yet could understand.

"You are well, cousin?" the Indian asked.

"Yes," Sandrine replied. "What are you doing here?"

"I was worried about you. I knew that you were in trouble." He hugged Sandrine tightly to him, but she pulled away. "What is it?"

Sandrine shook her head. "It's nothing. I'm fine." She reached up to touch his face. "I can't believe you're here. Did you bring Shining Bird?"

"No."

"You rode all this way alone?"

"I am not alone, Bright Star," he said, looking past her to Wade. "It is good to see you, Colter."

Wade walked forward. "I'm sorry, I don't—" He stopped

when he heard the whinny of another horse. Without warning, the horse and rider came into the clearing and Wade looked up. The man glanced at him for an instant and then his eyes fell on Sandrine. When she looked up at the rider, she shook her head and stepped backward, stumbling.

"No," she said, her face pale.

"I am sorry, cousin. I meant to warn you," Little Bear said, holding Sandrine.

Wade stood next to her. "What's wrong, Sandrine?" he asked, looking at her face.

But before she could answer, the rider had dismounted and walked to Sandrine. He reached out and touched her cheek, smiling wistfully. "I never thought I would see you again, Bright Star," he said.

Wade watched as Sandrine's eyes filled with tears, and then her legs buckled. The man caught her before she fell, and she cried out as he held her. "You were dead. I saw you die," she said, looking up at him.

"I did not die. I am here. I am here to take you back with me."

Wade knew then who it was. It was Lone Wind.

Wade watched, powerless to do anything as Lone Wind lifted Sandrine into his arms. He was amazed at the way she looked so at home with the man, the way she rested her head against his chest, the way she held onto him. Lone Wind spoke to Little Bear, and he nodded.

"Where is your lodge, Colter?" Little Bear asked.

Wade looked at Little Bear. "It's up the trail a bit. It's a cabin."

Little Bear spoke to Lone Wind. Lone Wind walked past Wade, ignoring him. Wade watched him as he walked up the trail with Sandrine in his arms as though she was his.

"I am sorry, Colter. I know this must be strange for you," Little Bear said.

"You have no idea," Wade said, shaking his head. "She told me Lone Wind was dead."

"My cousin told you about Lone Wind?"

"Yes. What is he doing here?" Wade couldn't contain the anger he suddenly felt at the intrusion of the stranger.

"He wanted to make sure that all was well with Bright Star."

"I think he wants more than that," Wade said angrily, kicking at the dirt.

"He will respect the fact that you are married to my cousin."

"He doesn't seem to be respecting it now," Wade said, staring at the now empty trail.

"If Bright Star told you about Lone Wind, then she told you that there were strong feelings between them."

"Yes," Wade said, nodding. "But she told me he was dead."

"He thought it best that she believe him to be dead."

"You mean she wouldn't have come back here if he'd been alive, is that it?" Wade shook his head. "I don't need this. Since you're here, you take care of her. She doesn't need me anymore." Wade started up the trail to the cabin, but Little Bear took his arm.

"Wait, Colter. Before we go to your lodge, I wish to talk to you. It has been a long time. I have missed you, my friend."

Wade stopped, sighing deeply. When he turned to look at Little Bear, he could see the look of sincerity in his eyes. "I know all about you, Little Bear, yet I don't remember you." When Wade saw the puzzled expression on Little Bear's face, he explained what had happened to him.

Little Bear listened in amazement as Wade talked. "You do not even remember Bright Star?"

Wade shook his head, watching Little Bear's face as the Indian realized he was telling the truth. "No."

"Yet you seem . . ." Little Bear shrugged his shoulders. "You seem to be bothered by Lone Wind."

"I don't like the way he came in here and . . ." Wade stopped.

"I don't know, Little Bear. Maybe she does belong with him. I can't be the man I used to be. I'll never be able to love her the way I used to."

"Then you will learn to love her in a new way, yes? I believe you already have."

Wade caught Little Bear's eyes, then quickly looked away. He walked down toward the stream and stood, arms crossed, staring into the water. Little Bear was just as Sandrine had described him: smart, strong, and loyal.

"Are you trying to remember, white man?"

Wade jerked his head around, narrowing his eyes. "Why did you call me that?"

"I always called you that when we were boys. I did not like you much then."

"I didn't like you either, did I?"

Little Bear grinned. "No, I do not think that you did."

"You saved my life." Wade didn't remember the circumstances exactly, but he knew that Little Bear had helped him more than once.

"Yes, I saved your life. You fell into a half-frozen river." Little Bear shook his head. "Stupid white man."

Wade couldn't resist a grin. "I'm sure your cousin would say the same thing."

Little Bear clapped Wade on the shoulder. "It is good to see that you still have your sense of humor."

Wade sat down. "I suppose we should give them some time together."

"That is not necessary. She is your wife," Little Bear said, sitting next to Wade.

"She used to be my wife." Wade picked up some pebbles and rolled them around in his hand. "Tell me something, Little Bear. Were your cousin and I close? Did we care for each other?"

Little Bear was silent a moment, clearing his throat. "Are

you asking me if you and Bright Star loved each other, Colter?" Without waiting for an answer, Little Bear said, "The first time my cousin saw you riding with the wagon train when you were just a boy, she felt something in her heart for you. And each time you came back, the feeling grew stronger. You felt the same way about her. But I do not think you realized how much you loved my cousin until she was kidnapped by Bear Killer. You would have done anything to find her, and you did."

"And what about when she went to your grandfather when he was dying? How did she feel about me then?"

"She loved you still."

"But what about Lone Wind? If she loved me so much, how could she have loved him, too? How could she have even thought of staying with him?" Wade was surprised at the emotion in his voice.

"Bright Star was a long distance from you, Colter. You did not come with her. She was alone. Many times she was in danger, and each time Lone Wind was there to help her. She did not fall out of love with you, she just grew close to Lone Wind."

"It doesn't matter anyhow," Wade said, throwing the pebbles into the water.

"Why?"

"I'm leaving."

"Where are you going?"

"Don't know," Wade said, resting his elbows on his knees. "I may just get on my horse and ride until I find a place I like."

"What is it you are running from, Colter?"

"I'm not running from anything. I just want to get away."

"Is it my cousin you are running from?"

"Hell, no. Why would I be running from her?" Wade stood up, brushing off his pants.

"Perhaps you are afraid," Little Bear said, standing up next to his friend.

"What do I have to be afraid of?" Wade shook his head and started walking toward the trail.

"I think you are afraid of loving Bright Star."

Wade stopped and looked at Little Bear. "You don't know what you're talking about. I don't love Sandrine and I don't remember loving her. I think it's good that Lone Wind is here. If she loves him, she should be with him."

"I think you are playing a game with yourself, Colter," Little Bear said, brushing by Wade on the trail. "Stupid white man," he muttered again.

Wade followed Little Bear to the cabin, hesitating before he went inside. He took a deep breath and walked through the doorway. No one was in the front room. He walked to the bedroom. Little Bear was standing by the bed while Lone Wind was sitting on the edge next to Sandrine. He was gesturing angrily to Little Bear. When Little Bear saw him, he turned.

"How did this happen?" Little Bear asked.

Wade tried to explain, but before he could finish, Lone Wind stood up and walked to him.

"Why were you not there to help her?" he demanded in broken Blackfoot.

"I didn't know she'd been kidnapped," Wade responded. He clenched his jaw tightly. "I came to her as soon as I could."

"She should never have been left alone," Lone Wind said.

Wade narrowed his eyes. "Why are you here? Is it to see if she is well, or is it to take her back to your village with you?"

"If she is willing, I will take her," Lone Wind said, his voice hard.

"And if she is not, I won't let you force her."

"Stop," Little Bear said, stepping between the two men. "It is not your place to interfere, Lone Wind," he said.

"I will ask Bright Star if she wants me to leave," Lone Wind said, his eyes holding Wade's.

"No," Little Bear said, taking Lone Wind's arm. "Let her rest now."

"You stay with her, Little Bear." Wade glanced over at the bed, noticing that Sandrine hadn't spoken a word. "I'll go make us something to eat."

"And I will check on the horses," Lone Wind said, pushing past Wade.

Wade looked at Sandrine once more, but her face was turned toward the wall. It made him angry to think that there was nothing he could do about Lone Wind. He started for the door but stopped when he heard Sandrine call out his name.

"Wade."

He walked back to the bed. Sandrine was half-sitting, leaning on Little Bear's arm. She looked up at Little Bear. "Can you leave us for a few moments?"

Little Bear nodded, gently touching his cousin's cheek. "I have something for you from Running Tears," he said. "I will get it from my horse."

Wade stood by the bed, feeling angry and confused. He avoided Sandrine's eyes when he spoke. "Are you all right?"

"I'm all right. Sit down. Please."

Wade shook his head. "I'll stand." He crossed his arms over his chest, brushing his boot along the floor.

"I didn't know he was alive, Wade. I swear to you."

"It doesn't matter, Sandrine. I have no claim on you."

"That's right, I forgot. Or I should say, *you* forgot," she said angrily.

Wade looked up. Sandrine was sitting, her hands resting on the edge of the bed. She was obviously in pain but trying not to show it. Her cheeks were flushed and her mouth was set in an angry line. "I know that you loved him," Wade said, sitting down in the chair opposite Sandrine. "You would've stayed with him if he were alive."

"I was getting ready to leave him the night he got hurt." Her voice was soft and tremulous when she spoke. "I wanted to come back to you."

Wade felt the depth of her emotion, and he reached out, tilting her chin up. "I'm sorry, Sandrine. I wish I could remember. I wish I knew what it was like to love you the way everyone tells me I loved you. I wish we—" Wade stopped when he heard Lone Wind's voice in the other room, coming closer to the bedroom.

"Are you all right, Bright Star?" he asked, walking into the room and standing next to the bed.

"Yes." Sandrine looked at Wade and then at Lone Wind.

"Would you permit me to sit with you awhile?"

Sandrine glanced at Wade and then nodded. "Yes, I'd like that," she said, avoiding Wade's eyes.

Wade glared at Lone Wind and went into the other room. Little Bear was sitting at the table, going through one of his hide bags. Wade went to the cookstove and poured himself a cup of coffee. He sat down at the table, slamming the tin cup down, spilling some of the brown liquid.

"So, you no longer love my cousin, eh?" Little Bear said, pulling a small piece of rawhide from his bag.

Wade ignored him and took a sip of his coffee. "How long will you be here?"

"Why, do you wish me to be gone?"

"I don't care," Wade said, taking another sip of coffee. "I think I'll take off tomorrow."

"Where will you go, Colter?"

"I'll go home."

"And what is at your home, Colter? Have you a family waiting for you?"

"You know I don't," Wade said, wrapping his fingers around the cup. "I only have a half-finished house, a house that I was building for Sandrine before I lost my memory."

"You can still finish the house."

"I have no reason to finish it now." Wade stared past Little

Bear to the other room, but he couldn't see anything because Lone Wind had closed the door.

"So what will you do now that you are a free man?"

"What?"

"Well, it is obvious that you will let Lone Wind take Bright Star back to his village. You will no longer be saddled with a wife. Will you find yourself another woman, or will there be many?"

"Were you always this irritating?" Wade asked, finishing his coffee.

"What is this word?"

"You are like a thorn that gets stuck in the side and you can't get it out. That's what irritating means."

Little Bear considered the explanation, then nodded his head. "Yes, I have always been that way, especially with you and my cousin." Little Bear bent down and picked up another bag, handing Wade a piece of soft rawhide. "This is a gift from Running Tears. She told me to tell you that she misses you and she hopes that you will one day bring Bright Star to visit them."

Wade unwrapped the bundle. It was a shirt made out of the softest hide he had ever felt. He looked up at Little Bear. "How did she make this?"

Little Bear shook his head. "You truly do not remember? She scrapes it free of the flesh, then she puts on a mixture to soften it. She stretches it out so that it can be worked, then she chews on it. My aunt worked many hours on this, Colter."

Wade nodded, running his fingers over the blue beads that were sewn along the neck and down the front of the shirt. "This is incredible work."

"They are her favorite colored beads. You were always very special to my aunt. Do you remember her?"

"No," Wade said, looking at the shirt. "At least, I don't think so."

"But you remember how to speak our language."

"Yes, but I don't have any memory of having learned it." He ran his fingers over the beads again. "I have a memory of you and me playing in the sun all day and I got badly burned. It was Running Tears who took care of me, wasn't it?"

"Yes, it was," Little Bear said, smiling.

"What? Why are you laughing?"

"I thought my aunt was going to beat me."

"Why? It wasn't your fault that I got burned." Wade knit his eyebrows together. "Or was it?"

"I simply suggested that you take off your shirt while we played. I said it would be cooler."

"But you were dark-skinned and used to the sun, and you knew that I would burn." Wade shook his head, a grin appearing. "I guess you were a thorn in my side, weren't you?"

"There were many times I made you look like the fool in front of my friends," Little Bear admitted, "but there were other times when I was proud that you were my friend. You were fearless. You would try anything. I am sure you would have fought by my side until death if I had asked you."

"I guess I wasn't very smart," Wade said, laughing.

"You were very smart, but there were times that you were not guided by your brain, especially when my cousin was around. You would do anything to try to impress her."

Wade put the shirt on the table, stood up, and put his cup on the stove. "It won't work, Little Bear."

"I do not understand what you are saying."

Wade walked back to the table. "I know what you're trying to do. You're trying to make me remember my past by telling me things that happened. But it won't work. I've tried to remember, but there's nothing there."

"You just told me a story from when we were boys, and you also can speak our language. How is this possible?"

"It doesn't mean anything. The doctor said I might remember a few things, but I might never get my memory back." Wade walked to the front door. "I can't live my life worrying about what kind of man I used to be or thinking about the woman I used to love." Wade glanced toward the bedroom door once more and walked outside, knowing he had to get away from Sandrine as soon as possible.

Wade reined in his horse as he rode into Jim and Rose's yard. Danny and his dog were nowhere in sight, and the place was uncharacteristically quiet. He dismounted and tied up his horse, then peered into the window. It looked like no one was home. He opened the door and went inside, checking all of the rooms. The place was empty. He rubbed his face. He was exhausted and had been hoping to get one of Rose's home-cooked meals. They were probably in town, he thought, and they'd be back soon.

He walked over to the sofa and sat down, then lazily stretched out, propping his boots over the edge. He took off his hat and rested his head on a pillow, covering his eyes with his arm. It had been a long ride; more than that, it had been a long two weeks. As much as he didn't like to admit it, it had been hard to say goodbye to Sandrine. When he saw her with Lone Wind today it had stirred something inside of him that he didn't understand, and he didn't like. She'd gotten tears in her eyes when he said goodbye and he'd almost changed his mind, but he knew it was best for him to go. What could he offer Sandrine? Nothing really. A home, maybe, but not love, and he knew that was what she wanted more than anything.

He tried to clear his mind, but every time his body started to relax, he saw Sandrine's face. She had such incredible blue eyes, eyes that demanded so much from him. He sighed deeply, feeling his body relax into sleep.

"Wade. Wade."

At first the voice seemed to be coming from a distance, then it grew louder, more insistent.

"Wade. Wake up."

Wade opened his eyes. Jim was bent over him, his face white and tense. Wade met his old friend's eyes and saw fear and sorrow. "What is it? What's wrong?" Wade sat up, rubbing at his face with his hands.

Jim paced the length of the room and then whirled and started back, ignoring Wade's question.

"What the hell's the matter, Jim?"

Jim frowned and shook his head. Wade could see that his eyes were watery. His face had a stubble at least three days long, and his work clothes looked like he'd slept in them. A flash of fear ran down Wade's spine. "Where are Rose and Danny? What happened?"

Jim paused in his pacing. He faced Wade for a moment without speaking, his expression bleak, then he dropped into the chair that was next to the sofa, covering his face with his hands.

Wade's feeling of fear intensified, and he clutched Jim's arm. "Has something happened to Rose or Danny?" He repeated.

Finally Jim looked at Wade, nodding his head. "Rose is unconscious; she's been like that for days. Danny's fine. He's staying with the Fosters."

"Where is Rose?"

"She's in town, staying at Doc's. He said it was too dangerous to move her."

Wade recalled his own injury and that Doc had allowed Jim and Rose to bring him here. Rose must be in bad shape if she wasn't allowed to be moved. "What happened, Jim?"

"It's a goddamned nightmare," Jim muttered, covering his face again. "Rose went into town to visit Emily, to take her some things." He looked up and shook his head. "You know Rose, she can't stand the thought of anyone suffering. Anyway, she was inside the cell with Emily, visiting with her." He shrugged his shoulders, a dazed look in his eyes. "I guess she turned her back and Emily hit her on the head with a brush that Rose had brought. Jesus, she hit her so many times," Jim said. "There wasn't a lot of blood, but Doc said she could be bleeding inside her head. Even if she does wake up, Doc says she might not be the same. He says she probably suffered some damage."

"No," Wade said, shaking his head. "Not Rose." Pain stabbed his chest, and he felt as if he couldn't breathe. Rose was like a mother to him. No, she was more like a big sister. He'd been there to help her deliver Danny, and they'd had a special bond because of that, he'd been told. But he didn't remember any of his past friendship with Rose. All he knew was how kind and loyal she'd been to him since his accident and how close he felt to her now. "Can I see her?"

"It won't do any good, Wade. She can't hear you."

"You don't know that for sure."

"Stop it," Jim said angrily, standing up and pacing the room again. "We don't live in some big city, Wade. It's not like we can just call in some fancy surgeon to operate on Rose and make her well."

"We can take her to a surgeon," Wade said.

"Doc said she can't be moved, I told you."

"Then I'll bring one here," Wade said, getting up and standing next to Jim.

"You can't do that in time, Wade. Be realistic."

"I am being realistic, Jim. If Rose can't travel, then I'll bring someone here who can help her."

"I don't know . . ."

Wade heard the dismay in Jim's voice, and he stopped. "I'm sorry. I don't mean to push."

"It's okay, kid," Jim said, smiling weakly as he sat down again.

"You hungry? Want some coffee?"

"You sound like Rose," Jim said sorrowfully.

Wade didn't know what to say. He sat back down on the sofa, leaning forward, his elbows on his knees. "Where's Emily?"

"They haven't found her. She took our wagon and drove it about five miles out of town. The sheriff found it, but there was no sign of Emily. She just disappeared."

"How could she just disappear? She's from the East. She doesn't know about covering her tracks."

"It's obvious there's a lot about Emily that we don't know," Jim said, sitting back in the chair. He shook his head. "First Sandrine, now Rose."

"Sandrine will be all right."

"Where is she?"

"She's at the cabin with Little Bear. She wasn't quite ready to make the trip." Wade decided that Jim didn't need to know about Lone Wind.

"What're you doing here anyway? I didn't think you were coming back until Sandrine was completely well."

"She's safe with Little Bear. Besides, I wanted to check on you and Rose. It's a good thing I did. I might've never found out about her." He put his hand on Jim's shoulder. "So what do we do about Emily?"

"I don't know. My main concern is Rose."

"What about Danny? Is he safe with the Fosters?"

"Yeah, you know how big that family is. I told them not to let Danny out of their sight. Emily would be a fool to try to go there."

"Is Rose safe at Doc's?"

"When I'm not there, a deputy is. She's well-guarded."

"Good. I'd like to see her tomorrow, if you don't mind. After that, I think I'll ride out and see if I can figure out where Emily's gone to."

"It won't do you any good."

"Maybe not, but I'd like to try anyway."

Jim nodded and stood up. "I'm tired. I'm going to get some sleep. You know where everything is."

Jim walked into the bedroom, and for the first time, Wade noticed that he looked old and tired, and it saddened him. He lay back down on the couch, staring up at the ceiling. He owed Jim and Rose a lot; the least he could do was try to find Emily before she caused anyone else any more hurt.

He closed his eyes but sat up suddenly, his mind racing. What if Emily had gone back to the cabin to find Sandrine? Logic told him that Emily was no match for Little Bear and Lone Wind. Still, he had underestimated her before, and Sandrine and Rose had paid the price. What if Little Bear and Lone Wind went hunting and they left Sandrine alone? He shook his head, knowing that that wouldn't happen. Lone Wind wouldn't leave Sandrine alone. He was too protective of her. Feeling relieved, he lay back down and closed his eyes, trying to relax. But all he could see was Emily's face, contorted in rage.

Sandrine watched Lone Wind as he brushed his horse. He was acutely uncomfortable staying in the cabin, and he used any excuse to be outside. He had been kind and understanding to her, and for a few days it was as if they had never been apart. But as the days wore on, Sandrine realized how different they really were. When she had been in the Crow camp, it had been easy for her to adjust to the life there. She was used to a similar kind of life because she had grown up living in a Blackfoot camp. But it was different for Lone Wind. It was apparent to her now that he could never get used to any other kind of life but the one he had always known. While she loved visiting her people, she had become accustomed to the white world and did not want to leave it. And then there was Wade.

He had taken care of her when she was so badly beaten. He had held her and had listened to her cry over and over again. It had almost been like before, like nothing had ever changed between them. She had even seen him soften toward her. She had caught him staring at her numerous times, and she knew that he was becoming attracted to her. But she also knew that he was scared and wasn't ready to settle down again. She looked up and smiled when she saw Little Bear walking up the trail, his hands filled with berries. He stopped in front of her and dropped them into her lap.

"Eat them. They will make you strong," he said, sitting down next to her.

Sandrine ate some of the sweet berries and wiped her mouth. "Are you happy?"

Little Bear reached over and took some berries from Sandrine's lap. "Are you asking if I like having a wife and children?"

"Yes, I guess that's what I'm asking."

Little Bear popped some more berries into his mouth and nodded. "Yes, I like it very much. I find that my heart is not so cold anymore."

Sandrine looked at her cousin and smiled wistfully. She had forgotten how much she had missed him. "I don't think that your heart was ever cold," she said, putting her arm through his and leaning her head against his shoulder. "I miss you. I wish you were closer. Sometimes I want to speak what is in my heart, but I can't. There isn't anyone I trust as much as I trust you."

"What about Colter?"

"You know it's not the same with us. I don't think it will ever be."

"The same is not always good. There is nothing wrong with change, cousin."

Sandrine looked at Little Bear. "Do you think I could make a life with Lone Wind?"

"That is something you must decide for yourself."

"Tell me what you think, Little Bear. Please." Sandrine

watched Little Bear as he stared ahead of him, his eyes narrowed. Then he turned to look at her.

"I think when you came to visit grandfather, you were angry with Colter. You felt sadness after grandfather died, and when you went to the Crow camp, you felt an emptiness inside of you that needed to be filled. Lone Wind was there and Colter was not. I think that you confused love with need."

Sandrine started to speak but stopped and thought about what Little Bear had just said. He had voiced her own thoughts. "My feelings for Lone Wind are strong."

"I believe that to be true, but are they as strong as your feelings for Colter? This is the question you must answer, cousin."

Sandrine took her arm from Little Bear's and bent her knees, wrapping her arms around them. She rested her head on her arm, staring at Wade's blue shirt. She rubbed her cheek against the cloth and closed her eyes. She was able to see everything about him.

"Lone Wind is a good man. I did not want to believe that at first because he is Crow. I now know differently. He is a man of honor."

"I know," Sandrine agreed.

"And Colter is a good man, also a man of honor. It is a difficult choice."

Sandrine shook her head. "Wade doesn't want me," she said, fighting to keep the emotion from her voice.

"He struggles with many things right now, cousin. You must give him time."

"Time won't make any difference," she said, suddenly feeling angry. "I should just go with Lone Wind." Little Bear made a grunting sound and Sandrine looked over at him. "What? Why are you making that face?"

"The berries, they are sour."

Sandrine hit Little Bear in the shoulder. "Stop playing with me."

"You want words of wisdom from me, cousin, and I have none. I am not grandfather and I am not your mother."

"But you know me," Sandrine said.

"Yes, I know you."

"Then help me, Little Bear."

Little Bear reached into Sandrine's lap and took the rest of the berries, munching on them thoughtfully. When he was finished, he wiped his mouth and looked at her. "It would not be right to go with Lone Wind only because you believe Colter will not take you back. If you go with Lone Wind, it must be because you want to be with him. If you go for any other reason, you will be dishonoring yourself and him."

"I care for him, Little Bear," she said, looking at Lone Wind again.

"Do you care for him enough to share his robe at night, to bear his children, and to live in a Crow camp for the rest of your days?" Little Bear clasped Sandrine's shoulder. "You spent half of your time growing up in a Blackfoot camp, Bright Star. You know it is not easy. Would you be able to give up the white world forever?"

Sandrine watched Lone Wind for a moment longer, then looked away, unable to face the truth of what Little Bear had said. "I dreamt of him when I was hurt."

"I dream of many things."

"He said he would come to me and protect me, and he did."

"Do you think that you had a vision, cousin? What do you want me to say, that the Great Spirit means for you and Lone Wind to be together because you had a dream? If that is what you wish to believe . . ." Little Bear shrugged his shoulders and stood up. "I am going back to the cabin. You should decide what you are going to do, Bright Star. I miss my family and I wish to return home. If you are going to come with us, we should leave soon." His voice was firm.

Sandrine watched Little Bear as he walked away. They were close in age, yet he had always seemed so much older and wiser. She stood up and walked through the grass to Lone Wind. He turned when he saw her and smiled slightly, continuing to brush his horse.

"Little Bear says that we should leave soon," he said without looking at her. "I think that he misses Shining Bird."

Sandrine clenched her fists at her sides. "I won't be going with you, Lone Wind," she said. When he didn't answer, she stepped closer, touching his arm. "I won't be going with you. I'm going to stay here."

Lone Wind stopped brushing the horse and turned to look at Sandrine, his dark eyes betraying no emotion. "Will you stay with the white man?"

"No, I'm staying because this is where I belong."

"This is not where you belong, Bright Star," Lone Wind said, turning back to the horse.

"I thank you for coming here," she said, again touching his arm. "My heart is full to know that you are alive. But I cannot go back with you. I am not Crow. I cannot live in your world."

"You lived in my world once before," he said, turning to face her.

"I was there because of Gray Wolf."

Lone Wind dropped the brush. "But you stayed because of me," he said, pulling her into his arms. "I will not lose you again."

Sandrine looked into Lone Wind's dark eyes. She remembered how she had felt about him, and now she knew why. He had saved her life and she had felt grateful; she had also felt lonely. But now she was back where she belonged. She felt strong, and she knew she didn't belong with Lone Wind. Even if she never had a future with Wade, she would still live in the white world. She took his hands and moved them away from her. "You and I are so different, Lone Wind. I'm part Blackfoot, but I'm also half white. I could never live in a Crow village the rest of my life."

"I think you could," Lone Wind said.

"No, I couldn't," Sandrine said impatiently. When Lone Wind tried to reach for her again, she brushed his hands away. "I don't love you, Lone Wind, and I know you don't love me."

"How could you know such a thing?"

"Because," she said gently, looking up at him, "I am not the woman who was in the Crow camp. I'm different now."

"How are you different?"

"I can live on my own here."

"What about the white man? Will he watch over you?"

Sandrine turned away. "No, he won't."

"Your heart is still full of him, is it not?"

She took a deep breath and turned back to Lone Wind. "Yes, it is, but I'm not staying because of him. Do you understand that? I'm staying because this is where I belong."

"Will you return to your mother's people?"

"No, I don't belong there either. I will visit my mother and her people, but this is my home now."

"I want you to be happy, Bright Star."

Sandrine nodded. "Don't worry about me. I want you to go home. Find yourself another woman, a woman who will be a good wife, someone who will give you many children." She reached down and took off the silver bracelet, handing it to him.

Lone Wind took the bracelet and touched Sandrine's cheek. "Are you sure you are not that woman?"

"Yes," she said, smiling weakly, "I'm sure."

Lone Wind nodded. "If that is what you wish, I will return home. But I will never forget you, Bright Star." He put his arms around her.

Sandrine rested her head against Lone Wind's chest, closing

her eyes. Perhaps it was easy to say goodbye to Lone Wind because she knew he was alive and would go on with his life. Now she had to find a way to go on with hers.

Fifteen

Three days had passed since Wade had come back from Frank's cabin, but it seemed longer. He'd tried to help Jim, but there was no consoling his friend. Wade had gone to visit Rose and was shocked by how pale and vulnerable she looked. He had held her hand and talked to her as if she could hear every word he was saying, but she never moved. It didn't really hit him until he left Doc's house and was riding back to his ranch. Tears welled up in his eyes, and he felt a heaviness in his chest. He remembered the feeling; he had felt the same when his parents had died.

He rode along the ridge that was above Jim and Rose's ranch, and continued on past, following the narrow trail that led toward his place. He knew that even though he was letting Emily get a head start, it was better this way. If he had found her any sooner, he probably would've killed her. Every time he pictured Rose's pale, expressionless face, he felt a rage well up inside of him. What he needed was one more day, a day at his own ranch, then he would be able to leave calmly, purposefully. He would find Emily, and when he found her, she would answer for all the sorrow she had caused.

When he reached the hill above his ranch, he reined in, looking at the lush, green valley and mountains beyond. This was the first time the view gave him no joy. His eyes teared up again as he thought of Rose lying so still, and especially when he thought of Danny and Jim possibly having to go on without her.

Sighing heavily, he kicked his horse and guided the animal down the trail that led to the big house. He barely glanced at it as he rode into the grass and dirt yard. He sat astride his horse for a few minutes, staring down into the valley, letting his mind wander. It was then he saw movement down below. He sat up straight and strained his eyes to see. There was a person walking along the stream.

He turned his horse and guided it down the hill into the valley. As he got closer to the stream, he could see who it was. Sandrine was walking barefoot in the water, her skirt held up around her knees. She was still wearing his blue shirt. When his horse nickered, Sandrine turned around, putting her hand up to shield her eyes. She raised her hand in a half-wave and then quickly lowered it to her side. He felt an odd mixture of feelings wash through him, and he reined in his horse, averting his eyes to hide the intensity of his response to her. He was so glad to see her. He didn't know why she'd come back, but he was grateful that she had. He swung off his horse and walked to the stream.

He met her eyes and almost smiled when she flushed and looked away. She was a beautiful woman. Whatever else he had been before the accident, he had been lucky to have a woman like Sandrine. "Why are you here?"

Her gaze was level, in spite of the girlish blush on her cheeks. He watched as she drew in a quick breath as though she were about to speak, but then she didn't. Her eyes held his, and he felt a wave of desire so strong that he stepped toward her before he could stop himself.

"Are you all right?" He searched her eyes.

"Yes," she said softly. After a moment she looked away, blushing again.

Wade couldn't take his eyes from her. He always thought that she was beautiful, but now, knowing how close he had come to almost losing her, he found her irresistible. It was all he could do to keep from touching her. He stared at the clear water rushing over her feet.

"What's wrong? Do you want me to leave, Wade?"

Without speaking, he bent and pulled his boots off, refusing to question his own impulse. He waded into the cold water and took Sandrine into his arms. She didn't resist but returned his embrace, surprising him with her strength. Then, after a moment, she pulled away.

"Lone Wind has gone back home."

Wade traced the curve of her cheek with his finger. "Why would he ride all this way and leave without you?"

"I told him I wanted to stay here. Near you."

There was no mistaking the invitation in her voice and her eyes. Wade pulled her into his arms and held her tightly against him. He felt her breath, quick and warm, against his neck, and he felt his desire ignite. The water swirled around their legs as he found the warmth of her mouth with his own. Afraid that she would pull away from him, he held her even tighter, caressing her body with his hands. Trembling with passion, he finally released her. Searching her eyes for any uncertainty, he undid the buttons of her blouse and slid it back off her shoulders. He bent to kiss her again, running his hands from her wrists up to her shoulders, then back down again. As he kissed her more deeply, he felt her eagerness, and he groaned. Lost in the softness of her skin and the sweetness of her mouth, he traced the curve of her back upward to her shoulders with both hands. It took him a moment to realize that she had stiffened within his embrace, and he remembered. Gently he turned her around and saw the ugly red welts that crisscrossed the lovely smooth skin of her back.

"No," she said, trying to turn in his arms, but he held her to him.

He leaned forward, gently kissing the welts on her back, and he felt her body tremble. He dropped to his knees in the cool water, and he pulled her with him. He continued to kiss her back, and slowly his hands caressed her breasts. Her head went back against his shoulder and he heard her moan softly. He wanted to take the time to explore her, to get to know every inch of her, but his desire was strong.

Suddenly he stood, pulling her with him, and he walked to the bank. Quickly he took off his clothes and faced Sandrine. He could see the desire in her eyes; he could see in her eyes what he had forgotten. He took off her blouse and her skirt, and reached underneath her slip and slipped off her underwear. His hands still on her hips, he drew her to him, kissing her passionately. As soon as his body touched hers, felt its warmth, his desire grew stronger. Slowly he lowered himself into the high grass as he held onto her, pulling her on top of him. He kissed her again as he moved his hips against hers. He ran his hands up and down her long legs, caressing the softness of her inner thighs until he felt her move against his hand, and finally her moans became too much for him. He entered her slowly, making sure she was ready to receive him. When he felt her settle herself on him, he thrust himself harder and deeper inside of her, feeling her take all of him, and he heard himself groan. He sought Sandrine's mouth and kissed her deeply, hearing her tiny moans of pleasure as they moved in unison. As he moved faster and faster, he felt her body shudder, and she cried out. Wade thrust as deeply as he could, rising to meet Sandrine's hips, his hands on her waist, until he couldn't control his desire any longer. Finally he let himself go, burying his face in her breasts.

Wade didn't move for some minutes. Sandrine still lay on top of him, her head resting on his chest. He could feel her heart pounding against his. Unwillingly he took a deep breath and eased Sandrine to the ground. She was still dressed in the thin, white slip, and it was still wet from the stream. She had pulled it down over her legs, but it clung to her body, and he could see her breasts pressing against the material. He reached out for her, pulling her to him. She rested her head on his chest, and he stroked her long dark hair. He wondered if this was the way it had been between them before.

"We should probably get dressed," Sandrine said, suddenly sitting up. She sat with her arms crossed in front of her chest.

"This is my land. Anyone who comes on it will be trespassing," Wade said, drawing her back to him. He reached up and brushed his fingers across her cheek. "I don't want you to leave yet."

"I'm not leaving. I just think we should get dressed."

"Wait," Wade said, holding Sandrine close to him. He kissed her lightly, enjoying the softness of her lips.

Sandrine pulled away. "What if Rose or Jim comes?"

He held her at arm's length, feeling his body tighten.

"What? What is it?" she asked.

Wade could hear the worry in her voice. He sat up and reached for his pants, quickly pulling them on. He held out his hands to Sandrine and helped her to her feet. He squeezed her hands gently before he released them. "Rose has been hurt."

Sandrine's face went white, and she searched Wade's eyes. "Hurt? How badly?"

"She's been unconscious for days."

Sandrine shook her head, pressing the back of one hand to her lips. "Not Rose . . . What happened?"

Wade started to speak but hesitated.

Sandrine put her hands on her hips. "What? Don't try to hide anything from me."

Wade almost smiled as he watched her anger turn to embarrassment as she realized that she was dressed only in her slip. She snatched up her skirt and stepped into it clumsily. He reached out to steady her, but she glared at him, and he took his hand from her arm. A moment later, she was buttoning her blouse with quick, snappish movements. The damp cloth would not slide over the buttons easily, and the hem of her wet skirt swung heavily. Her eyes were impossible to read now, the anger clouded with worry and something else he couldn't identify. Wade knew that she was probably feeling confused. And so was he. Their lovemaking had been wonderful. It was as though his body remembered hers; they had moved together so passionately, so easily. But whatever they both felt, it had to be set aside for now.

"If you stare at me for one more minute without talking, I swear I'll ride straight out to Jim's now. He'll tell me the truth."

Wade shook his head. "They're not out at the ranch. They're with Doc in town. Rose can't be moved."

"What happened?" Sandrine demanded again.

"Emily did it." Wade watched her face carefully, seeing the disbelief fade into an anger so intense that it almost frightened him.

"Where the hell is she?"

"No one knows."

"Why haven't you gone after her? What's the matter with you?"

Wade knew there was no point in trying to explain to Sandrine that he had been afraid that he would harm Emily. "I've been with Jim. I wanted to make sure he was all right."

Sandrine was staring into his eyes, and for a second he felt ashamed. She obviously thought that he should have already found Emily. "I'm sorry, Sandrine—"

"You *are* going to go after her, aren't you?"

Wade nodded curtly. "Of course."

She narrowed her eyes. "Why haven't you already?"

"I already told you . . ." Wade trailed off. He bent to pick up his shirt. "I don't owe you an explanation. Jim and Rose are like family to me. I will find Emily."

Sandrine held his eyes. "You'd better."

Wade almost took a step backward, surprised by the resolve

in Sandrine's voice. "I'm leaving in the morning. She can't be all that far away."

"How do you know?" Sandrine snapped. "She could be on her way back to Boston."

"What the hell's the matter with you?" He watched as Sandrine fought with her blouse buttons. It took him a moment to realize that this time she was trying to unbutton them. Finally she tugged the shirt off over her head. For an instant he was distracted by the outline of her lovely breasts beneath the thin cloth of the slip. Then abruptly she turned around, and the sight of the scars on her back made him catch his breath.

"This is what's the matter with me," she said angrily, turning to face him. "If you don't find Emily, I will."

"I'll find her," Wade said, his voice softening.

"I want to go with you, Wade."

"No," he said, shaking his head. "It's not a good idea."

"Why?"

"Because you're not that strong yet."

"I'm strong enough."

"No," Wade said adamantly. "I don't want you riding with me."

"I can track as well as you. Probably better since you don't remember how."

He glanced sharply at her, not sure if she had intended to insult him, but choosing to ignore her comment. "You're not coming with me, and that's that." He picked up his boots and socks.

"I don't need to go with you. I'll go on my own."

Wade dropped his boots and walked to Sandrine, holding her wrists tightly. "I don't want you riding with me, Sandrine. I don't want you anywhere near Emily."

"I'm not afraid of her."

"Well, you should be afraid of her. She almost killed you

and Rose." He loosened his grip on Sandrine's left wrist and held it up. "Where's the bracelet?"

Sandrine shrugged, avoiding his eyes. "I gave it back."

He tilted her chin up so that she was forced to meet his eyes. "I know it meant a lot to you. Why did you give it back?"

"It didn't belong to me," Sandrine said, her voice low.

"You do mean to stay then?"

"I told you that I did."

Wade nodded, feeling relief flood through his body. He lowered his mouth to Sandrine's, lingering for a moment. "Let's go to the cabin." Wade didn't wait for her to argue. He took her hand and held onto it tightly as he walked toward the cabin. When he reached the door, he opened it and led Sandrine inside. He walked toward the bedroom and sat on the bed, pulling her onto his lap. He sought her mouth and kissed her passionately. He didn't want to think about Emily now; he only wanted to think about how much he wanted Sandrine.

"I have something I need to do first," Sandrine said, standing outside of Doc's house.

"What do you need to do? I thought you were going to see Rose," Wade said impatiently.

"I am going to see her, but I need to get something for the room first. Just a little something to cheer it up. I won't be long." Sandrine smiled and waved, lifting up her skirt in one hand as she headed toward the center of town. When she was far enough away from Doc's, she dropped her skirt and hurried along to the first saloon she saw. Without hesitating, she pushed open the doors and went inside. It was fairly quiet, and there were just a few men playing cards at one of the tables. She walked to the bar, ignoring the look of surprise on the bartender's face.

"Can I help you, ma'am?"

"I'm looking for Nick Boulton. Have you seen him?"

The bartender shook his head. "Can't say as I have. He hasn't been in here in a few days. You might check on down the street at the Silver Nugget."

"Thank you," Sandrine said, turning to leave.

"Excuse me, ma'am, I couldn't help but overhear that you were asking about Nick Boulton."

Sandrine turned at the sound of the voice. A woman in a plain brown dress was seated at a table playing solitaire.

Sandrine walked to the table. "That's right."

"What do you want with him?"

"I want to offer him a job."

"A job?" The woman twisted her mouth and shook her head. "The last woman who offered Nick a job almost got him thrown in jail."

"I know," Sandrine said, pulling out a chair and sitting down. "Look, I need Nick's help. I need to track down the woman who hurt a friend of mine."

"You're talking about Rose Everett, aren't you?"

"Yes."

"And you're the woman Nick told me about, the one he kidnapped and then saved."

Sandrine nodded. "Yes. I promised him if he helped me, I'd pay him some money and I'd give him a job. I just need to find him."

"He said you'd come. He said you had honest eyes." The woman set down the cards she was holding in her hand. "He's probably over at the stables. They usually let him stay in an empty stall if they have one."

"Thank you," Sandrine said.

"Nick's not a bad sort, you know. If he was, you'd be dead."

"I know," Sandrine said, standing up. She held out her hand. "My name is Sandrine. Thank you for your help."

The woman nodded and shook Sandrine's hand. "Good luck. From what I hear, it's going to take a lot to catch that woman."

"We'll catch her," Sandrine said, nodding to the bartender as she headed out of the saloon. She hurried down the plank sidewalk, almost knocking over a woman who was carrying an armful of packages. With a quick apology, Sandrine hurried on her way until she reached the stable.

A tall, gangly young man was standing out in front brushing a stocky buckskin. "Can I help you, ma'am?"

"Yes, I'm looking for Nick Boulton."

"Haven't seen him," the young man said as he continued to brush the horse.

Sandrine nodded and, ignoring the protests of the young man, pushed by him and went into the stables, walking up and down each side until she found Nick. He was asleep in the last stall on the left, his bed a pile of hay. She unlatched the gate and walked inside. Squatting down, she shook Nick until he opened his eyes. "Nick, do you remember me?" She waited until recognition dawned in his eyes, and then she continued. "I promised you money and a job." She reached into her purse, handing him some bills. "I owe you a lot more, and I'll pay you when we get back."

Nick sat up and leaned against the rough-hewn wood stall. He rubbed his hands over his face in an attempt to wake himself up. "You don't owe me nothing," he said. "I never shoulda kidnapped you. You almost died because of me."

"No," Sandrine said gently, reaching out to touch Nick's arm. "I'm alive because of you. She would've surely beaten me to death if you hadn't stopped her."

"Yeah, but—"

"Nick, we don't have time to argue. Emily has hurt a friend of mine and she's escaped from jail. I need you to help me track her down."

"You want me to help you?"

"Yes. Are you interested?"

"Yes, ma'am. Tracking is one thing I'm good at."

"I know." Sandrine stood up. "I want you to get some coffee and food and get packed. Meet me at Doc's in two hours."

"Yes, ma'am."

Sandrine started toward the gate but stopped. "I want you to be thinking about Emily, Nick. Think about anything she might have said to you, places she's been or would like to go, anything. All right?"

Nick nodded. "Miss Sandrine?"

"Yes."

"Thank you for keeping your promise, ma'am. No one has ever done that before."

"You're welcome, Nick. I'll see you in two hours." Sandrine left the stable and started down the sidewalk, so lost in thought that she walked right into Wade. "Oh," she said, trying to hide her nervousness.

"Did you find whatever it was you needed?" he asked, looking past her to the stables.

Sandrine took Wade's arm and guided him back toward Doc's. "I had to speak with someone."

"What the hell are you talking about, Sandrine?"

"I hired Nick Boulton to help you track Emily."

"Are you crazy? The guy's a drunk."

Sandrine stopped. "The man saved my life. If he hadn't been there, I'd be dead right now."

"Have you forgotten that he's the one who kidnapped you?" Wade said angrily.

Sandrine tried to ignore the stares of the people who passed them on the sidewalk, and she steered Wade toward an alley. "I haven't forgotten that it was Emily who was responsible for my kidnapping. I don't want her to get away with this, Wade."

"She won't."

"Nick's good. As I recall, he led you on a merry chase." Sandrine tried to keep from smiling.

"I don't need his help," Wade said angrily, stepping back onto the sidewalk.

Sandrine hurried after him, grabbing his arm. "Please take him with you, Wade. I promised him a job, and this is perfect. Please."

Wade stopped in front of the telegraph office. "Why do you trust him, Sandrine? For all you know, he's the one who could've led Emily out of here."

"I trust him because he saved my life. He didn't have to, but he did." Sandrine reached for Wade's arm. "I owe him this at least." She watched him. She could tell that he was debating with himself. "He does whatever I tell him to do or he goes back, got that?"

"Yes," Sandrine said, nodding agreeably.

"And I want to leave right after we visit Rose."

"I told him to meet us there in two hours. Is that all right?"

"I guess it'll have to be," Wade said impatiently, heading down the street.

Sandrine quickly followed him, hurrying. Just as she caught up with him, Wade stopped abruptly and turned. Sandrine walked right into him again, reaching for his arms to keep from stumbling.

"Tell me something," Wade said evenly, his eyes never leaving hers.

"What?" Sandrine said, squirming slightly under Wade's intense gaze.

"Was it always like this with us?"

"What do you mean?"

"Were you always able to get what you wanted?"

"No," Sandrine replied defensively. "Not always."

"I bet," Wade said, walking faster.

Sandrine kept pace with Wade as they walked to the other side of town. When they reached Doc's house, Wade knocked on the door. A moment later, a deputy answered the door. He nodded to Wade, and they went inside. They were met by Doc's wife, a pleasant older woman with gray hair and a good-natured smile. She immediately offered them both tea and led them to Rose's room. Doc's house was a big two-story home. He and his wife lived on the top floor, while the bottom had been converted into his office and a four-bed hospital. During one cholera epidemic, the parlor had been filled with cots and bedrolls and the house had had as many as thirty people in it.

"Here you are," Doc's wife said, leading them to Rose's room. "She's the sweetest thing, isn't she? I say a prayer for her every day."

Sandrine watched the woman leave and then followed Wade into the room. Jim was seated next to Rose. Sandrine was shocked by his appearance: he had gray circles under his eyes, his skin was pale, and his face looked gaunt. He stood up, and Sandrine went to him, wrapping her arms around him. "I'm so sorry, Jim," she said, looking up at him.

"It's good to see you up and around. That would make Rose real happy."

"How is she, Jim?"

Jim shrugged. "She wakes up sometimes but only for a few minutes. Doc says that's a good sign. I just want her to wake up for good."

"She will," Sandrine said. "Rose is a strong woman." She took Jim's hand. "Why don't you let Wade take you to get something to eat. You look like you could use it."

"No, I don't want to leave Rose."

"I'd like to sit with Rose if you don't mind," Sandrine said gently.

"Come on, Jim. A visit with Sally ought to perk you right up."

Reluctantly Jim nodded, bent down and kissed Rose on the cheek, and left the room with Wade.

Sandrine sat in the chair next to Rose, reaching over to rub her cheek. She was warm; it was a reassuring feeling. She picked up one of Rose's hands, trying to still her tears. "Life out here sure isn't easy, is it, Rose? From the time I was a little girl, my family taught me about hostile Indians, drunken cowboys, and wild animals. But I was never prepared for anything like Emily. Sweet Miss Emily Dodd from Boston." Sandrine turned at the sound of the knock on the door. Doc's wife was standing holding a tray.

"Where are the men?" she asked.

"They've gone to get something to eat. We thought Jim needed to get out for a while," Sandrine replied.

"Oh, dear," she said, staring at the tray. "Would you care for some tea? I have some nice cake here, too."

"I'd love some tea," Sandrine said, starting to get up.

"No, no, you stay there. I'll bring it to you. Sugar?"

"Yes, please," Sandrine said, smiling at Doc's wife.

"Did Jim tell you that Rose has woken up several times? My husband says that's good." She handed the cup and saucer to Sandrine and went back and sliced some cake.

"If anyone can get through this, it's Rose," Sandrine said, sipping at the hot tea.

"That's what the young lady last night said."

Sandrine stared at Doc's wife, putting the cup back on the saucer. "What lady?"

"There was a young woman who came to the house last night. She wanted to visit with Rose, but no one is allowed to see her but Jim, Wade, you, and Sally. It's too bad. She really seemed to want to see Rose."

Sandrine set the saucer on the night table. "What did she look like?"

Doc's wife straightened. She looked thoughtful for a moment, then she shrugged her shoulders. "I really don't know. It was dark, and the light on the porch isn't real good. Besides, her hair was all tucked up in a bonnet."

"How tall was she? Was she as tall as I am?"

"No, no, she was much shorter. Shorter even than Rose."

"Did you ever meet Jim's niece Emily?"

"No, I never did, but everyone has already told me what she looks like. If you're asking me if the woman who came here last night was her," Doc's wife shook her head, "I honestly don't know. I didn't get a very good look at her. She kept her face lowered, and the brim of the bonnet pretty well covered it."

"What about her voice? Was there anything distinctive about it?"

"Now that you mention it, it did sound kind of strange. She sure wasn't from these parts."

"Where do you think she was from?"

"East maybe, but I can't be real sure."

Sandrine nodded her head. "Did you watch her when she left? Did you see which way she went?"

"No, dear, I was so tired I just shut the door and went to bed."

Sandrine nodded, accepting the plate of cake from Doc's wife. She picked up the saucer and sipped from the cup. So Emily had come here, but why? Why would she risk getting caught just to see Rose, or was she trying to get inside to make sure Rose never woke up?

"Can I get you anything else, dear?"

"No, thank you very much. This is wonderful."

"You just holler if you need anything."

"I will," Sandrine said, watching as Doc's wife left the room. She turned back to the bed and took Rose's hand in her own. It was so strange to see her good friend so lifeless, so still. But she knew if anyone could recover from something like this, Rose would. Doc's good care and Jim's love would pull her through. Sandrine smoothed Rose's hair back from her brow. "I'll find Emily, Rose, and I'll make sure that she has to face the consequences of what she's done. I won't let her get away with this." She kissed Rose on the cheek and left the room. No matter what it took, she'd find Emily. She'd made a promise to Rose, and she was going to keep it.

Emily paced the floor impatiently. She couldn't stay in this place forever. She crossed the room again and parted the curtains so that she could see the street without being seen. With the tricks that Ruby's girls had shown her, she was pretty sure that no one would recognize her anyway—at least not from a distance. But she didn't want to take any chances. She glanced in the ornate gold-framed mirror that hung on the wall. She looked like a stranger, even to herself. Her hair hung smooth and straight, blond against her skin. Instead of her usual high-necked blouses, she wore a green flounced dress, cut low over her breasts. She reached up and touched one of her heavy gold earrings. She almost giggled. If her parents could see her now, even they wouldn't recognize her. Her mouth was painted full and red, and the kohl smudged on her eyelids made her eyes look bigger and more seductive. She wondered if Wade would like her like this.

She smiled. It had been very clever of her to think of hiding in the brothel. Ruby, the madam, had been easy enough to buy off. She had even liked the idea of fooling the sheriff and the rest of the strait-laced citizens of the town. As long as Emily didn't cause any trouble among the other girls, she knew that Ruby would let her stay indefinitely. Emily reached out and touched the smooth surface of the mirror. It was the perfect disguise and the perfect hiding place. No one would ever suspect that she was here.

Wade sipped at his coffee, unsure of what to say to Jim. He'd never seen his friend like this. The man who had taught him most of what he knew about life and who had led wagon trains full of frightened people to safety seemed helpless as a child. Wade drew in a breath. It was useless to keep saying that Rose would be all right. Worse yet, it might not even be true. And as helpless as he seemed, Jim was not a child. He was a man, stricken by the prospect of losing the only woman he had ever loved. Wade leaned back in his chair. There was nothing to say. All he could do was sit with his old friend and maybe try to get his mind off Rose for a few minutes. "You sure Danny's all right? You want me to bring him into town?"

"No," Jim said. "I don't want him to see his mother like this. It'd scare the pants off a kid that age."

"I think you're wrong, Jim. I think Danny should see her. He's big enough to understand, and it's what Rose would want."

"How do you know what Rose would want?" Jim asked, looking up sharply.

"You're not the only one who loves her," Wade said, his voice even.

Jim's face softened. "I know that, and I know you mean well. I just think it's better if Danny stays away for now." He shook his head. "Last night I really thought she was going to speak to me. She opened her eyes, and for a second I could've sworn she knew who I was. Then she slipped away again." He struck the table with his fist. "Doc said it was an encouraging sign, but in an odd way it just made everything harder for me. She was so close, but now she's gone away again."

Wade could only nod and look away. The pain in Jim's eyes was more than he could take. When he saw Sally coming toward the table, he smiled at her gratefully.

"So what is it, my cooking?" she asked, patting Jim's shoulder.

"I guess I don't have much of an appetite," Jim said.

"Well, I think you'd better get one," Sally said, pulling out a chair and sitting down at the table. "You know how much it hurts my feelings when people don't eat my food. Besides, what happens when Rose wakes up and finds you like this? Lord, man, you look like hell."

Wade watched Jim as his old friend looked at Sally and shook his head. "Damn you, Sally, did you come over just to cheer me up? I don't want to be cheered up." Jim smiled weakly.

Sally leaned forward to touch Jim's hand. "It doesn't do Rose any good for you to wear yourself down, Jim."

"I'd forgotten, you've been through this, haven't you?"

Sally nodded and glanced at Wade. "It was a long time ago, but it seems like it was yesterday. All you can do is take care of yourself and hope for the best."

Wade watched as Sally raised Jim's hand to her mouth and kissed it. She was an extraordinary woman. Already Jim's eyes had softened, the hard-glazed weariness fading away. Sally had that effect on people.

Sally glanced at Wade. "So am I supposed to guess?"

"Guess?"

"About Sandrine. Where is she and is she all right?"

Wade smiled. "I thought you knew everything that went on in this town, Sal. You tell me."

Sally straightened up, smoothing her skirt. "Well, I did hear from Betty that Rose had some visitors today. Two men and a woman, she said. I assume the woman was Sandrine."

"You assume right," Wade said, grinning. "She's okay, Sal. She's all healed up."

"No thanks to Emily," Sally said angrily, quickly glancing over at Jim. "I'm sorry."

"That's all right. If I saw Emily right now, I'd probably strangle her myself."

"Speaking of Emily, I'm going to see if I can pick up any of her tracks. Sandrine thinks she's going with me, but I told her she can't."

"She can stay with me," Jim said, then shook his head. "On

second thought, that probably isn't a very good idea. She'd probably be safer here in town."

"I think you're right," Wade agreed. "Can she stay with you, Sal?"

"Of course she can stay with me. It'll be like old times." She narrowed her eyes. "Where do you think Emily has gone?"

"I don't know. She could be anywhere by now."

"Would she have tried to get on a train and go back East?" Sally asked.

"I don't think so," Wade said, shaking his head. "For some reason she wants to see Sandrine dead, and I don't think she'll leave until she can get close to her again."

"Yep, I think Wade's right. In fact, I don't even think she's left the area."

"Sandrine never did anything to hurt her," Wade said, shaking his head again.

"Yes, she did, Wade," Sally said gently. "Sandrine loved you, and what's worse, you loved her back."

Wade met Sally's eyes for a moment, then quickly glanced away. Love. He hadn't thought of putting a name to what he felt for Sandrine, but it made sense. When he had come into the cabin and seen her bleeding, he would've done anything to help her. And making love to her had been unlike anything he'd ever felt with any woman, he was sure. Maybe Sally was right, maybe he did love Sandrine.

"Well, I should be getting back," Jim said, reaching into his pocket.

"Don't you dare, Jim Everett," Sally said. "Your money isn't good here."

Jim leaned over and kissed Sally's cheek. "Thanks, Sally. You're a good friend." He stood up. "You coming, Wade?"

"Yeah," Wade said, still thinking about what Sally had said. "Why don't you tell Sandrine to go on over to my place when she's done visiting Rose?"

"Thanks, Sal," Wade said, hugging her. "I hope old Frank realizes what a prize you are."

"Don't you worry. I remind old Frank of it every chance I get," Sally said, smiling.

Wade followed Jim out of the restaurant and onto the sidewalk. They walked in silence back to Doc's and stood outside talking for a few minutes. Wade tried to string the conversation out; it was good for Jim to get out of that close little room. When they finally went inside, Wade peeked into Rose's room and almost swore out loud. Sandrine was gone. "Where the hell did she go now?" Wade said shortly.

"Just take it easy. I'll go on out and ask the deputy. She had to go by him first."

Wade nodded, sitting down next to the bed and taking Rose's hand. "I know you can hear me, Rose. I know you've been resting, but it's time for you to wake up. There're a lot of people who depend on you. You can't leave us now, Rose. Not now." Wade closed his eyes and rested his head against her hand, allowing himself to feel the sadness that he'd been carrying around for days.

"Wade."

Wade jerked his head up as Jim came back into the room. "Did he know anything?"

"He said she met Nick Boulton and they went off together."

"Sonofabitch," Wade mumbled. "I told her not to go after Emily. Do you think she'd listen to me?" Wade kissed Rose's hand and gently put it back on the bed. He stood up and walked to Jim. "Did he say which way they rode?"

"They didn't ride. They walked."

"What?" Wade paced around the room. "I can't go tracking Emily unless I know Sandrine is safe."

"I know that. You go look for her."

"I'll let you know what's happening," Wade said. He stopped by the front door and questioned the deputy once more. Satisfied, Wade left the house and walked through town until he reached the stables. He questioned the stableboy about Nick, but he said he hadn't been back, nor had he seen Sandrine. Wade stood outside the stables, looking up and down the street. So they were still around town. He headed across the street to the saloon. If he wanted answers, this was the place to start.

Emily sat up abruptly when she heard the knock. She hurried across the room, asked who it was, then opened the door. Ginny came inside, barely looking her seventeen years. "What is it?" Emily asked impatiently.

"You know that woman you were asking about, the one with the dark hair?"

"What about her?" Emily snapped.

"She's downstairs. She's asking questions about you."

"She's downstairs? Is she alone?"

"No, she's with Nick Boulton."

"Hmm," Emily said, walking across the room. She turned around and walked back to Ginny. "Tell her to come back tonight, alone. Tell her you have some information, but you want her to bring some money, say, one hundred dollars."

Ginny shook her head. "I don't know. If Miss Ruby found out, she'd be awfully mad."

Emily grabbed the girl's shoulders. "Listen to me, Ginny. Besides the one hundred dollars that woman brings you, I'll give you one hundred more. Miss Ruby doesn't have to know anything about it."

"Miss Ruby knows about everything around here."

"Just tell her you're doing me a favor. That's all she has to know." Emily walked to the chest of drawers and took out her purse. She handed Ginny some bills. "Here's fifty dollars. I'll give you the other fifty when you bring her to my room tonight."

Emily watched as Ginny tentatively stuck out her hand and took the money.

"What time should I tell her?"

Emily thought for a moment. "Tell her to come back at seven. Miss Ruby won't even be out of her room by then."

Ginny nodded. "All right."

Emily did not permit herself to smile until Ginny had left. This was more than she could have hoped for; better than anything she could have planned. Sandrine was going to come to her.

For the hundredth time, Sandrine thought about finding Wade and asking him to help. She knew he was still in town. She had seen him twice at a distance and had managed to duck into shops before he had seen her. Now he was back at the Half Moon, and if she got lucky, she would be safely at the brothel before he came out. Nick was waiting for her at the stables. She told him to wait for her until she was done at Miss Ruby's.

She was starting to like the big man, and she could tell that he liked her. He was going to be the perfect partner in what lay ahead. He could track as well as Wade, and she wouldn't be distracted by the intensity of her own feelings. In fact, she wanted more than anything to get out of town without Wade seeing her, without him interfering in any way with what she needed to do.

Sandrine stepped off the plank sidewalk, glancing behind her. She wasn't accustomed to frequenting the brothel; in fact, she'd never been in one in her life. She felt odd, as if she was doing something wrong. She was grateful for one thing—the girl had said to come early, so there was little chance that she would run into any men that she knew from town. Most of the men got liquored up before they came to Ruby's, and getting liquored up took some time.

BRIGHT STAR'S PROMISE

She walked a little faster, picking her way through the dust as she crossed the street. As she got closer to the old two-story house where Ruby had set up her business, she had to fight the urge to run. As silly as it seemed, it felt wrong, and she only wanted to get this over with. With a final glance behind her, she pushed open the heavy door and went inside. The sudden dimness made it impossible to see, and for a moment she simply leaned back against the door, waiting for her eyes to adjust. To her great relief, the drawing room was nearly empty, with only two of the girls lounging on the ornate sofas.

"Is Ginny here?" Sandrine asked, then cleared her throat and repeated herself in a louder voice.

One of the girls looked up. "I think she's upstairs."

The girl's voice was indolent, and she looked away the moment she had finished speaking.

Sandrine glanced toward the stairs, then back at the girl. "Which room?"

Before the girl could answer, Sandrine heard the rustle of skirts on the stairway and looked up. Ginny was coming down the staircase. When she saw Sandrine, she almost stumbled, then recovered. "You're early."

"Do you have that information for me?"

Ginny glanced around. "Not here. Upstairs."

Sandrine followed the girl up the curving staircase. The banister had been ornately carved and would've been beautiful if it had not had to compete with the deep red carpet and the black and gold brocade that had been hung over the walls. The smell of cheap perfume hung in the air, and the sound of giggling seemed out of place. On the top landing Ginny motioned for Sandrine to follow her, and they started down a wide hallway. Portraits in gilt frames were hung on the walls, and Sandrine was sure that they had come with the house when Ruby bought it after old Mr. Jensen died. She looked up into the faces of the prim ladies and stern-faced men and wondered if any of them could have ever imagined what their ancestral home would become.

Ginny stopped abruptly in front of one of the doors, but instead of opening it and going inside, she gestured. "In there. I'll come back for my money."

Before Sandrine could say a word, Ginny had gathered her skirts and was off down the hallway. Sandrine watched her go, then stared at the door. So. It was one of the other girls who really had the information. She should have asked. Now she would have to pay twice. Or, she thought wryly, maybe Emily herself was behind this door. Sandrine smiled. Proper Emily in a brothel. There were some things that were impossible to imagine. Emily might be capable of murder, but her strait-laced Boston upbringing would never allow her to come here.

Sandrine reached out and knocked on the door. There was a muffled reply, and the door swung open. A blond woman stood in the dim interior, motioning Sandrine to come inside. Sandrine hesitated, looking past her into the dimly lit room. Unless she was hidden in the wardrobe, Emily was not here. Chiding herself for allowing the first girl to cheat her, Sandrine went into the room.

"Close the door." The woman's voice was husky, barely audible.

Sandrine shut the door and stepped forward. "Do you have some information for me?" She watched as the woman nodded slightly, turning away from her. She waited for a minute, but when the woman didn't answer, Sandrine spoke again. "Do you have information for me? I want to find out about the woman who escaped from jail. I have your money."

Sandrine watched as the woman turned and slowly walked toward her. Sandrine squinted in the dim light. There was something very familiar about her. When she stopped just two feet away, Sandrine could only stare at her—at the bright green dress and garish makeup, at the bleached blond hair and cheap jewelry.

"What's the matter, Sandrine, don't you recognize me?"

Sandrine felt an icy chill go up her spine at the sound of Emily's voice. Involuntarily she took a step backward. She couldn't believe her eyes; she couldn't believe that Emily would go to so much trouble just to lure her here. "God, you're mad," she murmured.

Emily stepped closer. "Wade never really loved you, you know."

"And he loved you?" Sandrine laughed harshly.

"He loved me before you came back," Emily said as she stepped closer. "When you came back, you ruined everything."

Sandrine looked at Emily's eyes; she remembered that look. Emily had had it the night she had almost beaten her to death. But Sandrine refused to be cowed by the woman. "You're going back to jail, Emily."

"And who's going to take me? You?"

"You're going to pay for what you did to Rose."

Emily shook her head. "Poor Rose. What a fool."

"That's enough," Sandrine said angrily, reaching out and tightly gripping Emily's arm.

"Let go," Emily said between clenched teeth.

"No, not until you're locked up again." Sandrine started to guide Emily toward the door, but Emily yanked her arm free.

"I should've killed you when I had the chance."

"Yes, you should've," Sandrine said, her voice hard, "because you won't get the chance again." Before Emily could react, Sandrine struck out, smashing her fist into Emily's jaw, knocking her backward. When Emily tried to recover, Sandrine struck her again, this time knocking her down to the floor. Emily rolled to her side, trying to get up, but not able to gather the strength. Quickly Sandrine scanned the room, looking for something with which to tie Emily. She found a curtain cord and yanked it down. She turned Emily on her stomach and tied her hands behind her, then she pulled her to a sitting position.

"You'll never get away with this," Emily said angrily, trying to twist away from Sandrine. "They'll never let you take me out of here."

"Do you think anyone here is going to risk their life for you, Emily? I don't think so. Get up," Sandrine ordered, yanking Emily to her feet by the rope.

"You're hurting me!"

"Good. Now start walking. And so help me, Emily, if you try to run away, I'll push you down those stairs so hard you'll never get up again." As they walked out of the room, Sandrine could barely suppress a smile.

Sixteen

By the time Wade had located Nick Boulton and tracked Sandrine to Miss Ruby's, Sandrine had already delivered Emily to the sheriff. Wade hurried to the jail, only to find Sandrine sitting in a chair on the other side of the sheriff's desk, drinking coffee. She and the sheriff were laughing easily.

Wade walked up to the desk. "Are you enjoying yourself?" he demanded angrily.

"I'm just having a cup of coffee with the sheriff."

Wade glared at her and then looked at the sheriff. "Where's Emily?"

"She's locked up, thanks to your wife. I'm thinking of hiring her on here. She does better work than most of my deputies." He laughed loudly.

"Do you think that's funny?" Wade said, staring at Sandrine. "I can't believe you went after Emily alone, especially when I told you not to."

Sandrine set her cup on the desk. "I think we should talk about this someplace else, Wade."

"No, you two use my office," the sheriff said, standing and taking his rifle from the rack. "I need to make my rounds."

Wade waited until the sheriff was gone and said. "You could've been killed."

"Yes, I suppose I could have."

"Why are you acting like this?"

"Like what?"

"Like you don't even care."

"I care, Wade. I'm just not going to spend all of my time being frightened."

Wade shook his head, leaning on the edge of the desk. "It was a stupid thing to do. If Emily had had a gun—"

Sandrine sat up straight. "Yes, and if you and Little Bear hadn't saved me from Bear Killer, or if Nick hadn't stopped Emily from beating me, I'd probably be dead right now. But I'm not, Wade. I'm very much alive."

Wade stared at Sandrine. Her blue eyes were sparkling and her cheeks were flushed pink. He remembered what it had been like to hold her in his arms and make love to her, and he was finding it hard to think about anything else.

"Did you hear what I said, Wade?" Sandrine asked.

"What? No." Wade shook his head, embarrassed that he had been caught staring at her.

"Have you told Jim that Emily is in jail? It might make him relax a little."

"No, I haven't told him yet. I guess I should do that right now." Wade stood up. "Do you want to come with me?"

"Yes."

Wade took Sandrine's arm as they left the office and walked down the street. It wasn't that late yet, and some of the cowboys were just getting started. He could hear the pianos from the two saloons and the raucous laughter of the patrons inside. But suddenly it didn't interest him. By the time they reached Doc's, Wade had gathered the courage to ask Sandrine something that had been bothering him since they'd made love that day at the stream. As she started up the walk to the house, he held her arm.

"Wait," he said gently. "There's something I've been wanting to ask you for awhile."

"What?" Sandrine said, looking at him. "You can ask me anything."

"I'm not quite sure how to say it."

"Just say it, Wade."

Wade cleared his throat. "Were you with Lone Wind?"

"What do you mean?"

"Did you sleep with him?" he asked, looking at Sandrine. The expression on her face quickly turned to anger.

"Does it matter if I slept with him?" she said, her voice angry.

Wade kicked at the dirt on the ground. "I guess it does or I wouldn't have asked," he said honestly, remembering how passionate Sandrine had been in his arms.

Sandrine pulled away from his grasp. "You're not my husband anymore, Wade; you haven't been for a long time. You forgot all about me, and you took Emily into your bed. I don't think I owe you any explanations." Sandrine started up the walk to Doc's house again, but Wade grabbed her arm, turning her to face him, his hands tightly clutching her shoulders.

"Emily was there for me. You weren't."

"So was Rose and you didn't sleep with her."

Wade sighed. "It's not going to change the way I feel about you, Sandrine. I just want to know." He watched Sandrine's face change and her eyes fill with tears.

"Why? Why do you need to know?"

Wade shook his head. "I just do."

Sandrine nodded her head slightly. "I can see that it already has changed the way you feel about me. You've made up your mind." Angrily she swiped at her tear-flooded eyes, looking at Wade. "All right, if you really want to know, I did sleep with Lone Wind. I shared his robe many times. I was his wife. I did whatever he asked me to do. And he wasn't the only one."

"What does that mean?" Wade asked angrily, his fingers digging into Sandrine's shoulders.

"There were others in the tribe, men who Lone Wind owed favors to. He loaned me out to them."

Wade shook his head, searching Sandrine's eyes. "You're lying. You wouldn't do that."

"How do you know, Wade? You don't remember the way I used to be. Besides, we Indians are a lot different from you whites." Sandrine pulled away and walked up to the house, and this time Wade didn't stop her.

He turned around, shaking his head. He couldn't believe it; he couldn't believe that Sandrine would do something like that. He couldn't imagine her with another man, being the way she had been with him, giving herself the way she had. He ran his hand through his hair, sighing deeply. He leaned on the fence, trying to make some sense of what Sandrine had told him. Would it really make any difference if she had been with other men? Would it change the way he felt about her?

"Wade. Wade, it's Rose." Sandrine's voice came from behind him, and there was an urgent sound to it.

Wade turned and saw Sandrine standing at the door. Without hesitating, he followed her into the house and into Rose's room, his heart pounding. But his fear quickly subsided when he saw Rose, eyes open, looking at him. He went to the bed and knelt down, kissing her on the cheek.

"God, I've missed you," he said, resting his head against hers. He could feel Rose's hand on his hair.

"Did you think you could get rid of me that easy?"

Wade lifted his head, quickly wiping his moist eyes. "You had me worried this time."

"Well, I feel like I've had a nice, long nap," she said, smiling. "But unlike you, I can remember everything. It must be awful for you sometimes, Wade."

Wade glanced at Jim and then at Sandrine. "It's only bad when I can't remember the important things." He took Rose's hand. "So what can I do for you? Can I get you anything?"

"You and Sandrine can go out to the ranch and make sure it's ready for me, 'cause I'm coming home tomorrow."

"Rose," Jim said gently, moving to stand next to the bed, "Doc hasn't said whether you'll be able to go home tomorrow."

"I don't care what Doc says, I'm going home." She looked past the men. "You know what that's like, don't you, Sandrine?"

"Yes," Sandrine replied softly. "I'll make sure the place is ready for you."

"Thank you." She looked at Wade again, reaching up to touch his cheek. "Don't look so worried. I'm all right. Actually I have a real hankering for a piece of Sally's pie. I don't suppose you and Sandrine could walk over there and get me a piece."

"Sandrine can stay here in case you need her help," Wade said quickly.

"I wouldn't mind if you two left Jim and me alone for awhile," Rose said practically in a whisper. "I think he needs to know that I'm all right."

Wade nodded, kissed Rose on the cheek once more, and stood up. "We'll go over to Sally's and get a bite to eat. We'll be back later."

"Don't forget my pie."

Wade walked out of the house with Sandrine, feeling relieved but drained. He hadn't realized before how much he loved Rose; she really was like family to him. They walked in silence to Sally's restaurant. Wade didn't know what to say to Sandrine. If what she had told him was true, would it really change how he felt about her? And what was it exactly that he felt for Sandrine? Was it love, or was it just the most overwhelming desire he'd ever felt for any woman?

When they reached the restaurant and went inside, Sally waved for them to sit down. Wade looked at Sandrine, but she ignored him. When Sally came to the table, Wade watched as Sandrine propped her chin on her hand. The two women smiled at each other. Wade felt shut out.

"Well, this is a nice sight. I could get used to seeing you two together."

"It's best not to get used to things, Sally," Sandrine said.

"What does that mean?"

"Never mind," Wade answered. "We have good news. Rose has come around. She's awake."

Sally put her hand on her chest. "Thank God," she said, closing her eyes for a moment. "Jim must be so relieved."

Wade nodded. "She wants some of your pie."

"I'll get her some right now."

"No," Wade said. "She wants to spend a little time with Jim. We'll eat dinner first."

Sally nodded, looking from Wade to Sandrine. "All right. I'll bring you both some coffee while you're waiting."

Again, Wade watched Sandrine as she thanked Sally and then folded her hands in her lap, looking past him. "Are you going to ignore me all night?"

"I don't think we have anything more to discuss," she said coldly.

"Sandrine, please," Wade said, reaching out to take her hand, but she snatched it away.

"I think you've already made your mind up about me, Wade. You think I'm not good enough for you."

"I never said that."

"You didn't have to." Again she avoided his eyes.

"I just needed to know. I . . ." Wade shook his head, not able to explain to himself why he felt the need to know if Sandrine had been with another man.

"It was the same after Bear Killer kidnapped me, you know," Sandrine said, her eyes staring past Wade.

"What do you mean?"

"After you and Little Bear came for me, I was so sick and so frightened. But you helped me get well. You helped me be strong. Then Gray Wolf married us and we came here." Sandrine shook her head. "But it wasn't the same once we got here. You treated me differently. I think you began to wonder about everything Bear Killer had done to me. I think it bothered you that another man had touched me." Sandrine's voice began to shake, and she cleared her throat.

Wade started to speak but stopped when Sally came to the table carrying two cups of coffee.

"Here you go. Dinner will be here soon. So can I do anything to help Jim? How about food? I'll take care of the meals for tomorrow, how's that?"

"Sure, Sal, that'd be great."

Sally leaned close to the table. "Is it me, or did it suddenly turn mighty chilly in here?"

"Wade and I were just having a discussion, weren't we, Wade?"

"About what?" Sally asked.

"He wanted to know if I've been with any other men. He seems to think it makes me less honorable if I have been."

"I didn't say that," Wade protested loudly.

"Listen you two," Sally said in a low voice. "Maybe you should have this conversation later. I don't think the whole town wants to know your business."

"I think you're right," Sandrine said, standing up and throwing her napkin on the table. "We certainly wouldn't want to embarrass you, Sally." Sandrine brushed by Sally and left the restaurant.

"Oh, my," Sally said, shaking her head. "I didn't mean to upset her."

"It wasn't you who upset her, Sal. It was me." Wade clutched the cup of coffee tightly.

"What happened, Wade?" Sally asked, sitting down across from her friend.

"I don't know. We . . . we've grown closer lately, and I just wanted to know if there had ever been anyone else." Wade shrugged his shoulders, hardly able to meet Sally's eyes.

"How could you ask such a thing, Wade? What's gotten into you?"

"I guess I just wanted to know if she ever felt the same way about another man. I don't know, Sally. I don't remember what it was like between us before the accident."

"And you think asking her if she'd ever been with another man would help you understand what it was like between the two of you? I thought you were smarter than that, Wade." Sally stood up. "I'll go get your dinner."

Wade stared into his cup of coffee as Sally walked away, feeling desperately lonely and wondering what his life might be like if he hadn't lost his memory.

Sandrine rode back to the ranch without waiting for Wade and without saying goodbye to Rose and Jim. She was hoping that Wade would stay in town and visit with Sally because she couldn't bear any more humiliating questions from him. She had swept, dusted, and cleaned everything in the house, as well as changed the linens on Rose's bed. Then she brewed herself some tea and sat down on the sofa, staring at the hearth. She forced herself not to cry when she thought of the look on Wade's face when she had lied about Lone Wind and the others. But she knew it was best. Wade would always think there had been something between her and Lone Wind; it was just easier to confirm his suspicions.

She sighed deeply, finally finding comfort in the fact that Rose had recovered and would be coming home the next day. She could use Rose's friendship now, especially when she didn't know what she was going to do.

Sandrine finished her tea and stretched out on the sofa, covering herself with the blanket that was folded on the back. She closed her eyes, trying not to think about Wade. Maybe she would go visit her parents for a time until she sorted things out. It would be good to be with them and her people again.

Sandrine felt her body jerk involuntarily at the sound of footsteps and the slamming of the door. She sat up, forcing herself awake. She blinked, disoriented. How long had she been asleep? Wade stood for a moment, staring at her, then he walked to the cupboard. He took down the bottle of whiskey and poured himself a glass, then walked over to the hearth, sitting down on the edge. Sandrine watched him as he sipped his drink, and she could tell by his eyes that he'd already been drinking.

"How was Rose when you left her?" Sandrine asked.

"She was fine," Wade said curtly, holding the glass to his mouth.

"Is Jim coming home tonight?"

"No, he's staying in town with Rose." Wade finished the glass and went to the cupboard to pour another.

Sandrine watched Wade as he sat back down on the hearth. He seemed angry and aloof. "Are you all right?"

"Me?" Wade laughed. "I'm fine. In fact, I'm great." Wade lifted the glass and downed half of it. "Let's see, I lost my memory, I got involved with a woman who almost killed you and Rose, and I learned that the woman that I used to love, the woman who was my wife, has been used like a whore." Wade laughed harshly. "Yeah, I'm feeling real good." He swallowed the rest of the whiskey and slammed the glass down on the rock hearth.

"I'm sorry I'm not what you thought I was, Wade," Sandrine said, throwing the blanket to the side and sitting on the edge of the sofa. "But you're not exactly the man I remember either." She stood up, picking up the blanket. She folded it and hung it over the back of the sofa. "I'll let you get on with your drinking." She started toward the guest bedroom but stopped when Wade stood up.

"Why don't you join me? We could have some fun."

"I don't like to drink, especially whiskey."

"Why not?"

"I saw too many drunken Indians and cowboys come into the trading post. They were always the same: their breath stank, they always managed to get into trouble, and they usually wound up destroying something of my father's."

"Guess you saw all kinds of men up there, didn't you?"

Sandrine stared at him. "What're you saying?"

Wade smiled. "I just wondered. Seems like you'd see a lot more men than women."

"There were women on the wagon trains. You know that—or you used to. Haven't you ever talked to Rose about how the two of you met?"

"Of course I have. I've talked to everybody I could. Don't you think I want my memory back."

Sandrine shrugged. "I don't know. Sometimes it seems like you're glad you don't remember."

Wade walked to the cupboard and grabbed the bottle.

Sandrine watched as he took a long swig and walked toward her. "You're not the man I fell in love with. You're nothing like him." Sandrine was sorry she'd said the words almost as soon as they left her mouth.

Wade stopped midstride and stood swaying on his feet. "I know you don't love me now, why should you? After all, I'm sure I can't measure up to Lone Wind."

Sandrine felt like slapping him. "It's none of your business what I did or didn't do with Lone Wind."

Wade lifted the bottle to his mouth and took a long pull of the whiskey. "Well, I think it is my business. I was spending all day, every day, building a house for us."

"Jim must have told you because I know you don't remember that."

Wade's face darkened. "You just can't miss a chance to remind me, can you?"

He took a quick step toward her, startling her, but he only reached out and lifted her hair off her neck. His fingertips brushed her skin. Sandrine felt her body react, and it made her angry. Who did he think he was? She pulled her hair free from his hands and smoothed it back into place.

"What's the matter, Sandrine? It's not like we've never been together before. You weren't so shy that day by the stream."

Sandrine felt her cheeks flush, and she forced herself to keep her hands loosely at her side. Why was he doing this to her? "Do you hate me?" she asked aloud.

Abruptly Wade took her into his arms. He held her tightly, even as she struggled. "Hate you?" he whispered against her cheek. "I could never hate you." Suddenly his lips were on hers, hard and demanding. He forced his tongue against her teeth, and in spite of her anger, Sandrine felt herself beginning to yield. "Did you fight him, Sandrine, or did you give yourself to him like you did to me that day by the stream?"

Sandrine stiffened and tried to pull away, the sting of Wade's words cutting her deeply. "Let me go."

"Why?" Wade said, his mouth touching hers again. "I know you want me, Sandrine. I've known it since you came back. It's always there in your eyes."

"What's happened to you?" she cried out. "What happened to the man I used to know?"

"He's gone. He's been gone for a long time." Wade backed Sandrine up against the wall, pressing his body against hers. "But I'm here and I want you." He held her head so she couldn't move it, and he kissed her deeply.

Sandrine struggled against him, trying to get free, but his body trapped hers against the wall. She managed to turn her face away, ignoring him as he kissed her neck. "I never thought I could hate you," she said, tears filling her eyes. She felt his body relax, and he loosened his hold on her. When she looked up at him, his eyes were cold and unfeeling.

"It doesn't really matter if you hate me, does it? You're my wife. We're married, remember?"

Sandrine felt her chest heaving, the anger building, and she raised her hand and slapped Wade across the face. "I'd rather be alone than be with you."

Wade took her hands and held them to his chest while Sandrine struggled against his hold. "Maybe you will be alone someday, but not now." Without warning, Wade picked her up in his arms and walked to the bedroom, dropping her onto the bed.

Sandrine rolled to the other side and stood up. "Don't touch me."

She stared at Wade, unable to believe this was the same man she had loved with all of her heart. As he started toward her, she moved backward, her legs touching the night table. She reached behind her and picked up a vase. When Wade came close, she tried to hit him, but he blocked the blow with his arm, knocking the vase from her hand.

He shook his head. "Don't stop me, Sandrine," he said, his voice low. He shoved her onto the bed.

Sandrine kicked at him, trying to get across the bed, but she felt Wade's grip grow stronger. Before she knew it, he had pulled her to him and turned her onto her back, pinning her hands above her head. "Don't do this, Wade. Please."

"Why not, Sandrine? You liked it before."

Sandrine tried to turn her head as Wade pressed his mouth against hers, but she could not. He kissed her deeply, exploring her mouth with his tongue. He traced a path down Sandrine's neck, then stopped. Sandrine closed her eyes, not wanting to see Wade's face or the look in his eyes. Desperately she struggled to get away from him, twisting and turning her body. But even as she struggled, she felt Wade's hands as they touched and stroked her, and slowly she felt her body betray her. She had loved him for so long that in spite of her anger and humiliation, he was able to kindle a fire in her that no one could.

"Sandrine," he whispered in her ear.

And Sandrine knew she couldn't fight him any longer. As her excitement built, she felt his hands clutching her buttocks, lifting her hips as he entered her. She cried out loudly as he drove himself into her and she dug her fingernails into his back through his shirt.

She heard him mutter her name over and over, and for a moment she pretended to herself that he had said it lovingly. As Wade moved faster and faster inside of her, Sandrine tried to fight him, tried to make her body fight the urge to meet his. But she couldn't. As he drove himself harder and deeper into her, she cried out, holding onto him, saying his name until she felt him explode inside of her and both of their bodies came together in a rush of passion.

They lay still for a few minutes, and unconsciously Sandrine reached up and ran her fingers through his hair. Even after the way he had acted, she couldn't hate him.

"You're an incredible woman, Sandrine," Wade said, rolling over onto his back and fastening his pants.

Sandrine smiled to herself, suddenly feeling hopeful.

"I can see why Lone Wind came back for you."

Sandrine's stomach tightened; she felt as if she'd been punched in the face. "Get out," she said, her voice tremulous.

"I'll get out, but you haven't seen the last of me."

Sandrine turned her head away as Wade brushed his fingers over her breasts. She heard his footsteps as he walked to the other room and then outside to the porch. She turned over and buried her face in the pillow, sobbing uncontrollably.

When Jim brought Rose home the next day, Sandrine made sure that neither of them could guess that she couldn't stand the sight of Wade. She didn't want to ruin Rose's homecoming, so she hid behind a sweet smile and treated Wade as politely as she could. She had made a big lunch, and the four of them ate and talked until it was obvious that Rose was ready for a rest. Then as Rose blushed, Jim lifted her into his arms and carried her into the bedroom. Their love was so apparent that it made Sandrine ache to watch them.

She stood up quickly and began clearing the table, then poured a pot of boiling water into the dish basin. As she began washing the dishes, Wade stood up and walked over to her. She felt him watching her, and suddenly the memories she had been trying to avoid flooded into her mind. How could she have given into him so easily? How could her body have betrayed her?

"Do you need any help?" he asked, standing next to her.

Sandrine shook her head. For an instant she hated him. He acted as if nothing had happened between them. What's worse, he acted as if he'd done nothing wrong. When she felt his hand on her arm, she glared at him. "Don't touch me."

"What's wrong? I thought after last night—"

"You thought what?" Sandrine demanded, her voice low but harsh. "You thought you could treat me like any common whore and I'd be grateful."

"You didn't seem to mind last night. You enjoyed it, Sandrine."

She dropped the plate she was holding into the water and faced Wade. "Leave me alone. I don't want to talk to you."

"You're going to have to talk to me sometime."

"I don't ever have to talk to you if I don't want to."

"Once Rose is well, we're going to live together. You can't ignore me all of the time."

"I'm not going to live with you."

"Where you going to stay? Here?" Wade shook his head. "These people need their privacy, Sandrine."

Sandrine started to answer but stopped when she saw Jim

coming from the bedroom. She turned back to the washbasin and picked up one of the plates.

"The house looks great, Sandrine. Thanks for all the work you did."

"You don't have to thank me, Jim," she said quietly.

"Why don't you let me take over," Jim said, taking her hands from the washbasin and handing her a towel. "Rose wants to visit with you for a few minutes before she naps."

Sandrine nodded, drying her hands and going to the bedroom. Rose was lying on her back, her arm over her eyes. "Rose, you awake?" she asked quietly.

"Yes, I was just covering my eyes. They're a little sensitive to the sun. Sit down for a bit, Sandrine."

Sandrine sat down in the chair that was next to the bed, sighing without realizing it.

"You all right?"

"Yes, I'm fine."

"Sure you are. It hasn't been that long since you were hurt, and here you are, hunting down Emily, bringing her in, and coming out here cooking and cleaning. I'm sorry, Sandrine."

"Don't," Sandrine said, taking Rose's hand. "I'd do anything for you, don't you know that?"

"Yes, as a matter of fact, I do."

Sandrine met Rose's smile, knowing she was referring to Jim's old gambling debt. "Don't make me out to be such a saint, Rose. I'm not, you know." She lowered her eyes, staring at the floor.

"You look tired. When was the last time you slept?"

"I got some sleep last night."

"Not much, I reckon."

"I'll be fine, Rose. Stop worrying so much. How are you feeling? Any more headaches?"

"No." Rose fixed her eyes on her friend. "What is it, Sandrine? There's something wrong."

"Nothing's wrong." Sandrine avoided Rose's probing eyes.

"It's you and Wade, isn't it? I could tell at supper. You two were just a little too polite to each other."

Sandrine shook her head, running her hands over her face. "I feel like such a fool," she said, her voice breaking. "I keep thinking that he's going to remember the way he used to love me, but I know now that isn't going to happen." Sandrine started to cry, but she quickly wiped the tears away. "I'm so sorry, Rose. I didn't mean to do that in front of you."

"If you can't do it in front of me, who can you do it in front of?" Rose asked gently, rubbing Sandrine's arm. "Tell me what happened."

"I can't. It's too humiliating."

"I'm your friend, Sandrine. Your friend."

Sandrine met Rose's eyes, and she couldn't hold back the tears. As quickly as she could, she told Rose about the previous night and the day that she and Wade had made love by the stream. When she was finished, she was too embarrassed to look at Rose.

"I'm sorry, Sandrine," Rose said gently. "But you have no reason to feel the way you do. If anyone should be embarrassed, it's Wade. If I wasn't lying in this bed, I'd knock some sense into that addled brain of his."

"You can't say anything to him, Rose. Promise me."

"Why shouldn't I say something to him? It's about time someone did."

"No, you can't. It's something I have to work out all on my own."

"That's just it, Sandrine, you shouldn't have to work it out on your own. You should be able to work it out with Wade. That's what marriage is, a partnership."

Sandrine shook her head. "I don't think Wade really understands about marriage, Rose. He doesn't understand about the give and take."

"Well, he sure understood the take part last night, didn't he?" Rose said angrily. "Damn him!"

"It's not his fault entirely," Sandrine said, her voice weary. "Fact is, I wanted him to make love to me." Again she avoided Rose's eyes.

"Look at me, Sandrine. Please."

Sandrine looked up, wiping at her tear-filled eyes again. When Rose took her hand, Sandrine grasped it tightly.

"I want you to listen to me. It's a natural thing, in fact, it's a downright good thing for a wife to desire her husband. Marriage would be awfully boring if there wasn't any desire between two people. You shouldn't feel badly about wanting Wade. My lord, Sandrine, you've loved him since you were a girl. The only thing that's confusing here is Wade. You fell in love with one Wade, and now he's another man entirely. How are you supposed to know what to feel?"

Sandrine nodded, clutching Rose's hand in hers. "I just know that I love him and he doesn't love me at all," she said sadly.

"I'm not sure he even knows what love is anymore, Sandrine. Somehow, he lost it along the way."

"Not completely," Sandrine said. "When he saw you had finally awakened, he was so relieved. He loves you and Jim so much, Rose."

"Maybe, and maybe there's hope for him still. I know he cares for you, Sandrine. When he found out you were kidnapped, he almost went crazy. I just think he's afraid."

"Afraid of what?" Sandrine asked.

Rose shook her head. "I don't know. Maybe it's just as simple as the fear of the unknown. Since he has no memory of the past, he doesn't know what love is really like. Maybe it scares him." Rose patted Sandrine's hand. "I wish I knew. I wish I could help you."

"You can help me by getting well," Sandrine said, leaning

down and kissing Rose on the cheek. "Thank you for listening to me, Rose. You're a good friend."

"Sandrine, I—"

Sandrine shook her head. "Don't you worry about me. I just want you to rest and get strong, all right?" Sandrine stood up and went to the door.

"Sandrine."

Sandrine turned. "Wade may have lost his memory, but he hasn't lost his ability to learn."

Sandrine shook her head. "What do you mean?"

"Maybe you can teach him how to love again. Maybe it's that simple."

Sandrine nodded and left the room. She closed the door, leaning against it for a moment before she walked back to the living room. Wade and Jim were on the porch; she could hear their voices. The dishes were washed and dried. Sandrine made sure everything was straightened up and the vase of wildflowers she had picked fresh for Rose was put back on the table. Then she walked toward the open front door, nervously running her hands up and down her skirt. When she stepped out onto the porch, both men glanced at her, but she only smiled at Jim.

"How's Rose?"

"She's wonderful," Sandrine said, pretending not to see Wade as he stood up and offered her his chair. Instead she leaned against the railing, facing Jim. "You're lucky to have a wife like Rose."

"I know," Jim said, running his fingers through his hair. "I never realized just how lucky I was until I almost lost her." He looked at Sandrine and Wade. "I've often thought about you two. If you hadn't been there, Wade, to help her deliver Danny, she might not have made it. And if you both hadn't looked for her after her husband died, she might've died, too. You're Rose's family, both of you. I can't imagine anything that would make her happier than if you two told her you were moving back in together."

"Jim," Wade said slowly, obviously trying to find the right words.

But Sandrine interrupted him before he could finish. "I don't think that will be happening, Jim. No matter how much Rose wants it to." She turned abruptly and went down the porch steps, walking to the barn. Quickly she saddled her horse and led it into the yard. She mounted up and guided her horse up the path and away from the ranch, then she kicked her horse into a run. She felt the wind in her hair and the sun on her face, and she wanted only to forget. She closed her eyes and imagined for a moment that she was a girl, riding with Little Bear out on the prairie, without a care in the world. This was not the life she had imagined or dreamed about with Wade.

She reined in when her horse tired, slowing to a canter and then a walk. She had ridden eastward, across the valley where Jim grazed his cattle. She felt a pang as she looked at the lazy animals standing in the pasture, chewing at the tall grass and flicking away flies with their long tails. Calves played alongside, occasionally running around in circles, then flopping down for a quick rest. She remembered the first time she had seen a cow and how shocked she had been. Her grandfather had described the white man's animal and told her that he kept it close to him for food. It was hard for her to imagine anything like that, but when the first wagon train had come to the trading post, she had seen a cow with her own eyes. She had expected it to be large and ferocious like the buffalo, but instead it was clumsy and slow-witted. With the other children of her village, she had gawked and laughed.

She smiled, remembering herself as a shy and unworldly girl. That had been long before she had ever dreamed she would live in Paris, long before she had ever thought about marrying anyone. For an instant she wished she could be that young girl again, the one who thought that life in a Blackfoot camp was all there was to the world.

When Sandrine neared the pond, she dismounted and let her horse drink. She knelt down and splashed some water on her face, then cupped her hands and drank. Letting her horse graze, she sat, stretching out her legs and looking around at the muddy tracks left by the cattle and horses that led up to the water's edge. She narrowed her eyes when she spotted tracks that made her catch her breath. Moving forward, she ran her fingers over the distinct prints and nervously looked around her. Mountain lion. The big cats weren't usually out in the daytime, but the tracks looked fresh, as if it had just come for water. She stood up and followed the tracks around the pond, stopping suddenly when she saw a dark stain on the mud. She stooped down and ran her fingers over it, realizing as soon as she had that it was blood. Either the animal had killed or it was wounded.

Sandrine followed the tracks away from the pond through the thick grass. She could see a spattering of blood on the grass. The trail of blood thickened until she saw what she had suspected. A young steer carcass was in the grass, and its blood had soaked the area around it. It was a fresh kill. She followed the cat tracks for awhile, glancing continuously over her shoulder. When she realized that the tracks led into the rougher country of the foothills, she stopped and went back to her horse. She mounted and kicked the animal into a gallop. She rode fast. She hated to tell Jim. The last thing he needed was to be worrying about his stock.

She rode into the yard, slipping from her horse. Wade and Jim were still on the porch, and she took the steps two at a time.

"Where you been, girl? You look all tired out." Jim said.

"I think you've got a cat on your hands, Jim. I was out by the pond on the eastern edge of the valley, and I saw tracks. I followed them and found a carcass, freshly killed."

"A cat?" Wade asked. He looked at Jim. "Have you ever had a problem with them around here?"

"I haven't, but I know some of the other ranchers have in the past."

"You're sure it was a mountain lion, Sandrine?" Wade asked.

"Yes, I'm sure. I've seen their tracks before. I know what they look like," she said curtly.

Jim shook his head. "I haven't been looking after the herd lately. I wonder if it's just a one-time kill or if it'll be back."

"That depends," Sandrine said, leaning back on the railing, feeling Wade's eyes on her.

"On what?" Jim asked.

"If it's hurt, it can do anything. Cats that've been wounded have been known to attack a man. On the other hand, if it's just hungry, this may be the only time." Sandrine shook her head. "Something bothers me though."

"Don't keep me guessing," Jim said.

"The carcass had barely been touched."

"Where did you first spot the tracks?" Wade asked.

"By the pond, then I followed them toward the foothills."

"You didn't see any other dead cattle?" Jim asked, sitting up straighter.

Sandrine shook her head. "No, but then I didn't look." She stared at both men. "I think the cat's wounded and has gone back up into the hills."

"How do you know?"

Sandrine shrugged her shoulders. "I don't know anything for sure, Jim. I didn't really take that close of a look."

"But you saw something," Wade said.

Sandrine barely glanced at Wade before continuing. "I saw some blood by the pond and in the grass around it. It could've come from the cat trying to wash itself off after it killed the steer."

"But you don't think it did, do you?" Wade said, standing up and walking over to her. "What exactly did you see?"

Sandrine glared at Wade for a minute, then decided to put her anger aside. "It was the way the blood spots fell, as if from a wound. And the blood I saw on the grass was high up on the blades. If the animal had just killed, it would've had blood on its paws, and that blood would've gotten on the ground."

"How much blood was it? Are you sure of what you saw?"

"If you don't believe me, check the tracks for yourself."

"I will," Wade said firmly.

"Good, I'll stay here with Rose," Sandrine said.

"No, you go on ahead with Wade," Jim said. "I'd kind of like to be here when Rose wakes up."

Sandrine nodded. "All right."

"I think we're pretty lucky you found those tracks."

"That's all it was, Jim, luck. I'm not that good of a tracker. I just picked up a few things from my grandfather and cousin."

"More than a few things," Wade said.

Sandrine looked at him, but his voice hadn't been harsh or cruel; it almost sounded like he was genuinely complimenting her.

"Wade, you have a good rifle?"

"I have one, but I'd feel better if Sandrine had one, too."

Jim got up and went into the house. Moments later he returned. He handed Sandrine a rifle and some shells. "Don't do anything foolish, all right?"

"I won't," Sandrine said. She waited until Wade had saddled his horse before she mounted up and led the way out of the yard, never looking back at Wade as they rode toward the pond.

When they neared the area where she had seen the carcass, Sandrine reined in, not wanting to obscure any tracks that the cat might've made. "Over there," she said, pointing to where she had seen the dead steer.

"Stay on your horse," Wade ordered as he dismounted and walked to the carcass.

Sandrine watched Wade as he squatted down by the dead

steer, running his fingers along the prints and studying the grass. He walked to the pond, examining the tracks that were there. Then he walked in a wide circle from the pond toward the foothills. Sandrine sat on her horse, content to watch Wade and to remember. He had always taken pride in his ability to track, and his pride was well-founded. Even her mother's people admired his skill. As he walked up the slope, Sandrine saw him stoop time after time to get a closer look at the tracks. Suddenly he straightened, and she could see that he was scanning the horizon. Then he walked back to the carcass. Finally he started back toward the horses.

"Well," he said, nodding his head, "you were right. Except for one thing."

"What?" Sandrine asked.

Wade looked up at her, pushing his hat back away from his eyes. "I think there're two of them."

Sandrine looked at Wade. "That's why they're hunting during the daytime."

Wade nodded. "They're probably mates. If one is wounded, the other one is hunting for it."

Sandrine shook her head, scanning the area around the pond and underneath the trees. "Do you think they'll come back?"

"It's hard to figure. I remember once when we were coming through the Dakotas, a cat kept attacking our stock. He followed us for three days until Clint shot him."

Sandrine stared at Wade, barely able to swallow. "Did you hear what you said, Wade? You just told me something you remembered all on your own, something that Jim didn't tell you."

Wade looked dazed, slowly shaking his head. He looked up at Sandrine. "I do remember it, too. Clearly. Clint brought the cat into camp and hung it up for everyone to see. Jim was angry at first, but Clint did it because he wanted those Easterners to realize how dangerous an animal it was." He shook his head. "I can't believe it."

"Do you remember anything else?"

"Not really. I remembered something that Little Bear and I had done together, and your mother's name sounded familiar to me."

"That's it, though," Sandrine said, trying to keep the disappointment from her voice.

"Sandrine, I'm sorry. I can't pick what I want to remember. If I could, I'd—"

"Don't," Sandrine said angrily. "Don't say things that we both know you don't mean, Wade. I think it's pretty clear how you feel about me. Especially after last night." She jerked her reins, turning her horse around. She felt hurt, angry, and confused. She kicked her horse into a gallop, but Wade leaned out of his saddle and caught her reins, forcing her horse to a stop.

"Wait, Sandrine."

Sandrine sat on her horse, staring at the trees, wishing that she weren't alone with Wade.

"Would you at least look at me, please?"

She waited for a few moments, then slowly turned her head toward Wade, her eyes set in a cold stare. "What do you want from me?" She then laughed harshly. "I think you've made that all too clear."

"Sandrine, I'm sorry about what happened last night. I didn't mean for it to happen. I was drunk and I was mad."

"Mad? What right did you have to be mad?"

"When you told me about Lone Wind, I guess I went sort of crazy. I couldn't stand the thought of you being with another man."

She looked away, not wanting Wade to see the tears in her eyes. She hadn't expected this from him, and she hated him for it. Every time she made up her mind about him, he did something to make her feel differently.

"I don't expect you to forgive me right away," he said. "I know I'll have to earn your trust again."

"I don't think we should be talking about this right now, Wade. We should be getting back to Jim's. He'll want to know about the cat." She kicked her horse into a canter, not waiting for Wade. She didn't want to hear any more of what he had to say; already her feelings had been laid bare.

Seventeen

Sandrine stayed with Rose while Wade and Jim rode to the neighboring ranches, alerting them to the danger of a wounded cat. While she waited for the men to return, Sandrine cooked supper. Just as she had finished setting the table, she heard the horses and went to the door. The men had dismounted and were heading toward the house.

"Smells good, whatever it is," Jim said smiling as he came through the door.

"Sure does," Wade agreed.

Sandrine met Wade's eyes for a brief moment, then turned away and walked back to the cookstove. "Did you find out anything?"

"Not much," Jim said. He walked to the cupboard. "I swear I had two bottles of whiskey in here. Oh well," he said, uncorking a new bottle and pouring himself a small glass. "You care to join me, Wade?"

"No, I don't think so, Jim. I've had enough of that rotgut to last me a long time."

Sandrine quickly glanced at Wade and then back at the stove. "So no one has seen a cat?"

"No one," Jim said, walking to the table and sitting down. He glanced back toward the bedroom. "Rose all right?"

"Still sleeping. She woke up once and had a little soup, then she fell right asleep again."

"Good," Jim nodded.

Sandrine carried the large pot from the stove to the table, ladling out bowls of stew. Then she brought a freshly baked loaf of bread and some butter, and she sat down in the chair next to Jim.

"Looks good," Jim said, dipping a piece of bread into the stew.

"Thank you."

"I didn't realize how hungry I was," Wade said.

Sandrine didn't respond. She dipped her spoon into the bowl. "Are you going to ride after the cat, Jim?"

"I don't think so," Jim said, taking a spoonful of stew before continuing. "If it comes back again, then I'll worry. But right now, Rose has to be my main concern."

"We could go after it," Sandrine said.

"What 'we'?" Wade asked.

"You and I. We could track it."

"No, you're not tracking any mountain lion. I won't allow it."

"And we all know you have to have things your own way, don't we, Wade?" Sandrine said angrily.

"That's not what I meant, Sandrine. It's just too dangerous, that's all. You've been through too much already."

Sandrine slammed her hands down on the table. "Well, I guess you know better than anyone what I've been through."

"You're acting childishly," Wade said impatiently.

"Stop, the both of you," Jim said finally. "Sandrine, I agree with Wade. If that cat is wounded, it could do anything. You said so yourself. I don't want you being put in any danger." He stopped for a moment, wiping his mouth with his napkin and then folding it and setting it down on the table. "Look, I don't know what's happened between you two, and I'm not sure I want to know. But I can't have either one of you upsetting Rose. She loves you both. She doesn't need to hear you fighting."

Sandrine looked at Jim and then lowered her head, feeling

like a selfish child. "I'm sorry. I didn't mean to cause a problem for you."

"Sandrine," Jim said gently, leaning over to put his arm around her. "You couldn't be a problem even if you tried. We love you. It's just that I need to take care of Rose right now, and I don't want her upset. I don't mind telling you two that I don't like hearing you fight either." He shook his head, looking from Sandrine to Wade. "I swear, you two got along better when you were just kids. You seemed a hell of a lot more levelheaded." Jim pushed himself away from the table and stood up. "I'm going in with Rose now."

"What about supper?"

"There's plenty. I'll eat later."

Sandrine waited until Jim went to his bedroom and closed the door, then she stood up, threw her napkin on the table, and cleared her plate and Jim's, but left Wade's. Without glancing at him, she went outside to the porch. She paced the length of it twice before she stopped at the railing, staring out at the darkening sky. She knew Wade would follow her outside, and she would be ready for him. When she heard the sound of his boots on the porch and the door close behind him, she didn't turn around to face him. But she felt him close to her, and she hated the way his closeness made her feel.

"I think you and I better come to some sort of understanding," Wade said.

Sandrine closed her eyes for a moment, listening to the sound of his voice.

"Would you say something?"

Finally she turned. "What do you want me to say? You tell me."

"That's just what Jim doesn't want us to do."

"Then why don't you tell Jim what you did to me last night? Maybe then he'd understand why I can't stand the sight of you." She turned away from Wade and leaned on the railing again.

"As I recall, you didn't fight me all that much."

Sandrine clutched the railing, feeling her cheeks burn. She was thankful that it was almost dark and Wade couldn't see her blush. He was right, of course. She had fought at first. At first. But later, she had wanted him to make love to her, and he had known it. She felt him move closer. His body was barely touching hers, but he may as well have been holding her in his arms. She closed her eyes, trying to force away the gnawing ache that was in her belly.

"Maybe it was just my imagination, or maybe I was just too drunk to remember what really happened. Maybe you didn't want me to make love to you."

Sandrine took a deep breath and straightened, turning to face Wade. "What you did last night was not 'making love.' You came here drunk, and you forced yourself on me. You can call it anything you want, but you still forced yourself on me."

Sandrine looked up at him, able to see his gray eyes in the light that shone from the window. There were still times that he reminded her of the boy she had known long ago, the boy she had first fallen in love with.

Wade lifted his hand and barely brushed his fingers across Sandrine's cheek. "I guess I had to think you wanted me to make love to you last night because that makes it easier to live with. Otherwise, what I did to you is pretty ugly."

Sandrine looked away, not wanting to meet Wade's eyes. He still had so much power over her.

"Look at me, Sandrine. Please."

She sighed deeply, shaking her head. "Talking won't change anything, Wade. We used to have a life together. We used to love each other. But that's over now, and we'll never get it back. I think I finally understand that now." She started past him to the house, but he held her.

"We can't ignore each other forever. Sometime soon we're

going to have to decide what to do. We are still married, remember?"

"We don't have to decide anything. We were never really married, Wade."

"What do you mean?"

Sandrine shrugged her shoulders. "I don't think a marriage performed by a Crow warrior is considered legal." She turned away from him. "Besides it was based on a stupid wager: if you won, I would have to marry you. I think you meant it as a joke. I don't think you ever really intended to marry me. You regretted it as soon as it happened. You loved me, but you were sorry you had married me."

"That's not what Jim and Rose told me."

"Well, it's the truth. You barely spoke to me after we left the renegade camp. The marriage was fine while we were there, but when we came back here . . ." Sandrine shook her head. "Well, this is the white man's world. I should've never agreed to it."

"I didn't give you much choice, did I?"

"I could've said no even after I lost. It was all in fun anyway."

"But I wasn't going to let you say no. I was serious about that game. I was going to make you marry me somehow."

"I think you're imagining things, or Jim's put ideas into your head."

"No," Wade said, holding Sandrine's arms, forcing her to face him. "I know that I wanted you to be my wife. I know that I didn't want to lose you again."

Sandrine looked into Wade's eyes, but he seemed to be looking past her. Had he remembered something again? She shook her head and stepped back. "Don't believe what other people tell you, Wade. You don't remember what we had together, and I don't think you ever will."

"It doesn't matter what we used to have, Sandrine. There is something between us now. You can't deny that."

"There isn't anything between us, Wade. You want a woman who'll share your bed, and that's about it. I want more than that. I want a husband who'll love me and who wants to share his life with me."

She stopped, her voice shaking. It was too hard being around Wade. Without saying another word, she walked past him and back into the house. She went to the guest room and stood against the door, her whole body trembling. She couldn't stay this close to Wade. There was no future with him, and the only way she could ever get on with her life was to get away from him. She nodded. She'd stay for awhile, help Rose and Jim, and then she would go back to her parents. And from there, who knew what she'd do? She knew only that she had to start living again, and she had to start living without Wade Colter.

Wade and Jim rode out early the next morning to check on the stock, and they found another steer that had been killed. The animal had been partially eaten, and like before, its carcass had been left. They searched the area, but there was no sign of the cats.

"Dammit," Jim muttered, rubbing his hand along his thigh.

"I'm going after them, Jim."

Jim nodded. "I'll go with you. Maybe we can round up some fellas to help us."

"No, I track better alone."

"Don't tell me what to do, boy. This is my land."

"What if one of those cats wanders into your yard one day when Danny's playing? You want to take that chance?"

"Of course I don't want to take that chance, but . . ."

"There're no buts. You can't go with me. If Rose knows you're out hunting a wounded mountain lion . . ." Wade shrugged his shoulders.

"All right, you've made your point. But you're going to need some help."

Wade shook his head. "I'm going after it alone. I can move faster that way. I don't want anyone tagging along who'll make noise and slow me down."

"What if there're two of them like you think? Then what're you going to do?"

"I'm not going to do anything stupid, Jim. I'm going to wait down here first, maybe use one of your calves as bait. If that doesn't work, then I'll go up after them." Wade looked around. "Why don't you get on back to the ranch? I'm going to check the tracks again, then I'm going to ride out to my place. Maybe I'll even do a little work today."

"I'm sorry, Wade. Since this thing with Rose—"

Wade held up his hand. "Don't say anything. I'd rather be with you two, you know that. There'll be plenty of time to get my place in order."

"What about Sandrine?"

"What about her?"

"What's going on with you two, Wade? You're barely civil to each other."

"Let's just say I have a lot to make up to her. If she'll even let me."

"She loves you, Wade. It's painfully obvious. The poor girl can't hide it no matter how hard she tries. The question is, do you love her?"

Wade's fingers tightened around the leather reins. "I don't know, Jim. I'm not sure I can ever love Sandrine the way she wants to be loved."

"Then maybe you just ought to tell her that. It'd be a cruel thing to let her think you might love her. Don't do that to her, boy."

Before Wade could answer, Jim was riding away. Wade rode his horse around the area once more, leaning down from the saddle to try to see if he had missed any kind of sign. When he was finished, he kicked his horse into a gallop, heading toward his ranch. He kept thinking about something Sandrine had said the night before—she had accused him of wanting nothing more than her body. She was convinced he didn't really love her. He was beginning to think that she was right.

Wade had made it to the ridge above his ranch without even realizing he had ridden that far. As his horse made its way down the trail, he saw flashes of white between the trees that puzzled him. He kneed his horse into a canter. There were men in the yard. They were working on the house. Wade pushed his hat back from his forehead, frowning. The walls were up and the roof was finished; the entire house had already been whitewashed. He reined in and dismounted, ready to yell at someone. But before he could, he saw Frank sitting on the porch, a cigar in his hand.

"Well, I was wondering if you were ever coming back here," Frank said, looking around. "I'm growing kind of fond of the place myself. I was thinking of making you an offer."

"What the hell are you doing, Frank?" Wade shouted, pacing back and forth in front of the porch.

"You said you wanted some of my men to help you finish building the place, so when you weren't here, I decided to go ahead without you."

"Dammit!" Wade said angrily, throwing his hat on the porch and walking inside. He couldn't believe Frank had gone ahead with *his* house. But when he looked around, his anger quickly subsided. It was exactly as he had wanted, including the curved staircase that led to the second story. Heavy beams supported the high ceilings, and the floors would eventually be cleaned and polished. He walked to the staircase and took the stairs in long, easy strides. He glanced into the guest room and then walked down the hallway and stood in the doorway of the big bedroom that faced the valley and mountains. This was the bedroom that was to be his and Sandrine's. He stepped in, looking around. It was huge. Double doors led to a balcony, and there was a large window on the north side of the room.

"What do you think?" Frank asked from the doorway.

Wade turned around. Frank was leaning against the doorjamb, his cigar in his mouth. "I should beat the hell out of you."

"Yeah, but you won't. You like it too much," Frank replied, a twinkle in his eye.

Slowly Wade nodded. "I have to admit, I do. It's a lot more than I expected from a gambler and a bunch of cowpunchers." He turned to face Frank. "It's exactly how I imagined it would be."

"You remember?"

"I don't know, Frank. Either I remember, or maybe someone told me about it. It's hard to tell anymore."

"Well, it doesn't matter as long as you're pleased."

"How did you know what I wanted?"

"You forget that Sal and I knew you and Sandrine when you were planning this place. You were so excited, kept talking about a second story with a bedroom as a surprise for Sandrine. I figured you probably still wanted to give that to her. Least you could do."

Wade narrowed his eyes. "What's that supposed to mean?"

"I just mean that a woman like Sandrine deserves better than that little cabin down in the valley."

"Yeah," Wade said, walking over to the balcony.

"I think you ought to marry her again."

"What?" Wade said, turning around. "What did you say?"

"I said I think you ought to marry her again. Make it legal this time."

"Why the hell is everyone always meddling in my business and telling me what I should do with my life?" Wade said angrily, looking away from Frank.

"Maybe because you haven't done such a good job of it on

BRIGHT STAR'S PROMISE 401

your own." Sally's voice startled him, and he whirled to face her. She walked into the room, setting a basket on the floor. "That's one of the smartest things you've probably ever said, Frank."

"About Wade marrying Sandrine again?"

"Yes, I think he should."

"Would you two stop talking about me like I'm not here," Wade said. "I'm not going to marry Sandrine—not now, not ever. It's over between us. I don't love her."

"If you say so," Sally said, kneeling down on the floor and opening the basket. She took out a blanket and spread it out, setting out plates and utensils. "Both of you sit down. I've brought lunch."

"I'm not hungry," Wade said curtly, turning back toward the window.

"Stop acting like a child, Wade, and get over here," Sally ordered.

Wade shook his head impatiently and walked over to the blanket. He sat down, picking up a piece of bread. "It's nice of you two to build my house and plan my life for me. Is there anything else I should know?"

"Yes, I stopped by the ranch and invited Sandrine to lunch."

"How did you even know I would be here?"

"I didn't. See how nicely things worked out?" Sally said, smiling at both men.

"She's hard to say no to, isn't she, Wade?"

"She's a little too pushy for me," Wade said, chewing on his bread. "I like a woman who—"

"Oh, let me guess," Sally said, putting her finger to her chin with a thoughtful expression. "Maybe someone like Emily, perhaps. Someone who's adoring and loving until you cross her, and then she tries to murder everyone around you."

"I think maybe you struck a nerve with that one, Sal," Frank said, a grin on his face.

Wade's mouth twisted in anger. "I like this. I'm being judged by a known gambler and cheat, and a woman who slept with more than her share of men after her beloved husband died." As soon as he saw the hurt look on Sally's face, Wade regretted his words. "Sal, I—"

"Everything you said about me is true, Wade," Frank interrupted, "but I think you owe Sally an apology. She's one of the finest women you'll ever know, and she's been a good friend to you."

Sally smiled at Frank, tears in her eyes. "Thank you, Frank, but I don't need you to defend me. If I'm going to condemn someone else, I should be ready to be condemned." She stood up, straightened her skirts, and cleared her throat. "If you gentlemen will excuse me, I have to get back to the restaurant."

"Sally, wait," Wade said, standing up and grabbing her arm before she could leave the room.

"It's all right, Wade. I'm a grown woman. I can take it."

Wade followed Sally as she walked down the stairs and out into the yard. As she started to get into her wagon, he took her arm and held her back for a moment. "I want you to walk with me. Please."

Before she could answer, Wade guided Sally down the trail to the valley. They stopped by the stream, near the place where he and Sandrine had made love.

"This isn't necessary, Wade. Besides, I have to get back to the restaurant."

"The restaurant will be fine without you." Wade let go of Sally's arm and walked around in circles, trying to gather his thoughts. "Everyone tells me what a good man I used to be, only I don't remember that. The only thing I know is the way I am now. It's kind of like being compared to a twin; everyone expects me to be like him." Wade shook his head. "I wish I was the old Wade; it would sure make things a hell of a lot easier. I'd remember you, Frank, Jim, and Rose. Mostly I'd remember the way I used to feel about Sandrine."

"How do you feel about her now, Wade?"

Wade shook his head. "I don't know, Sal. I know I care for her and I desire her more than I ever thought I could desire a woman, but love . . ." Wade shrugged his shoulders. "She wants a husband, a man who can love her without question. I don't think I can give her that."

"What can you give her then?"

"That's just it, Sal, I don't think I can give her anything." Wade walked to the stream and stood staring at it, remembering the day he'd made love to Sandrine. She had been so incredibly passionate and beautiful; he was surprised that any woman could give herself so entirely to a man.

"Are you all right, Wade?"

Wade turned when he felt Sally's hand on his back. "What?"

"I asked you if you're all right."

"I'm fine."

"I don't think you're fine at all. I think you're spending too much time trying to convince yourself that you don't love Sandrine when I know that you really do."

"How is it you know I love her, but I don't?"

"Simple," Sally said, smiling coyly. "If she didn't mean anything to you, you would've told her it was over a long time ago, kind of like you did with me and Emily. But you haven't done that, have you, Wade?" Sally nodded. "That's what I thought. You're afraid if you tell her, she'll go away and you'll lose her for good. This way, she's around until you make up your mind what you're going to do." Sally put her arms around him, hugging him affectionately. "I'll always love you, Wade. You were there for me at a lonely time in my life. You were a good friend and you were honest. I know you didn't mean what you said up there. You're just hurting inside."

"Sal—"

Sally put her fingers on Wade's mouth. "The best advice I could give you, as your friend, would be to stop being so afraid. Love isn't all that frightening. In fact, it's kind of nice." Sally kissed him on the cheek and turned away.

Wade watched Sally as she walked up the hill, a grin on his face. Frank was right; she was one of the finest women he'd ever known. And she was a good friend. She would always tell him the truth. He stared at the stream for a few minutes, then walked back up the hill toward the house. Frank was helping Sally up into the wagon.

"I'm following Sally back into town. The men know what they have to do."

"That picnic is all laid out for you upstairs," Sally said. "Enjoy it."

"Thanks, Sal," Wade said, watching as Sally turned the wagon around and guided it up the trail toward the ridge. Frank rode his horse behind until the trail widened enough for him to ride alongside her. He watched until they were out of sight, and then he turned back to his house. His house. He looked around again, watching as the men hammered on the heavy beams. He looked down at the valley and at the distant mountains. He felt such a sense of peacefulness here, of belonging. It felt right to be here.

He saw his hammer where he'd left it, and impulsively he picked it up. It felt odd that his house had been finished by other people. He glanced around. No one had put up the rest of the porch railing. He took off his shirt and grinned. It would feel good to do something on the house again. He scooped up a handful of nails from the tin near the door and went to work. The planking was cut and stacked; all he had to do was nail it together. He worked section by section, surprising himself. He drove the long nails with clean, easy strokes. The hammer felt balanced and comfortable in his hand, and he found himself enjoying the physical labor. The clean, sharp smell of the fresh-sawn lumber was both familiar and strange. When he stood back and appraised his work, a sudden, detailed image came into his mind. The porch reminded him of the verandas on the houses he'd seen in Missouri. He shook his head. He was remembering again, only he was remembering the wrong things. He brought more wood up to finish the railing. He had just gotten back into the rhythm of the work when he glanced up and saw Sandrine ride into the yard. He could see the look of surprise on her face as she stared at the house. When she dismounted and walked to the porch, he went back to his work.

"What brings you out here?" he asked nonchalantly, setting the next rail in place.

"Sally invited me for lunch, but I see she isn't here."

"She and Frank already left." Wade drove some nails until the rail was set, and then he began on the next one.

"The house looks wonderful."

Wade stood up finally, putting the hammer down. "Is it how you imagined it would be?" He watched as Sandrine stepped onto the porch and looked inside. He saw her face brighten when she looked up at the high ceilings and the staircase leading to the second story.

"It's beautiful," she said, smiling.

Wade was charmed by the look of happiness in her eyes. He took her hand. "I want to show you something." He led her up the stairway to the second story and to their bedroom. Sandrine stood at the doorway, speechless. He thought he saw tears in her eyes. "Go on in," he said, gently pushing her forward. He watched as she walked around the large room. Then she went through the doors and onto the balcony. Wade followed, standing next to her as she leaned on the railing and stared out over the valley. "You haven't told me what you think."

"I can't believe it," Sandrine said, her voice low.

When she looked at him, Wade wanted to take her into his

arms. Her blue eyes sparkled brightly, and the sun made her dark hair shine. "Are you hungry?"

"I'm always hungry," she replied.

"Good, Sally left lunch for us." Wade took her arm and led her to the blanket. He poured some water into Sandrine's glass and then into his. He looked inside the basket. "Let's see what we have. Bread, cheese, meat, fruit, and, of course, pie." Wade took the contents of the basket out and set them on the blanket. He watched Sandrine as she put some meat and cheese onto a piece of bread and folded it together, taking small bites. She took a drink of water, and some of it dripped down the corner of her mouth.

Without thinking, Wade reached out and wiped it away. He gently touched her lips for a brief moment. He could see the pink flush that crept over her cheeks, and she smiled shyly. Wade found her almost irresistible. But he had to resist her. The last time he hadn't, he had hurt her deeply. He looked away, pretending to be interested in the room. It killed him to be so near to her.

"I think you'll like it here. It's exactly the way you planned it," Sandrine said.

"Yes, it's a good house."

"I'm happy for you, Wade. You deserve this."

Wade stared at Sandrine, his eyes wide. "Why do I deserve this?"

"Because you've wanted this for a long time. I remember the first time you brought me out here and showed me this land." Sandrine nodded her head. "I'm glad it's finally happened."

Wade took one of Sally's napkins and wiped his mouth and hands, throwing it down. He couldn't play this game anymore. "I don't deserve anything without you, Sandrine."

"Wade, don't," she said, shaking her head and looking away.

"I want you to live here with me. This is your house, too."

He saw the look of fear in her eyes as she tried to meet his gaze. "I understand if you don't trust me right now."

Sandrine stood up, walking out to the balcony. Wade watched as the wind lifted her heavy dark hair from her shoulders and tossed it around. He walked up next to her. "You're afraid of me." It was a statement, not a question.

"Yes." Sandrine's voice was muted.

"I don't blame you. How can I expect you to trust me when I don't even trust myself?"

Sandrine turned to face him. "It's all right, Wade. You don't owe me anything. You've already apologized for the other night."

"God, you're an exasperating woman," Wade said, pulling Sandrine into his arms. "Don't you understand that I'm asking you to marry me again?" He watched Sandrine as the words sank in, but he saw no joy in her eyes. He felt her body stiffen. Nodding grimly, he released her. He gripped the railing, his fingers tightening as he spoke. "You're not going to forgive me, are you?"

"This doesn't have anything to do with forgiveness, Wade. I could learn to forgive you for what you did the other night. I know you didn't mean to hurt me."

"Then what is it?" he demanded angrily.

"If I'm going to marry you, I want to know that you love me." She looked at him. "Do you love me, Wade?"

Wade met Sandrine's eyes for a moment, then he glanced away. That was the one question he couldn't answer. He wanted Sandrine, and he wanted to be with her, but did he love her?

"It's all right," she said softly, reaching out to touch his arm.

"I don't know what to say." He met her eyes again, afraid that he would find contempt there or, worse yet, pity. But there was only kindness. He put his hand on her cheek. "I know I don't want to be apart from you."

"I think you don't know what you want."

Wade started to get angry, but he knew she was right. He studied her face for a moment, then turned abruptly and looked out across the balcony railing. Everything a man could want was right here—open sky, good pastureland, plenty of water. There was only one thing missing. He glanced at Sandrine. There was a good chance that he would never be able to convince her to stay with him. Why should she unless he could convince her that she was loved?

Sandrine moved toward the doors. "I should be getting back now. Jim might need my help."

Wade watched her, wanting her to stay a little longer. "I'll be going after the cat tomorrow." He almost grinned when she turned around and faced him, her eyes wide with concern.

"You're not going alone, are you?"

Wade shrugged. "If I go alone, I have a better chance of finding it."

"But you said you thought there were two of them."

Wade nodded slowly. "I think there might be."

"And you're going alone? What about Jim?"

"I don't want him worrying about anything but Rose."

"What about me?" Sandrine whispered.

"I don't want you worrying about anything either."

"Then why did you even tell me?" Sandrine whirled and faced the door, but she didn't move toward it.

Hesitantly Wade reached out and touched her shoulders. He could feel her tense, but she did not move away. "Sandrine . . ."

She shook her head. "Leave me alone."

He tightened his grip on her shoulders, wanting to reassure her, touched and relieved that she cared. For an instant the gesture felt so familiar . . . then the familiarity was gone and only the tension between them remained. He lifted his hands. "I'll be fine."

Sandrine faced him. "Just like you were fine the time you

and Little Bear went after that pack of wolves. If Little Bear hadn't been there to help you, they would've torn you to pieces."

"Little Bear brags too much. That's not how it happened." Unbidden, an image flooded Wade's mind. As clearly as if it was happening in front of him, Wade could see Little Bear, his back against the rough bark of an ancient pine, the wolves circling, wary of his flashing knife. "Little Bear's the one who would've died if I hadn't helped him." He said it without boasting.

"But Little Bear said—"

"He was lying. We were both lying."

"But why?"

"Little Bear was afraid of what your grandfather would think. He didn't want him to be ashamed of him."

"How would you know anyway? Did you talk to him, or are you remembering again?"

Wade shook his head. "It's not actually like remembering, it's like pictures that come into my head. They're not really connected to anything. I don't know any more than I just told you."

"You seem to be remembering everything. Everything except us." Her voice broke.

Wade shook his head. "I have no control over that. It's not something I'm trying to do." He slammed his fist against the railing. "Do you think I like going through life without a past?"

"Sometimes I think you do."

"What's that supposed to mean?"

"I think it's convenient for you, Wade."

"What the hell are you talking about?"

He watched as Sandrine smiled sadly, shaking her head. "I think it lets you off the hook."

Wade stared at her, waiting for her to finish. She took a deep breath. "Maybe you wouldn't be happy settled. There was Emily, and—"

"What about Lone Wind?" Wade interrupted. "We were married when you were with him."

"We were married when you were with Emily."

Wade sighed deeply. "I'm getting tired of having to apologize for everything." Frustrated and angry, Wade pushed past Sandrine and left the room. He did not stop until he had untethered his horse and swung into the saddle. Only then did he look back at the house. She wasn't on the balcony. Damn that woman. She didn't even care enough to watch him ride away. He kicked his horse into a gallop, trying to push Sandrine from his thoughts.

Sandrine was waiting for Wade in the barn early the next morning, her horse saddled and ready. It was still pitch dark, a couple hours before dawn. But she had slept in the barn, not wanting to miss Wade when he left.

"What the hell are you doing here?" he asked, saddling his horse.

"I'm going with you," Sandrine said, holding her reins.

"You're not coming with me, Sandrine," Wade said as he cinched the saddle. "And that's final."

"If you don't take me with you, I'll just follow you anyway."

Wade dropped the stirrup and took the reins, leading his horse into the yard. "You'll just slow me down." He swung up into the saddle.

Sandrine mounted, following Wade out of the yard. "I won't slow you down. In case you don't remember, I used to hunt with you and Little Bear all the time. Sometimes I could pick up signs better than either one of you."

"This isn't a game, Sandrine. I'm going after a dangerous animal. I don't want you getting hurt."

"I won't get hurt," she said stubbornly.

"Suit yourself," Wade said angrily, "but don't expect me to wait up for you."

Sandrine stayed close behind Wade, able to see his outline in the pale moonlight. She looked around her. She had never liked riding at night. When she was a girl, her grandfather had told her stories of the ghosts of the dead who walked the earth when it was dark. She hadn't believed the stories during the day, but in the darkness it was possible to believe anything.

She guided her horse carefully along the ridge and down the narrow trail that led to the valley. She thought of the house, their house, and how wonderful it looked, and she thought of the plans she and Wade had made together. It seemed like a lifetime ago. Things were so different now. She reined in when Wade's horse spooked, nickering nervously. She waited in silence, looking around her. Her horse shifted uneasily from hoof to hoof, tossing its head. Then she heard it—the cat's shrill, heart-stopping scream. Her horse pulled at the reins, blundering into Wade's horse.

"Keep him still," Wade whispered, walking his horse forward.

Sandrine held onto the reins tightly, keeping her horse's head high. Only when Wade had moved forward did she allow her horse to go. When they reached the place where they had discovered the first carcass, Wade dismounted, handing his reins to Sandrine.

"They'll probably come back here," he said, his voice low. He took a coil of rope and headed toward the nervous herd.

Sandrine squinted her eyes, trying to follow Wade's movements. If the cat attacked him this far away, she couldn't see well enough to get a shot off. After what seemed like an eternity, he came back leading a calf that was bawling for its mother. He tied the calf to the trunk of a stout tree and walked back to his horse. Sandrine handed him the reins, and he mounted up. They rode to a nearby stand of oaks that was upwind from the tethered calf and dismounted. There they could conceal the horses and themselves.

"Here," Wade said, handing Sandrine one of the rifles he had brought.

"What about you?"

"I have another one," he said. He walked away from her almost silently through the scrub and wild grapes. He kept pausing and sighting along the barrel of his rifle, and she knew what he was doing. He was looking for the best place to stand so that he would have a clean shot. Finally he stopped under an ancient oak with heavy low-hanging branches and sat down, his rifle resting across his knees.

Sandrine sat next to him, gripping the stock of her rifle tightly. She listened intently but could hear only the rustling of mice in the dry leaves and the screech of an owl far off in the darkness. She glanced over at Wade. He was still, intent on watching the calf. Sandrine felt her heart pounding, but she didn't move. She leaned back against some branches, and she eased her legs out in front of her.

"You shouldn't be here," Wade whispered. There was no anger in his voice this time.

"I didn't want you to have to do this alone," Sandrine said, pulling her legs close to her body.

"I'm a grown man, Sandrine. You don't have to worry about me."

"I'll always worry about you," she said, unable to keep the tenderness from her voice. She rested her chin on her knees, setting the rifle down on the ground beside her. She felt Wade's arm go around her, and she smiled in the darkness. It had been a long time since he'd just held her.

"I guess I'll always worry about you, too," Wade said, pulling her into the circle of his arms.

Sandrine closed her eyes as Wade stroked her hair. She couldn't imagine ever feeling like this with any other man. Forcing herself to be strong, she took a deep breath and leaned close to him, kissing him fully on the mouth. "I love you," she said, not caring if he responded or what he thought. "I've always loved you."

She kissed him again, and this time she felt Wade return her passion. His arms tightened around her, and their kiss deepened. But Wade pulled away suddenly, taking her hands in his. Sandrine was overcome by sadness, and she tried to pull away. "I know what you're going to say," she said softly.

"No, you don't."

"You're going to tell me that you care for me but you don't love me." She felt her eyes fill with tears, and she lowered her head, not wanting Wade to notice that she was crying.

"You're wrong, Sandrine," Wade said, lifting her chin and kissing away her tears. "I've been thinking about what my life would be like without you," he said, his voice low. "And I finally realized I wouldn't have a life without you. I don't know why it's taken me so long to figure it out." He leaned forward, his mouth close to hers. "I love you, Sandrine. I want you to be my wife." He lightly brushed his lips against hers.

Sandrine rested her head against Wade's, reveling in the words she thought she would never hear from him again. "Are you sure? I don't—" She felt Wade's fingers on her lips.

"I'm sure. The past doesn't matter to me anymore. What matters is how I feel about you now. I can't imagine that I loved you any more before than I love you right now, at this very moment." He pulled Sandrine into his arms and held her tightly. "That big house will mean nothing if you don't share it with me."

Sandrine began to cry again, and this time she didn't try to hide it. She buried her face in Wade's shoulder, and she let him hold her. It seemed as if she had waited a lifetime for him to tell her that he loved her. As she settled into the comfort of Wade's arms, she was quickly reminded of the reason they had come out here. The frantic bawling of the calf cut into the stillness. Wade pulled away and picked up his rifle, looking through the branches. Sandrine grabbed her rifle and squatted next to Wade, squinting at the clearing. At first she saw nothing. Then, at the outermost edge of her perception, she thought she did. A moment later, she was sure.

"Don't move," Wade whispered. "He may have already caught our scent."

Sandrine nodded, finally able to see the cat as it hunkered down, moving slowly toward the calf. She watched it edge closer. then pounce on the defenseless calf. The calf's screams of pain filled the night. Wade squared his stance and raised his rifle, taking aim. She held her breath, watching. When he squeezed the trigger, her whole body jerked at the sound. Then there was only silence, and the darkness. A moment later the calf began to bawl again, a low, tortured moaning.

"Stay here," he said as he started forward.

Sandrine caught at his sleeve. "Don't go out there, Wade."

His answer was terse. "I can't let the calf suffer like that." He moved out of the cover of the trees. He held the rifle in front of him as he walked. Sandrine held herself very still, listening. The only sounds were Wade's footsteps and the thudding of her own heart. She saw him stop, his rifle raised, as he approached the body of the cat. After a moment, he lowered the rifle, obviously satisfied that it was dead. Then he moved toward the calf. Sandrine heard the muffled shot as he put the calf out of its pain.

Sandrine breathed a sigh of relief and started toward the clearing, but Wade's yell and the high-pitched scream of a mountain lion stopped her. Sandrine stood frozen, swaying in disbelief, then raised her rifle, straining to see. A second cat had attacked Wade. Quickly Sandrine ran toward him. He was wrestling the animal, struggling desperately to keep it away from his face. She took careful aim, refusing to let her hands tremble. She steeled herself against the cat's angry snarls and squeezed the trigger. The cat fell sideways, rolling off of Wade. Sandrine dropped the rifle and ran to him. "Are you all right?"

"A few bites and scratches, but I'll live."

"Are you sure?" Sandrine asked, reaching out to him.

"Just help me up, will you?"

Sandrine took Wade's arm and put it around her shoulders, helping him to his feet. She could feel the blood as it dripped down his arm and hand. "We need to get you back to the ranch now."

She helped him to his horse. Once he was up, she mounted. "Are you sure you're all right?"

"I'm fine." Wade said.

It didn't take long to realize that Wade had slowed down and was lagging behind. He was more badly hurt than he would admit. By the time they reached the ranch, he was hunched over in the saddle. Sandrine dismounted and ran to his horse, helping him down. She put her arm around his waist and guided him into the house. Jim was standing by the table fixing breakfast, a look of shock on his face when he saw them.

"What the hell?"

"We got the cats," Sandrine said, getting Wade to the sofa. "But one of them got Wade."

"I'll get some water and clean cloth," Jim said.

Sandrine tried to hide her fear when she saw how red Wade's shirt was. He had already lost a lot of blood. Carefully she unbuttoned the shirt and managed to take it off. When Jim brought the bowl of water, she took the wet cloths and cleaned Wade's wounds. "Bring me some whiskey, Jim," she said, her voice strong.

"That whiskey's for me, I hope," Wade said.

"It's for your wounds," Sandrine said, nodding to Jim when he handed her the bottle.

"You're not pouring that stuff on me."

"Here then," Sandrine said, putting the bottle to Wade's

mouth. "Take a few drinks if it'll help, but I'm going to have to put some on them."

"No," Wade replied stubbornly after he took a drink.

"Dammit, Wade. You know better than I do that the cat could be carrying all kinds of disease. What if it'd just eaten an old carcass? Do you want that in your body?"

"I'd listen to her if I were you, Wade," Jim said, standing by the sofa.

"I didn't ask for your opinion." Wade grimaced as he shifted positions. "Give me another drink then." He held the bottle to his mouth, took a long swig, then closed his eyes and nodded his head. "Go ahead."

Sandrine quickly surveyed Wade's wounds. He was badly gashed on his chest and forearms. She poured the whiskey over the ragged edges of each wound. She did it quickly, without pausing, then held the bottle to Wade's mouth once more. "Take another drink," she said gently. Then she took a clean cloth and wiped his face and hands, making sure there were no other cuts that she had missed. When she started to stand up, Wade reached for her hand. "You're not leaving, are you?"

"No, I'm not going anywhere."

"Good. I wouldn't want to lose you when I just found you again," he said, closing his eyes and clutching her hand.

Sandrine leaned forward, kissing his cheek. "Go to sleep."

"Did I miss something here?" Jim asked, bending down to pick up the bowl and dirty cloths.

"Just leave us alone, Cap," Wade mumbled without opening his eyes.

"Cap?" Jim mouthed to Sandrine. "He hasn't called me that since he was a boy." Jim narrowed his eyes. "Has he got his memory back?"

Sandrine shrugged her shoulders. "I don't think so, but it doesn't matter anyway. He's asked me to marry him again, Jim." Sandrine couldn't resist a grin. "He says that he loves me."

"That's it?" Jim asked, shaking his head. "That's not news to any of us who know Wade. We've all known he loves you. He just couldn't say it."

Sandrine watched Jim as he walked across the room. She glanced back at Wade. He was already asleep, his breathing even. She bent down and lightly kissed his mouth. She felt as if she were dreaming. She was almost afraid to go to sleep, afraid that she would wake up tomorrow and find out that Wade didn't love her. But she pushed her fear aside, choosing instead to believe that they would finally be together.

Wade tried to move, but he felt stiff and sore. He opened his eyes, finally realizing that he was asleep on the sofa. Then he felt the pain in his arms and chest, and he remembered what had happened. He started to sit up but stopped when he saw Sandrine asleep on the floor next to him, wrapped in a blanket. She hadn't left him. He reached down to touch her hair, and he was amazed by its silky texture.

"Wade."

He was startled by Rose's voice. He hadn't even seen her sitting at the table. He smiled when he saw her, and he moved to the edge of the sofa, carefully standing up. His body ached and throbbed, but he walked to the table and sat down. "It's sure good to see you up."

"I guess I could say the same for you. Are you all right?"

"I think so. I'm a little sore."

Rose looked at him. "Some of those gashes look pretty bad, Wade. I think you should go into town and have Doc look at them."

"Maybe later," Wade said, nodding. "Where's Jim?"

"He went out to check on the herd. Thank you for what you did last night. Thank you both."

"My pleasure," Wade said, smiling. "In fact, I owe those two mountain lions my gratitude. If I hadn't been out there hunting them, Sandrine might never have come with me." He stopped, looking down at the floor, feeling slightly embarrassed. "And I might never have told her that I love her."

"You finally told her?" Rose said. "It's about time."

"I guess I'm a little slow, Rose."

Rose put her hand on Wade's. "You were just afraid, that's all. You wanted to make sure that loving her was your idea, not just something we were all talking you into."

"I think I knew from the first time you brought her to see me at Frank's house, remember?" Wade shook his head. "God, she was beautiful, especially when she got mad at me. Never saw such flashing blue eyes in my life."

Rose grinned. "So are you going to have a real wedding this time?"

"Yes," Wade replied without hesitation. "I want the best for Sandrine. We'll have a wedding and a big old party to celebrate. I want everyone to know how I feel about her."

"Well, for a man who just almost got killed by a mountain lion, you seem pretty cheerful."

"I guess love will do that to a man, Rose." Wade looked at her, seeing just how frail she still looked. "How're you feeling, really? Should you even be up?"

"If I stay in that bed for one more day, I swear I'll die. And I miss Danny so much."

"How about if I ride out and get him today?"

"Nonsense," Rose said. "You're not riding anywhere like that. We'll wait a couple more days until you and I are a little stronger, then we'll pick Danny up and go into town. You know how he likes to eat at Sally's."

"That sounds good," Wade said, still studying Rose. Impulsively he took her hand in his and held it tightly. He'd liked her from the first moment he'd met her on the wagon train. He smiled. He remembered that now; it was all very clear to him.

His memories were coming back to him. He could only hope that they all would. His smile widened. For the first time since his fall from the horse, he felt good, so good that even if his memory never came back he knew he would be content with his life.

"Why're you looking at me like that? Do I look that bad?"

"No, you don't look bad. I was just thinking how much I owe you. You've been like a sister to me. You've been there for me even when I acted like a foolish ass, and God knows, I've done that enough times."

"Stop it, Wade."

"No, I want to say this, Rose. You and Jim are like family to me. In fact, you are my family. I don't know if I ever would've gotten to this point in my life without the two of you. I guess I just want to say that I love you, Rose, and I respect and admire you."

"Oh, Wade," Rose said, tears in her eyes. "Those are some of the sweetest words anyone has ever said to me."

"Well, it's been long overdue from me." Wade lifted her hand to his mouth and kissed it softly. "Thank you."

"You're welcome," Rose replied, smiling. "So when's the wedding?"

Wade laughed. "You're not going to let me get out of this, are you?"

"Not on your life. You owe that girl a big, beautiful wedding."

"Well, as soon as you and I are healed and our house is finished—"

"Your house? Hell, if you wait for that to be built, you'll both be old by then."

"It's almost finished now. You should see it, Rose. It looks great. Frank and his men have been working on it for me."

"Frank?"

"It was part of the deal I made when I gave him his house back."

"Well, I guess you weren't completely stupid when you got that place from Frank. Not only did you make some money, you got your house built to boot." Rose nodded her head. "You did real good, Wade Colter."

"Thanks, Rose."

"So you ready to plan a wedding?"

Wade nodded, glancing past Rose to Sandrine. Yes, he thought, he was ready to plan their wedding. He was more than ready. He'd been waiting for this for a long time. Longer than he could remember.

Eighteen

"If you don't stand still, I'm going to stick one of these pins into you."

Sandrine looked at Sally and shook her head. "I'm sorry, Sally. I don't know what's the matter with me," Sandrine said as she stared out the window of Sally's room.

"I don't know what could be the matter. In less than two weeks, you're going to marry about the most handsome man any woman's ever laid eyes on, you're going to live in a wonderful new house, and someday you're going to raise a big beautiful family. Don't tell me you're having second thoughts."

"No, I want to marry Wade. It's just that . . ." Sandrine shrugged.

"It's just that what?"

Sandrine fidgeted. "It's just that something is missing. I don't know what exactly."

"Hold still for one more minute. Let me pin the waist."

Sandrine stood impatiently while Sally finished pinning, then she stepped down from the stool. "Are we done?"

"Let me get a look at you. Stand back." Sally walked around Sandrine, nodding her head in approval. "It's a stunning dress, if I do say so myself."

Sandrine couldn't resist a grin. She walked to the mirror on Sally's bureau and looked at her reflection. Her dark hair was pulled back in a ponytail, and it contrasted startlingly with the stark white of the dress. The dress was made from a delicate

Mexican lace that Sally had bought years ago in Mexico City and never used. Sally had designed the dress herself, cutting a simple sleeveless satin gown, then covering it with the lace. The sleeves were long and sheer, coming to Sandrine's wrists, while the bodice of the satin gown was cut low, the lace covering it and tapering to the neck. The dress fell simply, with a slight flair at the bottom. "It's so beautiful, Sally," Sandrine said, smiling at Sally in the mirror. "You've done a wonderful job."

"Yes, I could be a seamstress besides running the restaurant. I'd be responsible for feeding and clothing everybody in town." Sally motioned for Sandrine to turn around. "Let's get it off you now."

Sandrine slipped out of the dress. While Sally hung it up, Sandrine got her clothes on. "So when are you and Frank going to get married?"

Sally walked to the table and sat down. "I don't think Frank and I will ever get married."

Sandrine sat down next to her. "It doesn't bother you, not being married?"

"I've been married, Sandrine. It was good while it lasted, but I don't think I'd ever do it again. It's good enough with Frank. He's not perfect, but he treats me well enough."

"I think he'd marry you today if you asked him to."

Sally seemed to consider what Sandrine said. "He probably would, but I wouldn't marry him. It's better this way."

"I wish I was more like you, Sally. You don't let anything or anyone control you. I envy that."

Sally shook her head. "Don't envy it too much, Sandrine. It can make for some very lonely nights."

"Sometimes I wish . . ." Sandrine stopped, lowering her eyes.

"What?"

Sandrine met Sally's eyes. "Sometimes I wish Wade and I were the way we used to be when we were kids. It was all so innocent then, so good."

"Maybe you remember it better than it really was, Sandrine. We all have a habit of doing that. Sometimes I remember my life with my husband, and I realize that it wasn't the best marriage in the world. But right after he died, I thought he was some kind of saint or something. He wasn't; he was just a man. Was your love for Wade any better then, or any stronger?"

Sandrine looked past Sally, recalling the times when the wagon train would come through the stockade. She could even remember the anticipation she had felt at seeing Wade. It was wonderful and exciting, but she knew what she had felt for Wade then wasn't real love. She had adored him, but that wasn't even close to the way she felt about him now.

She closed her eyes for a moment. She thought about Wade, and she felt her stomach tighten and her heart actually beat faster. God, how she desired him. The very thought of the way his hands touched her, the way his lips pressed against hers, and the way he made love to her made her feel giddy. But more than that, more than his physical presence, was the way he looked at her with love in his eyes. She loved him beyond all else.

"Are you all right, Sandrine? I swear, if you don't come out of it soon, I might have to call Doc to help revive you," Sally said.

Sandrine opened her eyes and smiled, feeling slightly embarrassed. "I'm sorry. I was just remembering."

"They looked to be nice memories from the color of your cheeks," Sally said, grinning impishly.

"Stop it," Sandrine said, standing up. "I should be getting back to the ranch. I told Rose I'd pick up some things for her."

"How's she feeling?"

"Stronger all the time. I think she's more excited about the wedding than I am."

"She probably is."

When Sally stood up, Sandrine put her arms around her and hugged her. "Thank you, Sally."

"For what? I didn't do anything."

"You've been a good friend to me and to Wade. We're both very lucky to know you." Sandrine thought she saw Sally's eyes moisten, but she quickly turned away and walked to the door, holding it open for Sandrine.

"Well, come back in a couple days and we'll get a final fitting on this dress."

Sandrine nodded. "Thanks again, Sally." She walked down the steps and out onto the street. She lifted her dress slightly and stepped up onto the planked sidewalk, heading toward the general store. It had been over a month since Wade had declared his love for her, and so much had changed. He and Rose were healthy again, and the house was finished. And Jim had received a letter from his sister in Boston. Emily was in a hospital for the insane. They had great hope that she would get the help she so desperately needed.

Everything was going well, yet Sandrine still felt a certain emptiness that she couldn't tell anyone about, not even Wade. She missed her family so much and had wanted them to come to the wedding, but Wade had wanted to get married before autumn, and she had agreed. There wasn't enough time for any of them to ride south. Besides, she knew her mother, and she knew she wouldn't be comfortable leaving the stockade or her people. Still, Sandrine had hoped that Little Bear might come for the wedding.

When she reached the store, she handed the list of Rose's items to Mr. Dawson, then looked quickly through the store to see if there was anything interesting or new. When Mr. Dawson had gotten all of the items together, Sandrine added some candy sticks for Danny, paid for everything, and left. As she headed toward the wagon, she stopped when she saw Nick Boulton. He was sitting in the alley between the newspaper office and the gun shop, his head back, his eyes closed. Sandrine walked to him.

"Nick," she said softly, not wanting to frighten him. When he didn't stir, she said his name again. "Nick."

Nick's head jerked forward then back again, hitting the wall. When he saw Sandrine, he squinted his eyes. "That you, Miss Sandrine?"

"Yes, Nick, it's me." Sandrine put her things on the ground. "Why don't I help you up?"

"No, ma'am, I don't think I could stand right now. I've had a little too much to drink."

"When was the last time you had something to eat, Nick?"

Nick shrugged his shoulders and shook his head. "Dunno. Yesterday, maybe."

"Why don't we get you up and take you over to the Half Moon. I'll buy you some lunch."

"I don't want you to do that, miss. I'm fine right here."

Sandrine watched Nick as he laid his head back against the wall, closing his eyes. She couldn't just leave him there. Twice he had helped her; once he had saved her life. Now it was her turn to help him. She squatted down next to Nick, shaking him slightly. "Come on, Nick, I want you to wake up. I'm not leaving here until you wake up, and come with me."

"Don't worry about me, miss. Eventually, the sheriff will find me and take me to jail. I get a good meal and a warm place to sleep over there."

"Is that what you want, Nick?"

"It doesn't matter what I want, miss. It's just the way it is."

"Well, you can change the way it is." Sandrine locked her hands underneath Nick's shoulder and started tugging at him. "Stand up, Nick. Come on." Even when Nick didn't move, Sandrine wouldn't give up. She kept tugging at the big man's arm, pulling so hard that she lost her balance and fell backward. Nick stared at her for a minute, then began to laugh. Sandrine laughed, too. "I guess we're not getting very far this way, are we?" she asked.

"I guess not," Nick agreed. "Why are you doing this? I don't understand it."

"You saved my life, Nick. I owe you for that."

"You've already helped me enough."

"I haven't done anything. You need to work and get out of this town. You need to use your skills, Nick."

"I don't have many skills, ma'am."

"You're a good tracker, and you're good with a horse. When Wade and I remarry, we could use a man that we can trust. Someone who'll look after the place, help us with the herd, and help us find lost animals or even rustlers."

"You're offering me to stay at your place?"

"Why not?" Sandrine said. "We have a small cabin that we won't be using anymore. It can be yours if you decide to work for us."

"You'd just give me a cabin like that?"

"No," Sandrine said softly. "You'd have to work for it, Nick. If I find you drinking and I don't think I can trust you, then I can't have you helping me out on the ranch, can I?"

"Guess not."

"You'll have to throw away the bottle, Nick. Can you do that?"

"Don't know. Never tried very hard before."

"Do you want to do it?" Sandrine asked, looking at the big man.

Slowly Nick nodded. "I think so. I've not had me much of a life. The only thing I was ever good at was tracking. I'm not sure I'd be very good at ranching."

"Well, you can try. If it doesn't work out, you're free to leave."

Sandrine watched as Nick attempted to get up, but he was too unsteady. She reached out quickly, trying to support him but she wasn't strong enough to pull him upright. When he fell, she could only fall with him, her purse swinging wildly from her wrist. Her skirt around her knees and her tailbone aching, she started to stand; then stopped. She looked up to see three strange men standing in the alley staring down at her.

"Well, well, Nick, you weren't thinking of running out on me, were you?" A tall man in a black hat looked at Sandrine, then back at Nick. "I thought I might find you here." He looked at Sandrine again. "You also didn't tell us you had such a pretty lady friend."

Nick put his arm protectively across Sandrine. "She is a lady, and she was just trying to help me."

"Doesn't look that way to me, Nick. Looks like she was rolling all over you," the man in the black hat said, laughing.

"Just leave us be, Rollie. I haven't done nothing to you."

"No, but you owe me some money, Nick. Fifty dollars, as I recall."

"Why don't you just leave him alone," Sandrine snapped, glaring at the man in the black hat. "I'll pay you the fifty dollars."

"You'll pay Nick's debt? You two must be good friends." Rollie looked Sandrine up and down. "My, you are pretty. Haven't seen you before in the saloon. You new?"

"She doesn't work in the saloon, Rollie. She's Wade Colter's wife."

"Wade Colter," Rollie said, nodding his head up and down. "Haven't seen him in awhile, but the bastard cheated me out of a lot of money awhile back."

"He wouldn't cheat," Sandrine said.

"He and Frank Lauter got me in a game. I lost, and those two wound up winning everything."

Sandrine looked at Nick. He hardly seemed able to focus. She looked past Rollie to the street. They were too far back in the alley for anyone to just happen to see her. Besides, not many people wanted to walk into trouble.

"Well, I tell you what, Nick," Rollie said, reaching for Sandrine's arm and jerking her to her feet. "I'll just take this pretty lady with me, and we'll call it even."

"No!" Sandrine shouted, struggling against Rollie's hold. She wrenched free and started to run, but Rollie grabbed her blouse, pulling her back.

"You're not going anywhere but with me," he said, wrapping his arm around Sandrine.

"Nick," Sandrine said, pleading with Boulton, but he simply lowered his eyes.

"Don't look for Nick to help you, little lady. He's more interested in where he's going to get his next bottle of whiskey." He nodded to one of the other men. "Give him some money for another bottle. I owe him that at least."

Sandrine watched as one of the men threw some coins on the ground and Nick picked them up, never looking at her. "Nick, what's the matter with you. Help me!" she screamed before Rollie put his hand over her mouth.

"You two lead the way," he said, grinning at his friends. "Let's have some fun with the little lady."

Sandrine forced herself not to cry out or to scream. She lay limp in his arms as he followed the others deeper into the shadows of the alley. Pretending to be helpless with fear, she waited until Rollie had reached the end of the alley, then she twisted hard, planting her feet. She jammed her elbow into his stomach. When he loosened his hold on her, she whirled away. One of the other men reached for her, but she leapt sideways, stumbling once, then running back up the alley. She ran as hard as she could toward the street, but the way out was blocked by Nick.

"Stop her!" Rollie called from behind Sandrine. "Stop her, Boulton, and I'll keep you in whiskey for a month."

"Get behind me, miss," Nick said firmly, taking her arm and pulling her behind him. "Get on out of here."

Sandrine hesitated for a moment, then ran into the street. She looked about frantically.

There was a group of men, as usual, sitting and talking outside the barbershop. She ran up to them, trying not to appear as desperate as she felt. "Do any of you gentlemen have a gun on you?"

One older man looked at his friends then at Sandrine. "I have a gun. Why?"

Sandrine reached into her purse. "I'll give you twenty-five dollars for it." She handed him the bills, still breathing hard, trying to keep her hands still.

"Twenty-five dollars?" The man's eyes grew big.

"Now, mister. I need the gun now." Sandrine almost snatched it from his hands. She quickly clicked open the cylinder and checked the chamber. It was loaded. "Thank you, sir," she said, whirling around and running. By the time she got into the alleyway, she saw one of the men down, his mouth bloodied, and Rollie and the other man were beating up Nick. She pulled back the hammer, and without speaking, she fired the gun into the air. When the men turned to look at her, she leveled the gun at them. "That's enough," she said, staring at Rollie. "I want you both to drop your guns and step away from Nick."

"Are you crazy?" Rollie asked, starting toward Sandrine.

Sandrine fired into the dirt at Rollie's feet. "Not nearly as crazy as you are if you take another step. Now do as I say." Sandrine watched as the one man unbuckled his belt and dropped it to the ground. Sandrine nodded toward him. "You, get down on the ground." When Rollie started toward her again, Sandrine raised the gun higher. "I'm not playing games."

"I don't think you have it in you to shoot a man," Rollie said.

"Don't count on it," Sandrine said. She glanced at Nick. "You all right?"

"I'll be fine, miss. Why'd you come back here?"

"I couldn't let you have all the fun, could I?" she said, still watching Rollie.

She could see that he was pretending to unbuckle his belt, but he wasn't actually doing it. She sighted down the barrel and readied herself. When he reached for his gun, Sandrine fired. He screamed and dropped the gun, clutching at his hand.

"Dammit!" Rollie yelled, shaking his hand and holding it against his chest. "You shot me."

"I told you to drop your belt and you didn't listen. Now take your gun out with your left hand and drop it. Do it, or I'll shoot your other hand."

"You'd better do it, Rollie," Nick said, getting to his feet. "Miss Sandrine has a real temper."

When Rollie dropped the gun, Nick picked it up. In one quick motion, Nick brought his arm back and then forward, hitting Rollie so hard that he was virtually lifted off his feet and thrown backward onto the ground. He moaned slightly but made no attempt to get up.

"You feeling better now, Nick?" Sandrine asked, smiling.

"Much better, ma'am." Nick wiped the blood from his face. "Why'd you come back? You didn't have to."

"Yes, I did."

"But I didn't help you."

"You wouldn't have let them hurt me, Nick. I know that."

"But I let them take you away . . ." Nick lowered his head. "I'm sorry."

"Don't be sorry, Nick. You helped me when it counted. Now, shouldn't we get the sheriff over here?"

"That won't do no good. Rollie will just say I owed him money and the sheriff will believe him."

"I guess I'll just have to tell the sheriff what really happened then," Sandrine said, glancing toward the crowd of people that was beginning to gather at the entrance to the alley.

"What's that?" Nick asked.

"I'll just tell him that Rollie and his friends tried to take me into this alley and rape me and you saved my life."

"No one will believe it, Miss Sandrine."

"Of course they will. Come on," Sandrine said, taking Nick's arm. But she stopped when she reached the street and saw Wade push his way through the crowd. "What're you doing here?" she asked, startled.

"I might ask the same of you," Wade responded tersely, looking at Nick and then down the alley. "What happened?"

Sandrine cleared her throat, shifting nervously. "Well, I—"

"Here's the sheriff," Wade interrupted. "You can explain it to him."

Sandrine looked up to see the familiar shambling figure of the sheriff. "Well, well," he said, peeking into the alley. "So it's Rollie again. Doesn't surprise me." He looked over at Nick. "What did you have to do with this, Nick?"

Sandrine stood in front of the big man. "He helped me, Sheriff. I was walking along, and those men pulled me into the alley. I screamed, but no one heard me except Nick. If he hadn't been there, there's no telling what might've happened."

"That true, Nick?"

"Of course it's true," Sandrine said before Nick could answer.

The sheriff rubbed the toe of one boot on the back of his pants leg, then looked at Nick. "You know, Nick, the last time I saw you today, you could barely stand. How is it you were able to come to Sandrine's aid?"

Sandrine looked at Wade, her eyes pleading.

Wade stepped forward, standing next to Nick. "I don't care how he did it, Sheriff. The fact is, he did it. Sandrine and I owe him a debt of gratitude."

The sheriff shook his head. "I don't know who owes who here, but I think it's time Nick got himself a job. If he keeps getting into trouble, I'll have to keep him in jail for a lot longer than a couple of nights."

"He already has one," Sandrine said quickly. "He's going to work for me and Wade on our ranch. Isn't he, Wade?" Sandrine said, narrowing her eyes as she looked at him.

"Yes, he is. And we'll make sure he stays out of trouble."

The sheriff nodded his head. "All right," he said finally. "You can leave, Nick. But I don't want to see you around here anytime soon. The rest of you folks, get on out of here. There's nothing to see."

Sandrine grimaced as Wade grasped her arm tightly, leading her to his horse. "The wagon is the other way."

"I know," he said angrily, stopping suddenly. "Nick, I want you to go down the street to our wagon, and I want you to drive it to our ranch. If something happens and you don't show up, I'll come find you myself."

"I'll be there, Wade," Nick said, walking away and glancing back at Sandrine.

"What're you doing?" Sandrine said as Wade put his hands on her waist.

"You're riding with me," he said, lifting her up onto his horse's back. "I'm not letting you out of my sight."

"You're being ridiculous," Sandrine said as Wade swung up behind her and kicked his horse.

"I'm being ridiculous?" Wade asked. "Every time I leave you alone, you get yourself into trouble."

"I didn't need your help. I got out of it just fine," Sandrine said angrily, pushing Wade's arms away from her waist.

Wade reined in as they reached the outskirts of town. "You scare me, Sandrine."

"Just what does that mean?" Sandrine said, twisting in the saddle so she could see Wade's face.

Wade jerked back on the reins until the horse stopped. "It means I've waited a long time to find you and I don't want to lose you," Wade said, lowering his mouth to hers.

Sandrine felt the gentle pressure of Wade's lips on hers, and she closed her eyes, feeling herself begin to give in to him. But quickly she sat up straight and opened her eyes. "What do you want, Wade?"

"What do you mean?"

"You want something," she said, nodding. "What is it?"

Wade brushed his fingers against her cheek. "I only want you, Sandrine. You're all I want." He kissed her gently again. "I don't want to find that you've been taken away from me again."

Sandrine looked at Wade, and she was touched by the sincerity in his eyes. "You don't remember the past, Wade."

"I may not remember, but I feel," he said, taking her hand and putting it on his chest. "I feel it in here. I know how much I love you, and I know that I don't want to be separated from you again."

Sandrine put her arms around Wade's neck and kissed him deeply. "All right."

"All right, what?"

"I'll be careful."

"That's not good enough, Sandrine."

"What do you want from me, Wade? I can't stop going into town. I can't be with you every minute of the day."

"I know that," Wade said gently.

"Then what do you want?"

Wade looked at her, his hand on her cheek. "I want you to be my wife again. I want to wake up next to you every morning. I want to hear you laugh; I want to comfort you when you cry. I don't ever want there to be a doubt in your mind about how much I love you."

Sandrine looked into Wade's eyes and was astonished by the love she saw there. She leaned back against him as they rode. She couldn't believe how her life had changed; it all seemed so simple now that she knew Wade loved her again.

When Wade guided the horse down the trail to their house,

she sat up, surprised. She had been staying with Rose and Jim. Rose felt like it was only fitting that she stay there until they were properly married again. "What are you doing?" she asked, but Wade didn't answer. Instead he reined the horse in in front of the new house and dismounted, lifting Sandrine down. Before she could say anything, Wade picked her up in his arms and carried her over the threshold into the house.

When they reached their bedroom, Wade set her down on the floor and shut the door behind them. Without speaking, he led her to the new fourposter bed. He sat down, his hands on Sandrine's hips. He pressed his face into her belly, and she ran her fingers through his hair. She closed her eyes as she felt his hands lift her skirt, deftly removing her underwear. Then his fingers caressed her, touching and probing, and Sandrine felt herself moving against his hand. She felt intoxicated.

"Sandrine."

When she heard Wade murmur her name, she grew more excited. Slowly she dropped to her knees, resting her head against his chest. "I love you, Wade," she said softly, lifting her head up. When he pressed his lips to hers, she heard herself moan. She moved against him, pressing her body so close to his that she could feel the warmth of his skin through his shirt. Gently he pushed her down to the floor, and he impatiently shoved her skirt up to her waist. She could feel the cold wood of the floor beneath her as she waited for Wade. She opened herself to him, making a small sound when he guided himself into her. He moved very slowly at first, and Sandrine closed her eyes, enjoying the slow, sensual feel of his lovemaking. But as their passion increased, Wade thrust himself more deeply into her, and Sandrine lifted her legs, wrapping them around his back, arching herself to meet him. "Wade," she whispered, and then said it more loudly. At first she was self-conscious, but then she couldn't help herself. Finally she called out his name, her voice filled with a sweet yearning. As he drove into her, hard and deep, Sandrine moved her hips to meet his every thrust in an abandoned rhythm that quickened, lifting them both into an ecstasy so intense that Sandrine cried out and felt Wade's whole body respond. Quickening his thrusts, Wade covered her mouth with his own, and Sandrine felt herself dissolving, exploding. An instant later the burst of passion consumed them both. Sandrine held onto Wade, her arms still wrapped around his back, his head still next to hers. Her body felt warm and moist, and she knew that her cheeks were flushed pink. She felt beautiful.

"I could stay here forever," Wade said finally, lifting his head and looking at Sandrine.

"So could I," Sandrine answered, kissing him. "I love this house."

Wade looked at Sandrine, his eyes heavy with desire. "I'm not talking about this house, Sandrine," he said, kissing her lightly. "I'm talking about you. When I am inside of you, I feel complete. God, how I love you, Sandrine," he said, his mouth covering hers.

Sandrine felt her desire surge again, and she didn't try to stop it. She had waited too long to hear these words and to feel Wade's love. She would never tire of hearing him say how much he loved her.

The wedding day had finally arrived. Rose and Sally had planned everything, except where the wedding would be held. Sandrine and Wade had already decided that they wanted to be married on the ridge overlooking their house. It was where Wade had first proposed to Sandrine, and it was where they had first planned their life together. Now it was finally going to happen.

While Jim, Wade, Frank, and Nick were helping to set up the

yard for the party afterwards, Sally and Rose were making sure that Sandrine looked beautiful.

"Explain to me again why I need all of these things?" Sandrine demanded, impatiently pulling on a pair of white stockings.

"Because you don't want it to be easy for him," Sally said.

"Sally!" Rose said in mock surprise, then she shrugged her shoulders. "Actually, Sally's right. The longer you make Wade wait, the more he'll look forward to . . ." Rose looked at Sally for help.

"You know, the more he'll look forward to taking you to his bed."

"I know what he'll look forward to, ladies. I've been married to the man before, remember?"

"Still, a little suspense never hurt," Sally said, holding up a delicate white slip. "What do you think of this?"

"I think it'll barely cover me," Sandrine said.

"Yes, that's what you want. Wade will love it."

Sandrine shook her head and laughed. "I think you two are more excited about this than I am."

Rose looked at Sally, and they both started to laugh. "What time is it?" Rose asked. "Wade wanted us to be finished by eleven so he could give you a present."

"He can't see me in my dress," Sandrine protested.

"He doesn't have to see you in your dress. Let's just get all the underthings on, get your hair fixed, and you can wear a dressing gown. He won't see you in the dress until you walk down those stairs."

"All right," Sandrine said. "What else do I have to put on?"

"Look at these boots," Rose said. "Aren't they wonderful? Satin. All the way from Boston."

"Boston?" Sandrine asked, raising an eyebrow.

"From Emily's mother. A wedding present. You must admit, they are beautiful."

"Look at these," Sally said, holding up a pair of short satin pantelettes.

"I've never seen any like those," Sandrine said, smiling as she ran her hand over the smooth material. "They're beautiful."

"I thought you'd like them. They used to belong to me. I thought I'd use them on my honeymoon night, but I don't think I'll ever have another one. I want you to have them."

"Are you sure, Sally?" Sandrine asked.

"Of course, I'm sure. Now hurry up and get dressed."

When Sandrine had finally gotten dressed and laced up her boots, Rose and Sally fixed her hair. Sally pulled it back in a loose chignon, letting tendrils fall around her face and at the nape of her neck. Rose fastened a strand of pearls around Sandrine's neck and handed her a pair of teardrop pearl earrings. After Sandrine had fastened the earrings, she looked in the mirror.

"What do you think?" Sally asked.

Sandrine shook her head. She couldn't believe the image that was staring back at her—the woman who sat at the dressing table was beautiful. Her eyes were a sparkling blue, her cheeks were flushed with color, and her smile was dazzling.

"You look so pretty," Rose said, hugging Sandrine from behind and resting her cheek against hers.

Sandrine took one of Rose's hands and kissed it. "Thank you for everything, Rose. I don't know what I would've done without you."

"You would've done fine."

Sandrine looked from Rose's reflection to Sally's. "And thank you, Sally. You've been a good friend to both me and Wade."

"Don't thank me. I'm just happy to see you two together. I figured he'd find his way back to you eventually."

Sandrine smiled at both women, not knowing what to say. They'd both been such good and loyal friends. She owed them a lot. She looked sharply toward the door when she heard Wade's voice outside.

"Are you ladies ready for me yet? I'd like to give my bride her wedding gift."

Sally walked over to the door and opened it. She looked Wade up and down as he walked into the room. "Well, well, you clean up nicely," she said.

"Thanks, Sal." Wade walked over to Sandrine. "Are you ready?"

"I think so," Sandrine said, standing up and taking Wade's hand. "You don't need to give me a present, you know."

"I want to give you the world," Wade said softly, barely brushing Sandrine's lips with his own. "Now I want you to sit down."

"Sit down? Why?"

"Just do it, please," Wade said, walking back to the door. "I'll be back in a minute."

Sandrine sat nervously on the chair, looking over at Sally and Rose. She couldn't imagine what Wade had gotten her. He'd already bought her the cookstove and the bed. Maybe he'd gotten her another piece of furniture for the house. She looked up when she heard Wade's voice outside in the hall again, and she smiled.

"I wish to hell he'd bring it in," Sally said impatiently. "I can't stand not knowing what it is."

"Me either," Rose agreed.

Sandrine saw Wade standing in the doorway, and then he stepped away. Sandrine blinked, her eyes stinging with tears. Her mother and father were walking into the room, and behind them was Little Bear. Sandrine stood up, hurrying across the room to her parents.

"I can't believe you're here," she said, tears streaking her face as she clung to her mother.

"I could never say no to Wade. He said that I had to be here for you today," Running Tears said.

"Thank you, Mother," Sandrine said, kissing her mother on the cheek.

"And what about me?" Luc said, holding his arms open.

Sandrine went into the circle of her father's arms, resting her head against his chest. "Thank you, Father. I could not have asked for a better present."

"Ah, *chérie,* I would not have missed this day. Not for anything." Luc kissed both of Sandrine's cheeks. "Now, I should be leaving you. You must get dressed. I am looking forward to this wedding and the celebration after. I hear there are many good card players here."

Sandrine laughed. "Too many."

"I will go, too," Running Tears said.

"No, stay here, Mother. Please. I want you here with me."

Running Tears nodded and went to stand by Rose and Sally.

"So, there is nothing left for me, eh?" Little Bear asked, walking forward. "Twice I have made this trip to see you, twice I have left my wife and family. And what do I get?"

Sandrine stepped forward and wrapped her arms around Little Bear. She felt him pull her into his arms, and she began to cry.

"Do not, cousin. There is no need for tears on this day," Little Bear said gently.

"How did you get here?"

"Colter. I guess he is not such a stupid white man after all."

"But I don't understand—"

"Do not trouble yourself about it now, cousin. Prepare yourself for your marriage to Colter. We will talk later."

When Little Bear started to pull away, Sandrine held onto his hands. "I love you, Little Bear. You have always been my best friend. The day is perfect now that you are here."

Little Bear nodded and then grinned. "It is good to know that the day is now complete."

Sandrine smiled and kissed him on the cheek. "You take my father and wait with the others. And stay out of trouble." Sandrine smiled at her father and Little Bear as they left the room.

She walked to the door. Wade was waiting for her there, and she shook her head. "How can I ever thank you?" she said, trying to control the emotion in her voice.

"I don't want your thanks," Wade said, lifting her chin up and kissing her softly. "I only want you to get dressed. We have a wedding to go to." He lightly brushed her cheek, smiled, and walked down the hall.

Sandrine watched Wade walk away, and she felt her throat tighten. There wasn't anything he could have done that could have made her feel more loved.

"Are you going to stand there all day?" Sally asked, walking up behind Sandrine and taking her arm.

Sandrine took a deep breath and turned around. She saw her mother across the room, and she smiled. Rose and Sally were fussing like mother hens, and she could hear the voices of the men from down in the yard below. It was time. She had been waiting for this moment for as long as she could remember.

Wade tugged at his collar. How much longer could it possibly take for Sandrine to put on her dress? He looked down at the yard. There was still no one in sight.

"What is the matter, white man? You look as if you are about to undergo a test of your courage. Is it true that the white man's ceremony is worse than our Sun Dance?"

"For some men it is," Frank laughed.

"Don't be so hard on the boy," Jim said, clapping Wade on the shoulder. "It's not so bad being married. All a man loses is his friends, his money, and his right to a Saturday night poker game."

Wade glared at the three men and shook his head. "Does anyone have some whiskey? I could use a drink."

"Just happen to have one," Frank said, taking a silver flask out of his jacket and handing it to Wade. "Good thing Nick's down helping the women or we couldn't do this. Sandrine would never forgive me if I got him drunk before her wedding."

"Well, I'm not Nick," Wade said, taking a swig and handing it to Jim.

"Let's drink to . . . Oh, hell, let's just drink to anything we can think of," he said, taking a long drink and handing it to Frank.

"What about me?" Little Bear asked.

"I thought you Indians couldn't handle your liquor," Wade said, grinning.

Little Bear reached out, snatching the flask from Frank's hand. "You white men should be careful. I might scalp you all and run off with your women before the day is through."

Jim laughed, and in spite of his nervousness, Wade couldn't help but grin. Frank was clearing his throat repeatedly and was shifting from foot to foot.

"You look like you could use this, white man," Little Bear said, handing the flask back to Frank.

"Relax, Frank," Jim said heartily. "He'll only scalp you if you beat him at cards."

"This is your last chance to run, white man," Little Bear said, slapping Wade on the back so hard he had to take a step forward to keep his balance.

"What do you mean?"

"My cousin is coming now." Little Bear pointed.

Wade looked down at the house. All of the women were walking up the slope toward the ridge. Sandrine was holding onto Luc's arm, the other women were behind them. It was easy to spot Rose. She was trying to hold onto Danny as he struggled to break free and run up the hill. Nick and the preacher were following a little ways behind. As Sandrine drew closer, Wade found himself unable to take his eyes off her. Her dress flowed like mist as she walked, and her hair was a shining dark cloud that framed her face. His nervousness quickly subsided as their eyes met. When she kissed her father on the cheek and walked toward Wade, he couldn't see anything but Sandrine. He took her hand, and for a moment they simply stood there looking into one another's eyes.

The preacher cleared his throat. "Are we all ready?"

Wade nodded without looking away from Sandrine's face. As the preacher read the vows, Wade saw Sandrine's beautiful blue eyes flood with tears, and he wanted to hold her. He barely heard the preacher as he spoke, and Jim had to nudge him gently when the time came to recite his vows. He could see a flicker of laughter in Sandrine's eyes when he turned to face her, the ring in his hand. She raised her finger, and he slid the gold band on, saying a silent prayer that nothing would ever come between them again. Then he took her into his arms and kissed her deeply, never wanting to let her go.

"Do I get to kiss the bride?" Jim said, tapping Wade on the shoulder.

Reluctantly Wade let Sandrine go and looked up to see a circle of smiling faces. One after another, the men shook his hand, clapping him on the back, and wishing them luck. Sandrine was surrounded by a similar circle of the women, and Wade could hear her lovely voice as the conversation rose and fell around him.

He grinned when he saw Sally walking toward him.

"Never thought you'd do it," she said, taking his arm.

"I'm not as stupid as you think I am, Sal," Wade said, hugging her.

"I'd say this was about the smartest thing you've ever done," Frank chimed in, taking Sally's arm.

Wade nodded as they moved off. Jim and Rose came to stand beside him. Clutching Rose's hand tightly, Danny looked up at him, round-eyed.

"I'm so happy for you," Rose said, hugging him fiercely.

"Sandrine sure looks pretty, Wade," Danny said.

"Yes, she sure does, Danny," Wade said, bending over to tousle the boy's hair.

When he straightened back up, he saw Jim looking at him.

"I'm real proud of you, boy."

"Thanks, Cap," Wade replied, feeling his eyes sting. As they moved away, he saw Running Tears standing alone, away from the others. He walked to her and took her hands in his. "Do you know how much I love your daughter?"

"I have always known that," Running Tears replied.

"I will take care of her."

"I know that." Running Tears reached up and gently touched his cheek. "Give me many grandchildren."

Wade grinned as she walked away. He started toward Sandrine, but Little Bear was suddenly there, the humor in his eyes belying the serious expression on his face.

"So you have done it."

"Yep," Wade said.

"There is no turning back now, white man."

"I don't want to turn back, Little Bear. I love your cousin."

Little Bear gripped Wade's shoulder. "You have always loved her, Colter. Has it taken you until today to realize this?"

Wade looked at Little Bear, trying to think of a clever response, but he only nodded. "I guess it has."

"Go to her then." Little Bear smiled. "Everett and I will take the others down to the house now. It is fitting that you are alone for a few minutes with your new wife."

Wade nodded as he watched the people go down the hill in scattered groups of two and three. Then he walked to Sandrine and put his arm around her, pulling her close. They stood, side by side, looking down at the house, hearing the laughter of their friends and family. "Do you remember the first time we stood here together?" he asked.

"I remember, do you?"

Wade nodded. "Most of it, I think. It came back to me earlier today when I was up here with Jim picking out the exact spot for our wedding."

Sandrine smiled, looking into his eyes, and he could tell she was searching for something.

"What?"

She glanced away from him toward the house, then looked back. "Is it the same?"

"What do you mean?"

"Do you love me as much as you did that day?"

Wade pulled her closer, brushing back a tendril of hair that had come loose. "I love you more," he said simply. He kissed her, marveling once more at the soft sweetness of her lips. "Shall we go home?" he asked her, and he saw joy come into her eyes.

She nodded, and he took her hand. Together they turned and walked down the hill, hand in hand, facing the bright promise of their future.

WAITING FOR A WONDERFUL ROMANCE?
READ ZEBRA'S

WANDA OWEN!

DECEPTIVE DESIRES (2887, $4.50/$5.50)
Exquisite Tiffany Renaud loved her life as the only daughter of a wealthy Parisian industrialist. The last thing she wanted was to cross the ocean on a cramped and stuffy ship just to visit the uncivilized wilds of America. Then she shared a kiss with shipping magnate Chad Morrow that made the sails billow and the deck spin. . .

KISS OF FIRE (3091, $4.50/$5.50)
Born and raised in backwoods Virginia, Tawny Blair knew that her dream of being swept off her feet by a handsome nobleman would never come true. But when she met Lord Bart, Tawny saw at once that reality could far surpass her fantasies. And when he took her in his strong arms, she thrilled to the desire in his searing caresses . . .

SAVAGE FURY (2676, $3.95/$4.95)
Lovely Gillian Browne was secure in her quiet world on a remote ranch in Arizona, yet she longed for romance and excitement. Her girlish fantasies did not prepare her for the strange new feelings that assaulted her when dashing Irish sea captain Steve Lafferty entered her life . . .

TEMPTING TEXAS TREASURE (3312, $4.50/$5.50)
Mexican beauty Karita Montera aroused a fever of desire in every redblooded man in the wild Texas Blacklands. But the sensuous señorita had eyes only for Vincent Navarro, the wealthy cattle rancher she'd adored since childhood—and her family's sworn enemy! His first searing caress ignited her white-hot need and soon Karita burned to surrender to her own wanton passion . . .

Available wherever paperbacks are sold, or order direct from the Publisher. Send cover price plus 50¢ per copy for mailing and handling to Penguin USA, P.O. Box 999, c/o Dept. 17109, Bergenfield, NJ 07621. Residents of New York and Tennessee must include sales tax. DO NOT SEND CASH.

JANELLE TAYLOR

ZEBRA'S BEST-SELLING AUTHOR

**DON'T MISS ANY OF HER
EXCEPTIONAL, EXHILARATING, EXCITING**

ECSTASY SERIES

SAVAGE ECSTASY	(3496-2, $4.95/$5.95)
DEFIANT ECSTASY	(3497-0, $4.95/$5.95)
FORBIDDEN ECSTASY	(3498-9, $4.95/$5.95)
BRAZEN ECSTASY	(3499-7, $4.99/$5.99)
TENDER ECSTASY	(3500-4, $4.99/$5.99)
STOLEN ECSTASY	(3501-2, $4.99/$5.99)

Available wherever paperbacks are sold, or order direct from the Publisher. Send cover price plus 50¢ per copy for mailing and handling to Penguin USA, P.O. Box 999, c/o Dept. 17109, Bergenfield, NJ 07621. Residents of New York and Tennessee must include sales tax. DO NOT SEND CASH.

PASSIONATE NIGHTS FROM
PENELOPE NERI

DESERT CAPTIVE (2447, $3.95/$4.95)
Kidnapped from her French Foreign Legion escort, indignant Alexandria had every reason to despise her nomad prince captor. But as they traveled to his isolated mountain kingdom, she found her hate melting into desire . . .

FOREVER AND BEYOND (3115, $4.95/$5.95)
Haunted by dreams of an Indian warrior, Kelly found his touch more than intimate—it was oddly familiar. He seemed to be calling her back to another time, to a place where they would find love again . . .

FOREVER IN HIS ARMS (3385, $4.95/$5.95)
Whispers of war between the North and South were riding the wind the summer Jenny Delaney fell in love with Tyler Mackenzie. Time was fast running out for secret trysts and lovers' dreams, and she would have to choose between the life she held so dear and the man whose passion made her burn as brightly as the evening star . . .

MIDNIGHT CAPTIVE (2593, $3.95/$4.95)
After a poor, ragged girlhood with her gypsy kinfolk, Krissoula knew that all she wanted from life was her share of riches. There was only one way for the penniless temptress to earn a cent: fake interest in a man, drug him, and pocket everything he had! Then the seductress met dashing Esteban and unquenchable passion seared her soul . . .

SEA JEWEL (3013, $4.50/$5.50)
Hot-tempered Alaric had long planned the humiliation of Freya, the daughter of the most hated foe. He'd make the wench from across the ocean his lowly bedchamber slave—but he never suspected she would become the mistress of his heart, his treasured sea jewel . . .

Available wherever paperbacks are sold, or order direct from the Publisher. Send cover price plus 50¢ per copy for mailing and handling to Penguin USA, P.O. Box 999, c/o Dept. 17109, Bergenfield, NJ 07621. Residents of New York and Tennessee must include sales tax. DO NOT SEND CASH.

MAKE THE ROMANCE CONNECTION

Z-TALK *Online*

Come talk to your favorite authors and get the inside scoop on everything that's going on in the world of romance publishing, from the only online service that's designed exclusively for the publishing industry.

With Z-Talk Online Information Service, the most innovative and exciting computer bulletin board around, you can:

- ♥ CHAT "LIVE" WITH AUTHORS, FELLOW ROMANCE READERS, AND OTHER MEMBERS OF THE ROMANCE PUBLISHING COMMUNITY.
- ♥ FIND OUT ABOUT UPCOMING TITLES BEFORE THEY'RE RELEASED.
- ♥ DOWNLOAD THOUSANDS OF FILES AND GAMES.
- ♥ READ REVIEWS OF ROMANCE TITLES.
- ♥ HAVE UNLIMITED USE OF E-MAIL.
- ♥ POST MESSAGES ON OUR DOZENS OF TOPIC BOARDS.

All it takes is a computer and a modem to get online with Z-Talk. Set your modem to 8/N/1, and dial 212-545-1120. If you need help, call the System Operator, at 212-889-2299, ext. 260. There's a two week free trial period. After that, annual membership is only $ 60.00.

See you online!

KENSINGTON PUBLISHING CORP.